What the critics are saying about
THE DARKENING DREAM:

"Wonderfully twisted sense of humor" and
"A vampire novel with actual bite" — *Kirkus Reviews*

"Inventive, unexpected, and more than a little bit creepy — this
book has something for everyone!" — R.J. Cavender, editor of the
Bram Stoker nominated Horror Library anthology series

THE
DARKENING DREAM

Andy Gavin

Mascherato
Publishing

The Darkening Dream
Andy Gavin

Printed in the United States of America.
Mascherato Publishing
PO Box 1550
Pacific Palisades, CA, 90272
publishing@mascherato.com

For more information about this book visit: http://andy-gavin-author.com

Edition ISBNs
Hardcover 978-1-937945-00-8
Trade Paperback 978-1-937945-01-5
E-book 978-1-937945-02-2

First Edition 2011, v5.03f / lv1.0.

Cover Photo-Illustration copyright 2011 © by Cliff Nielsen
Jacket design by Pete Garceau
Book design by Christopher Fisher
Interior vector art by Original Force

This book is formatted in Arno Pro, an Adobe® font family designed by Robert Slimbach.

THE DARKENING DREAM

One:

Agitation

Salem, Massachusetts, Saturday afternoon, October 18, 1913

As services drew to an end, Sarah peered around the curtain separating the men from the women. Mama shot her a look, but she had to be sure she could reach the door without Papa seeing her. After what he'd done, she just couldn't face him right now. There he was, head bobbing in the sea of skullcaps and beards. She'd be long gone before he extracted himself.

"Mama," she whispered, "can you handle supper if I go to Anne's?" Last night's dinner debacle had probably been Mama's idea, but they'd never seen eye to eye on the subject. Papa, on the other hand, was supposed to be on her side.

Mama's shoulders stiffened, but she nodded.

The end of the afternoon service signaled Sarah's chance. She squeezed her mother's hand, gathered her heavy skirts, and fled.

The journey through Salem's bustling downtown took only ten minutes, but the Indian summer sun left her corset sticky and cruel.

A final two blocks brought Sarah to her friend's pre-Revolutionary house, a kernel of which dated to the seventeenth century. Wings, rooms, and gables had sprouted during the past two hundred years, and in its present form the house and stables were large enough for five family members, seven boarders, a decent collection of horses, and a dog.

Sarah entered without knocking. Mr. Barnyard, the Williamses' obese basset hound, rushed to greet her. After suffering his affections, she found Anne in the sitting room helping her mother with the mending. Several inches taller than Sarah, she wore her straw-colored hair in two looped braids, and possessed all the womanly curves Sarah found lacking in herself.

"What a nice surprise," Mrs. Williams said. "Sarah, I know you're not much for the needle, but some conversation would help pass the time."

Behind her mother, Anne stabbed herself in the chest with an imaginary dagger.

"I hate to disappoint you," Sarah said, "but I hoped to steal away your oldest daughter. Where's Emily? Can't she help?"

Mrs. Williams shrugged a padded shoulder. "Out back somewhere. If I hadn't whelped that one myself, I'd swear she's some sort of changeling. But take Anne, she's all thumbs today."

Anne set down the trousers she was sewing and tugged Sarah out the door.

"Thank God," she said, leading Sarah upstairs to the bedroom she shared with her younger sister. "It was so stuffy in there I thought my stitches might melt." She cracked the window, sat on the bed, and patted the quilt next to her. "What's brought you here on a Saturday? Shouldn't you be helping your own mother?"

Sarah pulled the door closed and sat next to her friend.

"I had to talk to someone. Your brother isn't going to barge in?"

"Sam's earning extra money at the cotton mill. Tell me."

"My parents ambushed me at *Shabbat* dinner last night."

"That sounds exciting," Anne said. "Attacked you with candles and loaves of bread?"

"Papa brought a man home with him unannounced. Not one of his usual cronies, a *gentleman*. In his twenties. His name was Chaim Hoffmann."

Anne squealed. "That's a mouthful. Was the fellow handsome?"

"I don't remember."

"Extra, extra! Sarah Engelmann forgot something!"

Sarah had to smile at that. She replayed last night's dinner in her head, trying not to grimace as the awkwardness returned with the imagery.

In her mind's eye, her parents and Mr. Hoffmann hung before her as vividly as if they sat in the room. His skin showed little evidence of exposure to the sun, his bearded face was thin, and his spectacles were twice as thick as her own.

Sarah blinked and the memory vanished. "Not handsome, not ugly."

"Then his manner was bothersome?"

She shook her head. "Gentlemanly enough. Clearly he was very bright. A student of Papa's friend."

"So what's the problem? Your mother married at eighteen. With your birthday coming up on us, your father's probably barely reining her in."

"I have to finish school," Sarah said. "And at least begin college. What's the point of having studied my whole life if all I do is settle down and start a family?"

"But it's exciting just the same. At least you have prospects."

"What are you talking about?" Sarah said. "Half the boys in school would cut off an arm to court you."

Anne sighed. "Even the thought of choosing is stressful. If it were all arranged it'd be easy. You're lucky."

Lucky? Sarah couldn't imagine one of Papa's friends' sons allowing her the freedom he did. Or the respect. They'd only want their table set and six brilliant sons to make them proud.

"I know what we should do!" Anne said. "With this heat and with your, um, stresses, we need a break. My lummox of a twin traded for a new filly this week. Why don't the three of us go riding tomorrow, take a picnic, make a proper outing of it?"

Anne was right. School had started only a month ago, and Sarah's life was already dominated by study.

"What time?" she said.

The girls drifted downstairs to find Mrs. Williams and Emily enter-taining a boy in the parlor. So close to becoming a man, he looked to grow four inches if you glanced away.

Emily's pink dress was disheveled but she appeared luminous just the same. Sarah worried about what was going to happen when she came into her own. Anne could be bold and outspoken, but she had a fundamental prudence entirely absent in her little sister.

The new boy rose to greet them. He was about the same age Sarah's brother would've been and almost as handsome.

"Charles Danforth." He extended his hand. His hair was much straighter than Judah's.

"Nice to meet you," Anne said, shaking hands. "You're a friend of Emily's?"

Emily looked like she wanted to take a bite out of someone.

"We both study Bible with Pastor Parris," the boy said.

"Charles is just leaving," Emily said. "He stopped by to bring us some of his mother's preserves."

Charles offered Sarah his hand, and she took it. The late after-noon sun streamed in through the windows and threw their shadows against the wallpaper. A sound rose in her ears, slow and mournful like that of the *shofar*, the ceremonial ram's horn blown to announce the New Year.

Sarah felt queer. Her mouth dry. Before her eyes the silhouettes on the wall contorted, human limbs and torsos shifting to form the shape of a leafless tree. The reddish hue of the sun — surely that's what it was — made the tree look as if it was drenched in blood. The horn continued to sound in her ears, loud but seemingly blown at great distance.

She released Charles' grip and the bloody tree vanished, in its place only the shadows of two young people who'd just shaken hands.

Two:

Dark Shadows

Near Salem, Massachusetts, Saturday evening, October 18, 1913

CHARLES TRUDGED DOWN the tree-shrouded lane, heading home. His visit to the Williamses hadn't gone the way he hoped. Just last week Emily had offered to kiss him behind the chapel, then stomped on his foot when he tried. She really wasn't very nice to him, but she brightened his time at church, in itself a small miracle. Just today — before she turned bratty — they'd been mocking the pastor's habit of raising his voice as he said certain words, like *damnation* or *purification.*

Charles could see farmhouses in the distance and a half-collapsed old barn hunkered a couple hundred yards from the road. A rising chatter of high-pitched shrieking and leathery flapping made him stop and turn.

From the barn flew hundreds, perhaps thousands, of tiny dark forms. They poured out of gaps in the decrepit roof and high eaves like thick columns of smoke. Twisting languidly upward, they braided together into a larger column before passing overhead. He craned his neck to watch their crisp black silhouettes against the dusky sky.

Bats. Just bats living in an abandoned barn. They left their roosts at sunset, flying off to feed on the warm evening's rich insect swarms. Charles took a deep breath and resumed his walk — more briskly than before.

Then he heard the voice.

The sound whispered in his head, not his ears, a soft caress made audible, issuing from all directions and none at all.

Stop, come to the trees. The tone was rich as milk straight from the pail, yet powerfully masculine. He stopped and walked off the road toward the trees. As he entered the darkening copse, a shadowy figure flitted from trunk to trunk.

Don't look at me, keep walking. The figure winked at the edges of his vision as he continued forward. Why couldn't he turn his head?

Here, stop. He stopped.

Someone approached from behind. A powerful scent encircled him, fragrances of damp earth and exotic spices, of cinnamon, honey, almonds. One hand reached from behind to clasp one of Charles', the other placed itself on his hip — almost in an embrace.

Your chance has come. The beginning is as light as the end. Now the hand pulled Charles' arm to the small of his back and jerked it upward, lifting him off the ground. A hideous, wrenching crack was accompanied by hideous, wrenching pain. His arm and shoulder burned. His gut spasmed, and he pitched forward, gasping.

Savor the feeling. On your wedding night, you must cut the cat's head. The hand on his hip withdrew, leaving him dangling excruciatingly by his twisted limb. His attacker hadn't come around, but somehow was now before him. Charles felt a hand almost caress him — then slap him brutally across the face. His head slammed sideways; nails tore into his skin. The pain knocked out any other sensation. He felt himself ebbing away. Like coals in an untended hearth, he was fading, and only the agony remained. He was dragged further from the road, tugged by a hand twisted into his hair. Charles fought to dig his heels into the earth, then fought not to yield to the blackness that rose to claim him....

It was the pain that woke him.

Everything was still dark. Everything in his body still hurt. He was seated on the bare earth, legs extended. His pants and shoes were gone, and he felt the leaves and dirt under his naked buttocks and heels. His shoulder screamed as his attacker, the man whose face he couldn't see, stripped him of his shirt. Charles tried to lash out against limbs unyielding as ironwood. The man grasped his flailing hand, held it as a lover might, then bent the index finger back until Charles felt rather than heard the bone snap. Along with the pain came an absurd thought: so much for piano practice tomorrow.

The sacred hour has arrived. The passage stirs. Agony altered Charles' perception, rendering his assailant in staccato images, like a picture-show projector cranked too fast. For all his strength the man wasn't big, little taller than Charles himself. The only parts not clothed or swathed in black were his hands — and his face, featureless in the twilight but so pale it made Charles think of his dead grandmother's sun-bleached snuff box feeding termites in the attic.

Rise to heaven. The man gripped his bare shins and lifted Charles into the air. His limp arm flopped painfully against the ground. He felt rough bark scrape against his naked back and rope burn his ankle as it was lashed to the tree. His face nearly kissed the man's black suede boots, square-toed but with peculiar high heels. Again he tried to scream.

Quiet. His breath exhausted, only the smallest animal noise emerged from his throat.

One leg securely fastened, one leg to go.

Pain reminds you that you're alive, the voice whispered. Two hands grabbed his free leg, one on the thigh, the other on the calf, and with another terrible crunch, the man twisted at odds to the direction of his knee. Blood seeped from where the bone pierced the skin.

A thousand pardons, I neglected to measure the tree. Charles vomited and then, because he was upside down, choked on it. Stomach acid drooled downward into his nostrils.

Gradually he became aware of a sound, a note from some titanic horn, slow and mournful, loud yet seemingly blown at great distance. He searched for its source. Below him — well, above him — was a brilliant dark orange and purple sky, clouds lit from the sides with an intense red light. Would that he could just step down into these cottony platforms. Hanging by his ankles, he could make out the gnarled roots of a great tree overhead. Warm tickles crawled across his face, dark liquid dripped off and fell upwards toward the twisted canopy of roots.

The man stood silhouetted against the luminous backdrop, his legs planted in the ground above forming a V, his features melding into the fading light.

Even in death, lost strength may be found. The man stepped toward him, and his dark shadow blotted out the heavens.

Three:
Sounding Call

Salem, Massachusetts, Sunday morning, October 19, 1913

SARAH SAT BOLT UPRIGHT in bed, her heart racing, her ragged breaths sawing at the silence. Silver daggers of moonlight lanced through the dormered window. The desolate trumpeting of the horn lingered in her head. She inhaled deeply and held, listening.

From outside she heard the rustle of trees, the chirps of nighttime insects, the clopping of horse hooves on cobblestones. She struggled to hold onto the filaments of memory that bound her to the nightmare. All but the tree slipped away. The leafless form stood alone amid dry brown grasses. The sky behind it glowed stark orange, and the blood-stained bark glistened with something black and damp.

She threw off her heavy quilt and padded to the window in her nightgown, the old oak floor rough under her bare feet. The yard and street below were peaceful, the newly installed electric streetlights mixing their warm yellow glow with the cold moonlight.

Was her subconscious simply reprising yesterday's trick of the eyes? She massaged her shoulder and knee. Both ached faintly, she must have slept in an awkward position.

Daybreak would arrive soon enough, and further sleep seemed futile. She began her morning prayers, standing straight in the center of the room, feet close together, bobbing gently at the waist.

Dressed in her house clothes, Sarah pressed her hand against the cigar-shaped silver *mezuzah* on her doorframe, then kissed her fingers. Superstitious habit, but touching the prayer box brightened her mood. She went downstairs to Papa's study — time to relent after giving him the cold shoulder all yesterday.

She took a moment to gather herself while glancing out the rear-facing window. In the yard, the familiar bushy shape of the sycamore soared at least fifty feet into the air. She'd read somewhere that the root systems of trees are as big or bigger than their branches above ground. If this were true, the growth probably extended underneath the house. And the tree in her nightmare had been a sycamore—

The faintest echo of the horn tickled her consciousness.

She yawned to clear her head and forced herself through the door.

Joseph Engelmann sat behind his desk, surrounded by papers and books. Thick ringlets of curly brown hair snaked downward from his small black cap until they blended into his beard.

"*Tateh ist es ich.*" Sarah said in Papa's native Yiddish.

Her presence didn't seem to register immediately. He must be teaching today — he wore a brown wool suit, a starchy white shirt, and the burgundy bow-tie with white polka-dots she'd given him on his fortieth birthday. The tie looked good on him, adding a little color and drawing attention away from a belly straining to free itself from his vest.

Eventually her voice penetrated. He looked up at her through his bifocal glasses, shoved an empty plate into a drawer, and brushed crumbs from Mama's pastries off his beard.

"You've forgiven me, I take it?"

Sarah, not ready to jump directly into the awkward space hanging between them, switched topic and language.

"I had a nightmare," she said in Hebrew. "If God, *Hashem,* tries to tell you something, wouldn't He send signs, or dreams?"

Papa could never resist a theological question.

"So the Torah tells us, but from a more modern perspective, 'Every dream will reveal itself as a psychological structure, full of significance.'"

She sighed. Papa had made her read Freud's *Interpretation of Dreams* last summer — in German — and she remembered it well enough.

"But the good doctor also likened a nosebleed to a woman's monthly cycle."

That earned her a smile.

"You rather the Lord sent an angel to make His point?" Papa said.

"Would the angel appear as a pretty young boy with wings?" she asked in Greek. She expected points for pairing the word *angelos* to his Hebrew *mal'akh,* both connoting messenger.

"Undoubtedly any angel, even a pretty one, would be smitten by my lovely daughter. However, God, is of *Atziluth,* of the highest world, and we are anchored in *Asiyah* the lowest."

"Now, what would you say if *I* stuck Hebrew words in a Greek sentence?"

"Enough. Mama tells me you're going riding today," he said in Latin. "With Anne and Sam?"

She felt much better. Talking, even so artificially, had returned them to stable footing.

"The twins and I have a picnic planned." Sarah settled back into English. "Mama was kind enough to relieve me from laundry duty." Thank God. She hated chapped hands.

"You deserve at least a little time with your friends. I monopolize far too much of it."

"I don't mind, I like to study," Sarah said. Plus she'd eat a wool jacket before letting anyone else get a better grade.

Papa nodded. "I'm sorry you were unnerved the other night, and I won't force anything on you, but marriage is a *mitzvah.*"

"Can't we just let events unfold?" she said.

"I didn't just pluck any young man off the street, you know. Rabbi Hoffmann and I have been friends for sixteen years and his son is the second brightest young scholar in New England."

Sarah made a study of her slippers.

She entered her mother's seat of power — the kitchen — wearing taupe riding pants and a ruffled white blouse with a high collar.

"Sarah, sit down and have some breakfast before you go, and if I thought it was going to make any difference, I'd mention it's inappropriate to be out in public wearing trousers."

Rebecca Engelmann was a plump, pretty woman with soft curves and merry eyes — nothing sharp about her except on occasion her tongue.

"Mama, everyone goes riding and cycling in pants these days. This is the twentieth century, remember?" Sarah helped herself to a roll and some pickled herring.

"Well, take a hat at least. Everyone isn't the only daughter of the Rabbi Josef ben Jacov ben Yitzhak."

"He really isn't a rabbi anymore," Sarah said. "We can call him Herr Professor Doctor Engelmann instead."

"Very amusing," her mother said. "But watch what you say outside this house. Your father treats you too much like a son, letting you think what you want, say what you want, study the *Zohar* even. You may be a brilliant scholar, but the effect on your manners is another matter entirely."

"It's pretty obvious why — since he started teaching me after…" Sarah caught the words before they left her mouth, but her mother still flinched.

"Whatever am I going to do with her?" Mama said. "She has such a tongue on her, learning things no woman has a right to know."

"It wasn't me who took that fruit from the tree," Sarah said. "I'd have given the serpent a smack on his scaly little *tuchus*."

Her mother tried to hide her smile. "What sort of scholar will want to marry a girl with such a smart mouth? At least when you end up alone, you'll have your books to entertain you."

"Fine with me," Sarah said.

"That public school has spoiled what your father didn't," Mama said.

"So why'd you send me there?" Sarah asked.

"They refused you at *yeshiva* because of your lip."

That stung! But then her mother's straight face broke into a grin.

"Seriously, Mama!" Sarah said. "Why?"

"Seriously, Sarah! You'll have to ask your father."

Sarah didn't think she would, at least not yet.

After finishing her fish, she crossed the room and wrapped her arms around her mother's softness.

"Sorry, and thanks for letting me go today. I owe you double the chapped hands next week," she said.

Mama hugged her back. "Just help me pack lunch for the three of you."

Sam waited on the brick sidewalk with his bay gelding behind him while he adjusted the saddle on what must be the new filly. Anne was some distance off, trotting her chestnut mare back and forth along the quiet street. Sarah still wasn't used to Sam's recent transformation. The lanky boy she'd known forever was now a man over six feet tall, with broad shoulders and reddish-blond stubble.

"Good morning, Mr. Williams," she said. "What's the new filly's name?" She put down her pack and approached the roan slowly, one hand extended toward its muzzle.

"Morning, Miss Engelmann." Sam drew the words out to mock Sarah's formality, then grinned. "She's Peach Melba, or just Mel if you like."

The filly did have the coloring of a white summer peach, a dappled reddish-pink layer of fur underneath pale white. Her spotted nostrils flared gently at Sarah's touch, but she seemed docile enough when stroked on the velvety soft nose.

"I like her; she's beautiful," Sarah said, looking up.

"When I saw her at the fair, I thought of you."

Papa's comments about marriage ricocheted back into her mind. How was attraction supposed to feel? She'd never given the whole business much thought, which was odd, given her penchant for over-thinking. Sam was clearly not "the second brightest young scholar in New England," but he was sweet — and handsome. For a second, she allowed herself to imagine being kissed. But the phantom kisser in her mind didn't look like Sam. Or anybody else she knew.

"Anyway," he added, "we wouldn't have much of a ride if you didn't have a horse."

"Papa thinks they're too much bother," she said. "But he's been leering at those brochures from the Ford Motor Company. Oil, steel, and belching smoke are more to his liking than manure."

Anne stopped prancing and maneuvered her horse to join them.

"Sam, get that pack on the horses. Nothing fun's going to happen here on the street five minutes from our house."

Sam snapped to attention, "Yes, ma'am!"

Since Salem's 48,000 or so souls were mostly packed inside a dense urban core, it didn't take Sarah and her friends long to leave the houses and factories and reach the surrounding rural neighborhoods.

"I was riding this way the other week," Sam said, "and I noticed a big meadow with a pond and southern exposure — perfect for a picnic."

He led them past a low farmer's wall and across a grassy stretch to an unpaved lane. An eight-foot hedge blocked out most of the view to the left. As they rode by, the morning quiet was shattered by a loud crack followed almost immediately by a metal ping. A small flock of geese took noisily to wing from behind the hedge and climbed diagonally into the sky.

Mel gave out a whinny as Sarah came to a sudden stop behind Sam's horse.

"Rifle shot," Sam said. Sarah caught the faint scent of gunpowder.

Anne smirked. "And I thought breakfast just wasn't agreeing with you."

Sam threw his sister a dirty look. He held out one palm toward the two girls, leaned forward to whisper something to his horse, then slid off. He really did have a way with animals. Sarah spoke six languages, but Horse wasn't one of them.

Twenty feet in front of them, the hedge was interrupted by a little gate. Sam crept to this opening, peered in, and called out.

"Hello there, sorry to—" Another shot rang out. "Disturb you. Didn't mean to mess up your shot, sir."

Anne grabbed the reins of Sam's horse as she passed.

Sarah saw through the gate into a large space overgrown with grasses. Striding toward them was a young man, compact and wiry, with fair skin, dark curly hair, and just the hint of a goatee. He was dressed in peculiar baggy black trousers tucked into knee-high boots, and a loose white linen blouse with an old-fashioned embroidered vest. Slung over his shoulder was a long rifle on a thick leather strap. He looked vaguely familiar.

"I apologize if my gunfire disturbed you." His voice was slightly accented. "I only just arrived in America this summer, and in my homeland a little target practice is almost a national pastime."

Sam examined the gun on the young man's shoulder. "I haven't seen a bolt action like this before."

The young man swung the weapon off his back. "It's a Mannlicher-Schönauer, Austrian-made for the Greek army." He fussed with the mechanism. "There's an interesting rotating bolt action—"

Anne directed her horse's nose onto Sam's shoulder and her attention to the newcomer.

"Aren't you in my Natural Science class?"

He studied their faces. "Indeed, and we've forgotten our manners! My name's Alexandros Basileus Palaogos." He performed a funny little bow, leaning on the rifle for support. "But please, call me Alex."

Sarah tried to visualize each of her own classes. No wonder he looked familiar. She found him sitting in the back right corner of first period Senior English. Her own desk was in the front left, near the teacher.

Sam smiled. He shared that science class with his sister. "I'm Sam Williams, the corrector of our manners is my twin sister Anne, and this young lady is Miss Sarah Engelmann."

Alex — who she'd never really paid attention to in school — shifted his attention to her now, and Sarah felt more heat on her skin than the morning temperature warranted.

"Have you been to the Acropolis?" Of course she was showing off her conversational Greek. "Or to the Oracle's cave at Delphi?" She'd never traveled beyond Boston, but she desperately wanted to visit Europe.

"Yes, on all accounts, although your grammar is more suited to Sophocles than the streets of Athens." His Greek was perfect — and why shouldn't it be? "But your charms bring to mind golden Aphrodite."

At once prickled and flattered, Sarah wasn't about to let the newcomer get the upper hand. Using a proper if awkward dactylic hexameter, she said, "Good thing I'm laughter-loving Aphrodite as well, if you're going to throw epithets from Homer around."

Alex laughed. "I'm being rude yet again," he said in English and glanced at the twins.

Anne moved her horse closer to Sarah's. "We've come out of town for a ride and a picnic," she said. "If you've had enough of killing innocent cans, you're welcome to join us."

Sarah felt a little stab of jealousy. Ridiculous. Realistically, she was going to have to start considering Papa's *yeshiva bucher* selections soon enough.

"Bring the gun," Sam said. "I've a pistol. After we eat we can shoot targets for pennies."

The newcomer had better have money. Sam had taken the state fair marksmanship prize three years running.

"Let me fetch Bucephalus," Alex called back over his shoulder as he turned toward his barn.

Now that took the cake. The young man had named his horse after Alexander the Great's stallion.

Four:
Picnic

Near Salem, Massachusetts, Sunday, October 19, 1913

ALEX JOGGED TO THE BARN and started the process of wrestling Bucephalus into his tackle and harness. He wanted to rush back as fast as he could. His life right now was boring, and he knew it.

The move to America had been exciting: the train ride across Europe followed by the luxurious ten-day party that was the steamer crossing. But after unpacking last May, he'd settled into a monotonous regimen. He read, wandered around the yard, rode Bucephalus, or played chess with tight-lipped Dmitri. In the evening or early morning Grandfather was more likely to be awake, but even when they did talk, the old man was usually distant and distracted.

All summer Alex had planned a sojourn into town to see the modern shopping district, old colonial houses, and the nineteenth-century wharfs that once received pepper from Sumatra. He'd even read the *Scarlet Letter* and *The House of the Seven Gables*.

But he never went. He didn't relish outings by himself and couldn't convince Grandfather or Dmitri to join him. At school, whether Irish, Italian, French, or Polish, everyone stuck with their own, and while there were other Greeks, he'd nothing in common with them.

Today's excursion would make for a welcome change. Sam seemed nice enough, and hell, if he'd been bound to a post and forced merely to watch either young lady, he'd have counted the day well spent.

After cinching the saddle tight, he paused for a moment to give Bucephalus a carrot. The stallion was everything you could ever want in a horse, but it was good to remind him of that sometimes. Alex grabbed his rifle, mounted, and trotted the big black out to the gate.

Fortune was with him, they'd waited.

The blond girl was terrifyingly beautiful. Slender except for the bountiful, beautiful curves of her hips and breasts, her skin carved from alabaster.

"With that outfit," she said when he and Bucephalus pulled up, "we'd better not run into the police. They might think we're out to rob a train."

But it wasn't Anne who'd really caught his eye.

It was Sarah — lovely too, if not in the same league. She was a little thing, barely five feet tall, with fiery energy and quick motions that made the dark coils of her hair quiver. In riding clothes she looked different than the girl in his English class who always had her hand up, and today, while batting at him with her pedantic Greek, the intensity of her gaze had made him feel something he rarely did with others: noticed.

"I think he looks more like *Battle for the Balkans*," the object of his attention said.

Alex glanced down at himself. Perhaps the vest and the two crossed ammunition belts were a bit much for Massachusetts.

"Pay the chittering birds no mind." Sam's face was all grin as he nimbly dodged a swing of his sister's riding crop.

They set off down the road, Sam leading his bay into a graceful trot. He straddled that Apollonian line between handsome and pretty — and Apollo had a twin sister, too, but Anne didn't look much the huntress. When Sam casually flipped himself around to speak to her, riding backward for a moment, Alex was impressed. He'd ridden as long as he could remember and he would never think to try such a maneuver.

After thirty or so minutes they crested a gentle slope strewn with wild grasses and autumn flowers. At the bottom a small cow pond was ringed by trees and low brush.

While Alex and Sam wiped down the horses and posted them to graze, the girls spread some blankets and unloaded the packs. There were sandwiches made from thick beef, pickled cucumbers and tomatoes, an extra loaf of bread, fig jam, a glass jar containing what looked to be noodles, something akin to apple strudel, and a jug of cider. Each item was carefully wrapped in butcher paper, right down to plates, silverware, and even three small glasses.

"Whoever prepared this lunch was both generous and assiduous," he said.

"My mother," Sarah said, "is a woman who holds any task to exacting standards."

"So, Alex," Anne said as they settled on the blankets with their food, "what brought your family to Salem?"

"It's actually just my grandfather and his manservant Dmitri. My parents died when I was little."

An uneasy silence hung in the air.

"I'm sorry," Anne said.

"It's not a problem." There was a time when this subject had made Alex angry, but in recent years the feeling had faded to a hollow ache. In some ways, he missed it — even a negative emotion might be better than none.

"I don't remember my parents. And Grandfather, he's an antiquarian, a dealer and collector of old things, a historian of sorts. The market is poor in Greece. Salem has old houses and people who buy old things."

"He's a historian?" Sarah said. "My father teaches religion and history at the college."

"Greek history is Grandfather's specialty." Alex chuckled. "And that's full of religion. He loves the late Middle Ages so much he takes the fall of Constantinople to the Turk rather personally. Every year on May 29th he lights candles and mourns."

Anne uncrossed her legs and stretched luxuriously across the blanket. "Pardon me for asking, but what happened on May 29th?"

Sarah's arm half rose, as if she were in school. Alex swallowed his smile.

"In 1453, the Turkish Sultan Mehmed II captured and sacked the city of Constantinople, modern Istanbul. The Byzantine Empire collapsed, and the last Roman Emperor, by this time really a Christian Greek king, was killed."

Alex was speechless. He'd never met a boy who could rattle off such facts — let alone an American girl — and Sarah's animated hand movements were mesmerizing.

Anne elbowed her in the ribs. "Sarah's father isn't the only lecturer in the family."

Sign him up for her class. "She's correct," he said, "and it was a very sad day, when my people came to be ground under the heels of the Ottoman Turk." He stood up. "Since you've been so generous with your morning and your lunch, I'd like to share a tradition from my homeland."

He walked over to his saddlebag and rummaged for the small cloth-wrapped bundle.

"Ouzo, from the island of Lesbos, birthplace of Sappho." He returned to the group with a dark green bottle. "Our national drink. It's traditionally consumed with friends before or after a meal."

He dumped the water from each glass and poured the clear liquor.

"Foreigners often find the taste… unusual." He held his cup toward the group. "To new friends, *opa*!"

They clinked glasses. Alex tossed the contents down his throat and awaited the reactions of the uninitiated. Sam, who had also taken his in one gulp, rewarded him with bulging eyes.

Five:

Afterglow

Near Salem, Massachusetts, Sunday, October 19, 1913

AFTER SAM'S REACTION, Sarah gave her cup a sniff and discovered a licorice-like smell with a medicinal note. She took a sip. A warm anise fire burned its way into her mouth and spread through her sinuses. The sensation was more like a tonic than wine. She forced herself to swallow, and a ball of sinking fire traveled down her throat. She took another sip.

The conversation continued, but Sarah soon felt light-headed and distant. She drank wine on holidays or at Sabbath dinner with her family, never anything out of doors or in the daytime. Alex was asking the twins about their family. Anne told him about the boarders at their house in town. Sam told him about the horses he tended. Their voices sounded like a phonograph with the volume turned too low. Sarah looked around. The whole world felt lazy. Even the gnats churned above the grass in languid gyrations. She stood up, her feet swollen and prickly.

"I'm going to take a walk around the pond to clear my head. Anne?"

"Why not? You boys can talk about guns or dynamos or something."

"Ladies, enjoy yourselves." Alex turned to Sam as soon as they moved away. "I'll get my rifle. We can put some pine cones on a stump. What firearm did you bring?"

"A Schofield Model 3 revolver, like Jesse James used. My uncle brought it back from out west."

"A genuine cowboy weapon," Alex said. "May I try it?"

"As long as you've got coins to wager." Sam's face was all grin.

Sarah and Anne strolled across a thick carpet of grass that soon gave way to the ivy-covered stretch under the trees. Their boots crunched hidden twigs as they picked their way over to the narrow cattle path ringing the pond.

"I'm floating like a dandelion in the breeze," Anne said. "That licorice drink...."

"It's not just the alcohol — I've been feeling weird all day. Last night I had a nightmare about a bloody tree."

Her friend swooned in operatic terror. "Stop my heart in its tracks: a bloody tree!"

Sarah swatted at her. "There's more to it. Yesterday when we met Emily's friend I thought I saw the same tree in the shadows on the wall, and this morning I realized it looked like the big sycamore behind the house. Maybe God's trying to send me a message."

"Sarah, how much of that stuff *did* you drink?"

She smiled, not wanting Anne to think she was serious, even if she half was. Behind them in the distance, shots rang out as the boys practiced their marksmanship.

"Enough of that," Anne said. "Tell me what you think of Alexandros." Of course she didn't pause or wait for a reply. "I think he fancies you, and he's handsome in a goaty Mediterranean way."

"Anne, he's not even Jewish. And *goaty*? What kind of person is goaty?" Religion aside, the picnic had been fun, and she was pretty sure their new friend was no small cause in the effect.

"Well, the curly hair and that little bit of dark beard on the chin, goaty. Not a Billy goat but an Alexi goat. Baa!"

Anne placed her index fingers to the sides of her forehead like horns. There ensued a fit of giggling, punctuated by an occasional bleat from one girl or the other.

More gunshots rang out in the distance. Anne glanced back.

"I hope that awful tonic didn't rob the boys of too much common sense — they'd better aim away from our direction."

They were roughly halfway around the emerald-green pond when Sarah saw something white protruding from a large mass of brush.

"What's that?"

Anne turned to look and Sarah forced her myopic eyes to focus. It was a naked human leg, jutting from the undergrowth. Unnaturally white, not even the slightest hint of skin color, splattered and streaked with a dried brownish-red blood. The limb was twisted grotesquely at the knee, the joint bent oddly, perpendicular to the direction of the ankle.

Anne screamed.

Sarah stood paralyzed by fear. Anne's scream went on and on until, finally, she stopped to breathe. Her face was almost as pale as the leg before them.

Sarah took Anne's hand — warm and clammy. Behind them, a loud rustling in the brush injected further terror until she saw Sam and Alex crash through.

"You two okay?" Sam said between heavy breaths.

Anne threw her arms around him while Sarah pointed at the thicket.

Alex swung his rifle off his shoulder to aim at the brush, stepped closer, and returned the weapon to his back.

"That poor soul's done with violence for this life," he said.

Good Lord. A dead body. Sarah had never seen one, not even when Judah died — her parents hadn't allowed her into the room.

Sam joined Alex in examining the form under the brush.

"This is no accident," he said. "We should summon the authorities."

Sarah straightened her broad hat and brushed at her pants. She needed something practical to focus on.

"Sam's a fast rider. Maybe he should find a house and ask them to call the police. The rest of us can wait here." With the body. She shuddered.

Sam glanced at Alex. "Will you girls be okay here with him?"

Did he mean the Greek or the corpse?

Alex turned his eyes to the ground.

"We'll be okay," Sarah heard herself say.

"I'm over the worst of it," Anne said. "Alex has his gun." She tried to smile.

"Hurry, Sam," Sarah said. "And remember to look for a house with telephone wires. We're pretty far out of town."

"In Greece," Alex said, "you could ride for a whole day to find a telegraph."

Sam snorted. "I don't suppose it'll take that long."

They watched him sprint off in the direction of the horses.

Alex stepped toward the body. "Let's see what we have here." He leaned down to clear brush off the remains.

"What're you *doing*?" Sarah said. The deceased belonged to God now — and the police.

But she spoke too late. Alex heaved the tangled ball of vegetation off the cadaver and to the side. Anne gasped.

The body of a boy lay naked in the dirt, belly up, covered only by a few remaining sticks and leaves. His eyes stared at the sky, his face frozen in bewilderment. His skin was bluish-white. One arm was twisted behind his back, the shoulder bulging unnaturally. On the opposite side his mangled knee was twisted, lending him a ghastly diagonal symmetry. Gashes scarred his wrists and ankles, and a deep gouge split the side of his torso. There was surprisingly little blood, though flies buzzed about the wounds, crawled in and out of his nostrils and mouth.

Oh, God. The crust of blood around his lips made Sarah think of Judah. In those last months, when the consumption had all but eaten him from the inside, she would sit by his bed and hold a damp cloth to his bloody mouth as he shuddered and coughed his life away.

Anne whimpered nearby.

"I think it's Charles," she whispered.

Sarah forced herself to look at the face. She'd met Charles only that once, yesterday, and the dead boy's face looked different — like a wax mannequin's — but it was him, at least the material part of him. His soul, she hoped, had moved on to some better place.

The slow tone of the mournful horn rose out of nowhere to sound in her ears. Charles' lifeless face lifted slightly, his right eye winked at her, and he raised an arm to point at a leafless tree glistening with black wetness in the warm afternoon sun. Blood slicked the trunk and roots.

Sarah jumped back. The little shriek that passed her lips sounded like someone else's.

"Are you all right?" Anne's voice severed the horn blast.

She looked around. Sunlight streamed in through the thick foliage to dapple the unstained bark of the mossy tree. The startled birds resumed their songs and Charles' ashen body lay still on the leafy dirt.

She wasn't crazy. But she should have warned him yesterday. Somehow, for some reason, God had sent her a sign, and she hadn't listened.

Six:
Paradise Lost

Near Salem, Massachusetts, Sunday afternoon, October 19, 1913

ALEX SHIFTED HIS WEIGHT from one foot to the other. It seemed inappropriate to comfort the girls — he had, after all, only met them today. He tried to distract himself by studying the body again, eyes drawn repeatedly to the boy's nearly hairless manhood, lying there like a pallid little worm. Sarah and Anne had likely never seen any man naked, and certainly none like this one. He pulled a silk handkerchief out of his vest pocket, unfolded it, and draped it across the organ in question.

"Thank you, Alex," Anne said. "I feel so bad for his mother. Who could've done something so horrible?"

Alex had seen his grandfather dissect enough crimes to make an attempt at an explanation.

"The body was concealed, and someone wrenched that leg and arm with tremendous force. It's possible he had a machine accident and someone dumped him here."

He didn't really think it was an accident, and he was far less calm than he appeared. Anne's screams had triggered one of his old memories: a woman wailing, her shadowy face illuminated by firelight. Knowing that to chase the image into the labyrinth of his mind would only lead to a headache, he forced his thoughts elsewhere.

"It wasn't a machine," Sarah said. "Look at the wounds on the wrists and ankles, the big slash on his torso." She paused for a second. "Could they be stigmata?"

Could she be right? There was something ritualistic, even Christlike, about this killing. The body lay there, pale shoulders twisted, rib cage protruding, arms extended, macabre. He tried to watch Sarah without looking directly at her. First she talks about the fall of Constantinople, then stigmata?

Anne shivered despite the bathhouse air. "Alex, can I borrow your jacket?"

An hour later, Alex heard a siren, followed by the distant growl of an auto-mobile. Sam arrived not long after, accompanied by two men in uniforms and a third in a dark suit.

"Inspector George Finn," said the gentleman in the suit. He looked back and forth between the brush pile and the body itself. "One of you removed that?"

"I did," Alex said. "Only a leg was showing, and I thought it best to make sure he was dead, not merely injured."

The inspector nodded. "From the look of him, since yesterday or last night. Rest assured, we'll get to the bottom of this. One of you mentioned you knew the boy's name?"

Anne said, "It's — I mean he was — a friend of my younger sister, Charles Danforth. He even visited our house yesterday."

"I'll need more details on that," the inspector said. "Do you know where he lived?"

Anne shook her head.

"There are Danforths about a mile from here, sir," one of the officers said. "I think they have a son about this age."

"If you know the house," the inspector said, "take one of the motorcars and head on over. Don't mention anything about a death.

If they have a son, and he's missing, ask them to come to the station at..." He glanced at his pocket watch. "Five o'clock. That'll give us enough time to document the scene and bring the body downtown. Please try to be tactful."

After the police released them, they walked quietly back to the horses. Bucephalus bit playfully at Alex's shoulder when he adjusted the bridle. Yesterday, he would have considered the stallion his only friend.

The picnic earlier had been great fun, and he'd even enjoyed losing thirty cents to Sam. He hoped the disturbing turn of events at the pond wouldn't sour his new fellowship. The fates could be cruel, tempting the starving man with a feast and then snatching it away just as he approached the table.

Seven:
School Days

Salem, Massachusetts, Monday, October 20, 1913

ALEX ROSE ABOUT AN HOUR before the sun. Grandfather's intermittent sleep wasn't predictable but his predawn activity never varied, making this quiet window of time the only one the three bachelors consistently spent together.

He wound through the maze of staircases and twisty corridors that honeycombed his new home. Built by some mad baker-turned-architect, its gothic revival style and turret-like tower lent it a haphazard appearance not unlike a giant gingerbread house. To this Grandfather had added his own taste for the baroque, a hodgepodge of medieval trunks and benches juxtaposed with Viennese and Venetian cabinets — all undercut with dizzying non-figural carpets. Dark portraits of dour old men and dying saints scowled down from ornate framed perches.

In the breakfast room, Alex found the usual morning fare: olives, feta made fresh with milk from Dmitri's precious goats, and a plate of deep-fried dough balls drizzled with honey. He snagged one of these treats and a slab of the white cheese, stuffed them both into his mouth, and enjoyed the contrast of sweet and salty. The high whistle and wonderful aroma of brewing coffee drew him into the kitchen.

Dmitri was taking the pot off the stove with a rag. The Albanian was closer to seven feet than six, and Alex wouldn't hazard a guess as to his real age. In the fifteen or so years he remembered, perhaps Dimitri's unruly black beard and banana-sized mustache had taken on a bit more white, and certainly his huge frame carried twoscore more pounds, but he didn't really look any different.

Seeing Alex enter, he plucked a porcelain coffee cup out of a cabinet with an almost dainty two-fingered grip. He held the little octagonal pot a full two feet above the cup, pouring without spilling a drop while pivoting 180 degrees. The hairy giant presented this offering with a low bow and one of the characteristic flourishes that for him took the place of conversational pleasantries. While Dmitri understood Greek more or less fluently, he was laconic to an extreme, and when he did speak, it was in short bursts of his incomprehensible mountain tongue.

Alex thanked him before sipping the chewy coffee.

"Is Grandfather about?"

The Albanian clasped his hands together and opened them like a book.

"Ah, reading," Alex said. "I'll bring him while you finish setting the table."

He crossed the dark hall and entered his grandfather's even darker library.

The old man sat in his wheelchair by the cold fireplace, snoring gently, a large book on his lap and a candle smoldering on the side table. His tall and elegant frame was cloaked in his favorite scarlet and gold damask robe, cinched with a braided gold belt. His sleeping face was long and attenuated, crowned by a lengthy mane of hair still thick and lustrous though its color had bleached to a bone white. Long spider-like fingers steepled the tome he'd been reading, and narrow slippers of purple velvet protruded from under the robe's hem. In sleep his face looked slack.

He startled. Fierce intensity snapped back into his figure and piercing intelligence into his gaze.

"Good morning, Alexandros," he said in Greek. "Ready for another week at your new American school?"

"Ready enough, Grandfather. Shall I push you to breakfast, or would you like to walk?"

The old man caressed one of the wooden wheels.

"I'm not feeling my strongest today."

"You haven't been eating enough." Alex began to maneuver the bulky chair. "You lost too much weight on the ship."

He half-remembered a time when the hair had been more gray than white, and Grandfather had stood on his own. A little stab of pain jabbed Alex in the temples. By the Father and the Son, he hated mornings.

"My diet does not agree with me like it once did," the old man said. "The wine no longer tastes of the fruit but only of dry dust and decayed earth. Enjoy the bright flavors of your youth, for eventually all things are wearisome. Would that the eye never has enough of seeing, nor the ear its fill of hearing." A grin made his face look all the more cadaverous.

With Constantine Palaogos' cryptic allusions, partial comprehension was only to be expected. He wheeled Grandfather through the dining room, as the old man thought the kitchen too bright and fit only for servants. Once settled in his accustomed place, he glowered at the food, making no attempt to help himself.

Alex sighed and sat, grabbing a few olives to munch on.

Dmitri set Alex's abandoned coffee before him and handed his employer a cup of dark liquid, saying only one word: "Basil." Alex shared this middle name with his grandfather, and it was Dmitri's private appellation for the old man. The big servant settled comically on the tiny stool he preferred, reminding Alex of a Russian dancing bear.

They hadn't spoken the previous evening.

"Yesterday I made some American friends — from my school — but while we were out enjoying the day we stumbled on a tragic scene."

Constantine's eyes glittered; the macabre was guaranteed to pique his interest.

"Tragic? Tell me about that first, then I'll want complete descriptions of each companion."

Grandfather preferred detailed reports, which he blamed on his years as a military officer. Alex dutifully summarized.

"I saw no obvious motive for the killing, but the condition of the cadaver, the cruelty of the attack, the ritual arrangement of the corpse…. I did wonder: could it have been one of them?"

The old man's narrow face brightened.

"You were right to suspect more than the usual variety of meanness," he said. "But I've not heard of a ritual that fits this description, although there are as many ceremonies as practitioners. Crucifixion is, of course, an important element in many ancient European sacrifices. There were no distinguishing attributes? Markings? Figures? Herbs?"

"Just the body," Alex said.

When they'd lived in Constantinople, a certain Pasha-come-police-magistrate had approached Constantine for help with these types of murders. Surprisingly, given how Grandfather felt about the Turks, he'd always been gracious and helpful. His interest in morbid criminality apparently outweighed his political aversions.

"Perhaps the ritual was only symbolic, not necessarily efficacious," he said. "It's also interesting that one of your new friends observed a relationship to the stigmata. And a female?"

Alex laughed. "The world's changing on you, Grandfather. I read in the paper about women starving themselves in protest for the right to vote."

The expression that crossed Grandfather's face was like that of a man discovering a long overlooked cheese in the ice-box.

"Allowing women the franchise would be like expecting fish to speak."

Alex's sinuses filled with snorted coffee grinds.

"Some Greek you are," he said when he recovered.

Constantine's yellowing old eyes narrowed.

A sliver of rising sun peeked above the horizon as Alex headed for the Highland Avenue trolley. He enjoyed the brisk walk until his reverie was disturbed by a neighbor's German Shepherd barking at him incessantly. Dogs made Alex nervous, particularly pointy-eared dogs with ill-natured temperaments. He was chased for at least a quarter-mile, escaping only when the streetcar drowned out the barks, shrieking and rattling around the corner. He swung onto the crowded trolley and clung to a pole while the dog continued its pursuit, losing ground and eventually reaching some territorial limit.

As the vehicle rolled into town he marveled again at the contrast with Greece, and not just the wood and brick buildings. New England buzzed with energy, smokestacks and construction, a constant reminder of the infestation of factories and businesses. People here didn't revel in past glories — they worked, fashioning the raw materials borne in on trucks and carts into finished goods. Americans were clearly fond of the whole process, judging by the time and money they spent flitting about the insane variety of shops.

The buildings grew more residential near the new high school, where Alex spied a handwritten sign, "Special Assembly, 7:00 a.m., Hawthorne Hall." He let the current of students pull him inside. Brick walls and terrazzo flooring amplified the boisterous conversations. He'd been forcing himself to think in English, but his lack of fluency hit home with every babbled sentence.

"Alex! Abandon hope, all ye who enter here."

He swiveled too slow to avoid a jovial blow to the back. Sam stood with his twin and another girl who looked like a miniature reflection of her.

"Let me introduce our baby sister, Emily," Anne said with a big grin. "I'm embarrassed to say that your surname escapes me."

"I'm not a baby anything. I'm fourteen." The girl gave Alex a theatrical curtsey. "I'm embarrassed to say God made me Anne's sister."

"Ignore them," Sam said. "Sarcasm is a Williams family trait. In England, two hundred years ago, some ancestor insulted an important lord, and onto the boat they shoved her."

He gave Anne a push. She stumbled right into Alex and he barely managed to grab her arms before they ended up in a decidedly public embrace.

"Thanks," she whispered, and turned to kick Sam in the shin.

She was still grinning when the surrounding babble quieted and Principal Burnsworth took the stage.

"It is with great regret that I inform you of the tragic death of one of our entering freshmen, Charles Danforth...."

The low murmur of the crowd rose to a cacophony as the student body exchanged rumors.

"Quiet, please.... Quiet! Thank you. Memorial services will be held at the Tabernacle Third Congregational on Wednesday...."

"Do you think they'll let us see Charles at the funeral?" Emily whispered.

The girl looked so young and innocent. Her long blond hair was like her sister's, and her skin almost a crystalline glaze. Even at fourteen, she was heartrendingly fetching.

"Don't be morbid, Emily," Anne said. "They won't have an open casket." She turned to Alex. "It's not something Congregationalists usually do."

Charles had been Emily's friend. But condolences always lay awkwardly on Alex's tongue, making him think he should feel more than he did.

Thirty-odd desks were bolted to the floor in Alex's first class, all facing the teacher's desk. Mrs. Fletcher nested behind this inglorious failure of the cabinetmakers' art, plump, wearing a pleasant expression and a ridiculous tweed hat.

He spied Sarah in front, next to the casement windows that showcased a brick wall. Alex's assigned desk was in the back, but the one behind her was empty.

"Is this seat free?" he asked as he approached from behind.

"I'm sorry," she said in falsetto. "It's reserved for Mr. Palaogos. Most people are intimidated so close to the front."

She'd remembered his surname.

"I'm not." He took the seat. "And I'm happy to see you again. I didn't notice you at the assembly."

She turned her head so he was speaking to her profile. It was a nice profile.

"I ditched," she said. "I suspect Mr. Burnsworth had no brilliant new wisdoms." Alex saw half a smile.

"The man could bore paint off a wall."

They both laughed.

"Have you learned anything else about the poor boy's murder?" Sarah asked. "The newspaper didn't say anything new."

Alex had a sudden urge to share some details from his conversation with Grandfather. A lifetime of family secrecy clashed with his desire to say something, anything, that might impress her. He shrugged — mentally. *Hubris* led only to *nemesis*.

"The funeral's on Wednesday," he said. "Emily's going. I assume you know her?"

"Of course, ninny, only since she was two." From her, the insult was endearing. "Their church is a peculiar place. Reserved and cold, so unlike the Williams themselves. Basically, it's Puritan. They changed the name, but it's the same congregation. And the pastor, he's actually descended from the minister who tried the Salem witches! Isn't that creepy? But then I'm not Christian, so I can't help thinking of Torquemada."

Alex's head began to buzz. Sarah was pushing a lot of information at him, and her soapy smell was distracting, took the edge off his thinking. If not a Christian, what was she?

"I don't know much about American churches," he told her. "But if you need information on fussy Orthodox patriarchs, I'm your man. Tales of old martyrs are my grandfather's idea of bedtime stories."

Sarah raised the eyebrow he could see. "The man sounds more and more interesting. Nothing like thumbscrews and hot pokers to send you off to sleep."

"Well, now—"

A boy kicked his desk. "Wop, you sitting behind the Christ-killer?"

This sort deserved to be stomped faster than an Athenian roach. Alex stood up.

"Apologize to the lady," he said.

It happened fast. The bully shoved Alex's shoulder with his palm.

He shoved back. Hard. Caught off guard, the boy tumbled backward into a bolted desk, couldn't regain his balance, and crashed to the floor.

Everybody in the class erupted in laughter.

Except for the bully and Mrs. Fletcher.

Which was how Alex ended up having a private audience with Principal Burnsworth.

After what amounted only to a stern warning, Alex found Sam in the cafeteria waiting for his plate of overcooked food. In Greece, nothing was so organized or institutional. Today Alex received split pea soup, bread and butter, veal stew with vegetables, lima beans, milk, and a strange confection called a raisin layer cake.

"Sarah and I have been friends a long time," Sam said as they each handed over a nickel. "But my sister could use a hand on the reins."

Americans were so blunt. "If Paris had met Anne instead of Helen," Alex said, "there'd have been no Trojan War."

"I assume that means you think she's pretty?"

"An understatement."

Sam beamed and slapped Alex on the back again. He might end up with a bruise.

Sarah and the Williams girls were already seated. Anne was regaling Emily with advice about her teachers, and Emily looked bored. Sarah had brought her own lunch, a sandwich and an apricot.

"You don't like the school food?" Alex asked.

"My mother packs mine — religious dietary laws. I can't eat milk and meat at the same time, or pork at all."

That made him think of the incident with the bully.

"I hope what happened this morning isn't a regular occurrence."

"It was just words," she said. "I'm sorry you got in trouble."

"Boys can be mean." He had a knife scar on his thigh to prove that. "They're just as bad back home and we didn't even have—"

"Jews?" She giggled.

Sam sat next to his sisters, but he kept glancing at Alex and Sarah.

"I never knew any. My grandfather says everyone draws power from their own faith."

"That's very enlightened."

"I'm not sure that's the right word for him." Alex smiled. "But Greeks have lots of rules, too. The faithful are advised to avoid olive oil, meat, fish, milk and dairy products every Wednesday and Friday, and to fast for forty days before Christmas, and forty-eight before Easter—"

"No special restrictions for the third Monday in October?" She looked at his plate.

"Probably some saint's day. We haven't followed all those since I was little."

"I *was* kidding," she said.

"It's still hard for me to identify sarcasm in English," Alex said.

"We can offer you plenty of practice," Anne said.

Alex couldn't help but laugh with the rest of them.

Anne banged the table with both hands to get everybody's attention — which, of course, she already had.

"Lots of folk are going to the Willows on Thursday night. Let's go while we can — it's closing for the season soon, and there's talk of instituting a curfew because of the murder."

Whatever the Willows was, it had to be more exciting than another macabre evening with Grandfather.

Eight:
An Unusual Conversation

Salem, Massachusetts, Wednesday, October 22, 1913

ANNE HAD BEEN RIGHT about the funeral, Charles' coffin was closed. He'd been Emily's only friend in the youth group bible study, but he was finished studying now. Thinking about him gave her a peculiar sensation, not so different from riding down the big hill of the Willows water chute. It made her want to cry and at the same time pulled the corners of her mouth into a grin.

Pastor Parris' gaunt face was crowned by a slick of brown hair combed back from his high forehead. When he grew animated — as he always did when denouncing sin — this sheet often tumbled across his face, only to be swept back, immediately and compulsively, by one hand or the other.

The pastor was always nice to her because she helped out around church. Sometimes he'd bless her with warm hands that made her skin crawl a little. But his sermons, even the hair-flipping kind, could be awfully repetitive. He seemed to take the whole hell thing very seriously. Emily had a fantasy about hell she liked. She was nude and a bunch of red-skinned demons cooked her up for dinner. It didn't hurt. Usually they cut her open and stuffed her insides with fruit and stale bread. Sometimes they boiled her naked in a big pot. Thinking about it made the place between her legs buzz. Besides, she was going to heaven, so it really wasn't an issue.

The boring part done, everyone milled about to offer condolences. Emily stood to the side with the twins, who were arguing. They did that a lot, particularly if no one else was around. Evidently, Emily counted as 'no one else.'

"Sammy, if that little bit of sand you're hinting about has even begun to put on a layer of pearl, I'll cut off your head before you can blink."

Now that sounded like an interesting hell-type sermon.

"I can't help what I feel, *Annie*." They hardly ever used their nicknames any more.

"Your feelings aren't even real," Anne said. "We've all been friends forever, and it's going to stay that way. You know you're competitive — it's probably just because we met Alex."

"I'm not competitive," he said. "And I like Alex, and it's great to have another man around. I might be a better shot, but I never saw a finer horse than Bucephalus — his riding ain't bad, either."

He smiled at her. Emily knew that smile. He was up to something.

He said, "You like horses. Maybe you two should go riding."

Anne glared at him, but before she could say anything their parents returned.

"Mommy, I need to ask the pastor about one of our Bible assignments," Emily said. There weren't any, but her mother wouldn't know that.

"I wanted to thank you for delivering such a nice service," she said. "Charles was my friend."

Pastor Parris looked down at her. "I have to go back to the parish and close up. Have a good evening, Emily."

"I can help if you like."

"That won't be necessary. I'll see you Sunday."

Disappointing. If she went straight home, she'd have no excuse to avoid chores or homework. The schoolwork she'd eventually have to do, but if she dodged the chores long enough, Sam would take care of them. She drifted back to her parents.

"I volunteered to help the pastor close up."

Technically it wasn't a lie. And anyway, if they made the twins include her no deceit would be—

"Fine, Emily," her mother said. "Just be home before dark."

Emily dawdled in the old graveyard near the church, long full now. The new cemetery where Charles was buried was a few blocks away. Funny to think of a graveyard full up, packed with bones. She played at jumping from grave to grave, trying to land wherever she thought a skull might be — six feet under, of course. By the time the pastor returned to enter the small wooden building, the sun had almost set.

She crept over to the church door and peered into the sanctuary. The central room was dark, the orange glow from the sky streaming in through the high windows. The pastor must have gone into his office, so she slipped inside. She walked slowly down the middle aisle on her toes, trying not to let the old floorboards betray her. Halfway to the altar, she slid into a hardwood pew. She folded her good dress carefully and sat, studying the altar and its single plain crucifix.

Perhaps she should leave before the pastor returned. A loud flapping from the entrance sent her beneath the pew to lie on the wooden floor.

The church door swung open with a loud squeal. Heavy boots clomped on the floorboards as someone strode down the aisle toward the altar. Her vantage on the floor allowed her to see only the shoes as they passed and then stopped, perhaps fifteen feet away. She'd never seen boots like these, black, with high heels, like a woman's, but square-toed and fuzzy, as if made of suede. Adorned with a fancy pattern. Black on black.

She heard the pastor's door creak and his lighter footsteps.

"Evening, sir," he said. "There are no services at this time, but may I help you?"

The boots rotated to face him, but their owner remained silent. Then Pastor Parris spoke again.

"This place is forbidden to your kind."

The stranger made a noise she'd never heard a person make, like a tomcat guarding its food.

"The crucified god holds no power over me. I spit in his blood and grind his host under my boot."

Despite the nasty words, the man's voice was smooth and calm, soft, like the ringing of small, deep bells. For the first time today, Emily was scared.

Pastor Parris' brown leather shoes took two steps closer to the boots.

"This is no papist palace. Be gone! Before I tumble you back into the pit."

The man made the cat noise again. Emily thought it might even be a laugh. Then she heard his voice again, but it couldn't be said to come from any particular place in the church, instead echoing all around her. *Come to me, John Parris. I have crossed the great water with a message for you. I have braved sea, sun, and rats to set you to this task.*

It was all Emily could do to remain on the floor. She had the strongest, most senseless urge to crawl into the aisle and run to the dark stranger. The pastor's movement stopped her, his brown leather shoes advancing on the funny black boots.

Come to me, the voice that wasn't exactly a voice repeated.

The shoes edged even closer.

Come.

The stranger called the pastor across the small space that still separated them like a man coaxing a kitten.

Then everything got weirder.

The pastor's feet shuffled like a carnival performer's. He shouted something in Latin. Emily heard a whoosh and a bright light flashed from the direction of the two men. Even though the wooden pews sheltered her, it left searing colored dots across her vision like she'd been staring into the sun. The high-heeled boots vanished, and a hideous shrieking cry rang out, accompanied by the leathery flapping she'd heard earlier.

The pastor's shoes stepped backward, and he continued his Latin chant. Emily wondered what had become of the stranger, but she didn't dare move. When the pastor came back he was preceded by flickering shadows and light — he must have brought a candle.

The terrible noises stopped, and the funny boots stepped down onto the floor, as if descending from a set of invisible stairs. Emily reminded herself to breathe. The boots stood much further back now, at the far end of the altar from the pastor.

The bell-tone voice spoke again. Not the funny everywhere voice but the regular odd one.

"So my employer sent me to the right man."

"Who do you serve?" the pastor said. "What does he want from me?"

"I'm no one's servant, fleeting one," the strange voice said. "But the Painted Man and I are partners when it serves our interests. I've brought his Eye, so that he may see and know you."

Emily risked a peek.

With a rustling metallic rattle, something sailed through the air toward the pastor, who caught the object with a little wooden rod. It settled and dangled on a golden chain. She couldn't see it clearly, but it looked like a blue and gold necklace. She lowered herself carefully back to the floor.

"What do I do with this?" the pastor said.

"Keep it. He wants to keep an eye on you,"

"And this task?" Pastor Parris said. "Why would I even consider any bargain with your sort?"

"We'll speak of the details another night. Perhaps when there's not a child lying between your pews."

Emily had to bite her hand to stop herself from gasping. She was in big trouble now.

"Do try to keep your… vices under control," the pastor said. "I have a parish to keep clean, so kindly refrain from making a mess."

The boots turned away. "Why would I ever want to do that?" their owner said.

He walked down the aisle toward the door as briskly as he'd entered. Emily cowered as he passed then continued out into the full darkness of the night.

The pastor followed him to the door and latched it shut.

"Emily, my pet?" He turned. "Is that you on the floor?"

Nine:

The Willows

Salem, Massachusetts, Thursday evening, October 23, 1913

AFTER SUPPER ON THURSDAY, Sarah walked the quarter-mile to the Williamses' house. The Indian summer was bound to turn soon, but for now it lent the evening air a sultry thickness. Mrs. Williams was inside the kitchen baking with Emma, their Negro cook. The room felt like an oven but smelled delicious.

"I'd give you a hug," Anne's mother said as Sarah closed the screen door, "but I have a pear pie in my hands. Follow me into the dining room so those vultures can sink their talons into it. I don't suppose you want a piece?"

"You know I can't, but it looks gorgeous."

She followed the big woman through the double-hinged doors. The room was full, not just with the family and boarders but also Alex, all looking rather satiated. There were no seats at the table, so she dragged a side chair next to Anne.

"We should get going," Sarah whispered. "More time before dark."

"Almost finished here," Anne said. "The men demand pie for the road."

"Alex ate with you?"

"And you pretend not to be interested. Sam invited him, then all but chained him to the chair across from me, but don't worry, I'm waiting for the tall, blond, and pliant type. We—"

The doors swung open and Mr. Barnyard, the family's basset hound, bounded in. He went straight for Emily, his favorite, then proceeded to press his huge head into the lap of each person around the table. Alex pushed back his chair and stood up. Mr. Barnyard, not to be denied his introductory crotch sniff, forced him into the corner.

"What's the matter, Alex?" Sam said. "Something hounding you?"

Alex tried to laugh. "I just don't like dogs."

"He only wants to say hello," Emily said.

Alex allowed Mr. Barnyard his fun but held his hands awkwardly in front of him as if trying to restrain himself from pushing the dog away. Sarah sympathized. She had nothing against Mr. Barnyard, but he did have a tendency to leave foot-long strands of drool on your clothes.

Mr. Williams jumped into the pause in the conversation.

"Kids, do you really think this outing to the Willows is such a good idea with a homicidal maniac on the loose?"

"Don't worry, Pop." Sam started clearing the table. "It's a public place and nothing's going to happen on my watch."

The trolley line to the Willows was an older one, horse-drawn, not yet upgraded to overhead power. Still, the journey wasn't long, and they arrived with at least two hours of daylight left.

The thirty-five-acre amusement park occupied a wooded peninsula jutting out into Salem Harbor. Sarah came two or three times a year, always with her friends — Papa didn't care for public amusements. As usual, she saw people dancing in the big pavilion. In winter the boards were pulled aside and the floor slicked with ice. They still danced, on silvery blades instead of leathery soles. The muted sounds of the orchestra rippled the evening air, drifting among the buildings and trees to mix with the chatter of the crowd and the excited cries of children. The sounds of fun.

"Can we ride the water chute first?" Emily asked. "Mommy says I shouldn't, but if we have time to dry, she'll never know."

"Sounds like a plan," Sam said.

"Sam," Anne said, "if Mom doesn't want her to—"

"I'm not a baby," Emily said. "I can do what I want."

Sarah put her arm on Anne's shoulder. "It's just a water ride."

The shoulder relaxed. "You're right," Anne said. "But Emily's been acting strange. She disappeared after the funeral and pretends she doesn't remember. No one forgets a whole afternoon, not unless they were drunk as a skunk."

"Methinks more sulk than sot," Sarah whispered.

Anne sighed. "Sorry, Emily," she said, loud enough so everyone could hear. "Go ahead. I won't tell Mom."

"Thanks, Sarah!" Emily called from up ahead.

"And *you* even get the credit," Anne said.

"Has she started bleeding yet?" Sarah let the distance grow between them and the others.

"She hasn't told me, but I've seen extra bloody rags in the laundry."

"It was traumatic for me," Sarah said. "Coming as it did after Judah…. Do you know, I can barely remember several months from that fall?"

"Feels like a lifetime ago. Next, we'll be getting married." Anne elbowed Sarah. "We know who you like, confess it!"

Sarah elbowed her back. "You have to be kidding. Now that I've rejected Papa's local offering, he'll probably betroth me to some thirty-year-old rabbi from Budapest." She glanced ahead of them. "Besides, *he* isn't even Jewish."

"And you consider yourself a modern woman!"

"Hey Em, don't stand up when we go over the hill," Sam said as he paid a quarter for five tickets and they joined the long line waiting for the water chute. "Last year the sign at the top lopped someone's head right off."

"Did not," Emily said.

"Did so. It tumbled into the bushes right over there."

"He's just trying to scare you," Anne said.

"Why would I do that?" Sam raised his eyebrows and grinned at them. "The risk is half the fun. A couple years ago four people died when a funny-track train on Coney Island shot off the tracks."

"Our resident authority on amusement park fatalities," Anne said.

"My father told me about a park like this in Vienna," Sarah said. "It has a wheel so big they use carriages instead of seats — you can see the whole city when you're at the top. I can't recall if it was the first in the world or the largest."

"When I was a year old," Alex said, "my grandfather brought us to Vienna for business. I don't remember, of course."

"What year was that?" Probably he was older, but Sarah didn't want to ask him outright. "My father used to work at the Hofburg Palace. But my parents left in '96, after my mother became pregnant with me."

"1895, so they would've still been there," Alex said. "Did your father work for the kaiser?"

She knew it! He was a year or two older, perhaps nineteen.

"Not directly. He was a secretary for an important rabbi — a liaison between the Jews and the empire. Papa never liked court, but he met Kaiser Franz Josef a couple times."

They reached the front of the line, where the fake logs beckoned. Sam tapped Sarah on the arm, but Emily grabbed his and dragged him into a boat. Since none of the craft held more than two, this left Anne, Sarah, and Alex in a slightly awkward situation.

"You two ladies ride together," Alex said. "I'll go solo."

He'd been a gentleman, but then Sarah had never ridden with a boy, and it might be fun to try. Maybe another time.

The boats left the platform, bumping along the wood and steel channel. The water smelled briny, which made sense, given how close they were to the ocean. At the hill, the craft snagged on a chain, tilted back, and slowly clicked upward. Sarah's stomach fluttered in anticipation. When they crested the top she could see the whole peninsula below, rows of white willows along the strand of restaurants and gaming booths.

Anne sat in front. Sarah, stomach clenched despite her having done this before, gripped Anne's waist as they began to fall. Anne screamed, and Sarah heard a matching cry that must be her own. When they crashed into the pool she ducked down low but couldn't avoid the arcing salt water.

"Glorious!" Alex said as they left the platform. "Nothing compares back in Greece. Unless you count jumping off cliffs—"

A running figure shouldered into him, knocked Alex backward off the platform into the shallow lagoon, and ran off into the crowd. But not before Sarah recognized him as the same boy that had insulted them Monday in school.

Alex floundered waist deep in the brackish water, sputtering, and Sam reached over the edge to grab his hand.

"Welcome to America." He hauled Alex back onto the platform.

"It's a warm evening, perfect for a dip," Alex said.

Sarah couldn't understand how he took it so calmly.

"It was that moron from Mrs. Fletcher's class," she said. Alex had been punished at school for defending her, and now this.

"I'll dry," he said, then added in Greek, "Wise men learn from their enemies."

With the sun a memory, the park was now bathed in light thanks to hundreds of electric bulbs — an ethereal glow, as Sarah experienced it. Despite Alex's unexpected swim and her soggy clothes, she was having a fantastic time. They rode the carousel, which made Sarah feel a little silly, but Emily still liked it. She really was on the cusp, very grown-up, very much a child.

"Hey, Alex," Sam said as they walked away from the ride, "you ever had an ice cream cone?"

"I've had ice cream," Alex said. "What's a cone?"

"You don't know?" Emily said.

"Actually," Anne said, "they're pretty new. I remember when Hobbs over there first introduced them. They even make a big deal about being the first."

"Well, Alex should try one," Emily said. "I want chocolate."

As the initiate, Alex had to get his cone first. He chose vanilla.

"I don't know about the cone part, but the ice cream sure is good," he told Sarah. "You want some?"

"I do... but I can't."

"Oh, I forgot." He smiled. "But I don't see any meat here."

"I wouldn't be surprised if there's lard in the cone — it's used so often in baking," she said. "Still, I wish I could eat all this stuff, it looks so good."

Kosher ice cream was hard to find. Mrs. Hoffmann, the wife of Papa's friend, had made some when Sarah's family visited Boston.

"Do you think God will send you to hell if you eat it?"

She laughed. "I don't even believe in hell, but *Hashem* — that's God — keeps the accounts in balance. Not that life doesn't sometimes seem unfair."

"Like Emily's friend?" Alex said. "I don't know what Charles did or didn't do, but he got the bum side of the scale."

Or Judah, who a week before he died, had been thrilled by a toy train Papa made for his sixth birthday.

"And Job," Sarah said. "He was tested with heavy sorrow, even though he was a righteous man." She reached over and poked Alex's jacket. Merely damp. He prodded her padded sleeve in retaliation.

"I seem to remember Satan as being the instigator of Job's suffering."

"I don't believe in the devil, either," Sarah said.

"I do."

Most Christians did, she supposed. The conversation was so delightful it hurt. But Anne had brought her a paper cup of water from the ice cream stand, and she enjoyed watching the carousel while her friends enjoyed their cones. Horses, camels, and lions spun around and around. Each one was different, with manes and tails of real hair. In the center of the contraption was a miniature village, complete with little wooden houses, churches, trees. She'd never noticed all the detail before.

The steam calliope attached to the carousel wound down its boisterous tune, finishing on a single extended note. A long mournful whistle blast Sarah knew all too well.

Nervously she sipped her water. It tasted meaty, salty, perfumed. Not like water at all. The liquid in the glass was dark—

She flung the cup away, spitting to try and clear her mouth. Her friends turned to her, concerned.

Then she saw him.

He stood on the other side of the carousel, appearing and disappearing in the gaps between the horses. It was Charles, the boy from the Williamses' parlor, the boy from the pond.

The dead boy.

He wore a dark Sunday suit. His light brown hair was disheveled and his face gaunt and streaked with dirt. The little hairs on Sarah's arms stood up as if electrified. The steam-powered organ note droned on.

Beside her, Emily gripped Sarah's arm and pointed across the spinning horses.

"It's Charles," she said. "He's not dead."

Everyone else stopped eating and turned to look, but the boy was gone, vanished into the night. The music had resumed its usual cheerful melody.

"I don't see anything," Sam said. "I know this has been a hard week, Em, but Charles is in heaven now. You went to his funeral, so—"

"I saw him!" Emily yelled. People were looking at her. "Sarah, you did too, right?"

As surely as she'd seen the silhouetted tree branches, red with blood. And heard the horn.

"I don't think Charles made it to heaven," she said. "Yes, I saw him."

"See!" Emily looked excited, not scared.

"Sarah," Anne said, "don't encourage her. It must've been another boy."

"It was him, I know it!" Emily said. "The far side of the carousel."

"Calm down, ladies." Alex spread his hands. "Let's just go look — but together, all right? When people get excited and run off alone, bad things happen."

The other side of the carousel was closer to the big pavilion with the skating rink and restaurant. They milled around the crowded area, which looked perfectly normal to Sarah. No dead boys here.

Sam was gripping Emily's hand. Suddenly, she lunged against it, straining like a dog on a tether.

"Up there!" She pointed. "On top of the restaurant!"

Rows of tiny electric lights ringed the two-story pavilion, giving enough illumination to the roof to reveal a pale figure scrabbling sideways like a crab across the beach. He scurried, starting and stopping, clinging between starts to the vertical eaves. Then he was up and over, out of sight behind the lip.

"What the hell was that?" Anne said. "Let's get out of here."

"We have to find him!" Emily tugged at her brother's grip again.

"I don't know what was up there," Sam said, "but it can't be Charles. Dead boys don't scurry across restaurant roofs."

"Unfortunately, sometimes they do," Alex said.

Sarah looked away from the roof to Alex. What did he mean by that?

"There has to be some explanation," Sam said. "Maybe an Italian acrobat practicing his trade." He released Emily and mimed a tight-rope walker.

"Charles is my friend," Emily said.

"*Was* your friend, Emily." Alex loomed over her. "If you want to see the sun tomorrow, stay away from him."

"Who are you to boss me around?" It was hard not to laugh at Emily's angry stance, hands balled up and placed on her not quite straight hips.

"Do you know something we don't, friend?" Sam asked Alex.

Emily dashed off into the night.

"Damn it!" Sam bolted after his sister.

The rest of them wove after him through the thinning crowd. Sarah glanced at the pavilion roofline, looking for any sign of the apparition. Nothing. Inside the building, people danced to the orchestra's rendition of *The Garden of Roses*.

It was darker here, less public. No more well-lit kiosks — utilitarian sheds now lurked in the blackness, which was pierced by a wail that sounded distant, inhuman.

Emily was fast, much faster than Sarah and Anne, but her brother caught up with her as she passed through the doors of a wooden shed. Sam tackled her, tumbling them both into a heap of limbs and straw. On their heels, first Alex and then the older girls careened through the doorway.

Inside, it was dark but by no means quiet. Sarah smelled horse, hay, and manure. She heard some of the big animals shuffling and snorting. Worse noises reverberated from the dark depths: slurps, squeals, heavy thrashing thumps. Something was eating, gorging itself. It all sounded very wet.

"We should go back and get the police," Anne said.

Alex grabbed a pitchfork and shovel leaning against the wall.

"This isn't a matter for the police."

Sam took the shovel Alex offered, but first he placed Emily's hand in Anne's and folded the older sister's fingers around the younger's, pressing hard.

"Do *not* let her go. Emily, am I going to have to tell Mom you died a silly little girl?"

Emily cocked her head, listening to the awful wetness.

"I'll behave. Promise."

"We need some light," Alex said.

"How about this?" Anne flipped a switch.

With a pop and hum, dangling electric bulbs sparked to life one by one. The slurping noises briefly gave way to a growling hiss.

Alex and Sam crept forward, makeshift weapons in hand. Sarah tiptoed behind. White-faced, Anne stood with Emily by the door. No agitated horse head poked from the last stall, and it was here that the boys stopped. The pony in the adjacent pen reared and bucked, wild with terror, its muzzle streaked with foam.

Alex gestured to Sam to make ready, then pulled the stall door open.

The thing inside struggled with a thrashing horse, crouched low over its long neck and head. The boy's skin glowed milky in the dim light. His church jacket was muddy and his white shirt soaked red. Bone-colored nails grown into long talons gripped the dying animal. The boy's face, buried in living flesh, lifted to reveal features roughhewn in approximation of life. He resembled Charles, or perhaps his ghoulish *doppelgänger*. Black lifeless eyes bored into Sarah's soul. His bloody distended mouth snarled, long canines protruding from rows of teeth too numerous for the jaw, then he bent back to his meal.

Sam stepped into the stall, raised the shovel high, and brought it down sideways onto the creature's skull with the full force of his weight. There was a sickening crunching sound and a spray of blood as the steel blade chopped into the boy's cranium and sheared off a huge flap of skin, hair, and ear.

The creature emitted a hideous shriek and reached to yank the shovel from Sam's hands, nearly toppling him. Moving unnaturally fast, he broke the wooden shaft in two and sprang upward. A mixture of fluid and bone rained downward.

Sarah looked up to see the thing scuttle across the ceiling, leaping from rafter to rafter. In seconds, he'd traveled past them to the door. Anne threw herself and Emily into a bale of hay as the thing dropped, then fled outside into the night.

Sarah's breath burned in and out so hard her throat hurt. Her worldview churned around the inside of her skull. She tried to readjust and realign, to make sense of it. Now she knew, with total and complete certainty, that monsters were real.

Everyone else seemed just as dazed. By the exit, Anne rose, dusting hay from her skirts.

"Oh my God, blessed Jesus, what kind of crazy man was that?"

"Let's go after it!" Sam said.

"No need right now," Alex said. "I know where we can find it later."

They all looked at him.

"What aren't you telling us?" Sarah said.

Alex sighed. "That was a *vrykolakas*, what you'd call a vampire. A young one, buried only yesterday, risen for the first time this night or the last."

"Huh?" Sam said.

"Like Dracula?" Emily asked.

"Perhaps, but this one is so young it's feral, like a rabid dog." Alex was looking at Sarah. "The hunger for blood has driven it mad, so it doesn't talk or think. It only kills and feeds. Evil is like a seed: it needs time to grow after it's planted."

"What are you even *talking* about?" Anne said.

"Dracula's the villain from this great novel the librarian thought I'd like," Emily said. "He's an evil Romanian count who's dead but drinks the blood of beautiful—"

"Mom would be furious to find you reading that nonsense," Anne said.

"Nonsense?" Alex said. "Do you believe your eyes? Is the blood in our hair a figment of your imagination? Vampires are rare, perhaps, but they're real enough. The world is full of the unknown, swimming like fish under the surface of normalcy."

"I was over here. I didn't see it," Anne said.

"Why didn't you tell us before, Alex?" Sarah said.

"Should I have said, 'Hello, my name's Alex, I believe in vampires'?"

"The man has a point," Sam said.

"I knew it was Charles," Emily said.

"How'd this happen?" Sarah asked. "I mean, he was a normal boy, then he was dead, and now he is … whatever he is. How?"

"Created by another vampire," Alex whispered.

"You've all gone insane." Anne was holding herself so rigid Sarah was surprised she could speak. "How can anyone be created?"

"Good Lord," Sarah said. "There're two of those monsters?"

"And the one we saw is just the baby," Alex said.

"One at a time, then," Sam said. "Alex, you said you knew where Charles would go? If he's undead, how do we make him all the way dead?"

"He'll return to his grave before dawn. They have to. But *we* will do nothing. You can all go home and my manservant Dmitri will deal with it."

"That's the best idea I've heard yet," Anne said.

The image of the gaping maw and the teeth flashed through Sarah's head. Conflicting emotions roiled in her gut.

"No. We'll see it finished."

She'd failed Charles in life — failed to pass on the warning God had sent her. She would not fail him in death, too.

"This is no task for women," Alex said. "I'm sorry if I offend you, but it's dangerous and bloody."

Anger washed the fear and questions right out of her head.

"Is that so?" she said. "I think we women know a bit more about blood than you do. We're coming."

"Sarah, please," Anne said. "Let's take Emily home."

Sarah kicked her friend's foot.

Anne glared back.

"I don't want to go home," Emily said. "Sam, tell them I don't have to go."

Ten:
Dead Again

Salem, Massachusetts, Thursday night, October 23, 1913

"ANNE, I REALLY, REALLY, *really* want to come," Emily said. The sisters hopped off the downtown trolley behind Sarah. The boys had gone ahead to Alex's. "And I'm not a little kid. I'm practically a grown-up."

"If I could stay behind, I would," Anne said. Sarah knew it was true. The difference between siblings was about more than just a couple years.

"I'll never get to sleep," Emily said. "I'll just lie there suffering in my bed till you get back. Why don't *you* want to go?"

Sam had labeled this tactic *tacking*.

"Because it's scary and dangerous," Anne said. "If you had any sense, you'd see that and I'd treat you more like a grown-up."

Sarah's own sibling arguments were more than seven years laid to rest, but she knew not to get caught in the crossfire.

"Anyway, you owe me for backing your fib," Anne said. "Where were you yesterday after the funeral? I saw the pastor leave — without you."

Emily stopped walking. "You lied for me?"

"When have I ever been a snitch? Seriously, Em, where were you?"

"I don't remember, honest. I heard you badgering Sam about Sarah, and the next thing I remember is walking home." She frowned. "I was probably daydreaming."

Anne seemed to give up — at least, she stopped asking questions. But Sarah had one for her.

"What were you saying to Sam about me?"

"I don't remember, either." Anne looked down. "Emily got me all flustered when she disappeared."

Not that flustered. Once they got rid of Emily, Sarah would get the story out of her.

When they reached the junction point between their two houses, Anne finally looked at Sarah.

"You still have blood in your hair. You might as well go home to wash and change."

"We need more practical clothes anyway," Sarah said. "I'll sneak out after my parents think I'm in bed. How are you going to keep Emily from following us?"

"Hey, I'm standing right here!" Emily said.

"I'll get Emma to help," Anne said. "She owes me. I don't tell Mother about her *juju*."

Sarah had seen Emma's dolls and charms. The island woman fed her little deities rum when she thought no one was looking.

"Okay," Sarah said. "I'll meet you on Essex Street in exactly an hour."

Sarah had taken a few moments at the Willows powder room to wash her face, and her dress was a dark color, so she hoped for the best. When she popped her head into Papa's study to say goodnight he barely acknowledged her. She grabbed her riding boots and headed upstairs.

Papa's renovations hadn't yet brought plumbing to the second floor, so the washroom water was cold. She stripped down anyway and scrubbed herself head to toe. The water in the basin turned reddish-brown — *ugh*. She tossed it out the window.

Back in her room, prowler outfits were in short supply, but she made the best of what her wardrobe had to offer. When she glanced out the coast was clear, so she stuffed stockings into her riding boots and threw them down into the yard.

Then paused. She'd almost forgotten her nighttime prayers. Tonight, she could use all the help God was willing to offer.

Afterward, she swung one leg to straddle the sill. The wooden shingles prickled her bare sole. Her room was in the front of the house, far from Papa's study, above the steep pediment of the porch. She gripped the window frame.

And looked down.

Anne and the boys would be waiting.

With a final silent prayer, she sprang across the small gap to the porch roof.

She made the leap easily but slapped the surface with a jarring full-body impact that knocked half the wind out of her. She slid down, scrabbling to grip the rough shingles, then rolled off the edge and fell six or seven feet onto the grass below.

She lay for a moment in the yard, her scraped hands and feet throbbing, then picked herself up and limped over to her boots.

Anne wasn't waiting on Essex. Sarah gave her a few minutes, then made her way slowly to her friend's house. All the lights were off, and a few pebbles tossed at her window got no response.

She sighed and began the thirty-minute trek to the Palaogoses' old Victorian mansion. A splinter stabbed her in the foot, and she imagined blood filling her boot until it overflowed. She kept an eye out for a place to take her shoe off but the road was pitch dark.

By the time she pushed open Alex's creaky iron gate and staggered to the barn she was in agony. Sam and Alex had set up portable oil lamps. Two canvas packs sat beside some shovels and a medieval-looking pike of sharpened wood.

"Where's Anne?" Sam said. "We're almost ready."

"Not coming," Sarah said. "She didn't have the guts."

"Anne turned yellow on us?" Sam said.

Sarah's last sentence echoed in her head. She stepped back into the shadows as if hiding would take it back.

And bumped into something hard and metallic. A shiny black automobile half hidden behind a haphazard wall of hay-bales.

She pointed. "Can we take that?"

"We just bought it," Alex said. "Dmitri's teaching me how to drive *next* Sunday."

Sarah sat on a hay-bale, tugged off her boot, and rolled down her stocking. She winced.

"If I don't get this splinter out," she said, "I don't think I can walk anywhere. Alex, I hate to impose, but do you have a clean rag and some water?"

"Sure," he said. "I'll be right back."

"Find out the time," Sam called after him. He lowered his voice. "I can't believe it. Anne always comes, even if just to complain."

Sarah managed to get her fingernail underneath the shard impaled in the ball of her foot.

"It *is* a lot to swallow," she said. "Maybe she just needs time to adjust."

He stepped closer. "Anything I can do to help?"

As long as they'd been friends, Sarah couldn't remember being alone with him.

"No thanks. I got the splinter out."

Alex returned with a wet cloth and a jar

"Three hours past midnight," he said, then sat next to Sarah. "I brought salve. May I?"

She offered him her injured leg. The scrapes on her foot stung while he cleaned them, but his touch was gentle. The whole thing was awkward and improper, and Sam was staring, but she was too exhausted to do anything about it.

Then Alex opened the jar. The most repulsive odor assailed her nose, likely a blend of rare herbs, goat feces, and hundred-year-old frog guts.

"Jesus Christ on the cross!" Sam cried. "What's in that stuff?"

"Dmitri never said, but it works."

Alex carefully took a dab of the yellow goo on the tip of a forefinger and gently applied it to Sarah's wounds. Despite the stench, the ointment was cool and soothing, and within seconds her discomfort receded. The sudden absence of pain, the touch of Alex's hands.... She closed her eyes and drifted.

"Sarah, are you all right?" Sam asked.

She felt her cheeks flush. She retrieved her leg and yanked her stocking back on.

"My foot's much better now." But her hands also stung. "Maybe I'll take some of that salve on these cuts, too."

Alex set to work, Sam watching him intently. Then he looked at Sarah.

"Our vampire expert says the undead will have returned to its grave by dawn," he said. "Which leads us to the plan—"

"Sunlight will burn it," Alex said, "but to make certain it's dead — for good — we need to put an ash stake through its heart, chop off its head, and boil it in wine or vinegar."

"Poor Charles," Sarah said. Anne would've said something funnier.

Alex put away the ointment, and Sarah took stock of herself. Her injuries no longer hurt, but—

"You don't have to come," Sam said.

Alex tried to catch Sarah's eye. She focused on the barn floor.

"I'm coming." She was supposed to be a part of this. "Will the creature fight back?"

"Hopefully, not very well," Alex said. "The devilish spirit that animates him is much weaker during the day."

"Splendid," Sarah said. "Breakfast with the damned." Finally, a line worthy of Anne.

The new Congregationalist graveyard was in the old section of town, walled off from the nearby streets by ancient trees. This morning, mist pooled in the low spots, shrouding the grassy spaces between the headstones. In the first light of dawn Sarah could make out Charles' grave, simply a rectangular patch of naked earth.

"The plot doesn't look disturbed," she said, "but at least the local theatrical troupe provided some sinister ground-fog."

She giggled. Her nerves must be getting to her.

"The vampire will be in its coffin," Alex said. "A young one wouldn't risk even a hint of sunlight."

"How did he pack the dirt behind him?" Sam asked. "Do they float down like ghosts?"

Alex shrugged. "I've only done this twice before, and those graves were stone crypts. Let's get to work before someone comes."

The digging took longer than expected, even though both boys worked quickly. Sarah watched the edges of the yard for intruders. Women's rights were one thing, but men were welcome to the hard labor.

Finally, she heard the soft thud of metal on wood. A few minutes later Sam uncovered the lid while Alex laid out some garlic cloves, a sword-like knife, and a burlap bag. He donned a pair of heavy leather gloves and grasped his wooden spear.

"Sam, use the iron hooks I gave you to open the box. Sarah, stand back." Alex positioned himself at the head of the casket, spear raised.

Sam worked the iron rod under the lid until it creaked and splintered. Next, he wedged the head of a shovel into the gap and stepped on the handle. The lid shattered with a loud crack. Sam batted the broken wood aside with the shovel.

Charles lay in his coffin, eyes closed. His fangs and claws were gone, his hands folded soft and clean in front of him. His clothes were filthy and torn, the blood on his shirt dried a dark brown. There were gouges in the side of his head where Sam had struck his skull, but the face was otherwise intact.

He looked so peaceful. Sarah's heart ached at the thought of what lay before them.

"They sleep deeply during the day," Alex said, "but see how even this early morning glow burns him?"

Dawn light now streamed through the trees and shadowy fingers reached back from the gravestones. Down in the grave Charles still slumbered in darkness, his white face and hands were turning pink, and small wisps of smoke coiled about his lifeless flesh.

"Brace yourselves," Alex said.

He raised the long spear. Sarah could see that his hands were shaking, but he drove the stake down hard into the boy's chest.

The creature's dark eyes — so different from the blue ones Sarah had seen in the Williamses' parlor — snapped open. He hissed and squirmed. Alex leaned into the spear, twisting it deeper. Pinned like a collection beetle, Charles flailed, limbs lashing out. Sunlight crept into the pit, and the smoke issuing from the body thickened. The soft hands transformed into wicked claws, and a forest of teeth sprouted from his mouth. Ropes of blood spat from his hideous maw and oozed from the point where the stake penetrated his chest.

Even impaled, he managed to stretch up a taloned hand to grope at Alex's foot. Alex tried to move away, but his grip on the pinioning spear tethered him to the creature.

"Sam, take the knife and cut off his head! Hit him hard."

Sam picked up the machete, examined its two-foot length, then looked into the grave.

"I can't reach from here!"

"Just stay away from the sharp parts, I'll try and keep him pinned."

Alex danced to evade the groping claws.

"I'm doing the best I can." Sam lay on the earth and stabbed down into the pit with the machete.

Sarah grabbed up one of the shovels and tried to whack at the hands reaching for Alex. Nervousness — and perhaps a general lack of shovel experience — caused her to miss her target.

"Watch the feet, please!" Alex yelled as he dodged the blow.

Sam wasn't faring much better. The vampire grabbed the tip of the machete, forcing Sam into an awkward tug-of-war, head and shoulders drawn toward the pit.

"Fool idea using the blade!" he yelled.

Sarah raised her shovel again but found herself frozen when her eyes locked on the thing below. Its flesh blackened and bubbled, making a sound like sausage in the pan. The smoke became a thick column, and she coughed and gagged on the fumes, dropped the shovel into the pit when her hand flew to her mouth. Thick pink vomit splattered her pants and hard leather boots. She turned away and wiped the strands off her face with her sleeve.

Sam jerked the machete free and moved towards her.

"No!" Alex yelled. "The head!"

Small flames sprouted from the vampire's clothing. The horrible hissing and squirming continued. The dead boy grabbed the shovel Sarah had dropped and swung it toward Alex—

Who released the stuck spear to avoid being clobbered. Flames leapt out of the pit as the vampire struggled to rise.

"I'll do it my way." Sam knelt, snatched up the other shovel and struck.

He missed the neck — the lower face collapsed with a sickening crunch and a burst of flame. The thing emitted a feeble hiss. Alex grabbed the bobbing stake and forced the vampire down while Sam swung again at the neck. This time the blade drove cleanly through blackened skin and bone like a carving knife through overcooked turkey. The head separated and rolled to the side. The body stilled, flames intensified, and acrid smoke poured upward into their faces.

Sarah gagged again. Her stomach empty, her painful contractions gave birth to only a thin stream of fluid.

Alex clung to the stake. "We need to boil the head. Sam, can you get it?"

"You've got to be kidding?"

But Sam used the shovel to push the charred, smoldering head up the side of the grave. The edge of the hole was ragged, and the skull kept falling off the shovel, thudding against the collapsing corpse. Finally, on the fourth try, he was able to flip it onto the grass above.

In seconds Alex had pressed the garlic bulb into what remained of the mouth and kicked the head unceremoniously into the burlap bag.

"Let's break off the stake and get this dirt back into the grave."

Eleven:

The Morning After

Salem, Massachusetts, Friday, October 24, 1913

SARAH RETURNED FROM THE GRAVEYARD feeling like a corpse herself. She trudged up her front walk, arms crossed to fight the chill. The hot spell had finally broken and dark clouds churned the morning sky.

Once in her room, she stripped off her clothes — they reeked of death and smoke — and shoved them under the bed. She fell asleep the second her face sank into the pillow.

Charles haunted her dreams. Smiling, teeth overwhelming his pinched pale face, dressed in his best Sunday suit, he held her hand and tugged her up a grassy hill. Sharp nails and cold fingers pressed against her palm. She heard the baying of wolves, and a dark bird of prey circled the sky.

At the crest of the hill, Charles paused before a lone sycamore, gnarled and bare of leaves. The sun just touched the horizon, throwing dark branches into relief against the heavens.

He gave me the dark gift, and you took it away. Charles' reddish mouth didn't move, so packed with teeth speech hardly seemed possible.

"What's the dark gift?" she asked.

He gestured to the east, where black clouds roiled across the valley. A tremendous horn blast sounded, a single note free from any notion of beginning or end. The frenzied howl of the wolves played counterpoint. Overhead, the ugly bird shrieked in response.

The horn has sounded, and I have opened the gates.

"What gates?"

Charles shrugged, sharp blades shifting under dark wool.

The passage is unblocked. What is lost will be found.

"Passage to where?"

The dead boy pointed to something behind her. She turned. Before the great tree, the green earth was scarred with a neat brown wound. Terror lofted from her belly into her throat.

"I pray that's *your* grave," she said.

The bloodless mask of his face was unreadable. His hair, slicked with animal fat, parted neatly in the center.

Only you can stop us.

She locked eyes with him, but the lifeless black orbs offered nothing. The horn was still blaring. A young woman with brilliant orange-red hair in braids stood beside the grave. She was dressed in a burgundy velvet gown, her breast emblazoned with a white doe cavorting amidst red tulips.

"Is this your grave?" Sarah asked.

The doe-woman gestured at the hole like a hostess offering a seat at a dinner table—

Charles shoved Sarah hard from behind, and she stumbled into the woman, dragging them both down into the pit.

Sarah lifted her face from the pillow.

Papa knelt beside her, his hand resting between her shoulder blades. Outside the window the sky was gray-white, rivulets of rain streaking the glass.

She jerked up. "Am I late for school?"

He picked up her hand and examined her nails, caked with blood-soaked dirt.

"Digging ditches?" He was smiling. "A night job, I take it."

"I slipped in the mud by the water ride."

"Is there anything else you want to tell me?"

A tempting offer, but on balance she thought not. He had his secrets, too, plenty of them. They'd long respected those private spaces in each other's lives, each trusting the other would confide if and when the time was right.

She shook her head.

"When did you come home? After midnight, wasn't it?" Sometimes he seemed aware of things only God should've known.

"I'm sorry, Papa." He really wasn't being unreasonable.

He rose and pressed his fingers to the *mezuzah* at her door, then kissed them.

"You'll be in the house by ten o'clock, Sarah, not a moment later."

"Yes, Papa."

The long-case clock in the hall began to chime. She counted the bells. Seven.

"You should get ready for school. I'll see you at *shul* for *Shabbos* services."

Friday again. The week had steamed past. The last thing she felt like was an evening in synagogue. Then again, maybe she could use a little extra credit with the Lord.

Papa gave her three quick kisses on the forehead and left.

Sarah threw back the covers. If he'd seen the scrapes her roof-climbing had left on her feet, she'd have more than a curfew from him. She peeked under the bandages. Much improved, although a whiff of the odor from Alex's salve lingered.

She glanced at her hands. She couldn't remember why she hadn't washed them, the trek home had been an exhausted blur. And that tumble down the dark dream-pit, fingers dragging through the dry dirt.... After last night, a nightmare was the least any sane person could expect, but this one was reminiscent of her original visions. Dreadful in appearance, dream-Charles had seemed almost brotherly in demeanor. And who was that redheaded girl?

When she stood, a wave of fatigue swept over her. Next time she helped destroy a living corpse in its grave, she'd better be doing it on more than two hours' sleep.

As soon as Sarah joined the others at the cafeteria table she pulled out her little journal. No need to write that Anne looked drawn and worried or Sam disheveled and tired. But it should be noteworthy that even Alex seemed exhausted. Emily looked unperturbed — excited, even — but then she hadn't gone vampire-killing with them.

"You'd feel better if you'd come." Sarah reached for Anne's hand, but Anne pulled it away. "It was terrible, but it's finished now."

"I got ready," Anne said, "but I just sat by myself in the parlor with the lights out. I didn't see anything, and I'm still terrified."

"Trust me," Sam said. "You'll sleep better knowing that thing is dead."

If only it were so.

Only you can stop us, Sarah scrawled in big letters that took up a quarter page of the journal — and didn't need writing down at all. The five words had burned themselves into her brain the moment she heard Charles say them.

"Alex, tell us what you know about vampires." Sarah glanced at the clock on the cafeteria wall. "You've got thirty-five minutes until class."

Twelve:
Unholy Feast

Salem, Massachusetts, Friday, October 24, 1913
and Santorini, Greece, February 1906

ALEX TOOK A DEEP BREATH and adjusted himself on the hard wooden seat.

"My first encounter with the undead was at the age of twelve, while we wintered on the island of Santorini. It was February second — the night of the Ipapandi forefeast."

"The what?" Emily said.

"Like Christmas, but different. When Mary and Joseph presented baby Jesus at the Temple. Anyway, we'd rented in the cliffside village of Oia, and the labyrinth of streets and the church square were lined with candles. Grandfather was busy, so I was alone, watching laymen reenact the story with candlelit effigies — Mary, Joseph, Simeon, the Righteous, and the Prophetess Anna — when this little waif, maybe two years older than me, appeared out of nowhere. She just hopped up onto the wall at my side."

Sarah's expression changed, subtly, and indecipherably — given his minimalist experience with the fairer sex.

"Her name was Maria." He took a sip of his milk. Her skin had been like fresh yogurt, her black hair tangled, her dress ragged, her feet bare. She'd been beautiful, and they talked for hours.

"After services, she asked my help with an errand. I had no idea what needed doing in the middle of the night, but I'd have followed her across the river Styx to Hades."

Now he could read Sarah's expression — and it wasn't good, but he continued.

"She led me across town to a small church, through an iron gate to a cluster of crypts. From between some graves she gathered up a rag-covered bundle then she took my hand and drew me into a central mausoleum and—"

"You followed her into a tomb?" Sarah said.

"Shhh," Emily said. "I want to hear the vampire part."

"Coming right up," Alex said, trying to keep his tone lighter than he felt. "I heard Maria's bundle make a strange noise, but when I asked, she silenced me. I was young and stupid, so I followed her down the dark stairs into a scene from a Rembrandt etching. The torch-lit sepulcher held marble sarcophagi, one with a throne of carved angels' wings. An old man sat there, dressed in a robe of silver and blue, with a high hat and jewel-studded breastplate. To his side hunched a crone, dressed in rags and leaning on a stick.

"When I met his gaze, I felt rubbed thin, my will stripped. I found myself a mute spectator to the play of my life. Maria tugged me forward, and she held up the bundle: a swaddled baby.

"'My lord Simeon, we present this child for your blessing, so that we might all be saved.'

"A dark radiance rolled off the old man as he took the infant and I still remember his words: 'Now instead of releasing your servant, Master,according to your word, in blood; for my eyes have seen your damnation, which you have prepared before the face of all peoples; a darkness for revelation to my people, and the glory of the night.'"

"That sounds like a passage from Luke," Anne said.

"It is," said Alex. "A perverted version. I'd found myself in the midst of an unholy feast, a dark parody of the Ipapandi, and it was about to get worse.

"Simeon's dark eyes devoured the torchlight, his hands became claws, and the mouth… you've seen what happens to the mouth. I was frozen. The old lady completed a similar metamorphosis, and beside me, Maria's beautiful face had become the maw of a beast. They surrounded the baby and their faces and hands soon glistened with blood."

Alex forced himself to swallow.

"When the deed was done, the old lady held the body aloft. 'Behold, this child is set for the falling of many, and for a sign which is spoken against. Yes, a sword will pierce through your own soul, that the world shall be consumed.'"

"Oh, God," said Sarah, her face pale.

Anne held her hands by her ears, as if she might need to cover them at any minute.

Alex licked his lips. "Their terrible feast complete, the teeth withdrew."

"And you just stood there?" Sam said.

"For a long time," Alex said, "I merely thought myself a coward. But now I believe Simeon held me in his glamour, my mind enslaved to his, and he no more worried about me than he would his own hand. For only then did he acknowledge me. 'So, Maria,' the master vampire said, 'you brought us a second treat, shall we save him for the afterfeast?'

"The girl argued on my behalf: 'Master, make him one of us. Give me a little toy of my own.'"

"That's arguing on your behalf?" Sarah said.

"I'll never know what Simeon would have done, for I heard a hissing crunch, and flames burst from Maria's breast. She hung there, then was engulfed in fire, the light from her burning body illuminating the figure behind her.

"It was Dmitri, who lifted the pole he'd impaled her with and tossed her aside, then slapped me from my trance. Next he waved a giant wooden cross in the direction of the two remaining vampires.

Their fangs had returned, but they slunk away, hissing and screeching as we backed up the steps."

His story left the table in stunned silence until Emily leaned in.

"Anne told me your parents are dead. Were they killed by vampires too?"

"Emily!" Anne hissed.

Alex felt the blood drain from his face and that crawling feeling in his testicles, not so different from being kicked between the legs. Hard.

"They died while I was little, and Grandfather won't tell me how. To be honest, I don't remember what happened."

Thinking about it, his skull began to throb and his brain felt thick as mud. The usual fragments came to him: terrible growls, thick mist, fire — he could almost smell the flames — and screaming, always the screaming. If he pressed deeper into his memory, his head would hurt so badly he couldn't even talk.

When he recovered, he noticed Sarah staring intensely at a page in her notebook.

"These monsters crossed our paths for a reason," she said without looking up. "We know they're real, and it's up to us to do something about it."

"Do?" Alex hadn't expected this.

"Yes." She tapped her little book. "To stop them."

Finally she met his gaze, her earnest face framed by dark ringlets. Hell, he was surprised she even believed him. And Sam was *grinning*.

"Yeah," he said. "Whatever made Charles is still out there. Should we go to the police?"

"My grandfather's been down that road," Alex said. "What proof do we have? A headless skeleton in a grave? They'll think we're insane."

"Or involved," Sarah said.

"As nasty as last night was," Sam said, "we did pretty well. Let's track the other one down and kill it."

"Sam, I don't believe this," Anne said. "Sarah's always on a mission, even if it's schoolwork. But you?"

Sam turned away from her. "Who wants to do it ourselves?"

Alex watched Sarah, Sam, and Emily raise their hands. Others knew. They believed. He raised his hand, too.

Anne looked like she'd just smelt sour milk. "Crazy. You're all certifiable—"

"Majority has it," Sarah said. "First order of business is to find this vampire, the one that made Charles. Since we're swapping secrets, I've got one myself. I was warned about Charles' death."

"What do you mean?" Anne said, glaring at Sarah.

"Remember that day on the pond? I was telling you about my dream. I never finished because we found the body, but when I met the living Charles I had a... vision, and I dreamt about it the night he died."

That certainly sounded peculiar, but Grandfather had told him about a witch in Athens who could dream the precise moment of someone's death.

"What did the vampire look like?" he asked.

"I didn't see him, or at least I don't remember," she said. "I saw a tree soaked in blood. I think Charles died on it, perhaps upside-down. I didn't understand it at the time, but there are connections between my dream and his death that just can't be coincidence."

He was about to ask her for details when Anne abruptly stood up.

"I can't take this anymore." She gathered her things and stormed off toward the cafeteria exit.

Sarah rose to follow, but Sam grabbed her wrist.

"Let her go. You said it yourself, she needs time to come around."

He was still holding Sarah's arm. All Alex could think about was how soft her skin must feel.

"I'll shoulder the load for the Williams girls," Emily said.

"Quiet, Em," Sam said. "Alex, Sarah. What's our strategy?"

Despite his concerns, he felt excitement kindle inside him. They were together in this. He thought back to the times he'd watched Grandfather and Dmitri track the creatures.

"Back home we'd get death records from priests to look for a pattern."

"Here, those are found in Town Hall," Sam said, "and newspapers have obituaries."

"Good idea," Sarah said. "I'll also go through my father's books for anything relevant. Who wants to help with the death records?"

"I will," Alex said. If they came to the banks of the Styx, he was ready to wade right in.

Thirteen:
Indecent Proposal

Salem, Massachusetts, Saturday night, October 25, 1913

PASTOR PARRIS FOUND THE SHORT MAN seated in the corner of the tavern. His invitation, delivered yesterday by a gargantuan colored fellow, had been quite specific. The Latin missive, scrawled on parchment with reddish brown ink Parris strongly suspected wasn't actually ink, said, "My dear Pastor John Parris, kindly allow me the pleasure of buying you a drink tomorrow night, exactly one hour after sunset, Salem Tavern. Eternally yours, Nasir."

Parris didn't know a Nasir, but he had no doubt as to the author.

The man was dressed as at the church, in black with intricate black embroidery. His skin looked old yet young, smooth yet fragile. He had a little pointed beard and thin brown mustache that reminded Parris of portraits of his own pilgrim ancestors. His fingernails were yellow, as were the whites of his eyes when he looked up. He neither rose nor offered his hand.

"Sit with me, Pastor John Parris." Parris couldn't place the accent. Like the scent — cinnamon and almonds — it was exotic.

But he took a seat. The cruel edges of his grandmother's cruciform bracelet cut into his wrist, and he hoped it was protection enough — if it came to that.

"What shall I call you?"

Parris didn't expect to learn his true name, if the creature even remembered it after all these centuries.

"Here in America I'm known as Alan Hammil Nasir. You may call me Mr. Nasir, or just Nasir if we're to become friends." His smile revealed small pointy teeth. "But we're not friends yet, are we? Colleagues of a sort, perhaps."

"No, not friends, Mr. Nasir, not at all," Parris said.

"I think we could be in time. We've much in common."

"Don't be so sure about that."

The barmaid materialized. "Gentlemen, what can I get you?"

"Nothing for me," Mr. Nasir said, *but my handsome friend would like a pint*. Parris was sure the man's lips had not finished the sentence.

The barmaid smiled at Parris, gave his shoulder a squeeze, and left.

Women never smiled at him, much less squeezed body parts.

"You brought the Eye?" Nasir said. "My partner would like to observe the discussion."

The silky voice was hypnotic, which made Parris all the warier.

"I have it."

He brought out the leather bag, sewn from the buttock skin of a human boy — if the seller hadn't cheated him. A week had now passed since he'd received the amulet, yet he'd not dared examine it, instead opting to leave it wrapped in black silk and tucked inside the bag. With such nonchalance as he could summon, he uncovered the gold and blue *Wadjet* Eye and placed it on the table.

"That bag smells delightful," Mr. Nasir said. "It must have been expensive."

The Eye blinked once from its place between the salt shaker and the menu. Mr. Nasir tipped his hat to it. Parris tried not to meet its gaze. The object was pretty enough, gold and lapis, with a curved brow above and two distinctive swirls below. Egyptian. Parris had researched the probable owner, and his skin crawled thinking about it.

"You called him the Painted Man. I've never heard that name, but I assume you're referring to the immortal Egyptian?"

Mr. Nasir nodded again at the Eye. "The Immortal, the Secret Advisor, Son of the Earth, the Painted Man, all one and the same."

Parris tried to swallow, but his throat felt dry. He was startled by a warm hand on his. The smiling barmaid settled a pint of ale in front of him.

Mr. Nasir continued. "My partner is, as you may know, a great locator and collector of unusual and powerful objects. He has recently — what he might consider recently — come into reliable information that something we want is here in Salem. We seek a man of your talents to aid us in obtaining it."

"Why would I help you?" Parris said.

"Out of the kindness of your heart?" The man's smile was disarming. He reached under the table and brought out a satchel, opening it to reveal a gnarled leather-bound tome. The book looked ancient.

"If you help us, you may have this." The man unlocked it to reveal a vellum page covered in dark scrawl.

Parris recognized the handwriting but scanned the text anyway.

"The last Knittlingen treatise?" These gentlemen knew him too well. "I thought it was lost or destroyed."

"What is lost can be found," Mr. Nasir whispered. "My partner acquired this not long after Dr. Faustus' death. It can be yours."

Parris reached for the book. Mr. Nasir snapped it shut and put it back in the bag.

"This thing you seek," the pastor said. "What is it?"

"A ram's horn." Mr. Nasir leaned across the table. "If we're agreed, I'll tell you more." His breath smelled of the grave.

"This horn. You and I would have to retrieve it from its present owner?"

"Your talents and associations can help with the arcane aspects, and I'll handle the guardians."

Mr. Nasir settled back into his side of the booth.

"After we retrieve the item I'll give you the grimoire." He patted the bulky satchel. "Then my partner and I will require you to use it. If accepted, this is an obligation of the contract. We seek to negotiate with a certain... personage."

He'd been staring unblinkingly at Parris for most of the conversation. Now he glanced across the room at the hearth fire.

"Do not name a demon!" Parris said. "Even you should think twice about that."

"I'm not a fool. Diodorus Siculus spoke of this individual." Mr. Nasir offered his toothy smile.

"What is your purpose in this?"

"Only my partner is free to reveal that." Mr. Nasir glanced at the Eye again. It blinked. "Rest assured, he has considered every eventuality."

"This all sounds quite dangerous," Parris said.

"Your line of work is not without certain hazards."

"I'll need time to think about you proposal."

"Of course, the centuries have taught me patience. When you're ready, tell the Eye. I'll find you."

"Are we done for now?" Parris asked. "Shall I put away your partner?"

"By all means, return him to that lovely little purse."

Paris glanced down to retrieve the amulet. When he looked up, the small man was gone.

Pastor Parris' house near the church was dark. Electric lights disturbed him, and his funds were meager, so he'd never installed any. He lit a single candle at the door.

He needed to ensure the Eye couldn't observe him at work. He placed the boy-skin bag inside a small lead coffer he'd procured for this purpose, draped a black sheet over one arm, and chanted:

> *Give me the power.*
> *Give me the dark.*
> *I call on you, the laughing gods.*
> *Let your blackness crawl beneath my skin.*

He dropped the cloth over the chest, making sure no portion of the container was visible. He extracted a knife from his pocket, made a tiny cut on one finger, and squeezed a drop of blood onto the black silk.

"Accept my sacrifice. Feed!"

He walked into the small living room and built up a good fire in the hearth. This whole Mr. Nasir business had him agitated. He'd been constipated since first meeting the man, and that always disturbed him, reminding him as it did of what'd happened to Grandmother Grace.

Perhaps he should call Betty. He needed to unwind.

After their time together, she left him tied to the chair in his bedroom. He wasn't comfortable, but he knew that pleased her. He felt relaxed for the first time in days, even though his wrists and ankles were covered in bloody ligatures, even though he felt wet and raw below. He couldn't check from his current position, but he hoped she hadn't done too much damage. It was going to be a busy week.

Betty lounged naked on his bed. The candlelight played over her bluish breasts and her dark red areola.

"My dear Toy, you had something serious to talk about?" Her thin blue tail danced above the mattress like a snake charmer's cobra.

"I've a choice to make." He told her about his meeting in the tavern.

"This man, he's a practitioner like you?" Betty asked.

"He's not exactly a man, my dear. He hasn't breathed in a long time."

"Older than me?" She was vain about her age.

"Aren't you nine years old?"

"Liar!" Her tail lashed him across his naked chest, leaving a red welt. Tied as he was, he could only wince. She wasn't really angry, just playful. "I was nine at the trial with my father, *your* — or shall I say *our* — ancestor. Aren't we naughty?"

She rolled over on her stomach, kicking her legs and waving her tail above her bare buttocks. She was 231 this year, his great-great-great-grandmother or maybe there were more greats.

"The one I met tonight is older," Parris said. "I saw him fly in the church."

She clacked her teeth. "I don't think they can do that unless they're very old, He has to be from before Luther at least, and few of them survived those years."

"At least several centuries old," he said.

"Strong, then, and clever. Is this book worth it?" she asked.

"It could mean everything. Johann Georg Faust made a deal with the devil, and his missing grimoire purports to explain how."

Her tail tickled him under his chin. "Surely you aren't foolish enough to try and follow in his footsteps."

He chuckled, from fear or her touch he wasn't sure. His relationship with Betty gave him certain advantages in the infernal realms, but with the book, he might be strong enough to command even a Duke of Hell. He shuddered. And if all went according to plan, that was what Mr. Nasir meant him to do.

"I'm a little lynx." She crouched like a cat. "We know in our bones not to mess with the big game. Do you know this Mr. Nasir's partner, the one behind the Eye?"

Despite the fire, Parris felt cold. "The undead calls him the Painted Man, but no credible tale of him exists after the French Revolution. He probably died in 1784."

Betty grew very still and didn't speak for a long moment.

"I met him once."

"Truly?"

"It was at Versailles, in 1757, I think. He called himself the Comte de Saint-Germain."

Parris nodded. "Legend has him taking that and countless other names, shadowy advisor to centuries of kings."

She slapped a buttock. "I'd seduced one of the younger sons of the Duc d'Orleans. It didn't end well for him, let that be a lesson to you."

"You're such a wicked whore, Betty. It's your infernal nature."

She wagged her tail at him.

"What was this *comte* like?" Parris asked. "I thought he was Egyptian, not French."

Now she used her tail to tease him, probing this place and that.

"He claimed to have existed longer than the world," she said. "And to have lived in Egypt and even China. On this occasion, he was talking to *le Roi*, Louis XV. This I remember, because he excused himself — who does that when talking to a king? — and came over to me. He had this peculiar walk, as if he floated above the surface of the floor. He warned me off."

"Why?"

"I think he knew what I was. He wanted me to leave. There was a brightness and a translucency to him, as if he'd been painted into the world with watercolors instead of oils."

"You think he had real power? Many believe he was a fraud."

"Let me put it this way," she said. "I and the young d'Orleans left that night for one of his estates. I wouldn't even allow the servants to pack."

This from Betty, who was more fearless than any man he knew.

"Why'd this Painted Man send a vampire to raise a demon?" she said. "Undead can't wager their souls. Goods that damaged are poor collateral."

Parris shrugged as best he could. "At least there's a market for our talents."

"What's in it for this little girl?"

"I think we can find something to please you," he said.

"We'll see about that."

She stood, bent over to retrieve her clothes, holding the pose to give him a good view, and crossed the room to the hearth. Only a few coals smoldered.

"What about me?" He shrugged his bound shoulders.

"A warlock of your repute shouldn't have any trouble with a wee bit of rope. Next time, let's play with that little pet of yours. Until then…."

Still naked, she blew him a kiss, stepped barefoot onto the hot coals, and in a flash of flame, vanished.

Fourteen:

Grist for the Mill

Salem, Massachusetts, Sunday, October 26
through dawn Thursday, October 30, 1913

ALEX PAUSED IN FRONT OF SALEM'S red brick neo-Italianate public library. He'd been thrilled at the thought of meeting Sarah alone, but now his stomach churned.

Notices plastered the foyer columns: "Public Safety Guidelines for the Current Crisis." He ripped one down and brought it into the reading room.

He found Sarah surrounded by stacks of newspapers, still in her school clothes. A pair of spectacles — he hadn't even known she needed them — pinched the bridge of her nose. She was so focused on a notebook filled with dense shorthand she didn't see him until he slapped the notice from the lobby on the table.

She glanced at him. "Oh, hi." Then the notice. "At least 'Stay at home after dark' is sound advice. We need to find this thing before it kills again."

"How can I help?" Alex pulled up a chair.

She struggled to unfurl a many-leaved map of Salem.

"I combed through two years of obituaries, making a list of possible unnatural deaths. A seventy-five-year-old, died in bed, okay. Hit by a trolley, okay. Dead in an alley at forty, bad. Died during daytime, off the list."

"That's a long list."

"Apparently one percent is typical," she said, "about five hundred a year. The rate's been steady for the last ten years but it's gone up fifteen percent since January."

"And no one noticed?"

"The paper blamed it on immigration and argued for an increased police budget." She handed him the notebook. "If you read out the address of each death, I can mark their locations. Maybe there's a pattern."

It was slow going, mostly because it took her a while to find each spot. He felt a stab of disappointment. He'd hoped the afternoon might entail something more than putting dots on a map. While he waited for her to pin down an address, he peeked at her notebook. Most of it was written in some alphabet he didn't recognize, but one sentence jumped out from a recent page: "Only you can stop us."

Halfway through, it was obvious the deaths weren't evenly distributed. He pointed to the biggest mass of dots.

"What's this group of buildings across from Derby Wharf?"

"The cotton mill?" She put her hand beside his, covering the cluster of suspicious deaths. "That place is a death trap. Besides those we marked, there were dozens of daytime incidents."

Her hand was warm and his head buzzed.

"It's also the biggest employer in town," she said. "8,000 people work there — including Sam. Let's go through all the deaths nearby."

She removed her hand and started to rifle through the papers.

Alex reached over and caught her hand.

"You're beautiful when you're excited about something."

She turned to look at him. Her brown eyes widened and her breaths were shallow. Best of all, she squeezed his hand back.

He was close enough to catch her scent. Breathing it in stopped thought and, for a moment, speech — which was hardly like him at all.

"You smell good," he said. "Like linen and roses."

Sarah smiled. "That's my mother's doing. When she folds my clothes, she puts rose petals in the drawers."

"I like it."

"My father complains that his suits smell of flowers, but I think he likes to be reminded of my mother."

He tried to slide his chair closer to her, and the legs barked against the tile floor.

Sarah jerked her hand away. "I can't."

"Can't, shouldn't, or don't want to?"

"Shouldn't."

"Then you want to?"

She blushed. "It's so complicated. My family's very close. Religion, courtship, they're all bound up together. I try not to think about it."

She reached over and patted his forearm with her hand.

"Let's be friends. I need one right now, especially since Anne is barely talking to me."

"Okay. You want to get back to the list of deaths?"

It wasn't the most romantic topic, but he'd pushed things as far as he dared, today. At least she hadn't slammed the door in his face.

Monday night at seven o'clock, Alex followed Sam through the gates of the Naumkeag Steam Cotton Company. The mill was a collection of brick structures with plain windows and column-like chimneys that belched coal smoke. All Sam's job called for was an able body and a willingness to work. Pay was by the bale.

"So what exactly are we looking for?" Sam asked as they joined the small crowd outside what he called the 'opening room.'

Alex shrugged. "Something that makes people dead."

They stepped into what Alex quickly decided was a snowstorm in hell. The temperature was over 100 degrees, the humidity high as an August afternoon just before a thunderstorm hits. His lungs immediately rejected the cotton fibers, and he found himself coughing amidst a thick cloud of them.

Pairs of men muscled huge bales off a belt and threw them in a line. Others broke open the cotton with pitchforks and machetes, while a third group tossed handfuls of the soft white stuff into the iron maws of a dozen machines that chewed chunks of cotton and excreted piles on the far side. Gears and belts whirled about, an ear-pummeling horde of infernal mechanisms driven by overhead drive shafts.

Alex and Sam worked side by side, feeding the row of machines.

"I wanted to ask you," Sam said, "now that no ladies are around. Did something else happen with the girl on the island? Something you left out?"

"We did kiss," he said. "Maria and I." In the burial chamber, on a limestone staircase leading down into stale blackness, she'd put her hand on his chest and pushed him into the stone wall. Alex could still feel the silky touch of her lips.

"I knew it."

Only five minutes since they'd entered the room, and already sweat drenched his body. Sam stripped off his shirt. Alex did too, but soon fibers coated his skin, making him feel like a tar-baby rolled in feathers. His eyes and nose stung, and the world didn't hold enough spit to get the cotton out of his mouth.

"Just a kiss?" Sam yelled.

Alex wished he could forget the surprise on her face when Dmitri's wooden shaft pierced her breast. He wiped sweat out of his eyes and yelled back. "Have you got a better story?"

The bigger boy laughed, soundless in the din.

"Last summer." He looked damn pleased with himself. "One of my mother's friends asked me over to chop firewood. Churchgoer, too. Fun while it lasted."

Did that kind of thing happen here in America? Alex shoveled more cotton into the device.

"Don't tell the girls," Sam said. "Especially not Sarah."

He nodded. Some things were just between men.

A barefoot boy approached them with a bucket of water and a ladle. Sam took the handle and passed it to Alex, who downed an entire tepid cup despite the cotton particulates coating the surface.

Resuming their work, Alex found he needed to concentrate. Rotating blades swept the cotton into the machine, spinning so fast they were almost invisible. All the nearby men had arms crisscrossed with scars, and one worker had only three fingers on his left hand. A careless move could be catastrophic. No more talk of kisses.

Or Sarah.

The next day Alex was so sore he could barely move, but he managed to slog through another uneventful night... for a dollar thirty-seven. Although the work was tedious and tiring, he got a certain pleasure from demolishing the bales, trying to optimize his motions so as to move the most cotton with the least effort. The third night, Sam had family obligations, leaving Alex to work alone.

Not long into his shift, an oiler — boys of about eight or nine who lubricated the spinning machines — tripped and pitched forward. Arms out to break his fall, one of his hands landed in the exposed gearbox.

For an instant, the boy's face was blank.

Then the screaming started. Only fifteen feet from Alex, his shrieks were barely audible above the constant mechanical roar.

All around, heads turned toward the commotion. The hand was buried to the wrist, but the gears still ground away. Blood squirted, slicking the cogs and staining the nearby cotton.

Early to reach the scene, Alex and another man grabbed the boy before he collapsed. The line supervisor arrived cursing and slammed the Stop button. Someone put a belt around the boy's wrist to serve as a makeshift tourniquet.

"Timmy, you damn fool!" the supervisor screamed. "Now this machine'll be off-line for hours. You two," he pointed at Alex and the other man, "get him out of there. You," pointing at a third, "get a fixer and the nurse."

Timmy's screams faded to whimpers, but his pale face was contorted in pain.

The man beside Alex took a loose bit of leather belt and offered it to the boy.

"Bite on this," he screamed over the din. "We're going to pull your hand free."

Timmy looked terrified, but he bit down on the leather.

"Slow or fast?" Alex asked. One hand rested on the boy's wrist, the other steadied him. The blood had stopped spurting, but the sticky fluid still oozed through Alex's fingers.

"Slow," the man said. A third worker tried to roll the gears in reverse to free the trapped limb.

It was in the midst of all this that Alex noticed a fellow watching from the shadows. He was tiny, barely five feet tall, and emaciated. His skin was pale, his hair plastered to his skull. His gaze was locked on the hand in the machine, but where others looked horrified, this man looked expectant.

As they wrestled to free him, Timmy stiffened and screamed, but Alex held tight. At last the hand — what was left of it — came free. The other man tightened the tourniquet while Alex held the boy's face against himself so he wouldn't see the hand. The two middle fingers were gone, and the gear had chewed into the meat of the palm.

Alex looked back at the man in the shadows. His face had a pinched look, and he licked his lips.

"Anyone have anything clean?" the older man yelled.

Someone brought a length of white sheet, probably one of the mill's products. Oil and grease from the gears coated the wound. The man with the sheet tried to wrap the hand gently, but Timmy still writhed in agony. Someone passed them a bottle of whiskey.

"Drink as much of this as you can."

"Okay, boys," the supervisor yelled, "show's over. Get back to work. You two, bring him to the nurse. Then back on the line or it won't just be the boy's pay I dock."

Alex returned to his place. He searched for the tiny man with the greasy hair, but he was nowhere to be found.

At the end of his shift, Alex was among the first out the door. He sprinted across the courtyard and stood where he could watch the workers filing into the night. It was very dark — the moon had set, but the sun had not yet risen. Most of the crowd drifted toward the pay office, but the short man with greasy hair broke off and made for a nearby gate.

Alex followed. He hung back, but his quarry paid little attention. The man had an odd gait, not fast or slow, a sort of scuttling shuffle. He left the factory grounds but instead of taking the road back into town approached the half-abandoned warehouse district by the old estuary wharves, where he ducked into an alley between brick buildings.

Alex peered down the narrow passage. It was dark, and he didn't see any movement. Slinking down the corridor, he heard a faint scraping sound.

He froze. Set into the cobblestones, a rusty iron grate covered the entrance to what must be a cellar. All around were muddy footprints. Alex knew he shouldn't be doing this alone, but he was too wound up to stop now. Besides, monster hunting wasn't so hard. What did Grandfather do but sit in his library?

With as much care as he could manage, he lifted the heavy grate to the side. His clothes were already filthy, so it didn't bother him to lie in the mud and peer into the opening. An old coal chute, by the looks of it. A lead-coated ramp led down into darkness. He pulled his hunting knife out of his small bag and jammed the sheath through his belt. Thus prepared, he lowered himself into the underworld.

The ramp was slippery, and he almost lost his balance, but by bracing his arms against the walls he stayed upright. While he caught his breath, he heard shuffling, accompanied by off-key singing.

Alex crept forward, bit his tongue and stopped when his knees banged into something hard.

The singing paused, then resumed. Soon, he heard a soft metallic sound and saw a dim light ahead. An opening revealed a cavernous room, where the small man squatted next to a rivulet of dark water, humming a low tuneless song. Beside him were an old oil lantern and a pile of small wet forms. Rats, barely alive. The man picked up a brick and smashed a rodent's head with a nasty wet smack.

Then the man, this real-life Caliban, stopped humming, brought the rat to his mouth and gnawed for a minute or two, then flung it away. Alex heard it splash in the distance. The man's small mouth was smeared with dark blood. Tiny white teeth gleamed.

Alex shifted to get a better view. He felt his knife slip through his belt. It clattered on the stone floor.

The man snuffed his lamp and the basement was plunged into darkness.

Alex snatched up his blade, leapt to his feet, and bolted for the only thing he could see: the coal shaft, now lit by the first light of morning. He hit the ramp running. His momentum and a few scavenged footholds carried him up and out into the alley. He paused to kick the grate back in place, then sprinted down the alley and onto the street. He jogged toward town, slowing only as his mud-stained form joined the early morning risers along a busier road. The sun greeted him like a long lost friend.

Fifteen:
I Smell a Rat

Salem, Massachusetts, Thursday, October 30, 1913

"I WAS THINKING…" Sarah's father leaned into her room as she packed for school.

"How unusual."

"Touché." He smiled. "That new friend of yours, the Greek boy? You mentioned that his father is also a historian, specializing in the late Byzantine."

Just like Papa to forget personal details but remember the academic.

"His name's Alex, and he lives with his grandfather — I think his name's Constantine — the antiquarian."

"I'd like to meet this young man," Papa said. "I was going to suggest we invite the boy and his *grandfather* over for dinner. How about Friday, November seventh?"

She was dying to meet the mysterious Constantine, having tried to peer into the house several times. The most evidence she'd seen of his existence was Dmitri's goat pen. She was *not* dying to subject Alex to her parents' scrutiny.

"I don't know."

"Try to contain your enthusiasm, Sarah."

"I'll ask him, but Alex's grandfather is really old, so he might not want to travel, and we can't very well eat over there. Which is a shame, because it sounds like they collect all sorts of wonderful things."

"It's settled, then. I'll tell your mother."

This morning Sarah had awakened thinking she heard the horn again. In her half-sleeping state she'd sensed something below her in the dark, something nasty and wet, but both sound and vision had slipped away when she looked at the pale dawn glow outside the window.

"Papa," she said. "Why do we blow the ram's horn on New Year's?" With the holiday only a month past, she hoped the question seemed innocuous.

Papa kissed his fingers and pressed them to the *mezuzah* on the doorframe.

"On *Rosh Hashanah*, the blowing of the *shofar* celebrates the coronation of God and the anniversary of creation."

Her horn hadn't seemed very celebratory. "Is that the only reason?"

"Do you have a year to add to your studies?"

"Papa!"

"Sorry. The blowing of the ram's horn reminds us of the *Akedah*, the binding of Isaac, where Abraham demonstrated his absolute faith in agreeing to sacrifice his son. But God provided the Ram in the Thicket and spared Isaac, allowing the ram to die in his place. This exchange forged the covenant with our people."

"The sound of the horn comes from *Hashem*?"

"Always. The *shofar* blast also recalls the trumpet blown by Moses at Mount Sinai, forged from a horn of the very ram sacrificed by Abraham. The Ram in the Thicket is eternal, one of ten special things God made on the eve of creation."

"If Moses used one horn from the ram, what about the other?"

"And in that day, a great ram's horn shall be sounded—"

"Isaiah 27:13," Sarah said.

"That's my daughter." He looked from her to the *mezuzah* and back again. "The Archangel Gabriel will bring that Horn to Elijah, and with it, the prophet shall sound the End of Days."

Sarah was distracted on the way to school and didn't find her focus until Alex told them all about the incident in the alley.

"Was this man a vampire?" she added. "He doesn't sound like Charles."

Alex shook his head. "As far as I know, when vampires eat they turn... well, you saw. He didn't do that."

"Damn," Sam said, "I should've gone to work last night. I'd rather have shared rats with that creep than eaten Aunt Edna's chicken."

Anne stayed silent. Sarah tried to make eye contact with her, then gave up and looked at Alex instead.

"You're sure he isn't undead?" Sarah asked.

She hadn't talked to him directly in four days — since the library — but she was going to have to tell him about Papa's invitation soon.

"He didn't seem undead," Alex said. "Remember, vampires actually *are* dead — cold and rotting corpses."

Sarah nodded. She had immersed herself in their lore, such as she could find. It was all pretty awful, but she had to admit that witnessing centuries of history had a certain appeal, if you could ignore the death and murder factor.

"How do they become vampires?"

Alex smiled at her before answering. She felt herself flush.

"I'm not certain," he said, "but it seems to have something to do with the blood. It's corrupted. Who knows if it's the person at all anymore, or if a demon moves in like a squatter in an empty house."

Something Charles had said tickled Sarah's brain. "Do they call it the dark gift?"

Alex shot her a look. "I'll be sure to ask one."

Sure, mock her God given revelation.

"Well, I think it sounds satanic," Emily said. "Pastor Parris would say it's a demon. He's always warning about letting the devil get a toehold in your soul."

"Certainly, creatures like what Charles became are evil," Alex said, "but as to whether they are literally spawn of the devil, I don't know. There are stories about vampires from ancient Greece, hundreds of years before Jesus. They called them *Lamia*."

"That doesn't prove anything," said Anne. "God has always existed. Maybe the devil has, too."

Sarah listened to them banter. She liked hearing Alex talk, even argue. If she was being honest with herself, she'd also liked when he held her hand.

"The nature of God and the devil," Alex said, "is unlikely to be resolved today. However, I have a theory about the rat man. Most of the time when a vampire kills a person, that's it, they're just dead, but since they're in-capacitated during the day, they need some mechanism for securing human help."

"Like Renfield in *Dracula*?" Anne asked.

"You read it?" Sam said. "I thought you didn't believe."

"I knew when you checked it out from the library you'd never open it."

"I would have. I just got busy."

"I read it first—" Emily said.

Sarah cleared her throat. Maybe Anne was starting to come around.

"Anne has a point," Alex said. "In the novel, Renfield's a crazy man whose condition Dracula exploits. Perhaps the same is true with the rat man, or maybe a person who's been fed on multiple times becomes something else, something halfway between human and vampire."

"Sucking blood — animal or human — is disgusting," Anne said. "Why am I even talking about this?"

"Because you stick with your own," Sarah said. "For better or worse."

Anne crossed her arms. "And I don't even get a wedding ring out of it."

"If — and it's a big if," Alex said, "this rat man is a vampire *sykophántēs*, then maybe he knows his master's location."

"Psycho-what?" Sam asked.

"He means sycophant, a slavish person," Sarah said. "Alex is just saying the rat man might know how to find the vampire."

The five of them gathered in the alley as the sun began to set. A breeze off the harbor carried the chill of oncoming winter, and Sarah was happy she'd chosen a heavy wool jacket and skirts. She pulled her hat down as low as she could and tucked herself into a boarded-up doorway, hidden from the rat man's grate.

Alex joined her, but she wished he'd chosen the other side. He opened his mouth to say something, and she put a finger to her lips, pointing at the grate. Clearly being invited to a family dinner had just egged him on.

He reached into his jacket and withdrew a four-inch wooden cross adorned with a grotesque ivory Jesus. Sarah waved it away, not even wanting to touch it with her gloves. He got the message and fished out a brown glass vial instead.

She eyed it warily.

"It won't bite," he whispered. "It's just holy water."

She sighed and took the bottle. Hopefully no one prayed to baptismal fonts.

As soon as the sunset began to fade, the grate rattled, and a small figure heaved itself onto the cobblestones. She hoped his willingness to brave the twilight was a sign he was still among the living.

Either someone made a noise or the rat man could smell them, because after a moment he crouched, sniffed the air, then bolted down the narrow alley.

Sam leapt out of his hiding place and threw himself onto the figure.

The stranger hissed and squirmed beneath his captor.

"Let me go, foul foal. Off of me you big offal. Master make mincemeat of you!" He spoke in such a bizarre blend of English and Greek that Alex was likely to be the only one to fully understand.

"What master?" demanded Alex in Greek. "*Vrykolakas?*"

"Luckless Nicolai, moorish master no want, send noxious Negros beat him big. Nicolai would serve the master for endless eternity, gallons of gold, limitless lifetime, he promised. Nicolai faithful."

Sarah edged closer.

"That guy's certifiable," Anne said over Sarah's shoulder. "I don't know why I agreed to come."

"Because you didn't trust Emily with us loons," Sarah reminded her.

Sam shook the man several times, but he seemed only half aware of his captors. If he was insane, Alex's vial of holy water shouldn't hurt him. Sarah splashed the contents onto him.

The man began to writhe and shriek like he'd been soaked with acid.

"Fiery tears of the son, it burns, it burns! Forgive me, master, forgive me, I perform putrescent, puerile!"

Nothing seemed physically wrong with him, but he kept contorting. Vampiric hysteria? He might not be undead, but he thought he was. Alex kicked at his scrabbling legs.

"Where's this master now?"

"Nicolai never betray the master, the master is lengthy life, fountain of forever! Forsake the rising son, what is left, only perilous promises."

Sarah almost felt sorry for him.

Sam knelt on his chest, pulled a silver cross from his pocket, and held it an inch from the man's face.

"Tell us!" he said.

Nicolai squirmed.

"Lictor of the lamb, nail of the Nazarene, keep it away! Close to Collins Cove, or Cove Collins close, far from his Caliphate, close to his crypt. Nicolai met the master on the wide water, the master needed him, needed his life, and promised eternal returns."

Sarah felt dirty, although it wasn't like they were actually hurting him. And more importantly, it seemed to be working.

Nicolai spat in Sam's face, grabbed Alex's leg, and bit down on his ankle. Alex yelped and jumped back, and when Sam relaxed his guard to look, the man wriggled out from underneath him and ran off into the deepening gloom.

Sam started after him.

"Let him go," Alex said. "We got what we came for." He hopped around, flexing his foot.

Sarah had to go to him. "Are you okay? Is his bite dangerous?" He smelled sweaty and pungent.

"He didn't break the skin."

"If he did?" Emily said. "Would you turn into a vampire?"

"I don't think so," Alex said. "I'd guess this master fed on Nicolai during his journey across the Atlantic. On a boat, there'd be nowhere for a vampire to run, and overhunting might draw unwelcome attention. I'm surprised the thing didn't kill him."

"Well, *I* might." Sam wiped his face with a handkerchief. "His spit smells like dead rat!"

Sixteen:
Housecall

Salem, Massachusetts, Saturday night, November 1, 1913

FOR THE HUNDREDTH TIME, Parris studied the peeling wallpaper of his dingy second-floor bedroom. One of these days he should turn his talents toward something more lucrative. He'd inherited some money from his grandmother, but neither his religious calling nor a predilection for exotic spell components helped the funds last. He crushed another roach as it sallied out from under the bed to cross the worn oaken expanse.

About an hour after midnight, too restless to sleep, Parris heard a tapping at the window.

Mr. Nasir hovered outside in the blackness between houses. Parris saw only his pale face and the claw prodding the cheap bubbled glass. Nasir smiled and waved as if they'd encountered each other on an afternoon stroll. The hand, however, looked older than the manicured pair that had rested idly on the pub table last week; instead, the fingers were ashen and unnaturally long, like the legs of a grotesque crab, the nails pointed and yellow.

Parris unlatched the window and slid the bottom half up.

"You called?" Mr. Nasir said.

The lead coffer housing the Eye was under the bed. Even the Painted Man shouldn't be able to see through that, so this morning Parris had taken the object out and beckoned to it. Apparently, the vampire had gotten the message.

Parris leaned out the window. The creature clung to the dark wood like some huge spider.

"Would you be so kind as to invite me in?" the vampire asked.

So that particular myth was accurate, or so Mr. Nasir wanted him to believe. Parris wasn't overly concerned for his safety. If this ancient predator wanted him dead, there was little he could do about it.

"Come in, Mr. Nasir."

Parris blinked, and the other man stood inside, unpleasantly close. Had he shut his eyes for more than an instant? Parris' nose twitched at the smell of spice and decay. Mr. Nasir's feet were bare, the gnarled pale toes at least five inches long, the thick talons scratching the cheap floor. The creature looked twenty years older than when Parris had seen him last. His wavy black hair was shot through with gray, his face creased with deep lines.

Parris frowned and settled into the room's only chair.

"You don't look well," he said. "Did something happen?"

"I'm merely hungry. I flew here from Boston and didn't have a chance to feed."

"You may sit on the bed if you wish."

"This place must be cheaper than a radish." Parris startled and nearly toppled off his seat. The vampire perched on the edge of the cot, one leg crossed over the other. Parris hadn't even seen him traverse the room.

"So you're ready for our venture?" Mr. Nasir asked.

"I was this morning, when I signaled the Eye. Alas, I assume we'll be working nights."

Mr. Nasir chuckled. "I like that you have a sense of humor."

Parris twitched. The vampire stood in front of him, pale face inches away, a cold hand on his shoulder.

"You swear to serve our order faithfully, and not divulge our secrets?" he said.

"In exchange for the grimoire, I do." Parris felt a tingle in his limbs. Such oaths were not sundered lightly.

"As soon as we retrieve the missing artifact, the book is yours."

"Then tell me what we seek."

"Long ago, it came to our attention that the Archangel Gabriel had left a certain artifact in mortal hands," Nasir said. "One of the Painted Man's ancient comrades has spent centuries trying to locate it, and several decades back he succeeded, only to have it snatched from under his nose."

A second Egyptian? "In the tavern you mentioned a horn."

"A ceremonial ram's horn, about this size." The vampire held his hands a foot apart.

"Doesn't the archangel want it back?"

Mr. Nasir's laugh sounded like a cat's screech. "This from the man that who just agreed to bargain with a Duke of Hell."

Parris' adam's apple attempted to find its way to his stomach. Truth be told, angels and demons usually left the mortal realms to their own devices.

"So you think the angel's horn is in Salem?"

"The Painted Man believes so."

This time Parris saw him move. Nasir drifted across the room to the window, more gracefully than any dancer, then paused at the open casement.

"Get dressed. We'll continue our discussion downstairs in fifteen minutes. I might grab a bite to eat while I wait."

Mr. Nasir was nowhere to be seen when Parris descended the staircase into his foyer. But a few minutes later, there was a knock at the door.

"Sorry," the vampire said when Parris let him in — notably without a second invitation. "I had to walk a few blocks to find what I was looking for."

He wore his boots again. The white was gone from his hair, as were the lines from his face. He seemed flushed with energy, if not exactly youth.

"What was that?" Parris asked, unable to help himself.

The smile grew no less horrifying with familiarity. "I settled for a Chinese boy. He was fresh enough, but a little sour. I've never been further east than Persia. I'm not sure I could tolerate the diet."

Parris himself had barely been past Hartford, Connecticut. Only that one trip to New Orleans — and that had certainly been worthwhile despite the rich southern food that had lashed him to the toilet for a week. A connection occurred to him.

"That evening, when we first met in my church, I'd just conducted a young boy's funeral service. Was that your handiwork?"

"What can I say? You've found me out."

Charles' death had caused Parris no small amount of trouble. Consoling bereaved congregants was tedious.

"Why'd you make such a spectacle of it?" he asked. "I assume he was just one of many, but that murder created quite a stir in the community."

"I was instructed on the manner. The Painted Man said it would stir the Horn from hiding."

"How?"

The vampire shrugged, an oddly human gesture. "The Egyptian paints with many colors, but the work is always masterful."

"You know only that it's in the city?"

"I've heard warlocks are good at finding things," Mr. Nasir said.

"Yes, but I've got to have something to work with. Do you have anything strongly associated with the Horn?"

The vampire's long fingers convulsed like an albino tarantula. "Indeed. While the Painted Man's lackey bungled the Horn's retrieval, he did recover a fragment of its golden decorations."

"That should serve. Can I see it? I'll need at least a week to prepare a spell." Formulations had already begun to swirl in his head.

"I have it in my treasury," Nasir said. "I'll send for you Friday after next."

Seventeen:
Pride and Prejudice

Salem, Massachusetts, Sunday, November 2, 1913

SARAH USED ALL THE LEVERAGE eleven years of friendship afforded to convince Anne to help with her plan. Two weeks had passed since the Charles-vampire had been killed, and she and her best friend still hadn't really made up. Sarah couldn't remember this ever happening before — at least not for so long.

"I can't believe you got me in trouble with Mom like that," Anne said as they walked east from her house. "Now I have to pretend to be writing a paper on the Salem witch trials."

"I'm sorry," Sarah said. "I didn't mean to stir things up."

Mrs. Williams was one of those ladies who knew everyone in town, so Sarah had invented a local history paper as pretext for finding a gossipy Collins Cove resident to interview. She hoped whoever they spoke to could tell them something about the neighborhood's newest undead resident.

"All this craziness only leads two places," Anne said, "the asylum or an early grave. And this pie is heavy."

Sarah took her turn with the cardboard box. Like her own mother, Mrs. Williams didn't believe in calling on someone empty-handed.

"This might be the first time I've *ever* lied to Papa. I've had my share of big league omissions, but nothing like this. If I have to sneak out at night again, he's going to start thinking I have a secret lover."

Anne raised an eyebrow. "Don't you? I see the way you and Alex look at each other."

At least they were talking about normal things. Sarah elbowed her.

"We aren't all as lustful as you."

Anne bent over in mock pain. "That's hitting below the belt. Particularly from an old maid like you."

Sarah didn't like that expression. "You're nine months older than me and I don't exactly see a ring on your finger. Besides, I've told you before, Alex isn't Jewish. He is, however, a gentleman, and very smart."

"I knew it!" Anne said. "You do fancy him. Are you going to wait for your parents to betroth you to some old rabbi?"

"There's nothing wrong with rabbis. My father was one, and my mother's father."

"I think you should say to hell with it, throw yourself at Alex, and become a wanton woman."

"Anne Elisabeth Williams," Sarah said. "Don't even say that. What if someone heard you?"

"You see anyone you know?" Anne asked. They were on Briggs, a quiet waterfront street close to their destination. "Besides, weren't your parents a love match?"

"So they say," she said. "They met when Papa moved to Prague to study with Grandpapa. But they're both so sensitive about his death, I've never found out any details."

Unbidden, the door of Judah's room opened in Sarah's memory. His tiny form lay in the bed, sweat beaded his sleeping face, little shudders rocked his body, tortured even in sleep.

Sarah blinked away her own budding tears. "After Judah died, the combined losses sucked some of the joy out of Mama."

Anne nodded. "I can't even think about my parents dying. Or even Sam and Emily, as much as they annoy me."

For a few minutes they strolled in silence.

"Isn't this the house we're looking for?" Anne said.

She'd stopped at a typical red brick and white trimmed Salem Federalist. The girls walked up the short stairs onto a columned porch and rapped the leonine door-knocker. A thin elderly lady in an old-fashioned dark dress opened the door.

"May I help you, girls?" Her voice was scratchy and her expression wary.

"Good afternoon, ma'am," Sarah said. "Are you Mrs. Catherine Stuart?"

"Why do you want to know?"

"My name's Sarah Engelmann, and this is my friend Anne Williams—"

"We're doing a school report," Anne said, "on the history of the Collins Cove neighborhood. My mother is friends with your daughter, and she — my mother, I mean — she said you know just *everything* about the area and are full of all sorts of *delightful* stories. She thought you'd be just the *best* source of information for us. So we brought you this cherry pie." She held it up.

"Of course I remember little Lizzy Williams," Mrs. Stuart said. "Come in, come in. I do love a nice pie."

Sarah was glad Anne had stolen her introduction. She could never have pulled off that girlish enthusiasm.

Mrs. Stuart ushered them into her parlor before retreating to the kitchen with the box.

"Your mother was a Lizzy?" Sarah said.

"It's the *little* part I find hard to imagine."

The old woman returned carrying a tray with three neatly plated pie slices, drinking glasses, and a milk bottle.

"So, what is it you'd like to know about the neighborhood? I know just *everybody*."

"Our report is on how recent immigrant arrivals have affected things," Anne said.

"For the worse, dears, for the worse," Mrs. Stuart said. "I know you Williams are old Salem stock like the Stuarts. All these new folk are just a *stain* on the town. It's unsavory. I mean, they don't speak English and they pack five families into a house that should properly have only one."

Sarah examined her pie. The dessert smelled lovely, but she really wasn't supposed to eat it. Explaining this to Mrs. Stuart was going to be impossible. And what if the dire portents in her dreams came true? Was she ready to die without tasting "Lizzy's" cherry pie? Mama was a great cook, but cherry pie wasn't in her repertoire.

She took a bite. It was good, really good. She hoped the richness in the crust was butter instead of lard. Hopefully God would forgive her minor slip-ups. She *was* trying to fight hideous evil for Him, after all.

In the meantime Anne was cooing her way through the conversation.

"I know, Mrs. Stuart, and some of them aren't even Christians." She nudged Sarah with her knee. "Or worse, papists."

"The Catholics with their intemperate ways and their gussied up churches — don't get me started."

Anne didn't. "Mrs. Stuart, recently I heard that some people came to Salem from really far off places."

"Well, now, there's this enormous Russian family just down the street. They must have twenty children living in one house. Or do you mean the Chinamen?"

"How about even stranger? What about colored people, not from the South but from somewhere really exotic."

Anne was good. The rat man had mentioned Negros.

Mrs. Stuart lowered her voice. "We do have that odd fellow in the white clapboard on Webb Street. I don't think he's a Negro himself, brown with a funny pointed beard, a tiny little man. He doesn't have a family — they do often send the menfolk over first — but he has these big Negro fellows working for him. I've never seen the like."

"You don't say," Anne said. "The Negros are foreign too?"

"And big as houses, with shaved heads. And *swords*!" Mrs. Stuart said.

"Swords?" Sarah said, spraying a few pie crumbs.

"They look like darkies from an *Arabian Nights* picture-show. No shirts, funny vests, and big curved blades."

"Part of a theater company, I expect," Anne said.

Eighteen:
Dinner Invitation

Salem, Massachusetts, Friday evening, November 7, 1913

ALEX HELPED HIS GRANDFATHER dress for dinner. The old man looked better, his skin tighter about his flesh. He even lifted his arms to help with his shirt.

"You had something to eat?" Alex said in Greek.

"Just a light bit of goat." The old man spoke in English, presumably practicing for dinner.

Dmitri's roast goat hardly qualified as light.

"Don't embarrass us tonight," Alex said. "Sarah is smart, perceptive—"

"When a young man warns his elders how to behave, that spells trouble. You like this girl." Constantine smiled, showing his yellow teeth.

"Maybe. I will say I haven't met a woman like her before."

"Plow the field where you like, that's a young man's prerogative. But take care where you plant your seed. Our bloodline—"

"Please, Grandfather, can we skip the lineage lecture tonight? No one cares about bloodlines anymore, not in America."

Grandfather gripped his arm. On this subject, he was like a dog in the manger.

"Alexandros, this is no insignificant matter, nor is it one of my eccentricities." He'd switched back to Greek. "This is a duty you inherit from your forefathers. Eventually, you must marry well and produce a male heir."

Alex sighed. "You know, if you actually told me *why*, perhaps I might take it more seriously."

"For now, you must trust me. Remember the last time you dallied with a girl."

"I've stood next to Sarah in the sunlight, so I hardly think it can be *that* bad. But I have a question for you, Grandfather. When one vampire makes another, do they call it 'the dark gift'?"

The older man's gaze could've punched holes in Alex's skull.

"Who told you this, Alexandros?"

"Sarah."

"Clever girl. How'd she know?"

Alex shrugged. "Probably read it. She reads a lot."

"That's not something one finds in books," Grandfather said. "Vampires too have their gods, but theirs is a dark covenant: blood for life. When the blood of a vampire is ingested by someone, and they die soon after, they are said to receive this 'dark gift' and rise again, undead."

"I'll make a point to avoid dying."

The pain that crossed his grandfather's face made him wish he hadn't made light of the subject. But then it seemed to Alex that this sadness was something more profound.

"Are you thinking about Grandmother?" he said.

"To see your love slain before your eyes is the worst kind of fate…."

Alex thought again of Maria's lips and felt a rare moment of kinship with the old man.

"But back to the dark gift." Grandfather pointed a long finger at him. "What aren't you telling me about your Sarah?"

Alex liked the way that sounded, *your Sarah*. Still, he should never have brought up the topic.

"That body we found three weeks ago, the boy? It was undead. It rose from the grave."

Grandfather's gnarled hands gripped the handles of his wheelchair. Alex had a peculiar feeling, as if he'd taken off his shirt during mass and everyone turned his way.

"You don't say." The old voice coiled to strike. "Your tone betrays a cockerel's pride."

"My friends and I took care of it. And yes, if you must know, it went very well."

"Foolish to involve them. You should have approached Dmitri."

"I can't always rely on you and Dmitri. No matter, the fiend is dead twice over. I even boiled the head in garlic and holy water."

"So you're a big game hunter now, having slain this fledgling? What of its maker? Will you and your friends be a match for one who's prepared, one who's not insane with the hunger?"

"We know what we're doing." Far from true, but pride *was* on the line. "We're getting closer to the maker."

"Are you?" The old man raised an eyebrow. "You've tracked the beast to its lair?"

"Well, we know he arrived last winter, and his *thralls* are blackamoors."

Energy gathered in his grandfather like the crowd before an execution. Ten years rolled off his face.

"You've caught an eel by its tail! You're not ready for al-Nasir."

Years had passed since Alex had seen him so excited. A distant memory surfaced: Grandfather, much younger, his hair only touched by silver, taking a long sword from the lintel of a door. Sharp jabs of pain lanced Alex's temples.

"Al-na-who?" he asked. "You know the creature?"

"Last I heard he was in Morocco. I didn't think they would send one such as he."

"*They?*" Alex said. Grandfather hoarded secrets like the Vatican hoarded relics. "I thought we came here to leave vampires behind. To start anew. What—"

"Desire and duty are different things," the old man said. "But yes, I knew one had been sent. It bodes poorly if it's al-Nasir."

"Is he the oldest vampire?" Alex asked.

"No, not *him*, praises be. But al-Nasir is formidable enough. Far older and more powerful than any you've known. He will drain you dry and crunch your bones beneath his boots."

Grandfather turned the chair and rolled it across the study — vigorous exercise — then opened the baroque cabinet with twisting columns carved like kneeling slave boys. He removed something from the boule coffer he unlocked with a key around his neck, then rolled back to Alex and offered him a silver wolf's head medallion, its eyes set with rubies the color of pigeon blood.

"Wear this — at all times, Alexandros, all times. It will not help you conquer this monster but it may protect you from him and his minions."

Alex slipped the leather thong over his head and tucked the amulet under his shirt.

"What can you tell me about this al-Nasir?" he asked.

"If you swear on the soul of your blessed mother to abandon this quest, I'll tell you something of him."

"I swear." Aeschylus had said God was not opposed to deceit in service of righteousness.

"I'll hold you to that," Grandfather said. "The creature is most likely Ali ibn Hammud al-Nasir, sixth Caliph of Córdoba. He died on the twenty-second of March, 1028."

Blessed Jesus, almost a millennium ago.

"Spanish, then?"

Grandfather shrugged. "In life he was a Moor, probably of Berber origin. *Ghazi*, a fanatical defender of Allah. Although we can be certain he no longer walks in Allah's light, literally or figuratively."

"You seem to know a lot about him," Alex said.

"I know what books tell of the man he was. But any creature that has survived nine hundred years of nights is *not* to be trifled with."

"Consider me impressed," Alex said. "Why is he here?"

"I'm not certain," Grandfather said, "but I received word that an old vampire had arranged to cross the Atlantic. A life defended for centuries is not lightly risked. If the one you found is truly the Caliph, it would be unprecedented. Legend describes him as a crafty robber of temples and tombs, most zealous in his pursuits."

"So what do we do?" Alex asked.

"*We* do nothing. Come, the sun has set. We'll be late for this *Shabbos* dinner of yours."

The foyer clock read twenty past six, and although the sun had left the sky, the heavens were still bright. Alex hurried outside to start the car.

He opened the water valve for the acetylene generator mounted on the running board. It took five minutes to build up gas for the headlights. He turned the key, slowed the timing, dragged the throttle down, and checked the hand brake. The Model T had an unpleasant habit of leaping forward when you cranked the starter, ill-advisedly located under the front bumper.

Now the true test. He gave the choke under the radiator a quarter turn, then gripped the starter crank, checking his thumb placement. Sometimes the car backfired, and a careless man could break his arm if the lever spun counter-clockwise. A few vigorous half cranks and the engine coughed to life. He skipped around and jumped into the driver's seat to adjust the timing before it stalled.

Dmitri materialized to reach over Alex's shoulder and gentle the beast with a deft touch.

When Alex knocked at the Engelmanns' a stocky bearded man wearing a black skullcap opened the door.

"Welcome," he said. "I'm Joseph Engelmann, Sarah's father."

"Alexander Palaogos. Sorry we're late, but my grandfather isn't as mobile as he used to be." Alex nodded at the curb, where Dmitri was situating the old man in his chair.

"You've got a motorcar?" Sarah's father lit up. "I've been saving to buy one, perhaps a 1914 series. Like having your own personal locomotive!"

"If you're a thrill seeker, Dmitri can give you a ride after dinner—"

"Constantine Palaogos at your service," Grandfather said from behind him. "I apologize for our tardiness. My fault, of course." He gestured at his frail legs. His yellow-toothed smile made him look like an elegantly dressed skeleton.

"Come in, join us," Joseph said. "*Shabbos* dinner is always tepid at best, it won't get any colder."

Alex and Dmitri manhandled Constantine's chair over the threshold.

Dmitri uttered only his favorite word, "Basil."

Sarah and a middle-aged woman, obviously her mother, waited in the foyer. Sarah wore a dark skirt and a high-collared white blouse, but her hair was down. She'd been cool when she extended the invitation, but tonight her smile was so warm, it almost hurt to look at her. Some animal part of him wanted to drag her off into a dark room and make her his own.

As the next round of introductions ensued, Grandfather was on his best behavior, for which Alex was grateful. It was a wonder the old man still remembered how to make social conversation since he never left the house.

A place in the dining room had been set for Dmitri, but he wouldn't take it, choosing instead to stand upright behind Grandfather's chair. The table was already laden with food, most of it hidden under china covers. A pair of lit silver candlesticks graced the center. Sarah's mother poured a raspberry-colored wine into Bohemian crystal glasses.

Joseph stood, raising an ornamental silver chalice, to say a couple of sentences in what Alex supposed was Hebrew. Sarah and her mother sipped in response. Grandfather, always partial to wine, downed his glass in one gulp. Alex sipped. The situation felt awkward, the wine peculiar, sweet, on the south side of mediocre.

Sarah's father took a loaf of shiny brown bread from a plate on the table, broke off a piece, and recited another blessing. He passed the rest of the loaf to Grandfather, dipped his piece in a small plate of salt, and ate it.

"Mr. Palaogos," he said, "do you have a blessing you'd like to say before beginning the meal?"

"Thank you, no." Grandfather looked amused. "As a boy I re-member whole days caught up in church pomp, but God and I now have a less … formal relationship."

Joseph nodded. "I myself am less attached to ritual than I was in Europe."

"Sir?" Sarah asked. "If I might be so bold, how long ago was that, when you were a boy?"

"Sarah!" Her mother looked shocked.

But Grandfather was in excellent humor.

"Leave an old man a few vanities. Let's just say that I look and feel truly ancient." He then addressed Mr. Engelmann in German. "I cannot help but notice by your accent that you're from Vienna."

Alex had no idea how many languages the old man knew, and he was able to mimic even the most subtle regional accents.

"Sarah told me we were probably in Vienna at the same time," Joseph said. "Rebecca and I met in Prague, but we lived in the capital between '90 and '96, before coming here."

"Did you also teach in Vienna?" Grandfather asked.

"No, I worked as an aide for a rabbi named Adolf Jellinek, and later his successor. I helped coordinate religious and cultural issues at court."

"Interesting," Grandfather said. "I was in the capital searching for pieces of Du Paquier porcelain. I visited the palace a number of times to catalog the imperial collections. Quite splendid…. Do you remember that impressive fire in the palace stables?"

"I was at court that day, yes." Joseph soaked a piece of bread in honey.

"Were you? What a coincidence. They struggled all night to douse the flames, as I recall."

"An… eventful day," Joseph said.

They paused while Sarah and her mother uncovered the dinner: beef brisket, stewed with carrots and sweet potatoes, green beans, and a mysterious egg noodle casserole with raisins. Sarah's mother set two heaping platters of the beef on the table but placed a smaller plate beside Mr. Engelmann, patting her husband's hand as she did so. When Sarah returned to her seat, Alex asked her about it.

"Papa doesn't like prunes," she said, "so she makes his brisket without them."

Alex took a bite of his own. The beef was a little sweet but good. He wondered if his mother had cooked anything special just for father.

Grandfather, who had the appetite of a pheasant, toyed with his food, all the while looking at Sarah, a peculiar expression on his face. It wasn't one Alex had seen before, and he considered himself adept at reading the old man.

Sarah also seemed to notice. "Mr. Palaogos, what happened to your wife, Alex's grandmother?"

Grandfather steepled his fingers. "In my youth, my brother arranged two marriages for me, but both women died in childbirth. I was not blessed in these regards, and neither infant lived. Years later, on a diplomatic mission to Venice, I met the love of my life. We married in secret, as her family didn't approve, and she bore me a son, from which Alexandros is descended. She, too, died tragically, so I believed myself cursed, and I never again sought the love of a woman."

"That's so sad," Sarah's mother said.

"He must like you," Alex whispered to Sarah. "He doesn't talk about my grandmother."

"What was her name?" She leaned in close to him.

Alex could smell her clean linen and roses scent, had to resist the powerful urge to bury his face in the curly halo enveloping her neck.

"What are you two whispering?" Sarah's mother asked. "You know it's not polite."

"I was just explaining what a *kugel* is," Sarah said.

Her mother looked concerned. "Oh, did you like it?"

For an instant Alex panicked — he had no idea what she was referring to. But then he noticed Sarah's hand in her lap, pointing at the egg noodle dish.

"Yes, very much," he said. "I'm just not used to starch with fruit in it."

Mrs. Engelmann smiled. "This one isn't my best. My dairy *kugels* are better. Cheese and butter are tastier than *schmatltz*."

When she turned away he whispered to Sarah, "What's *schmatltz*?"

"Chicken fat," she said.

As bad as the sweet wine was, Alex kept drinking. Before he knew it, they were caught up in a flurry of polite leave-taking at the door. He was going to have to make himself some strong Turkish coffee when he got home. The four teenagers had a clandestine rendezvous at midnight.

The image of Dmitri piloting the Model T would've been comical if Alex hadn't been terrified. As the giant plunged at breakneck speeds down the dark and bumpy dirt roads he seemingly sought out rather than avoided every pothole and ditch. The man was so large he barely fit into the driver's seat. The steering wheel mashed up against his chest and his elbows jutted out.

"What was that business about the fire at the palace in Vienna?" he asked Grandfather.

"It wasn't the fire that was important, but who started it."

"You don't think Mr. Engelmann did?"

The old man shook his head. "I doubt it. I had followed someone to Vienna. He was looking for something but he left disappointed."

"Followed him the same way you followed the Caliph here?"

"Those two serve the same master," the old man said in a voice that could have frozen the Aegean on a July afternoon. "Like roaches, they bring rot and disease to whatever they touch."

"What does Mr. Engelmann have to do with them?" Alex asked.

"For his sake, hopefully nothing. Did you notice the silver metal box on the door to his house?"

"No."

"Most Jewish houses have them, they contain prayers. But this one was unusual. It had extra symbols on it, allowing it to form part of a powerful warding spell."

"Who put it there?" Alex asked.

"Mr. Engelmann, I would assume," Grandfather said. "I think he's more than he appears."

If Sarah's father really was some sort of *magi* — a notion Alex viewed with a healthy dose of skepticism — what did that make her?

After they got home, Alex told Grandfather he was going out. Subterfuge wasn't necessary. As if in compensation for his own secrecy, the old man never asked after Alex's comings and goings. He felt guilty about bending his promise mere hours after making it, but if Grandfather stopped speaking in riddles, they could work together and be stronger for it. Maybe things would change after he tossed the Caliph's sun-roasted skull at Grandfather's purple slippered feet. But tonight, anyway, was just a reconnaissance mission to investigate the house the girls had located.

Alex arrived early at the west side of Salem Common and leaned against one of the cast-iron gateposts to wait. Sarah approached from the southeast wearing the same brown pants and dark jacket she'd worn the night they destroyed the Charles-creature. Alex was pleased with himself — he hadn't done half bad tonight. Just the other day they'd barely been talking, and at dinner they'd gotten along swimmingly.

"No trouble sneaking out?" he asked.

"I did much better jumping out my window, though I'm tired and tipsy from dinner."

Alex smiled. "Rooftop escapes — a useful skill for the modern woman. Did your family say anything about us?"

"Mama did happen to mention the importance of marrying a Jewish man. About sixteen times."

"Really?"

She laughed as she gave him a whack on the arm. "Consider it a back-handed compliment. They also thought your grandfather was smart and charming. A little strange, but we Engelmanns have a high tolerance for eccentricity."

Her proximity — she stood perhaps eighteen inches from him — and the echo of her touch on his arm were distracting.

"I'm glad to hear it. Grandfather was in good spirits. At home he can be a bit of a curmudgeon."

"I don't see that, though Dmitri's a quiet one. He just stood there—"

Her words went right in one ear and out the other. Part of him knew he should find a way to pass on Grandfather's warnings about the Caliph.

Instead, he leaned in and kissed her.

Nineteen:
On The Water

Salem, Massachusetts, Friday night, November 7, 1913

WHEN THE KISS HAPPENED, Sarah's first thought was whether or not she was doing it right. Neither of them was very tall, but she still had to stand on her tiptoes, so what was she supposed to do with the rest of her body? At least her lips seemed to manage.

It was over quickly, and she realized she'd closed her eyes — which meant she wouldn't be able to relive the whole thing in her memory, at least not her hyper-detailed visual memory. When she did open her eyes, she found herself staring into his. Close. Had he enjoyed it? She had. Her head felt a bit light and she realized she'd forgotten to breathe.

"Would it be all right if I did that again?" he asked. She supposed that meant he liked it, too.

She glanced around. A few strangers wandered across the common and another couple was kissing on a bench. Must be the spot. She leaned toward Alex. If her parents found out, Mama would hand Papa the knife to skin her alive. But given all the heaviness she'd been dealing with, didn't she deserve a little lightness for herself?

They kissed again. He placed one hand on her shoulder and the other on her hip. This time she kept her eyes open . . . .

From around the corner, Sarah heard the familiar sound of the twins arguing and pushed Alex away.

"Don't say anything," she said. "Fewer tongues to wag."

"I'm only here," Anne said, "so I can have a good laugh when this fellow turns out to be perfectly normal."

Sarah's head still spun like she'd stepped off the carousel but Alex was business as usual.

"Listen, we need to be careful tonight," he said. "This vampire, he isn't like Charles, careless and immature. The one's probably centuries old and very powerful. He might have magical powers, be able to change into animals, influence our thoughts, and so on. Tonight we just want to verify that the occupant of the house is undead."

Had Sam seen something? He kept glancing back and forth between Alex and her.

"I think I'll be going home now." Anne turned back the way she'd come.

"Not so fast, fraidy-cat." Sam held an arm out to block her.

"Sam, did you bring the mirror?" Alex said.

Sam pulled two brass cylinders from his jacket. He tugged on one to extend it.

"I had a better idea" He stepped past Alex to show the cylinders to Sarah. "I found a spyglass and periscope at a nautical parts shop. A couple hours in the school machine shop, and — presto." He screwed the two cylinders together so they formed an L shape.

Anne smiled. "Occasionally my numbskull brother has a good idea. The periscope is made with mirrors, so if we see this man through it — and we will — vampires won't show up."

They crouched behind a cluster of trees and looked across the street at the house Catherine Stuart had identified, a white clapboard with a small columned porch, on a narrow lot. The hour was well past midnight, but the inside lights were still on. Shadows periodically crossed the windows, the figures obscured by drawn blinds.

Sarah handed the spyglass to Anne.

"What now?" Sam asked.

"Patience, little brother." Anne was only a minute older. "I think we just have to watch and wait. Maybe we'll get lucky and see nothing."

Another hour passed.

"Oh my God!" Anne said.

"You see something?" Sarah peered through the gloom.

The front door opened, releasing someone onto the porch. A big man as far as she could tell, but even wearing her spectacles he was still blurry.

"Anne," she said, "pass me the spyglass."

"In a minute.... My God, he's huge. And strange! I can't tell what he's doing — maybe smoking — but I think he's a Negro."

"Let me see," Sarah said. This time Anne surrendered the brass tube.

She peered at the man's head — higher than the doorjamb, even though he was slouching. In the yellow porch light he looked as dark as the Williamses' cook Emma, and she was the darkest person Sarah knew. He wore no shirt either, only a shiny golden vest, and his shoes curled up at the toes.

When she passed the spyglass to Alex, his finger brushed against her calfskin glove.

"That's a Moor if I ever saw one," he said from behind the device. "This has to be the vampire's house."

"Only an evil henchman would dress like that," Sarah said. "And he's practically naked from the waist up."

"Come on," Anne said. "He looks like he's supposed to be guarding some sultan's harem—"

"Quiet," Sam said. "Another one!"

Sarah stared into the darkness. A second figure, similarly strange, sauntered past. He waved to the man on the porch, who joined him. Together they walked between the houses and toward the water.

"I've a friend who moors his rowboat around the corner," Sam said. "We could borrow it to get a better look from the beach side."

They collected their things and crept along Webb Street as it curved around the cove. Sarah heard water lapping against the rocks and smelled brine in the air.

Alex trotted up to walk next to her.

"Don't be so obvious," she whispered, then stepped forward to join Sam in the lead.

"Alex and Anne make a fetching couple," Sam said, glancing over his shoulder.

"Yeah, sure," was all she managed.

They passed through an open park and onto a stone jetty. An inky shadow floated in the darkness near the craggy shore. Sam took a kerosene lamp from his pack, lit it, then drew a small wooden boat halfway onto the rocks.

Alex squeezed Sarah's hand as he helped the girls into the bow.

"Take the stern," Sam told him. "I'll row from the middle. Can you untie the dinghy and hop in?" He maneuvered the boat so it was mostly in the water then climbed inside.

"No problem," Alex said. "I've fished from small boats my whole life."

He tossed the rope into the dinghy, gave it a running push, and using his momentum, threw himself into the stern. He ended up face first in Sam's lap, with his feet hanging off the back. Laughing, Sam pulled him the rest of the way in.

"Your whole life, huh?" he said.

Sarah stifled her own laughter. Alex tipped his cap to her.

Sam covered the lamp and rowed out into the inlet. Sarah was happy the twins were between her and Alex. She didn't regret the kiss, but it would seem weird if they knew about it — particularly Sam.

Soon they bobbed offshore from 70 Webb Street.

Anne had the spyglass again. She and Sarah huddled in the bottom of the boat, peering out over the prow.

"Two henchmen are on the porch," Anne whispered. "They look like they're waiting for the count's Cossacks."

Sam kept the craft pointed towards shore. The spyglass was passed around, but there wasn't much more to see. The big men lounged on the porch, immobile except for the occasional cigarette.

It must have been after two in the morning when they heard the soft rumble of an engine. Their dinghy rocked as a wake rippled past. A fishing boat, maybe twenty-five feet, motored toward the house.

It was Sarah's turn with the spyglass. She watched two dark figures on the deck toss ropes to the Moors on shore, who waded out to the boat. Two large crates were tossed down, and the Moors carried them up the beach and into the house.

No one on the dinghy dared speak. Sarah passed the spyglass to Sam and made out what she could without it. The Moors reappeared from inside the house, carrying something large between them.

"What do they have?" she whispered.

"Damned if I'm sure," Sam whispered back, "but I think it's a coffin."

"Ridiculous," Anne said. "Give me the glass."

Sam passed it to her. "If it's a coffin, why are they bringing it *out* of the house in the middle of the night?"

The light from the porch suddenly spilled across the beach, and now Sarah clearly saw the two Moors struggling down the porch steps with a long box between them. Alex took a turn, then passed the telescope back to Anne.

"There's another fellow coming out of the house," Anne said. She passed the spyglass to Sarah.

"Look through the mirror," Alex whispered.

Sam and Alex leaned forward. Sarah could just make out a figure, maybe two-thirds the height of the Moors. She took the periscope from Sam, screwed it onto the spyglass, and looked through it. "Oh my God. The Negro's talking to an empty porch."

Moving her eye to the side she saw two distant figures. Looking again through the periscope spyglass contraption, she saw the Moor standing by himself, gesturing at no one. She knew she should be afraid but felt only excitement. They'd found him.

Anne took the spyglass back. A fifth man came around the side of the house. He was very thin, taller than the vampire but tiny compared to the black giants.

"I can't believe it — that's Pastor Parris, from our church." Her voice quavered like a phonograph winding down. "He's talking to the... man with no reflection."

"Do you believe us now?" Sarah said.

"I don't know what's real and what isn't, but I guess I have to go with what I see. Or don't."

Sarah put her arm around her, then took the spyglass again. The new man was visible in the mirror.

"Only the little fellow's missing. The other one's human."

"Of course he's human, he's my pastor," Anne said.

"I'm starting to think we can't take anything for granted," Sam said from the back of the boat.

"Maybe he doesn't know he's talking to a vampire," Anne said.

Sarah looked at her. "It's the middle of the night, and he just watched them carry a coffin out of the house."

"Oh my God," Anne said. "Pastor Parris is pointing our way. They must have seen light bounce off the mirror. Put it down, put it down!"

Sarah threw the contraption into the bottom of the boat. Hopefully, the mirrors hadn't broken — they needed all the luck they could get.

"Alex, switch with me," Sam said.

The boys swapped, pitching the boat enough to slosh water inside. Sam spun it around with the oars and steered them back up the coastline.

Sarah heard a horrible shriek from the shore.

"The vampire's gone!" Anne said. "He just disappeared."

Goosebumps rose on Sarah's neck and back. She felt curiously in the moment. A funny thought popped into her head: Anne had used the word "vampire" without qualification.

"I think old ones might be able to turn into bats and fly," Alex said. He'd hunched himself down in the boat, his eyes darting back and forth across the sky. "I don't see him, but head out to sea as fast as you can. He won't want to fly over deep water."

Again the terrible shriek shattered the night air. Sarah imagined a giant bat with teeth like Charles soaring through the darkness.

Sam rowed out into the cove, his jaw set. The rest of them sat in silence, but Sarah counted Sam's soft grunts, the watery splashes, the clunk of the oars in their locks. Above and behind them, she heard an occasional cry. But as they glided over bigger waves, the sound grew fainter.

After what seemed like hours, Sam beached the dinghy at the western point between the inlet and the Atlantic. He and Alex pulled it out of the water and dragged it up the sand.

As they trudged ashore, Sarah noticed her boots were filled with cold water.

Twenty:
Golden Compass

Salem, Massachusetts, Friday night, November 7, 1913

PARRIS WAITED WITH ONE of the huge Moors on the vampire's porch. He'd been told not to enter the house. But he was curious, even if the smell wafting from the open door didn't exactly sell the place, reeking of charnel house gore and flesh left to rot.

He heard a leathery flapping accompanied by swirling currents of air.

"I see you met Ahmed," the vampire said, suddenly beside him. The pastor nearly lost control of his bladder.

"What was out on the water?"

"No matter." Mr. Nasir shrugged. "Let me introduce Fouad, my favorite."

Parris startled again at the sight of a new Moor, shorter and older, his hair stark white against coffee-colored skin. His yellow teeth were filed into points.

Parris forced himself to be sociable. "Nice place you have here."

"Are you in the market?" Mr. Nasir said. "I'm selling."

Breathing through his mouth, Parris peered across the dilapidated porch at the boarded-over windows. He glanced back at the beach and the rolling surf.

"But it has such a lovely view."

The vampire didn't look. "I purchased by correspondence. The sales agent exaggerated its charms, and I despise basements below sea level."

"He's helping you find another?"

"He's here now, inspecting the water table under the porch — six feet under." Mr. Nasir drew back his lips in what passed for a smile. "Fouad hired a new agent."

The pastor indicated his satchel. "Should we go inside?"

"Only the dead are welcome in my home."

The vampire barked at the older Negro in a language Parris didn't know. Fouad was gone in an instant and soon returned with an end table under his right arm and a small golden box studded with rubies and emeralds in his right hand. He placed the table in the darkest corner of the porch but held onto the box.

The pastor opened his bag and assembled his things. He jumped back when he found a cockroach scurrying over the wooden surface. Ahmed stepped forward, snatched up the insect, and popped it in his mouth. Parris tried to ignore the crunching sound.

"I'll need the piece of Gabriel's Horn."

Fouad handed the pastor the small box.

He held his breath as he opened it. Inside, nestled in velvet, was a fragment of beaten gold, perhaps an inch long, half coated in white wax.

Mr. Nasir backed away.

"Too holy for you?" Parris asked.

The vampire shrugged. "The archangel may have recited the Koran to the false prophet Muhammad, cursed be his name, but we are no longer on good terms."

Good to know. Nasir hadn't seemed in the least disturbed by the cross on the church wall.

Parris indicated the device he'd brought with him, now sitting on the tabletop. Also made of solid gold, it looked like a miniature water well.

"I had a jeweler craft this. Between the gold and the rush job, it cost me over four hundred dollars."

The undead waved his hand. "Sell that jeweled box if you like. I suspect this won't be our last expense."

At least the vampire wasn't stingy. The gems alone were easily worth two thousand.

Parris was almost finished. He used a pair of tweezers to wind some silver cord around the vampire's waxy fragment then suspended it from the arch of gold spanning the bowl of his device. He lit five white candles.

For a moment, the pastor feared he'd forgotten his knife. Judging by what he'd seen, he worried that any he might borrow would give him gangrene. But he found the blade at the bottom of his bag, half embedded in the loaf of bread.

"Before I begin," he said, "will the sight of blood cause you any... distress?"

Mr. Nasir's laugh was worse than his smile. "Good you ask, but I can control myself."

"Very well. Please stay back at least six feet, and do not interrupt or speak during the ritual."

The vampire and the three Moors retreated to the edge of the porch.

Parris steeled himself, crumbled some of the bread about the table, then sprinkled the crumbs with salt. He wrapped more silver cord around one wrist, cutting off the circulation to his hand, and chanted:

> *Bound and Binding. Binding, Bound.*
> *See the sight. Hear the sound.*
> *What was lost. Now is found.*
> *Bound and Binding. Binding, Bound.*

Parris felt the familiar tingling elation, like standing after kneeling for hours in prayer. He sliced into his bound palm and loosened the silver cord around his hand. As blood returned to it, so too did bright pain. Parris directed the flow of syrupy fluid over the artifact and into the bowl of the device. When it was full, he wrapped his hand in clean linen.

"It's done," he said.

The vampire peered at the device from his position. "That looked easy."

"It wasn't," Parris said, exhausted and lightheaded.

He was pleased to see the dangling gold fragment had spun on its silver cord to point west. He picked up the makeshift compass and rotated it. The pointer remained locked.

"Interesting," Mr. Nasir said. "It points at the Horn?"

"It should."

"And to think my Egyptian colleague has spent the better part of five centuries looking for the thing."

"If the Horn is in town, it shouldn't take long to find," Parris said.

"New ventures are best begun early in the evening." The vampire cocked his head. "Keep the compass until tomorrow night."

Parris packed his things and wrapped the device, carrying it separately. His spell preserved the liquid from evaporation but not spillage. It required a subtle command of the humors. Betty had taught him a lot about the humors, particularly blood.

Twenty-One:
Egyptian Mythology

Salem, Massachusetts, Saturday, November 8, 1913

TIRED... SO TIRED. The evening had left Sarah feeling like someone had beaten her over the head with a baseball bat wrapped in pillows.

She dreamt of the principal's office. It was nighttime, and the room was lit by a pair of torches mounted on the wall alongside school photos. Mr. Burnsworth, the principal, and Mrs. Fletcher, her English teacher, knelt on the floor. They both wore nun's habits, the Catholic kind with the black and white cowls.

Sarah lay before them wearing only a coarse linen shift. It was bunched under her armpits, tight across her tender breasts. Her pregnant belly was swollen to bursting, her legs were bare, her lower half naked and exposed.

A hideous long cramp surged through her abdomen. She screamed, but the voice didn't sound like her own.

"Quiet, bitch," Mr. Burnsworth said. "You'll wake the whole school."

Mrs. Fletcher leaned forward and wiped her brow. "Isabella, the baby's head!"

Isabella? Sarah looked down again. Long red braids tumbled over her shoulders. Her skin was fair and freckled, fairer than her own had ever been. On her dress, bunched as it was, she saw an embroidered doe.

The girl from the Charles dream.

As if in answer, a feminine voice echoed inside her head. *We're bound by blood and death, you and I. Blood and death. The Strength of God sings in our blood. The horn sounds our sacrifice, time and death mean nothing in the face of that.*

Sarah screamed again as the wave of pain crested. Hot fire burned between her legs. She sat forward to see around her distended tummy. The pain redoubled.

The door to the room rattled and shook. Faculty photos were knocked askew.

He comes, Isabella's voice said inside her head. *We must both die twice before we save each other.*

The wooden door exploded, swept open, and crushed Mrs. Fletcher against the case of sporting trophies. Sarah heard her bones crunch.

A monstrous bat filled the threshold. Man-sized, he glared with beady eyes dark as pitch. He entered slowly, long arms joined to his gray body by scabrous drapes of flesh. A horrible stench rolled into the room, the smell of rot mixed with spices and honey.

Meet the one you hunt.

The bat roared, revealing thousands of murderous teeth. The flexion of his ribcage forced his hideous wings into a parody of bird-like movement. His arm blurred and he slapped Mr. Burnsworth, whose head bounced off the wall and whose decapitated body crumpled to the ground.

Sarah squirmed on the floor, eyes wide, streams of the principal's blood running down her face. Her ichor-streaked bare legs found no purchase on the slick linoleum.

The bat-creature bent down, extended one clawed finger, and sliced her from groin to sternum. Pain beyond imagining. White heat. Red blood. He peeled back layers of meat and skin. She felt hideous tugging and his dead hands brought forth the tiny infant, crowned in gore. Almost tenderly, he severed the cord and gave the babe a squeeze.

My first killer, and yours. As fearsome as he is, he serves another.

The child wailed.

Her strength fading, Sarah reached out for the baby, but the monster set him out of reach.

My death, your blood, your death, my blood. I save you and you save me. Together we can stop them, but the price will be steep.

With his razor fangs, the monster bit into his own fingers, twisted the other hand into Sarah's raw guts to make her scream, and shoved his bloody digits into her mouth.

The dark gift. Together Isabella and Sarah gagged on the taste: exotic, meaty, salty, perfumed. The sound of the horn, slow and mournful, filled the room.

Sarah woke in her bed. She felt slick and wet below. Kicking off the covers she found her nightgown stained with blood.

A week early.

Pain knotting her abdomen and warm stickiness coating her legs, she curled into a ball and sobbed. That was no normal nightmare.

She rolled out from under the covers and crept to the light switch. Her nightgown was stained red to the knees, and she'd trailed bloody footprints from her bed. She grabbed her notebook and recorded everything she could remember using her usual Hebrew cipher. Flipping back, she found the page with *only you can stop us*. Underneath, she wrote *My death, your blood, your death, my blood*.

The window was ajar and the air was cold. She shut it, then stripped off her gown and used it to wipe the wetness from her legs and the floor. She balled the garment and sheets together, pulled on a fresh nightgown, and lay on top of her bare mattress. Even this was graced with a large dark stain, but there was nothing she could do about that.

She felt utterly alone. *Meet the one you hunt.*

She tried to pray but concentration was impossible. The bat creature — he had to be the one that made Charles — must be the same monster that'd chased them into the cove. Except this thing made Charles seem small and weak — house cat to the lion.

She heard the clock downstairs chime four. At least an hour before she should rise, but she was far too shaken to sleep.

A haggard young woman waited for her in the bathroom mirror. It wasn't the first time she'd tackled a day on three hours' sleep, but first she needed to wash, and the water was as cold as a mountain stream. Unfortunately, warm water this time of morning involved a trip to the cellar to start the water heater.

Sarah retrieved a pair of old work boots from the basement steps, pulled them over her bare feet, and lifted the kerosene lantern from its hook. The leather scraped against her toes as she shuffled down the stairs. The earthy smell of the dark cellar mixed with the odor of kerosene and the copper tang of her own blood.

The heater was one of Papa's newer gadgets, a three-foot tall copper cylinder that clung to the side of the water tank. She turned on the gas valve and lit the pilot light. Upstairs she heard the kitchen door open, probably their housekeeper Mary fetching wood. A gust of wind from outside slammed the cellar door shut.

Sarah felt herself in a bubble of lamplight enclosed by darkness. Oh, God, today was Saturday. She'd lit the heater on *Shabbat*. There'd be consequences, but this whole Cesarian by vampire gambit was plain unfair on God's part.

She shuffled back toward the staircase, but a dripping sound from the shadows caught her attention. In the back corner of the house, under what was probably her father's study, a network of roots had forced themselves through the stone wall that enclosed this part of the cellar.

Her heart raced as images flashed through her mind. Blood red sky below and roots above. She felt a coldness inside her, and the pain in her abdomen returned.

The horn blared. Everywhere and nowhere, the slow and mournful tone without beginning or end. The cramps forced her to her knees. She tried to breathe. The roots looked wet with blood. *My death, your blood, your death, my blood.*

The door behind her opened, and light spilled into the basement.

"Miss Sarah?" Mary's lilting voice. The sound of the horn faded, and with the added light she could see the roots were just damp with water, trickling down the wall.

Sarah managed to corner her father on the walk home from synagogue.

"You look tired," he said as they started off down the tree-lined street.

"Nightmare. I couldn't get back to sleep afterwards."

He raised a bushy eyebrow. "Anything you want to tell me about?"

We must both die twice before we save each other. Papa would know what to do.

She told him about the dream, leaving out the most ominous parts of Isabella's dialogue. After Judah, she wasn't going to plant those thoughts in his mind — or hers. She wasn't ready to reveal what had happened with Charles, either, so she didn't mention the first vision.

"It wasn't just a nightmare," she said when she'd finished. "It wasn't normal."

"What makes you think that?"

"The horn sounded like a giant *shofar*. I hear it sometimes — don't think I'm crazy — I heard it this morning in the basement."

"I believe you." He gazed into Salem Common as they walked along the fence-line. "God created demons to test mankind. If we don't resist evil with all our heart, we fail the test."

As fearsome as he is, he serves another. Somehow Sarah hadn't gotten the impression that Isabella meant God.

"So you think God sent these dreams?" she said. "He wants me to fight evil?"

"I think your dreams are significant." But he seemed more interested in the elegant afternoon strollers than her.

"What aren't you telling me?"

Now he turned back. "You remember the Horn we spoke about a week ago? The one from the Ram in the Thicket, the one that Gabriel keeps for Elijah?"

"I remember."

"I believe that's the sound you hear in your dreams." He took his pipe from his pocket, useless on a Saturday, and sighed.

"What makes you think it's the same?"

"Because God entrusted me with the Horn for a time."

If she hadn't seen the dead rise up and walk, she might've thought *he* was the crazy one.

"The Horn that signals the End of Days is in your desk drawer?"

He smiled sheepishly. "Not anymore."

As she contemplated this humdinger, a passing bicyclist honked.

"Explain, before my heart explodes in my chest," she said.

"Last night, Mr. Palaogos spoke of the Hofburg palace fire," her father said. "That particular morning, I was at court for an Imperial audience. God sent me signs and portents, so that He might lead me to the palace treasury. There, He revealed the Horn to me."

"Magical horns aren't real." The words sounded silly in her ears. "And wasn't Gabriel keeping it for Elijah?"

Papa returned his pipe to his pocket. "I'd have thought so, but while an archangel may never be late, it seems he may misplace things."

What is lost will be found. Charles' voice echoed in Sarah's head.

"That was it? God showed it to you, and you brought it home like a cake from the bakery?"

"Not quite." They turned onto their block. "Someone else was there, also seeking the Horn. I prayed, as your Grandpapa had taught me, and was able to make myself invisible to the wrongdoer."

God had made Papa invisible? Could He do that? Well, obviously He could, but could someone learn to ask Him? She almost tripped she was so excited.

"Can you show me how?"

"Perhaps," he said, "but don't get sidetracked. I need to explain what this monster was capable of. I watched him kill six innocent men that day. Him and his pets."

Another vampire? No, Papa had said he'd been there in the morning.

"Time for lunch," Papa said. They stood at the front door.

"You have to be kidding," she said. "What about the fire and the villain?"

"I'm just teasing," he said, "Let me grab a snack and meet you in my study."

She stomped to his office, every fiber of her being electrified. Finally she was getting some answers.

Papa returned with a plate of *rugelach,* one of them already in his mouth. Sarah helped herself to one of her mother's pastries while Papa settled himself behind his desk, leaving a trail of crumbs in his path.

"I was able to steal the Horn and escape to the stables, but the villain and his jackal-dog cornered me. I was trapped, so I used my *mezuzah* and the 27th Psalm to destroy his disguise."

Sarah pulled up one of the side chairs. "Disguise?"

"He wasn't a man. The Lord's Light exploded his head like a ripe pomegranate, revealing a giant black beetle growing from his shoulders. I blew the Horn, and he was destroyed by the fires of heaven. Unfortunately, so were the stables."

"You're not the Messiah or anything? I don't know if I could take that."

He laughed. "Let's hope not, but the Horn is God's Strength incarnate and has many uses."

In Hebrew, Gabriel meant 'Strength of God,' but strength also implied sacrifice, like the sacrifice of Isaac or the ram. *The Strength of God sings in our blood. The horn sounds our sacrifice.*

Papa took another pastry. "When Elijah sounds the Horn, he will use one of the secret names of God — unknown to me. As the world began with a *word,* so shall it end."

Papa dropped half his pastry into his lap and managed to stain his suit. Probably a good thing he didn't know the word that destroyed the Universe.

"Which name did you use?" she asked.

"*Ehyeh asher ehyeh.*"

Sarah knew it of course, so God had named himself to Moses at the Burning Bush. "I am that I am."

"I whispered the name into the Horn, and it became as a single note more pure than any sound I'd ever heard." A faraway look came to Papa's face. "The blare of the Horn threatened to sunder the very fabric of the world. Khepri burst into cold red fire and was consumed."

As he said this, she heard it, the slow and mournful sound of the horn from her dreams.

"Khepri? Was that the beetle man?" she asked.

Papa reached over to his bookshelf, pulled down two large volumes, and flopped them onto the desk. Cracking one, he thumbed through. Sarah glanced at the spine. *The Gods of the Egyptians Volume I*, by Sir Ernest Alfred Wallis Budge.

Papa turned the book so Sarah could see a color plate. An orange-skinned man holding a staff sat on a throne, in place of his head an enormous black scarab beetle.

The bottom of the page read, "The god Khepri."

"An Egyptian god?" she said.

He flipped to another page showing a hieroglyph of a little dog. The text read, "Anubis, jackal-headed god who receives the organs of the dead."

"*Hashem* refutes all other deities explicitly," she said.

"Of course. They can't be gods, not really." He closed the books. "But perhaps these ancient legends have some basis in truth — for this is certainly what I saw at the palace that day."

"Maybe he was some kind of sorcerer," she said, "a devotee of ancient Egyptian secrets."

"So you believe in sorcerers, just not gods?" He smiled.

"Aren't you one?" He had just claimed to have turned invisible and battled false deities.

"I prefer learned man." He folded his hands. "It doesn't matter what they were. Khepri's dead, and the Horn is safe."

"Where is it, then?" If it was real, she wanted to see it.

"Returned to the Garden of Eden and Gabriel's keeping." He turned away, setting the books back on the shelf. "I did as God bid." He sounded strange, his voice thick.

"How'd that happen? Gabriel knocked on the door one day and asked for it?"

"Not far from the truth. Hidden and not revealed." He wiped his eyes with his handkerchief.

"God is real."

He smiled. "You doubted?"

"Not really." If vampires and demonic beetles were real, God ought to be. "But believing in Him isn't the same as thinking he actually told my father to recover an angel's horn and destroy a monster."

"I know. I felt exactly the same when your grandfather first showed me what was possible when a righteous man entreats the Lord."

"You have to show me, too!" The idea thrilled her beyond comprehension.

He laughed again. "You already know most of what you need. It's a matter of opening your heart to God. The little rituals and trinkets are just helpful tools."

"So show me, please."

"Right now, we need to understand why you've been sent these dreams," he said. "I'm going to eat my lunch. Then I need utter solitude for several hours to pray."

"You aren't going back to *shul* for afternoon services?" she said. Papa never missed services.

"I can pray here, to ask the Lord for guidance — and to strengthen the protections on this house — so that evil finds it impossible to enter."

"Will He listen?"

Papa stood up. "He's been known to."

Twenty-Two:
Obstacles

Salem, Massachusetts, Saturday night, November 8, 1913

PARRIS AND MR. NASIR made their way across town, turning every so often to follow the direction of the golden compass finger. In about four hours, they found their destination: an ordinary home, wooden, in imitation of the seventeenth-century style.

"Interesting," Parris said. "Do you know anything about the occupants? The defenses?"

"Unfortunately not."

The vampire crept up to a window. It was nearly midnight, and Parris saw no lights on inside. He put the compass back in the wooden case he'd assembled that morning.

"I don't hear any heartbeats," Mr. Nasir said when he came back. "If no one lives here, I can break in and snoop around. Otherwise we'll have to wait for someone to return and convince them to invite me in."

"Go ahead." At least it wasn't Parris crawling around in the dark.

Mr. Nasir tugged off his boots and handed them to the pastor. Barefoot, he stepped into the shadows by the side of the house and faded into the darkness. Parris strained his eyes and finally spotted the vampire scuttling up the gray clapboard. The undead moved from window to window and eventually found an open one — who worried about intruders on the third floor? Parris watched him grip the sill and begin to pull himself in.

There was a blinding flash and a loud crack. A hot white trail shot away from the window and over the road. Behind him, he heard the thud of something hitting the earth, but there was no sign of Mr. Nasir.

"Over here," the distinctively accented voice called from across the street.

Parris crossed the quiet strip of cobblestones. The vampire lay on the muddy grass some thirty feet away. Even in the feeble light it was obvious that al-Nasir was badly hurt. His face was a mass of burnt and bloody skin, and a few inches of white bone poked out of his trouser leg at an odd angle.

"Jesus," Parris said, "are you—"

"It is no matter." The vampire spoke through ruined lips. "But keep your distance."

"Are you sure I can't be of help?" Parris asked.

"As a general rule, the living who wish to remain in that state do not approach wounded individuals of my kind. My weaker brethren might not be able to resist the sound of a beating heart under such duress." The vampire's tone remained calm, but the way he said *my kind* chilled Parris to the bone.

Incredibly — preposterously — Mr. Nasir rolled over into a crawling position, his broken leg flopping. He shoved himself back with his arms and sprang upright onto his good foot. His ruined features rippled in what Parris took for a grimace.

"On second thought," the vampire said, "lend me a shoulder."

Parris came around to his bad side. He breathed through his mouth, trying to avoid the nauseating smell of charred dead flesh. Mr. Nasir put one hand near his collar then reached down with the other to jerk his broken leg into an approximation of the correct position.

Parris still held the man's boots. "Do you want these?"

"Not yet. I need to recuperate and feed. I eat my fingers out of regret — I have delayed us."

"Does that normally happen when you don't have an invitation?"

"No, that was a warding spell," Mr. Nasir said. "I should've been more careful. It's designed to detect men of good character."

"You didn't measure up?"

This earned him the ghastly smile: way too many teeth, framed by burnt skin and rent lips.

"And to think," the vampire said, "I was once considered a moral paragon."

"What do we do?" Parris said.

"Now, my dear pastor, it's your turn."

Parris felt a spike of fear. "Perhaps I haven't had as many years to tarnish my own character, but it's unlikely to qualify as *good*."

Mr. Nasir brushed his fingers against the pastor's clerical collar, leaving bloodstains behind.

"Aren't all priests beloved of God?"

Parris bristled — he did believe, after all. Sadly, he knew where his road would lead him. Parris *loved* Jesus but he *feared* the other. And when push came to shove, fear always trumped love.

"You can at least examine the spell from outside," Mr. Nasir said.

They limped back across the street. By the time they reached the side of the house the vampire was able to put a little weight on his broken leg. He propped himself against a tree.

"Go ahead, take a look for yourself," he said.

Parris didn't have a lot of equipment with him, but he could try a little lychnomancy. He withdrew a white candle from his pocket, along with a match he struck against the brick foundation. He lit the candle and tried to relax. Squinting through the flame, he discerned a grid of ghostly lines, obvious once you knew where to look for them. On closer study, each line of power appeared to be woven from many other smaller, dimmer lines. This structure was clearly intended to keep out the likes of him — and the undead. After a few minutes, he blew out the candle and turned to the vampire.

Mr. Nasir appeared much improved. Mud still stained his tattered clothes, his face was likewise filthy, but his burns had dried and scabbed over.

"I can see the ward," Parris said. "It's enormous, strong, and hostile to both of us. If this is the work of a single individual he's a very powerful practitioner. To dismantle an arcane construct of this size would require detailed knowledge of its fabrication."

"I defer to your expertise," Mr. Nasir said. "Regardless, into the lion's den we must proceed. You must find a way for at least one of us to enter."

A worm of an idea began to wriggle its way into Parris' brain.

"I think I might know how to pass through myself," he said. "The ward is designed to evaluate the soul of the petitioner. You have none, and mine is mortgaged to you-know-who, but I might be able to borrow someone else's."

Mr. Nasir nodded. "I need to feed. See what you can do tomorrow."

Parris sighed. The vampire's hours were hardly conducive to a normal schedule. He was exhausted already.

The undead backed into the shadowy area beyond the streetlamp and vanished into the darkness like a bucket of water poured from a ship disappears into the ocean.

Twenty-Three:
Into the Breach

Salem, Massachusetts, Saturday, November 8, 1913
and Sunday morning, November 9, 1913

ON SATURDAY SAM HELPED Alex cut two long spear-like stakes and half a dozen shorter ones. They hammered together a collection of wood crosses, which Alex stashed in the Model T along with a machete-like blade, his knife, and a pistol. He considered taking the rifle, but the twenty-two semi-automatic was probably better at close range.

"Your sisters are getting the holy water?" he said.

Sam grinned. "They're going to sneak into a Catholic church with a canteen."

"Sarah's idea, I assume," Alex said.

"Something going on between you two?" Sam said. "I see the way you look at her."

"God made eyes for a reason," he said.

Sam looked at him intently but didn't say anything. He'd probably liked her for years.

But he wasn't the one she'd kissed.

The next morning, Alex accounted it a major victory when he stalled the automobile only three times on the way to Sarah's. Her mother answered the door.

"Is Sarah home?" he asked. "Some local farmers are offering cash for help with the harvest, and I thought she might like to join us."

"She told me," Mrs. Engelmann said. "Bring back some squash if you can."

"Yes, ma'am."

The parlor contained an upright piano and a glass cabinet filled with silver paraphernalia — church-like yet different.

Sarah bounded into the room. "I thought we were meeting at the Williams?"

"I was driving past."

They said goodbye to her mother. When they reached the Ford, he opened the door for her.

"Such a gentleman," she said. "Would you have done that last week?"

"Of course."

"I'm just teasing."

He went around front and started the engine, then coaxed the thing into motion. They zoomed forward and careened around a curve. Alex braked hard. Sarah flew forward in her seat, bracing herself with her arms.

"Is it always like this?"

"No," he said. "It's just me." He noticed a scratch on her wrist between glove and sleeve. "Did you cut your arm on the boat?"

"Probably." She glanced at her wrist. "I hurt myself all the time and rarely notice. The other night at dinner, you never told me your grandmother's name."

"Isabella. I didn't want to upset Grandfather."

Sarah didn't say anything. He glanced over, trying not to crash the car. She was staring off at nothing.

"Was she a redhead?" she eventually said.

Alex thought about the portrait in the library, Isabella with her orange braids. "How'd you know?"

"I dreamed about a redheaded Isabella the night of the boat."

"She's about your age in her portrait."

"A painting? Not a photo?" Sarah asked.

"The old man hates photos."

Alex pulled over and turned off the engine. Grandfather was the last thing he wanted to think about.

"We need to wait until Emily and her parents leave for church," he said, "or she'll know we misled her about the raid."

"We lied," Sarah said. "I don't like lies, but it's not safe for her to come."

"Not safe for us, either."

He leaned over and kissed her. She let him, then again and again until they were both breathing hard. Eventually, she gave him the tiniest push and pulled away.

"I'm not a good enough kisser?" he said. "We can practice some more."

"No, the kissing's fine. Better than fine." She laid a finger against his mouth, just for the briefest moment. When she took it away, the spot tingled. "But try not to act differently in front of anyone else."

If Sam had his questions, Anne had to be a couple steps ahead. "I'll do my best." He glanced at his pocket watch. "It's time to go."

He sped through the last couple of blocks. At the Williams place, he turned a hair too late as he tried to maneuver into position by the curb and smacked a front wheel into the raised line of cobbles.

"It's the driving that needs practice," Sarah said.

Sam was inside the foyer with jars of water, his pistol, and boxes of ammunition. Alex had a hard time looking him in the eye. At least the dog was nowhere to be seen.

Anne came down, swimming in oversized trousers, apparently having borrowed old ones from her brother.

"Ready for action?" Sam said, loading shells into his revolver.

"The lever on the right feeds gas to the engine," Alex explained to Sam as he drove. "The one on the left controls the spark timing. The right pedal brakes while driving, this big lever is your parking brake. Push the left pedal for the forward gear, middle pedal for reverse."

"Easy as rolling off a log," Sam said.

Personally, Alex found the whole process unnatural. But two or three near-death experiences later, he parked near an empty lot not far from the white clapboard house on Webb Street. He should tell them what he knew about the vampire. He'd intended to, last Friday, and again this morning. At first he'd been distracted — hell, he was still distracted. But the longer he'd waited, the harder it became to say anything.

They distributed the gear. Anne snatched up a cross and held one out to Sarah.

"I just can't."

Alex imagined her throat being shredded by a gray-skinned vampire.

"You need some protection. It doesn't mean you have to believe."

"I brought this *mezuzah*." Her hand touched a small silver cylinder nested in the frills of her collar. "It belonged to my mother's father."

Alex shrugged. "Probably has the same chance of working as the crosses. I'm not sure if we have to believe or just the vampire."

He should tell them — after he situated his equipment. He settled his satchel onto his back, making sure his smaller stake was accessible, blunt end first, with a jar of holy water tucked behind it. He would carry the large stake. He holstered the pistol on his right hip and the machete on his left.

"Take these." Sam offered both girls kerosene lamps. "We'll need our hands free."

He should tell them now, but he could almost feel Grandfather lurking in the shadows.

"Let's go," Sam said. He led them straight through the empty lot to the shoreline, then turned left on the beach. They only had to walk past one house to reach their destination. A good thing no one was about, given how strange they must look.

Sam strode right up the porch steps to the door from which they had seen the Moors carry the coffin. Alex stood just out of sight to his right. The girls hung back.

Out on the cove, fishing boats glided across steel blue waters.

Sam knocked.

No one answered. Sam tried the door — it was locked.

"Hold the screen open," he said. Alex pulled it back. The porch stank like something had crawled underneath and died.

Sam jumped down to the sand. Facing the house, he got a running start, took the steps in a single leap, and slammed his shoulder into the flimsy wooden door. With a crash, it burst open and the brass mortis lock ripped out of the half-rotten wood.

Alex followed him into the breach.

The room must have once been a sun porch, but now the boarded windows let in only slivers of light. A couple of crates were stacked against the walls. Underneath the peeling plaster they could see chicken wire and old lath. The stink wasn't just outside.

Sam raised his hand for silence.

They listened. Nothing except the girls opening the shades on their lanterns.

"The creature will be in the basement," Alex said, "or in some interior room. During the day it's unlikely to wake, even if we make a lot of noise. The Moors, on the other hand...."

He used his machete to pry open a crate, brought out a handful of what looked like gray ash. He let it run through his fingers and fall to the floor.

"Dirt," he said. "Probably from his original grave. No rest for the wicked without it."

Anne scrunched her face. Sam unbuckled the safety strap on his pistol, raised his stake, and proceeded into the next room.

The reek of rot and decay in the kitchen was so awful Alex had to breathe through his mouth to keep from retching. There were two wooden chairs at a tiny table, and on the table three bowls of God-knows-what, seething with maggots.

Something crunched under Sarah's boot. She moved her foot and a million roaches ran for cover. The one she'd wounded sidled off into a corner, leaving behind a trail of ichor.

Anne gasped. The hand holding her lantern was shaking.

"This house," she said, "lacks a woman's touch."

There was a letter on the kitchen table addressed to Mr. Alan H. Nasir. Alex's heart raced — Ali ibn Hammud al-Nasir. He looked inside.

"It's from an international shipping agent," he said. "And Nasir's a Moorish name." He hoped they didn't ask how he knew — they'd never trust him if he told them.

Sam found the door to the basement. If the upstairs smelled like a dead dog, what wafted out of the depths was like a sty filled with dead pigs.

"I guess we know where he sleeps," Alex said.

He would have preferred to call the shots himself, but Sam reached the door first, and that was that.

"Anne, come down right behind me with the light held high. Alex, you and Sarah stay up here, then follow when we reach the bottom. Keep an eye out behind you."

The stairs were old and steep and hard to see with the lantern swinging in Sarah's hand. The cellar walls were well-maintained, the stones freshly painted with a heavy coat of pitch.

"The creature probably chose this place because of the basement," Alex said. "That and the dual land and sea access."

"Not for the lovely southern exposure?" Anne said.

Halfway down, Alex saw more cockroaches skitter across the stone floor. Cobwebs draped the corners, and a millipede snaked along the wall. Crates littered the chamber, which had only one door. It looked recently replaced braced with steel bands that were already rusted in the damp. It stood ajar.

Anne screamed.

Alex rushed down the rest of the stairs. His heavy tread snapped one of the lower risers, and he landed hard on his right ankle. Pain lanced up his leg.

Anne pointed between two crates. Sarah's lantern illuminated a human skeleton — no flesh on the white bones, too small to be an adult's. More roaches perched on the half-shattered rib cage.

"I don't think he's expecting company," Anne whispered.

Alex limped toward the big wooden door. He could walk, but each step was painful.

"Or his guests don't leave alive."

Sam drew his pistol and edged behind.

Alex used his stake to pry the door all the way open—

To a different world.

Bright carpets covered every surface, forming a hodgepodge of clashing patterns in red, blue, saffron, white. Alex, who had a lifetime of experience with fine furnishings, recognized Berbers, Ottomans, Moroccans, Tabriz, Isfahans.... The room reeked of mildew. Antique glass oil lamps of Arabic design hung from the ceiling by brass chains. Some crates were open, filled with piles of exotic silk brocades or treasures of gem-encrusted gold.

Alex picked up a rhyton, a ribbed cup of solid gold with a base shaped like a kneeling and winged lion, a lovely example of the goldsmith's art. He slipped it into one of his jacket pockets. It should serve nicely if he needed proof for Grandfather.

The sarcophagus dominated the far wall. This was no pine box but a massive block of limestone. It looked old, carved in medieval Moorish or Islamic style, ornamented with tight patterns of flowers and leaves, every inch the final resting place of a Moorish Caliph turned vampire.

"Sam," Alex said, "it'll take two to get the lid off that sarcophagus while you or I stabs the vampire through the heart."

Sam swallowed. "Assuming by sar-co-whatever you mean that giant stone coffin, I can do the killing if you three can open it."

Alex nodded. The girls set down their lamps and positioned themselves by the foot end. Sam dragged over an unopened crate and climbed up. He held the long stake in both hands.

Alex gripped the lid.

"Don't try to lift, just slide it toward the door. One... two... three."

The cold stone ground into a slide — mostly on Alex's end — and fell over, crashing to the floor and exposing a huge bare black torso. Not the vampire, one of his servants.

Sam slammed the spear down, hard — and was immediately drenched in gore that spurted from around the deeply sunk shaft.

The bald Negro opened his eyes: bright yellow with vertically slit irises, like a black cat's. His ivory teeth were filed into sharp points. A rasping exhale escaped his lips, along with two gigantic centipedes. Alex tasted bile.

The man sat up. The stake wrenched free of Sam's grasp, and he was forced down from his crate. Anne and Sarah screamed. The Moor gripped the rim of the coffin and struggled to rise. The wooden shaft, impaled in his chest, wobbled back and forth as he managed to swing a leg over the side. The girls fled to the corner.

Sam and Alex emptied several rounds into the Moor. Alex's bullets tore into his torso just below the stake. Sam put two in his face, and at this range his forty-five caliber shells nearly shattered the great skull. A splash of red hit the carpeted wall. Small blood-covered forms writhed on the bright-colored wool.

The Moor fell to his knees. His ebony skin bubbled and rippled. A cascade of insects — maggots, cockroaches, millipedes, beetles, moths, and spiders — erupted from his face, chest, and belly. He deflated like a pierced bag of water, pouring forth a veritable river of many-legged life. Soon his baggy silk pants and curled slippers lay empty amidst a teeming mass of tiny creatures.

Behind him, Alex heard the squeal of the basement door and a thudding on the steps. He turned to see another figure descending into the dim antechamber.

"Sam, the door!" He leapt forward.

The two boys slammed the door on an angry face nearly identical to the one that had just dissolved. Sam threw the steel deadbolt.

"Now we're trapped in here!" Anne yelled.

The oak door shook.

"At least that thing's on the other side," Sarah said.

The door shuddered again.

"Get yourselves ready," Sam said. "Women in back."

Alex faced the door, holding his semi-automatic ready, trying desperately to stop the shaking in his hands. To his right, Sam cracked the Schofield and thumbed in two fresh shells.

The door buckled and fractured, tilted back out of its frame and up into the room behind. The enormous blackamoor squatted underneath, arms as thick as telephone poles tossed the slab of wood off into the corner.

The black man faced them, drew two curved swords, and charged into the room.

Alex felt his wolf's head medallion burn against his chest, and the Moor bowled past as if he wasn't there, knocking him to the side and sending the semi-automatic flying. Sam fired one round into the dark belly before the Moor knocked the forty-five out of his hands. He then threw Sam against the tapestries and swung his scimitar. Sam dodged, and the blade embedded itself in the carpeted wall where he'd just been.

The Moor yanked his weapon free and danced into a crouch. He poked at Sam, his face split by a huge grin. Pallid worms crawled from the bullet wound in his gut.

Anne crossed the buggy carpet and grabbed the semi-automatic. Apparently she knew how to shoot, because she fired the pistol straight into the giant's back. The arm not pointing the sword at Sam blurred into motion, and the big man batted the bullet aside with his second blade. The metallic sound rang in Alex's ears.

The Moor wagged this weapon at Anne as if he were scolding her. Sarah threw her long spear at him, but this too he slapped away, severing the wood into two pieces.

Alex grabbed his pack, drew his machete, and advanced. Again, he felt heat on his breast, and again the huge man didn't react. He reached into the pack, pulled out a jar of holy water, and hurled it at the Moor's back. The glass shattered.

The Moor's shoulders burst into green flame. He grimaced, then coughed a cloud of living flies in Sam's face. The unnatural blaze burned like a kitchen grease fire. Dark flesh sizzled. The big thrall tried to smother his back on the wall carpets, but they too burst into flame.

Sam snatched up his Schofield. "Everyone run!" He fired all five remaining rounds in the direction of the burning Moor, rapidly pounding the hammer with his left palm.

Alex took his cue and shoved the girls forward. He heard Sam behind him as he followed them up the narrow stairs, through the kitchen, out the door, and onto the beach. It all happened so fast he had no idea how many, if any, bullets had hit the big man.

They ran across the sand, breathing hard. Anne was out front, fear pushing her to new athletic prowess. Sam passed and caught up with her. Alex's ankle gave way. He cursed, then continued at a clumsy hop. Sarah heard him, darted back, and grabbed him around the shoulders. Together, they hobbled across the beach like a couple running the three-legged race.

Alex opened the car door and struggled with the key. Sarah was too winded to speak but pointed back at the house. A smoldering figure shambled up the road in their direction, huge hands clutching a single sword.

"Hurry!" Sam yelled.

Alex finished with the levers inside and limped around to the front, grabbed the crank, twisted hard. The car convulsed, and the starter whipped backwards and struck his thumb.

"*Xekoliara!*" Alex's thumb blazed in agony, but the engine turned over and coughed to life. Fiery pain rippled up his arm.

"Sam, you'll have to drive. I think I broke my thumb on the starter, and it takes two hands."

Sam climbed into the driver's seat. The blackamoor was only twenty feet away. Sam handed his empty pistol to Alex, released the brake, and pulled down on the throttle. The engine roared. The auto didn't move.

"It's in neutral," Alex yelled, clutching his hand. "The left pedal, all the way down!"

Sam stomped and gripped the wheel. The auto lurched.

"More spark, more spark!"

"You don't have to yell, I'm right here."

The Model T began to pick up speed. They pulled out onto the road — and heard a sickening thump on their roof.

"He's on top of us!" Sarah cried from the backseat.

The automobile cruised down the empty street. A big black arm, covered with suppurating burns and crawling with spiders, reached in the window and grabbed at Anne's hair. She screamed and hunched down.

Now the scimitar plunged through the roof into the front seat. Sam winced as it scraped along his shoulder blade.

"Slam the rightmost pedal as hard as you can!" Alex yelled.

Sam did, and Alex yanked the handbrake at the same time.

The hand of Zeus smacked them from behind as the Model T tried its best to stop. Alex braced himself with his feet, but Sam was thrown into the steering wheel and the girls were all but hurled into the front.

The Moor flew off the roof and crashed onto the cobblestones a few feet in front of them. Alex released the brake and pulled down hard on the throttle. The car surged forward and smashed into the big man just as he tried to get to his feet.

The blackamoor burst like a sail torn in high winds, releasing a cloud of pulverized insects. Red blood and yellow-green ichor splashed across the windshield, obscuring everything, and Sam was forced to stop the car in the middle of the road.

Alex glanced out the back. All that remained of the giant was a five-foot puddle of writhing bugs crowned by a swarm of flies and gnats.

Twenty-Four:
Heaven and Hell

Salem, Massachusetts, Sunday morning, November 9, 1913

Parris took five black candles from the box on the mantle, arranged them in a half circle around the fireplace, then sprinkled a line of dried garlic, lavender, and honey along the arc. He inhaled, held his breath, and hurled a handful of powdered sulfur into the fire. Orange flame mushroomed, accompanied by a cloud of black smoke. He squinted through tearing eyes at the now ignited candles and intoned:

> *Power of the warlocks rise, course unseen through the skies.*
> *Come to us who call you near, come to us who call you here.*
> *Down roads of fire and flame, come forth to bring pain.*
> *Blood to blood I summon thee, blood to blood return to me.*

He waited until the dancing flame began to shift, a shimmering curtain in front of a fiery tunnel. A small figure formed in the distance, flickered, slid closer. With one delicate hand, she parted the veil separating the realms, her skin the bluish purple of a corpse washed ashore, her black nails chipped as if she'd been hauling rocks.

"Betty." He bowed.

"Toy." She tiptoed over the line of candles and herbs to step into the room. "It's been too long since you let me out to play."

His manhood responded to the sound of her raspy voice and the thought of her tail tickling his skin.

Her lips didn't move when she spoke — the air in front of them merely shimmered, and sound followed. Her hair was jet black, her eyes red smoldering flames, and two small nubs of horn poked from her forehead. She was beautiful in her own way, willowy and well-proportioned. One merely had to overlook the complexion. And the attire. Her faded gray corset and tattered knickers were the only garments Parris had ever seen her wear.

"Did you miss me?" she said.

"I need your help," he said. "An ingredient for a hex. Mud from the banks of the river Lethe."

"Blessed waterway of oblivion," she said. "The reasons you love me are without measure."

Her frown hurt more than her whip. She ran her eggplant-colored tongue across her teeth then lifted her hand to brush his face. He shivered with pleasure, but she'd need more incentive.

"Remember my little pet?" he said. "The pretty one? We need to take something from her. Fast. The vampire is impatient."

"We?" She leaned close so their noses almost touched. Her skin smelled of sulfur.

"I'll use a binding of command," he said. "I know how you love that."

"If you're man enough." She slammed her hand into his crotch. "We can travel to the river right now. The gateway's still open." She glanced back at the curtain of flame.

"I have only thirty minutes until church," he squeaked.

"Time runs differently in the byways of the netherworld. We'll be back as soon as we leave."

She tugged him halfway into the fireplace. He grabbed the hand on his groin to retain at least some control. The flames licked at the fabric of his suit without singing it.

"The realms are myriad and vast," she whispered. "All suffering, all prayers made manifest. But no harm will come to you on my watch, so long as the price is paid." She pulled his hand between her own legs, into the dark place.

There was always a price.

Twenty-Five:
Aftermath

Salem, Massachusetts, Sunday afternoon, November 9, 1913

PAIN RADIATED FROM SARAH's nose deep into her head. She couldn't blink away the silvery fireflies dancing at the edge of her vision.

On the seat next to her, Anne sobbed and clutched at her. The auto was motionless, diagonal in the center of the road, the windshield splattered with revolting yellow and green never-mind-what. Sam looked shell-shocked, the back of his shirt torn and bloody. Alex turned to the back seat.

"You ladies okay?" he said.

"Is it gone?" Sarah's nose felt as big as her head. The last thing she remembered clearly was the Moor's scimitar stabbing through the roof.

"Dead," Sam said. "It exploded like a bag of bugs when the car hit it. In fact, it *was* a bag of bugs."

Anne looked up. "Oh, God. Sarah, your nose is all bloody."

"I must have smacked it on the seat when we stopped. How bad is it?"

Anne dabbed at it with a handkerchief.

"There's a lot of blood, but it seems to have stopped. Does it hurt?" She straightened Sarah's hat.

"The silverfish in my eyes seem to have moved on, and the pain's not so bad." Sarah could almost think in a straight line now.

Anne laughed — a semi-hysterical laugh but a laugh nonetheless.

"What's so funny?" Sam asked.

"It's just… those guys. You said 'bag of bugs,' and they're blackamoors and full of bugs, so they're *bugamoors*!"

Sarah found herself chuckling, which made her nose hurt, but it *was* funny.

"Bugamoor," Sam said. He started snickering.

Soon the three of them were laughing so hard Sarah found it hard to breathe. Whenever it died down, one of them would say "Bugamoor!" and they'd be off again.

Alex looked puzzled as he watched them. Sarah had the urge to pull him over the seat into the back.

"It's not *that* funny," he said.

"Bugamoor!" Anne said.

It would be nice to breathe again. Sarah tried to concentrate on something distinctly un-funny, like principles of accounting. When the last giggle finally died out, she was left with a pleasant cathartic feeling. And a sore nose.

Alex stuck his head out the window and peered down the street.

"Another car's coming. Sam, do you think you can drive?"

Sam pulled off his torn jacket and handed it to his sister.

"This is ruined, use it to wipe off Sarah's blood."

Anne scrubbed Sarah's face, bringing on a painful reminder of the silverfish attacks.

Sam took the coat back to clear a swath of bug guts from the windshield. He then balled up the nasty thing and threw it to the side of the road.

"We should go to our house," he said, climbing back into the driver's seat. "We can clean up there."

The car was still running. Sam popped the brake and rolled off as if he'd been doing it for ages. Sarah thought about Alex's struggles with the machine and sighed.

"How's your thumb?" Sarah and Alex were cleaning the car in front of the Williams house. The base of his finger was swollen and turning purple.

"I don't think it's actually broken," he said. "What do you call it in English when you wrench it but don't break the bone?"

"A sprain." She chose a bug-free spot, relaxed against the auto, and took his hand. "Tell me how bad this feels." She moved the digit back and forth, ever so gently. He winced.

"It hurts, but less than before." She couldn't help it. She enjoyed making him squirm. He retrieved his hand. "Sam, is there ice?"

Sam was inspecting the grill. "I'll get some from the ice shed. I was going for water anyway." He left with Anne.

She was barely out of sight when Alex grabbed Sarah's hand and pulled her to him for a kiss. His lips were salty.

"What if someone saw us?" She pushed him away. But only a few inches.

"I wanted to kiss you," he said.

Little bits of grit were in her mouth, and she tried to work them out with her tongue. Let it not be bugamoor grit. She wanted to smell him again. Silly. She glanced around. Anne was behind the house now. She leaned into him, stood on her toes to kiss him briefly, then put her face into the crook of his neck. He smelled of sweat, fear, and God knows what else.

She liked it.

"That wasn't so bad, was it?" he said.

She had to assume he meant the kiss, not their foray into the basement. She shook her head. Tears welled in her eyes. Eventually, she pulled away again. They held hands, but the auto stood between them and the house.

Sam returned first, carrying a bucket in one hand and a wrapped bundle in the other.

"I'm sorry, Alex, there's no way we can fix this perfectly," he said. "Your grandfather is going to notice the damage."

Alex took the bundle and held the ice against his thumb.

"He won't, but Dmitri will," he said. "It's not a problem. I'll just tell them that when I drove off the road and hit a tree, branches tore the roof."

"They won't take a piece out of your backside?" Sam asked.

"Grandfather doesn't care," Alex said. "Although if I'd broken one of his precious antiques? Well, those are art."

Sam shook his head. "So rich, the automobile is a toy."

Sarah washed the blood off her face and changed into a borrowed blouse. Her nose was still sore and puffy, but it didn't look serious. Maybe she should tell her parents Alex's crash-into-the-tree story, though she didn't want them to think he was dangerous.

The four of them reconvened in one of the downstairs living rooms, the one furthest from the boarders. Anne helped Sam clean the cut on his back. Sarah tried not to look. She hadn't seen Sam without his shirt in a long time, not to mention it was just plain awkward with Alex sitting right there.

Alex reached into his pack and took out a grubby jar.

"I brought some ointment. It'll help that cut heal."

After two weeks, the warm touch of his hands on her foot was still fresh in her mind.

Anne opened the container, grimaced at the smell, and slathered the stuff on Sam's back. He cringed.

"I know no one else is going to say this," Anne said. "I believe the whole kit and caboodle now, but we almost died. I don't know about the moral questions, and certainly vampires are bad, but what the *hell* — Jesus forgive me — are we doing?"

Sarah still remembered the bloody tree on the wall, the blaring of the horn, Isabella's grim delivery. In a logical world her friend might be right, but nothing about this was logical.

"If we don't do it," she said, "who will?"

Alex leaned forward. "I agree with Anne."

Sarah felt like her chair had been yanked out from under her.

"I know I was the one who started this," he said, "but we're in way over our heads. Those two bugamoors," he raised his good hand to quell the snickers, "were just *henchmen.*"

"We can't quit now," Sarah said. "We're all in it together." *Only you can stop us,* echoed in her head.

"Those henchmen are nothing compared to the vampire himself." Alex hesitated, and all of them looked at him.

"What do you mean, Alex?" Sarah said.

"I… that *thing* is vastly older and more powerful than we thought. He's almost nine hundred years old. Even if we fight him in the middle of the day, we'll be offering him a four-course meal."

"Just a damn minute," Sam said. "You sound awfully sure about this. How—"

"My grandfather knows the vampire."

"Knows?" Anne's voice was as sharp as Sarah had ever heard it. "What do you mean he *knows* him?"

Sarah felt like she'd been spinning out of control to the right, and someone hit her so hard she careened to the left.

"Why didn't you tell us?" she whispered.

Alex looked miserable — as well he ought.

"I wanted to."

"With the best intentions, the worst work is done," Sam said.

"You still haven't explained how your grandfather *knows* him," Anne said.

"It's not like he's met the vampire, but he has his sources. When I told him about the Moors he said they belonged to this undead Caliph he knows *about*. He insisted I stay as far away as possible."

"Good advice," Anne said. "You should have passed it on."

Sam glared at Alex. "We can't afford to fight or *hold back* from each other."

"Truth is, I don't want to stop," Alex said. "I know we almost died today, but there are two fewer monsters in the world because of us. We're not half bad at this."

Sarah considered throwing some of her own secrets into the maelstrom. Like dreaming of being pushed down a grave or having a baby ripped from her womb by a giant bat.

"We need more research and better planning," she said instead, "but this creature is a killer, and we just can't leave him to go on killing and killing, century after century. Someone has to end it."

"Count me out," Anne said. "I love you, Sarah, but I don't want to end up a forgotten little skeleton in some shore house basement."

"Good afternoon, kids." Mrs. Williams poked her head in. Sam and Sarah were still standing. "Everything okay in here?"

You could all but impale the tension in the room with a stake.

Alex stood and offered a half bow. "Good afternoon, Mrs. Williams. Everything's great. I hope you had a nice day at church."

"What a gentleman," she said. The phrase "gentleman liar" popped into Sarah's head.

Anne said, "Mom, where's Emily? She didn't come back with you?"

Mrs. Williams shook her head. "After services she stayed to help at the church."

Sarah met Anne's eyes and saw them widen with the same fear that filled her own heart.

"With Pastor Parris?" Anne asked.

"Who else?" Mrs. Williams said. "She should be home soon. I'm going to make lunch for her. Would any of you like some?"

Sam offered his mother a thumbs up.

"Yes, ma'am," Alex said.

"This is really bad," Anne said as soon as she left. "What if Emily is alone with him?"

"If anything happens to her," Sam said, "the man's going to meet his maker a lot sooner than he thought."

Alex sat back in his chair, then went right back to perching on the edge.

"Hopefully, Emily's fine—"

"What do you care?" Anne said.

"Let the man speak." Sam took his sister's hand. "Emily might be in trouble."

"You suppose the pastor's really in league with—"

"Mr. Nasir?" Alex said. Sarah realized there were others in the house — best be careful throwing around words like "vampire."

Mr. Nasir. It was weird to have a name for him, to think of vampires reading their mail at the kitchen table. Nine hundred years old.

Meet the one that you hunt. Had the giant bat licked brains and blood from Thomas Becket's broken head or drooled over bloody necks during the Reign of Terror?

"Emily's been spending a lot of time with the pastor recently," Anne said. "But he isn't a vampire. Maybe he was inviting this Mr. Nasir to join the congregation. It could all be a misunderstanding."

Sarah sighed. Freud called that denial.

Twenty-Six:
Breaking and Entering

Salem, Massachusetts, Sunday afternoon, November 9, 1913

Parris waited in the bushes. He'd circled the house with the compass, and all signs indicated the archangel's horn was inside. He held an opal wrapped in bay leaves in his hand — Albert Magnus, a thirteenth-century alchemist, had recommended this for invisibility.

Apparently Magnus was right, because when the bearded man in the brown suit and his wife emerged, they strolled away from the house without noticing him.

Parris tucked the opal away and put his hand on his jacket pocket, over the doll he and Betty had made this afternoon. He took a deep breath and drew a draught of energy, wrapping the soul about him like a winter cloak. It worked like the charm it was. Sure it was a little stinky — baked excrement, after all — but borrowing someone else's soul was the only way to circumvent the bearded mage's ward.

The front door was locked, but a small piece of moonwort from the kit in his satchel dealt with that.

He slipped inside, leaving the lights off. The house smelled of cooking fat. Better than Mr. Nasir's place, for sure. On the first floor he found a small office crammed with books and papers. A photo showed the bearded man, his wife, and a pretty girl with curly hair.

He scanned the books. They were in a vast range of languages and nearly all on religious or esoteric topics. Obviously the bearded man was well learned — his wards alone testified to that. Parris could feel them pulsing all around him, caressing his borrowed soul.

At least a third of the books were in Hebrew — Parris didn't speak the language, but he had a solid knowledge of the Hermetic Kabbala, so he knew the letters. A Jew, then. Something tickled his brain. He looked more closely at the photo. The man did look familiar, but ....

There were framed diplomas on the walls, some in Hebrew, some in German. Herr Doktor Josef Engelmann. Damnation! They'd met — twice. It wouldn't do to be caught and recognized. He'd best hurry.

He was about to leave when he spied the letter opener. It was brass and engraved with a German missive. He only read medieval German, but it was clear enough: "To my loving husband, Josef, December eleventh, 1898."

He shoved it in his bag. A sentimental object like that could come in handy if he needed to work against the man. Nothing personal, of course, but he needed the Horn to get that grimoire.

He removed a vial of water and an aspersing wand made of bound lavender from his satchel. The vial contained rainwater he'd collected on Ascension Day without ever allowing it to touch the ground. Pouring a few drops on the end of the lavender, he flicked the water around the room to erase any trace of his presence.

Back in the hall he lit a candle and peered through the flames.

The ghostly lines he'd noticed outside with the vampire were visible here as well. But from his new perspective inside the building, he was better able to see them for what they were. Metaphysical in nature, they echoed the structural form of another building. Enormous ghostly support columns, topped with pomegranate capitals rose upward to join a vast and awesome rectangular vault, supports shaped like giant angels reached their wings out to hold the phantasmal ceiling.

He observed a convergence of these lines beneath his feet, and the finger of the compass tilted down, so he looked for a cellar door, which he soon found.

The floor below was composed of loose dirt. The compass led him across the dank space to the far wall, where a thick cluster of roots broke from the packed dirt, gnarled fingers grasping after the damp.

This place felt thin. He sniffed, catching a scent like a sudden summer rain. His own hearth smelled similar — plus the sulfur, but none of that here. He squinted through the candle flame, whispering a few words in Latin.

The fabric of the universe had been pierced here. A gateway had been opened to some other world. He didn't think Mr. Engelmann had crossed into hell, but there were other realms out there.

Parris moved the compass back and forth along the wall. It swiveled, indicating a phantom spot in the center of the cluster of roots. He placed his hand there and held it steady. He could almost feel the threadbare reality.

The Horn wasn't here. This Hebrew magician had hidden it on some unknown celestial plane—

Click! Upstairs, he heard a lock tumble, a door open, and two voices talking. One male. One female.

Twenty-Seven:
The Bracelet

Salem, Massachusetts, Sunday afternoon, November 9, 1913

Sarah heard the Williamses' front door open and saw Emily pass by. A blur of pale blue church dress. She didn't stop or even look their way but went straight for the stairs.

Each riser creaked beneath her tread.

"Emily?" Anne called out. "How was church?"

There was a long pause before Emily's voice drifted down to them.

"I'm exhausted. Going to lie down."

The creaks resumed their upward plod.

"This is a first," Anne said. "She wants to nap?"

"At least she's home," Sam said. "Let's go up and get the real story."

Two windows looked out over the backyard in the sisters' room. Sarah hadn't been here since meeting Charles a lifetime ago, and it felt like greeting a friend who, once close, she hadn't seen in years. Emily lay on her bed in a cloud of blue satin, still wearing her boots and hat. Anne stroked her arm.

"Em, you sure you're okay?"

She didn't open her eyes. "I just want to sleep."

"You were helping Pastor Parris?" Anne said.

"Yeah."

"That's it?"

Emily nodded.

Sarah could smell Alex standing right behind her. She placed her boot heel on the toe of his shoe and put a bit of weight on it.

"Ouch! Why'd you do that?" Alex whispered.

"How could you, of all people, want to quit?" she whispered in Greek.

"This morning," Sam told Emily, "we went to the house over on Webb without you."

"Nice."

"I didn't quit," Alex whispered. "I thought you'd be mad at me for not telling about the vampire."

"I'm mad about both." Sarah pressed down with her heel again.

"Stop that!" Alex said. "I'm just being realistic, and you're using English diphthongs in Greek. It sounds ridiculous."

"The vampire wasn't there," Sam said, "but two big guards were. They're magic men filled with bugs instead of flesh. They tried to kill us, but we killed them."

"It was really repulsive," Anne said.

Emily nodded.

Anne bit her lower lip with her front teeth — an expression Sarah had for years privately named the blonde-bunny. She tried to pull her sister into a sitting position, but Emily lay like dead weight.

"Sam, help me get her up."

The two of them pulled her upright — with no help or resistance from her. She looked like a porcelain doll, not a live human girl. Anne slapped her hard, and Emily's head jerked sideways.

"Emily Elisabeth Williams, look at me."

Sarah said, "Take it easy, will you?"

"Leave me alone," Emily said, her tone so flat it gave Sarah goosebumps. "I'm tired."

"What happened with Pastor Parris?"

"I don't know… nothing. I can't remember." Sarah could see a red hand imprint on Emily's pale cheek.

"It was two hours ago," Sarah said.

"Seriously, I don't remember."

"Emily," Sarah said. "After Charles' funeral? You couldn't remember that, either."

Both times had been at church.

Emily shivered. "It's all hazy."

"I hate to state the obvious," Alex said from the door, "but this doesn't sound like a coincidence."

It was odd how his voice grated on Sarah now. She crouched down so her face was only inches from Emily's.

"Today, what was the sermon about?"

Emily sighed. "Sin? It's always about sin."

"What kind of sin?"

"Carnal sin," Emily said, "and how it soils the soul for the more holy relationship with God."

"What about after services. What happened then?"

Emily played with her skirts. "Everyone thanked the pastor."

"And after that?" Sarah said.

The girl reached down to her right leg, then jerked her hands back to her lap.

"He asked me if I could stay and help tidy up."

"Did anyone else stay?" Sarah asked.

"Matthew Lewis, but he left early."

Emily pulled up her legs and struggled to wrap her arms around her bulky skirts.

"What did you and the pastor do after Matthew left?" Sarah said.

Emily squeezed her arms at the elbows, her eyes darting back and forth.

"I can't remember," she whispered.

Her hand crept down to her ankle again and again. Every time, she pulled it back to her knee. Finally Sam reached under the skirts and grabbed her ankle. Emily had been slouching forward but now she arched back, threw her arms above her head, and pressed her palms against the wall.

Sam squeezed her ankle. She arched her back further — it looked to Sarah like she was rigid as a plank. She licked her lips, and a tiny moan escaped them.

"Emily?" Anne said.

It seemed a struggle for her to turn her eyes toward her sister. She was taking quick shallow breaths. Sam released her ankle. She went slack.

"Em, are you okay?" Sam asked. "Did that hurt?"

She took a moment to answer. "No. It didn't hurt."

"Something is seriously wrong here." Anne flipped up the bottom of Emily's skirts and started unlacing her right boot—

"NO!" she screamed. "Leave me alone!"

She squirmed and thrashed, managing to kick Anne and break free of her brother. She hopped up on the bed and retreated to its left edge, where she squatted like a cornered animal.

"Leave me ALONE!"

Emily's green eyes were wide and wild, her hat knocked free, amber hair going every which way. Clearly no longer sleepy but not in the least bit normal, she looked... feral.

"Is something wrong with your leg?" Sam asked. "Let Anne take off your shoe."

Emily shook her head. "No, I can't! Not allowed!"

Bizarreness upon bizarreness had been mounting since that afternoon when Sarah had met Charles, not twenty feet below where she sat now.

"Who won't allow it?" Sarah asked.

There was no answer. Emily huddled in the corner of the bed, a blue satin mouse in a pink floral wallpaper forest.

Alex came away from the door. "Sam, Anne. I don't think this is some kind of childish snit. I hope I'm wrong, but I think you're going to need to force the issue."

"Why should we listen to you?" Anne said.

But Sam turned back to Emily. "Let Anne take off your shoe, or I'm going to make you."

"Don't come near me!" She looked pitiful, and Sarah wished there was a better option. But they weren't exactly threatening to chop her arm off.

Sam lunged. He grabbed one of her legs and yanked her forward, then pinned her under his bulk. Still, she fought: limbs flailing, hands scratching, feet kicking.

"Sarah, help hold her down," Sam said. "Anne, you get the shoe. Alex, grab her if she gets away."

Sarah moved in. Emily was biting Sam's shoulder, but he held her head to the bed with one arm. One of her hands scratched at his ear, so Sarah grabbed it. Anne sat on Emily's right leg and resumed unlacing her shoe. Emily struggled and bucked, but there wasn't much she could do with her two-hundred-pound brother holding her down.

There were a lot of laces and an uncooperative subject, but Anne got the boot off. Through Emily's powder-blue stocking, the leg looked normal. Anne ran her hand down it, starting at the knee. As she touched the ankle, Emily convulsed.

"There's something on her ankle," Anne said. "I can't tell what."

"Then take off her stocking and look," Sam said.

There ensued a new and violent round of kicking, but Anne managed to reach up under Emily's skirts and find the stocking top. Alex turned away from the proceedings. Anne rolled the stocking off, and Emily went limp.

"Em, you playing possum?" Sam asked.

"Just get off of me," she said.

Her brother stayed where he was.

Emily had ceased trying to rip his ear off, so Sarah released her hand in order to get a better look. What she saw was a fourteen-year-old girl's leg, the usual five toes — and a peculiar circlet wrapped about the ankle. Bending closer, she saw that the thing appeared to be made of hair. It wasn't thick, just a couple dozen strands. The hairs — some amber, the others dark brown — had been braided and the ends knotted together.

"Who gave you the anklet?" Sarah said. "Has anyone seen anything like this before?"

"I've never seen one," Alex said, "but in Europe witches are said to construct bracelets or necklaces from human hair. There are probably countless uses for that kind of magic."

Sarah reached down and stroked the strand of greasy braided hair. Emily arched and tensed and moaned. Sarah pulled back her hand, and Emily's movements and moaning immediately subsided. But her face was flushed and sweaty, and she was panting.

"Emily," Sarah said. "What happened? Did I hurt you?"

"No." She gasped. "Do it again."

"Enough of this," Anne said. "Let's rip the damn thing off." She reached down, grabbed the bracelet, and pulled.

Emily screamed so loud Sam grabbed a small pillow and held it over her mouth. She writhed and twisted on the bed, and Anne struggled to hold onto the bracelet. Sarah saw bright scarlet welts like crimson ivy race up Emily's leg. They pulsed in time with her muffled screams.

Sarah grabbed Anne's wrist. "Stop it! Can't you see how much that hurts her?"

Anne let go of the bracelet, and her sister went limp. Within a few seconds, the welts faded to pale pink marks. Emily spit the pillow from her mouth.

"Don't do that again," she said. "It felt like you were sawing off my leg."

"Good idea, let's cut the thing off," Sam said.

"Bad idea," Sarah said. "If just pulling on it hurt, that might kill her."

"Emily, I'm sorry," Anne said. "Who put it on you? What's it for?"

"I'm scared, Anne." Emily looked terrified. "What's happening?"

"We don't know," Sarah said, "but we'll find out and fix it. Right?"

"Of course we'll fix it," Anne said, sniffing her fingers. "The anklet smells like licorice and something else. Sweet, like a medicine."

"Pardon me, but may I smell?" Alex said.

Anne offered her hand.

"You're right about the licorice," he said. "The other I think is calamus. Not surprising, but not good, either."

"What's calamus?" Anne asked.

Alex released her hand and Sarah smelled it, too.

"An herb. From India originally, I think. Used for thousands of years in countless tonics — named after Kalamos, a son of the river-god Maeander, it's used for spells of lust and control."

"And you know this how?" Anne said.

"There are too many unanswered questions here," Sam said. "Let's stay focused. We need to know what we're dealing with."

Emily's hysterical behavior reminded Sarah of her Freud readings. "In some way," she said, "either through subconscious defenses or magical intervention, Emily's memory has been blocked. We need to unblock it if we want to find out what happened."

"How do we do that?" Alex asked.

"I have a couple ideas," Sarah said. "I'm going to run home and get some things. I'll be back later. In the meantime, I want you to relax Emily. Dress her in some comfortable clothes, close the curtains. Maybe even give her some whiskey."

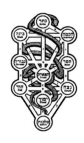

Twenty-Eight:
Clash of Faiths

Salem, Massachusetts, Sunday afternoon, November 9, 1913

"Sarah's spending a great deal of time with her friends of late," Rebecca said as she and Joseph stepped onto the front porch.

Joseph patted pockets, looking for his keys. He could never remember which one he'd dropped them in — it was the first pocket, but which was the first?

"That, I think, is a good thing. As much as I enjoy teaching her, she needs variety. You know, socialization."

He found the keys — scratching against his favorite pipe!

"Socialization had better not include any improper fraternization," his wife said.

He brushed her *tuchus*, opened the door, and tapped two fingers to the silver *mezuzah*.

A spark of energy burned his hand. He smelt something akin to sulfur.

"Rebecca. Go to the Kleins — stay there until I call."

She opened her mouth. He put a finger to her lips.

"Something's in the house," he said. She picked up her skirts and went.

Joseph raced into his study. He grabbed his father-in-law's prayer bag off the shelf, yanked it open, and pulled out the prayer shawl and the fuzzy top hat — no time for the complicated *tefillin*.

He returned to the foyer, raised his arms above his head, and shouted in Hebrew: "*The Lord is my light and my help; whom should I fear? The Lord is the stronghold of my life, whom should I dread?*" The structure of his temple-like ward seared into his retinas. A kind of ecstasy flowed into him. Four luminous walls girded the house, perfectly aligned as they were on the points of the compass. In each direction pillars shaped like angels spread their celestial wings.

"*When evil men assail me — to devour my flesh — it is they, my foes and my enemies, who stumble and fall.*"

A line of cold red flame raced from his feet past the kitchen and into the open cellar door. From the depths of the basement he heard a scream.

He followed the trail. Soundless tongues of fire licked his trousers but did not burn. At the top of the stairs he yelled, "*To my right Michael and to my left Gabriel, in front of me Uriel and behind me Raphael.*"

He leapt. The weight of his mentor's shawl lifted and the touch of feathers enveloped him. He landed lightly on the cellar floor. He raised his arms, and the foundations of his metaphysical temple poured light into the room.

Before him, surrounded by sulfurous smoke, writhed a blonde girl in a black suit with a clerical collar. Joseph grasped the *mezuzah* around his neck and shouted the *Shema*, the central prayer of his faith.

Brighter than bright, a searing white light from the silver charm bathed the girl before him, causing the figure to blur and waver. In her place was a gaunt middle-aged man carrying a bag, his spectacles askew and his frazzled hair smoking.

Joseph could still see echoes of the feminine form — his prayers had only muted the effect. What foul sorcery was this? All too reminiscent of Khepri and his waxen disguise. And he thought he'd seen this man before, too.

The priest reached into his bag and pulled out a brass knife. Was that the letter opener Rebecca had given him?

The man shouted in Latin, "Blade of my own, burn my joined flesh!" and pricked himself in the leg.

Pain seared Joseph's right thigh. He glanced down to see the fabric of his trouser leg burned away, black rot stained his flesh. The priest streaked past him and bolted up the stairs.

Joseph pulled off his prayer shawl and pressed it against the wound. The burn in his thigh cooled. Such was Rebecca's father's righteousness that his very clothing was drenched in God's love.

He limped up the stairs. When he reached the door to the street he saw the priest receding into the distance, running hard. Joseph was about to give chase when the man thrust a hand into his pocket and vanished.

Cursed warlocks.

He hadn't actually met one before, but the city was rumored to have its share. And he had thought it a good idea to move to a town named Salem!

He slumped against the door frame and pressed his forehead against the *mezuzah*. The false priest — he couldn't be a real man of God — seemed to have used somebody's soul, a young girl's by the look of it, to sneak through the defenses. When Joseph regained his strength he was going to have a nice long chat with *Hashem* and close that loophole.

As the adrenaline subsided he began to shake. He felt weak, his mouth dry. Clearly he needed a bit more exercise. He unwrapped his throbbing leg and saw the skin was red and peeling. A bad burn, but he'd heal. The real problem was this warlock.

When he'd checked the wards this morning he felt something. At the time he assumed some mischievous child had tried to open a window. Now he wasn't so sure. And no question what this priest was after down in the cellar.

Thankfully the Horn was gone, and fat chance some petty warlock could open a passage to paradise. Only on a day sacred to Gabriel was that even possible, and the next one wasn't until March. Still, anyone seeking the Horn could present a problem.

He remembered Khepri. Could this priest be the beetle god in disguise? Khepri had been able to steal the form of other men, cloaking himself in a suit of wax. But he was dead — turned to ash by the wrath of *Hashem* — and the priest didn't have a dog. Three times he'd faced Khepri, and three times the little silver dog had been with him.

Joseph shuddered. *Anubis, jackal-headed god who receives the organs of the dead.*

Twenty-Nine:
Training

Salem, Massachusetts, Sunday afternoon, November 9, 1913

PAPA WASN'T IN HIS STUDY when Sarah came home. She found him chopping wood in the back yard, looking ridiculous in a suit with the axe held high. This was doubly odd, since he rarely did physical labor. He had a white bandage wrapped around his right thigh.

"Papa, can you teach me how to enter a trance to increase receptivity and concentration?"

Back in Emily's room this crazy idea had come to her — a half-baked plan combining Freud's modern approach with Papa's ancient one.

He put the axe down on the carpet of colorful leaves.

"We have to talk."

"I promise to send Alex or Sam over to cut a month's worth of wood," she said.

"You command these young men at a whim?"

"Get your mind out of the gutter, Papa. They both owe me favors for helping them with schoolwork." That was true enough.

"Someone broke into the house today." He looked her in the eyes. "This was no ordinary intrusion. A warlock circumvented my defenses and entered our home."

Sarah stared. Witchcraft… Emily's bracelet….

"Oh my God. I think a warlock put some kind of curse on Emily — a Mr. Parris, the Williamses' pastor."

"I knew I'd met him before!" Papa's expression was somber. "But I couldn't place him until you mentioned it."

"You know him?" she asked.

He nodded. "I never liked the man. He seemed off, even for a Congregationalist. Tell me what he did to Emily."

"I'm not sure yet, that's why I want you to teach me the trance."

She told him about the anklet, and he told her about his encounter. Together they went into the house.

"Yesterday, after we talked," her father said in the mudroom, "I prayed to *Hashem* to protect our home. As you know, in Hebrew, the Great Temple in Jerusalem was called *Beit HaMikdash*, The House of That Which Is Holy. It makes an effective and popular esoteric model. I merely asked God to treat our house as if it were His."

"So our house is the Temple of Solomon?" she said.

He leaned the axe against the wall. "Not literally, and certainly not in any way normal people might perceive. But to a warlock like Mr. Parris, this house has become holy ground, and his profane soul is not welcome."

She stomped the mud from her boots, then tugged them off.

"But he *was* inside."

"I think he may have entered by borrowing Emily's soul."

"What did he want here?"

"What do you think?"

"The Horn?" she whispered.

He nodded. "We need to find out more. Meet me in my study. Change into all white. No metal, no jewelry, no leather, no shoes or socks."

When Sarah came downstairs she found her father placing a circle of white candles on the office floor. She watched in her knee-length white shirt with the tasseled fringes. It was one of her father's old ones, they didn't make them for women.

"Put on your grandfather's garments. His holiness imbues them even now." He handed her a pile.

She said the blessing, settled a prayer shawl over her shoulders, then studied the *tefillin*. Other than being white, the little boxes seemed typical. She took the proper box and wrapped the leather straps around her arm seven times. The straps of the other box she bound around her forehead, securing the little cube between her eyes. Finally, the arm straps were tightened about her left hand, forming the shape of the Hebrew letter *shin*.

Papa tapped the center of the circle. "Sit here."

She stepped over the candles, the carpet crisp under her bare feet. Papa lit the tapers. From his desk, he brought a wooden tray littered with small bone tiles carved with Hebrew letters and placed it on her lap.

"Realize you're about to serve your God in joy," he said. "Begin to combine letters, permuting and revolving them until your mind warms. Delight in how they move and in what ideas you generate. Through the combinations you will understand new things not attained by human tradition nor discovered through mental reflection."

"What am I looking for?" Sarah asked.

"You'll know when God shows you … or not," he said. "I'm going to call the police about Pastor John Parris, warlock extraordinaire. Then I'll be praying in the sitting room. I need to close the gap in the house defenses. Find me when you've finished."

Given the exercise, "finished" seemed a pretty elusive concept.

She tried to clear her thoughts and focus on the tiled letters. It was hard — soon her head began to nod. It had been a long day.

Sarah looked at the clock. An hour had passed. Examining the tiles she found they spelled in Hebrew, *The dark gift will make strength of your sacrifice*. Every tile had been used.

Her heart raced. It was terrifying and exhilarating. Her visual memory captured the phrase, then she rearranged the letters into a small section of a well-known psalm.

When she went to show Papa he was in the middle of praying. She didn't dare interrupt, but out the window she noticed it was dark. She still had to get back to Emily.

Sarah changed back into her street clothes and shoved the white garb into her bag. She peeked in on her father, but he hadn't moved. When she returned to the study, she paused before taking the prayer shawl, then fumbled with the desk drawer latch and added Papa's pocket watch to her satchel.

The ends would have to justify the means.

Thirty:
Blood Fury

Salem, Massachusetts, Sunday night, November 9, 1913

DUSK CAME, AND WITH IT, Ali ibn Hammud al-Nasir's return to consciousness.

He seethed and twisted in the darkness of his traveling coffin. The dirt of his homeland offered no solace. Nabil and Ahmed were gone, severed from him like the limbs he had imagined them to be. Allah, cursed be His name, heaped endless humiliations upon him.

Farther than the stars in the sky, to lose not one but two of his loyal servants to violence! Ahmed had been with him only thirty short turns of the year, but Nabil he had taken in 1811. Al-Nasir levered open the lid of his pine casket and sat up. His heavy breaths brought no oxygen to his desiccated heart.

He let anger bring his blood to a boil. Infidels, may he soon sever their filthy cocks!

His limbs became leathery and gray. He stretched his wings and flexed his talons.

"Fouad!"

Instantly, the old Moor entered the windowless sleeping chamber of the new townhouse. He slept at the door.

"Yes, most noble Caliph?" The big man spoke flawless traditional Arabic. Even now, well into his second century, his black skin covered an impressive array of powerful muscles, although his hair had gone almost entirely white.

"Fouad, someone has slain Nabil and Ahmed. Our beachside lair is likely desecrated."

"Woe upon them, terrible Master! May the whore mothers of those trespassers be fucked like the dog bitches they are!" Small white worms crawled from the corners of the big man's eyes.

"Well said." Al-Nasir patted the old Moor. "I go now to salvage what I can. Send Tarik. He must secure our treasures and my sarcophagus. I will meet him with further instructions."

Fouad was staring at the doorframe.

"Did you hear me, Fouad?" al-Nasir said.

"Yes, Master, of course." Fast as a desert snake, Fouad struck the wooden beam. He brought back a struggling spider, which he placed on his tongue.

Al-Nasir let him be. The huge eunuch had few pleasures available to him.

"Have you heard from the warlock? He was supposed to enter the house today, if we are blessed he will have secured the Horn."

"No word, Master."

"While I'm gone, find him and bring him here."

The vampire swept around two corners and unbolted the shutters Fouad and Tarik had installed on the window. He winced at the glow of twilight, as if he'd stood too close to a fire, then took to the air.

He beat his arm-wings to gain altitude, then veered east toward the coast. By feel, he followed the iron train tracks from the air. That coal-eating beast traveled faster than he could over distance, but in short bursts he was its better. He didn't trust the loathsome invention. Fruit of perverse science, its farts were fouler than those of a camel drunk on spoiled milk.

Al-Nasir circled the house on Webb Street three times before descending. His keen senses detected the dark stain on the street. Landing in the shadows between two nearby houses, he resumed his more comfortable, less alarming form. Pale nostrils sniffed the air. Any nearby humans remained in their houses, but no matter. He drew the shadows to him. None of these mortals had the strength of will to even remember him if they so much as caught a glimpse.

The bushes rustled, and he discovered what little remained of Ahmed. Al-Nasir plucked a millipede from the foliage and licked it to be sure.

Ahmed, the most recent of the hundred-odd slaves that had served him over the centuries, had been a fine specimen. Al-Nasir found him in 1876 in a Marrakech brothel — some mortals shared his taste for the boys who were men no longer. Although Ahmed was but a ball-less slave whore, a vessel filled by other men's seed, Al-Nasir made a glorious dark god of him, and now this — he crushed the millipede in his hand — was all that remained.

The vampire caught the scent of human blood. He let it pull him to a garment, smeared in gore, discarded behind the foliage. He sniffed carefully to sort through the complex bouquet. Crushed bits of Ahmed, a man's musk, and two strains of blood. One was from the man, presumably the garment's owner. The other he thought might be a woman's, but there was a subtle layered fragrance to her blood: jasmine, rose, and sandalwood.

Hmmm....

Before leaving for America, he had gone at the Painted Man's bequest to get the Eye and the portrait from the convalescing Khepri. While there, the beetle god's dung smell made its usual assault on his nose, but he'd also detected jasmine, rose, and sandalwood.

The archangel's stink. Even Khepri couldn't survive such a confrontation unmarked. Al-Nasir licked at the bloody remnant in his hands. The blood was dried, but he was certain. The beetle had lost the Horn, and the painted Egyptian had set al-Nasir to profane the archangel's feast day with that boy's sacrifice. Now this, literally intermingled with the death of his slaves. The vampire wanted answers. He must speak with the Painted Man soon.

Al-Nasir streaked down the street and into his former dwelling, batting the front door off its hinges. The place was useless now, anyway. Inside, he smelled human, but it was stale. Some flies that had once been Nabil buzzed about the kitchen.

The cellar door stood open, and al-Nasir leapt down the stairs, landing in the basement as gracefully as a cat. The door to his crypt had been ripped from its jamb. Former parts of Nabil crunched under his feet. His second-favorite slave no doubt died defending the treasures and sarcophagus. The vampire collected a few of Nabil's creepy crawlies. He wanted to retain a little of the old Moor inside himself, so he munched on the bugs as he surveyed the crypt proper.

The first thing he noticed was the cracked lid of his sarcophagus. His anger stoked hotter as he approached the coffin and sniffed. Ichor from his henchman had soaked the ancient earth that filled the limestone casket, but he sensed no effort at desecration. No holy charms, no oils or sacred waters. The infidels were either amateurs or too fearful to finish the job.

He remembered his first sip of Nabil, then a runaway living on the Cairo streets. Al-Nasir had snatched him from an alley and lifted him silently to a moonlit rooftop. The boy tasted of upper Egyptian and Mamluk blood, a delightful blend. It had been a tough choice. There was nothing so sweet as the taste of blood drawn all the way to the end, but in Nabil he sensed potential. With great effort, he stopped himself short. Instead, he offered the child a taste of his own blood, just a taste, then brought him to a back-alley cutter, easy to find in those happier days. The procedure was simple, whether it was ram, bull, stallion, or boy that was to be gelded.

Al-Nasir surveyed the hoard of gold and gems in his crypt. Nothing seemed to be missing, though a few things had been moved in the struggle, the treasure seemed accounted for. He picked up an Iznik dish, a tight pattern of knot-like shapes painted in blue on its translucent white surface....

His eye caught on one crate. Where was the lion-shaped Achaemenid drinking vessel? He snarled. The hand of at least two kings had held that rhyton. Suleiman the Magnificent himself had presented it to al-Nasir while he oversaw the Painted Man's interests at the Sublime Porte.

The vampire leaned down and breathed in. He caught the scent of a human male, not the one on the garment. He inhaled, memorizing the nuances of the man's odors.

If the precious goes, everything is cheapened. They would pay, these amateur intruders, for the deaths of Nabil and Ahmed, for daring to enter his private places. Ali ibn Hammud al-Nasir would retrieve his stolen goblet from their severed hands.

A creak of the floor above drew his attention. Faster than an *ifrit*, he was upstairs. It was only Tarik.

"When angels come, devils run away," al-Nasir said.

"Master!" The big man bowed low. He wore an ill-fitting modern jacket and trousers, curled slippers, and no shirt — probably no shirt could fit him. It was, even to the ancient vampire, an odd sartorial combination.

"Find one of those wagons they have now," al-Nasir said, "the kind that draws itself without horses. A big one. We need to move the sarcophagus and the treasure to the new lair."

"Yes, Master." Like Nabil, Tarik was a low-born Egyptian, and his gutter accent still colored his Arabic.

Of his current slaves, only Fouad had a real education. Al-Nasir grew depressed, realizing he now had only the two companions on this continent. Tahar still watched over his interests in Morocco, but that was literally half a world away. He might be forced to bring a new man into his service — in this forsaken place — how would he ever find anyone suitable?

The Moor returned in one of those noisy magical carts. It was well endowed with a canvas tent covering a copious storage area. Al-Nasir didn't ask how such an object had been procured in the middle of the night.

They maneuvered the coffin out of the cellar with ropes. Tarik was the largest and strongest of his slaves, one of the strongest al-Nasir had elevated. Of course, he himself was many times more powerful, but the lion was always stronger than the dog. They heaved the sarcophagus into the bed of the wagon, which even though it sagged under the weight, had a strong back. It took an hour to collect all the treasures and pull tarps over them.

"Master, I am sorry you must labor so," the big man said to him when they were finally done.

"No need to apologize, Tarik. Tonight we are in crisis." Losing Nabil and Ahmed had made him feel magnanimous. "Do you need a small drink to recharge your energies?"

"Oh yes, most perfect and generous Master."

He offered the big Negro his arm. The man bit down on his wrist, using teeth to tear a little flesh. Al-Nasir allowed him a minute to feed before pulling back his hand.

"Thank you, most illustrious Master."

"Enough, Tarik. There is so much more to be done. Take this thing," he waved at the vehicle, "and bring it to the townhouse. You are second in command here in the west now that Nabil is gone."

"Yes, Master, of course. Big shoes to fill, but I shall not let you down. *Salam alechem.*"

"*Salam alechem.*"

The Moor conjured the growling *djinn* that pulled the wagon. Man and machine rolled down the road, leaving behind an oily cloud.

Al-Nasir had hoped to begin his search for the light-handed miscreants involved in today's disaster. Unfortunately, it was getting late, and he still had the warlock to deal with. He sighed. One did not live 895 years after death by being hasty.

Thirty-One:
Cursed

Salem, Massachusetts, Sunday evening, November 9, 1913

EMILY LAY HALF ASLEEP on the bed when Sarah burst into the room.

"Men out!" She pointed to the door. "There's too much distraction."

Emily flung a hand over Mr. Barnyard, asleep on her bed.

"That includes you too, dog." Sarah could be so bossy.

Sam grabbed the basset hound by the collar and dragged him away.

"I'll have Anne write down anything we discover," Sarah told the boys, who slunk out, tails between their legs.

Sarah moved a chair in front of the door and jammed its back under the knob. "This is going to be an eclectic mix of techniques," she said. "Papa taught me a way of praying to increase perceptivity."

"What are you talking about?" Anne asked.

It was hard for Emily to concentrate. Was she coming down with something?

Anne sat on a nearby chair. Sarah handed her a notebook and pencil.

"You get to play secretary."

Sarah unlaced her boots and took off her stockings. She kept taking things off, even her brassière and bloomers.

"Jesus, Sarah," Anne said.

She pulled on a loose white man's shirt over her pale breasts and the dark triangle between her legs. Then took a little white beanie from a fuzzy velvet bag.

"Are you going to tell us what's going on?" Anne said.

Barefoot, Sarah climbed up on the bed and sat cross-legged between Emily's legs. She slapped the beanie on her head, pulled out a thin shawl from the velvet bag and wrapped it around her shoulders. She jabbered in some language that sounded to Emily like something was caught in her throat.

She brought out a pocket watch.

"Emily." Sarah dangled the device in front of her. "I want you to look at the watch. No matter what I say, what I do, or what you see or think, concentrate on the watch. When I put it away, we're finished, but until then, fix your eyes only on the watch. Can you do that?"

Emily tried to nod. Her head felt loose and wobbly.

"I want you to visualize yourself leaving for church this morning. You're wearing your blue satin dress. The sun is shining, and you and your parents are walking down the street. Tell me everything that happens. Slowly, and don't leave out any detail. Keep your eyes on the watch."

Sarah was chanting something. Emily couldn't understand a word, but the droning rhythm made her sleepy.

After services, the congregation had filtered out the church doors.

"Mrs. Williams," the pastor said to her mother. "Would you mind if your daughter helps close up? A number of the young folk are joining in."

Mommy was fine with it. Matt Lewis tagged along, which was annoying. Inside the church, the pastor opened a cabinet containing seven identical boxes.

"Emily, please take each candlestick from the altar and stow it in one of these. The boxes have numbers that match those on the candlestick bases."

She packed the candlesticks, which felt like they were made of lead. The pastor was pleased, but she'd swapped number three with number five and he made her fix it.

Matt locked the high windows along the sides. "Pastor, I have to go. My ma's expecting me for supper."

"Run along, then."

The pastor put his hand on Emily's shoulder. It tingled.

"What about you, Emily? Can you help me next door at my house?"

If she went, she could tell her friends she'd been inside. Mommy and Daddy would never miss her, and luncheon today was at the Cowton's. Their son's name stuck on your tongue, Cotner Cowton, and he snorted like a pig.

"I can help."

The house was right next to the church. Inside it felt old and tiny, only two or three dark rooms. The pastor lit a candle and locked the door behind them.

"Would you like some tea?" She nodded.

The tea was bitter but it made her feel very grown up. He dragged over two large trunks and packed things into a duffle — candles, books, lots of other stuff. He wrapped each item in a different cloth. Everything seemed to have its own cloth.

He didn't ask her to do anything. She felt kind of dizzy.

"Pastor, can I sit down?"

"Lie over there on that settee across from the fireplace." He was wrapping a skull.

Why did he have a skull?

Emily woke. She felt all groggy and her bed was hard and lumpy.

She opened her eyes. She wasn't in her room. The fireplace spilled soft red light from retiring coals. She must have fallen asleep on the settee.

The pastor needed to call the chimney sweep. His hearth drew poorly and smoke filled the room. It smelled like rotten eggs. Emily tried to rise, but her wooziness made her drop back down.

Pastor Parris entered carrying a tray of little bowls and jars, which he placed on a table.

His voice was different, relaxed but cold. Very cold.

"Betty, the vessel is awake. Time to play."

A raspy female voice spoke from behind Emily. "About time, Toy."

Emily tried to see the lady, but moving made her feel sick.

"Bring me some hair, then take off the vessel's shoes and socks."

He dragged a chair before his tray and poured something thick into one of the bowls.

Emily felt a tug and a sting as the woman yanked out a tuft of hair. The pastor sighed and took the strands.

The woman slid around to stand in front of the hearth. Her face was in shadow, but her eyes blazed. She was dressed in her underwear, just a corset and bloomers. Maybe she was a whore. Oh, God — a thin tail poked from a hole at her waist and snaked up and around like a cat's.

The woman walked to Emily's feet and unlaced her boots, pulling them off one at a time. She unrolled the pale blue stockings, too. Her touch was clammy and her nails jagged. Emily wanted to move, to kick, but nothing happened when she tried.

The pastor used scissors to sever a lock of his own hair. He looked to be braiding both the strands, because in the end he held up a single thicker ply. He tied knots in the cord while chanting a weird song:

> *Three times three I bind thee.*
> *I bind thee from above, I bind thee from below,*
> *I bind thee from in front, I bind thee from behind,*
> *I bind thee from yesterday, I bind thee for tomorrow,*
> *I bind thee in the night, I bind thee in the day,*
> *from birth to death do I bind thee.*

He dropped the knotted cord into one of his bowls.

"Betty," he said, "I'll need fluid from the vessel. Blood or urine. Don't make a mess. Some nail clippings, too."

Emily felt far away, not really here. She should be scared, but it was hard to even care.

The Betty-lady returned to the foot of the couch, and this time she held a knife. Now Emily wanted to scream, but no sound passed her lips. The woman shaved off some bits of toenail.

"Blood is probably easier," the Betty-lady said. "I don't see how I can get any pee unless I cut out her bladder."

"I can pee," Emily wanted to say, "You don't need the knife." But her mouth wouldn't open.

"Take blood, then," the pastor said, "just make the cut small, hidden."

The Betty-lady looked like she would've preferred to saw off Emily's foot. But she placed the edge of the blade between spread toes. The pain itself wasn't much, not as awful as the touch of the lady's cold skin. She squeezed Emily's foot, working some blood onto the knife as she might milk a cow.

"That's fine." The pastor took the bloody blade and stirred it into a bowl. He added the nail clippings, stood up, and unbuttoned his pants.

There was a wet splattering noise. He was peeing in his own pot like a horse on the street. The Betty-woman put her hands on her hips and laughed.

"Too timid to use the blade on yourself?"

"Just easier," he said. "It'll work the same either way."

"Toy, what's the point of all this?" the Betty-lady asked. "I'm getting bored."

"I'm not concerned with fun. I need to bind her life force. Mr. Nasir has been a gentleman so far, but I have a feeling he isn't forgiving of failure."

The woman dipped a finger in the crock, then brought it to her mouth. Emily wanted to gag.

"I warned you," the whore-lady said. "How's this going to help?"

"It's a binding of command, as I promised," he said, "but I should be able to draw the vessel's soul from the maquette instead of using my own. This should allow me to pass through that pesky ward without getting fried like Mr. Nasir."

The pastor added various things to the bowl and kneaded it with his hands. He lifted something lumpy from the container and set it by the fire. Emily didn't know what the thing was, but it was about six inches long with little arms and legs.

"It has to dry." He reached into another bowl and retrieved the cord of braided hair. He knelt and tied the bracelet around Emily's right ankle. His touch was warm and soft.

"All done," he said.

The lady scowled. "That's it, Toy? Anticlimactic."

"It always is, dear."

He reached out and caressed the bracelet. His touch made Emily warm in the middle. She stretched herself out. If only she could stretch further, it would feel so good.

He stopped. So did the new sensations.

"Touch it again, please," she wanted to say. "It was almost getting really good."

"Did you forget something?" The whore-lady offered the pastor a single rose, its petals dead and wilted.

He shook his head.

The Betty-lady gloated. "To commemorate our anniversary, the day your grandmother died. Such a messy end for a woman so obsessed with cleanliness."

The Betty-lady unbuttoned her corset. "Take me here, Toy. I want the girl to watch."

Emily felt a blast of warm wetness on her face.

She was back in her bed. Sarah sat between her legs, dangling a pocket watch from a chain.

Sarah sneezed again.

"Gesundheit," Emily said. "What are you doing here?"

"Emily, where are you?" Sarah asked.

"In my room, silly."

"Darn. My sneeze must have broken the trance. Do you recall the dark room with the pastor and the lady?"

The younger girl shook her head. "I told you, I can't remember."

"That's probably for the best."

Thirty-Two:
No Escape

Salem, Massachusetts, Monday before dawn, November 10, 1913

ABOUT TWO HOURS BEFORE DAWN Parris staggered up the stairs to the railroad platform, his duffle slung over his shoulder. He'd have to wait at least an hour for the train. He didn't care where it went. Boston, New York, Chicago, as long as it was far away. He'd known invading the mage's home would be risky, but he hadn't expected to lose all his hair to the fiery assault of a powerful Kabbalist. Witchcraft and demonology were both powerful arts, but they were indirect, employing various synergies and powers of others. Men like Mr. Engelmann, they stood in good graces with a *deity*.

Parris knew his own relationship with Jesus to be tenuous at best. If he had the grimoire, things would be different. Ancient demons might not be in the same class as God, but they were more willing to swing around the big guns.

A big Negro with white hair crested the platform and turned toward him, as if he knew exactly where to find him.

Parris tried to run, but it was pointless. His skin burned and chaffed, the duffle was heavy, and the Moor moved with super-human speed. The big man caught him by the shoulder, spun him around, and clocked him hard in the jaw.

The pastor staggered. Stars streaked his vision.

The Moor hoisted him above his head, duffle and all, and started back toward the stairs.

"You come," he said, his accent thick as mud.

Parris hadn't even known he spoke English.

Mr. Nasir was waiting when Parris arrived at the townhouse. It smelled like the beach house. He wondered if the new agent was buried under this porch, too.

"You swore an oath!" the vampire said. He looked older again.

"I panicked," Parris said. "I got inside, but the Horn isn't there. It's not even in this world. He hid it. We knew each other. I can't go back to my old life. He probably called the police, or worse."

"Stop babbling and explain yourself."

Parris told him about Mr. Engelmann. "It's there and not there. He made a hole in his cellar, years ago from the feel of it, and hid the Horn in some other place. There are so many realms, we'll never find it without a key."

"I still don't understand." The vampire wasn't smiling tonight.

"Think of the universe as an onion, with the normal or material world at the core. Heaven, hell, and all the places in between form myriad layers. Mankind has conceptualized endless mythologies, and each exists in a celestial realm."

"Like the places inhabited by *djinn* and *ifrit*?" the vampire said. "Their ilk are most capricious."

"I'm sure they have their weaknesses," Parris said. "Demons and angels, too. But to find a particular hell, one needs a guide, or a key. A person or thing that knows how to get there."

"In time, we shall make this *magi* open the passage," the vampire said. "But there is other news. My old lair was attacked, and one of these trespassers reeked of Gabriel. Maybe they know how to retrieve the Horn."

"Can you find this person?" the pastor asked.

"I've tasted their blood. I'll find them if I have to drain every soul west of the sea."

The vampire seemed to be growing as Parris watched, his fingernails and teeth at least.

"Fouad, prepare one of the extra rooms for our guest," Nasir said. "He'll be staying under your watch until he finds a way to our prize."

Nasir lost what little color he had. His hair thinned and became patchy, his frame more skeletal. The teeth and the claws became long and yellow. His eyes were pits, lifeless as the grave.

"You have disappointed me tonight," he said.

Parris backpedaled, but not fast enough to elude the old vampire. He felt a sting across his cheek. The monster stepped back, flexing his arms, his corpse-like ribs rising and falling. He brought his reddened talons to his mouth, the hideous tongue slithering across the pastor's blood.

You will find the way into this place, a voice screamed in his head. "Through the ward again, across the skein between worlds. The Horn will be ours. The demon shall be bound, and the very heavens shall quake and fall."

And Parris had thought they were becoming friends.

Thirty-Three:
Day of Atonement

Salem, Massachusetts, Monday morning, November 10, 1913

SARAH DREAMT SHE WAS IN a great hall. The high ceilings were covered with molded coffers, the floor was of spotted terrazzo, the walls adorned with rich tapestries.

A hundred guests sat at one side of a long, narrow table, the ram-headed man on a dais near the end. His body was wrapped in heavy robes, his shoulders covered in ermine, and his head crowned with a plume of ostrich feathers. He was old, his dark green muzzle peppered with white. One of his curling horns had broken off near the base.

The other guests seemed hazy, indistinct. Faces elaborate masks — some expressionless white, some checkered, others with long gilded noses and leering smiles.

Sarah sat next to the wolf. A purple and gold embroidered collar held his furred head high. He looked at her intently, his eyes red as rubies.

"My Lady Isabella," he said, "perhaps I was too forward in visiting your chambers last night."

She glanced down at her ball gown and saw the emblem of the doe.

Trust the wolf. It was Isabella's voice, in Sarah's head. *At the moment of the passage, his cruelty and kindness shall unlock everything.*

"I've no regrets, your excellency." Sarah felt her lips move, but the voice wasn't hers. "Are you enjoying your visit to our fair city?"

The wolf's long ears twitched, and he gazed out the arched windows at the crystalline blue lagoon.

"Be careful what you say. We're being watched."

Sarah followed his gaze to find the ram joined by two companions. The gray bat sat on his left, the giant beetle on his right.

I died twice, and the beetle's fire hurt more than the bat's cuts, Isabella's voice said.

The wolf's furry snout tilted in Sarah's direction. "The sun's glare drove me west, but I find the same dark advisors."

Livered servants set a domed tray before the couple, revealing a pastry-topped pie. A page in a colorful doublet wore Charles' face. *Only you can bear the dark gift unscathed.* He bowed theatrically then deftly sliced the pie with his sword.

Three white doves burst from the pastry, cooing loudly. They took flight, accompanied by applause from the guests.

The wolf poured red wine from a crystal decanter into a matching goblet. "Would you like some? The vintage is exotic and ancient, quite lovely."

Sarah accepted the glass. The wine was spicy, meaty, salty. She drained her goblet and took a few bites of the poultry-filled pie.

The wolf gestured again to the head of the table. The bat gorged himself on thick red wine straight from the pitcher, the beetle's ebony limbs were encrusted with tidbits of meat. The ram merely watched, head cocked to the side.

"Tell me about them," Sarah said.

"The bat has long flown through the dark sky, his own nature anathema to all he once held dear. I try to hate him, but he gave us what time we had. It's the beetle who took from me all that was mine."

"And what of the ram?"

"He looms behind them all, painted in sunlight yet never illuminated. Since before creation he has died and been reborn. Like me, revenge is all he has left."

Softly at first, she heard the low and mournful blast of the great horn.

"After I am gone, if another were to share my blood..." she heard herself say.

The wolf stood.

"My lady. Will you do me the honor of allowing me to kiss your hand?"

Now the blare of the horn reverberated through the hall.

"I don't bite." His gem-bright eyes gleamed.

The beast, for all his finery, was still a beast.

But Sarah offered her hand. He sniffed at it, his nose cold and dry — then without warning, nipped her fingers. It stung, and brilliant blood stained her pale sleeve.

Sacrifice is strength, and strength will save our souls, Isabella's voice said.

Sarah woke.

She lay very still, carefully holding the dream details in her head while she lit a candle to transcribe them into her notebook. The window was open, and the cold air nearly blew out the flame. Once she had down everything she could remember, she descended to Papa's study.

"How did you hurt yourself, Sarah? There's blood on your cuff."

She glanced at her left hand. Nothing.

"The other one," Papa said.

She examined her right.

"Just a scratch." She shuddered at the memory of the wolf. "I'll clean up after we talk."

Papa tapped his desk. "I know you borrowed my watch yesterday — and your grandfather's *tallus.*"

Sarah tried to swallow but her throat was closed.

"Last I checked, *thou shall not steal* was still in fashion."

"You were praying. I had to get back to Emily."

"You could've left a note — well, never mind — what did you find?"

Sarah told him, then waited while he retrieved some tobacco and packed his pipe.

"Combining the ritual I taught you with Freud's hypnotic technique was very clever, although it doesn't absolve you. I wasn't aware that disciplines could be hybridized like that."

Theoretician through and through.

"Emily's very sick," she said. "It started after a bracelet showed up on her ankle made of her hair braided with the warlock's."

Papa cradled his head in his hands for a moment.

"That sounds like traditional witchcraft, or perhaps a Creole spell. A binding, literally and figuratively."

"Would you know how to break the spell?"

He took a few drags on his pipe. "I'll do some research, but every occult system has its own style. Witchcraft is gimmicky, intricate, and what's more, I'm not expert with its mechanisms. Emily's very soul is caught up in it. To break the spell but leave her alive and untarnished.... I don't think I could manage that."

"Did you call the police?" she asked.

He blew two concentric smoke rings. He really was quite good at it.

"The sheriff searched the pastor's house. He appears to have vacated the premises."

"I don't think he's working alone." She told Papa what she knew about the vampire and about last night's dream. She concentrated on what had happened, as opposed to what was said or felt, editing out only the parts about her and Alex.

Papa blew another ring. "This is rather worse than I thought. You were very foolish to antagonize this foe."

As fearsome as he is, he serves another. Sarah thought of the bugs pouring from the Moor's flesh and the bat's claws slicing her belly. She scooted her chair forward and squeezed her father's hands.

"But you said God made demons to test us, that we must fight them."

"I was speaking in the abstract." He sighed. "This is my fault in more ways than you know."

She squeezed her eyes closed. Tears leaked onto her cheeks.

"Sarah, Sarah," Papa said. He rubbed her hands. "It's going to be all right. Monsters are real, evil is real, but so is God, so is love."

Slowly, she opened her eyes. "I don't know what to do. I thought I did, but it's not clear anymore."

He considered, stroking his beard. She found this familiar mannerism comforting.

"Like the monster I faced in Vienna, this undead and his warlock seem drawn to the Horn. They must be stopped, and Emily must be saved. This is why God has sent you these dreams."

"But how?" *We must both die twice before we save each other.*

"We'll be very careful." He squeezed one of her hands again. "So long as this vampire isn't invited, he cannot enter our house, and my defenses make it impenetrable to his minions."

"No strangers, no exceptions," Sarah said. "But what about Mama and Mary?"

"I'll talk to them," Papa said. "And no going out at night. You and your friends are to be inside an hour before dark." He jabbed his finger at her. "No exceptions to that, either!"

She bristled, but he was right.

Papa raised the object he'd been holding in front of him. It was a small silver *mezuzah*.

Here, O Israel!
The Lord is our God, the Lord alone.
You shall love the Lord your God with all your heart
and with all your soul and with all your might.

The *Shema*, the central prayer of their faith. A white light shone from the charm. Brighter than bright, it bathed her like the noon sun in summer. She felt as if her very soul had been laid bare. Then the light vanished, and Papa returned the *mezuzah* to his desk.

"What did you do?"

"Some secrets are merely truths, hidden and not revealed," her father said. "I'll show you some techniques that work well with the *mezuzah*, then you'll go to school. The world is a dangerous place, and I'll not leave you unprepared. But don't think, young lady, that I've let you off the hook."

Alex caught her hand as Sarah headed for the library. He pulled her off to the side so they stood alone on the edge of the schoolyard.

"What do you want?" she said.

"Are you still mad at me?"

She pointed at him. "You were supposed to stick by me."

He held up his hands, pleading. "I thought a little caution would be wise."

Hey! She was the one being shoved into graves and disemboweled in her dreams.

"The stakes are too high for caution. I've known Emily her whole life."

"Maybe I've a bit more in the game now, too." Alex glanced down. "This is the first time I've ever had to think about anyone other than myself and Grandfather."

She stepped closer to him. "So who do you have to think about now?"

"I don't know, maybe just the whole group of us." But he took her hand again.

This time, she let him hold onto it. She tugged him a little, and he pushed her to the wall and kissed her. Then kissed her again. She stood on her toes and pressed her forehead against his.

"Everything's more complicated than we thought."

"What do you mean?" he asked.

"While we were at the Williamses, Pastor Parris broke into our house. My father gave him a spiritual whupping. It's weird to think, but he has some serious righteousness on his side. He even taught me a spell."

His eyes widened and he let her go, stepping back. "What kind of spell?"

"More of a prayer, to God and the archangels for protection. But it works, if you believe."

He shook his head. "Grandfather warned me your father was a magician."

"Warned you? How'd he know?" Certainly it had been news to her.

"I'm not sure," he said. "This is just so much to take in, though I suppose it makes sense. I wish I had more faith in Jesus — then I could protect you, too."

Sarah laughed. This time she started the kissing. He didn't seem to object.

"We have to start being careful at night," she said when they stopped for breath. "Never go out after dark. Never invite anyone in. We need to make the Williams understand, too — it's going to be hard."

Alex laid his hand on her side, only inches from her left breast. She could hardly breathe, but she managed to speak.

"And talk to your grandfather. See if he can help with Emily."

He dropped his hand. "You owe me an explanation — how did you know my grandmother was a redhead?"

Sarah stepped back. "Oh… the dreams."

He caressed one of her cheeks with his hand. She wanted to just go limp and have him catch her.

"Am I in any of them?" he asked.

She told him about the Charles dream, the bat dream, and finally the banquet dream, leaving out the business of the Horn — that would take forever to explain.

"A ram, a bat, a giant beetle — and a talking wolf?"

"A dung beetle," Sarah said. "The ancient Egyptians believed Khepri dragged the sun across the sky like a real scarab beetle drags a ball of crap."

"Do you think it's possible," he said, "that your Isabella and Grandfather's are the same?"

"I've been considering that theory. When were they married?"

"I always assumed the 1860s," Alex said.

"I know it's awful to think about, but if it's true and that baby lived, he could've been your father."

Alex's eyes rolled up into his head. She put her hand on his neck — it was cold and clammy.

"Are you all right?"

"Just a terrible headache." His color started to return. "I get those sometimes."

Thirty-Four:
Icons

Salem, Massachusetts, Tuesday evening, November 11, 1913

ALEX WISHED HE'D WORN a sweater as he climbed the drafty spiral staircase inside the turret. Up top, Dmitri had planked over all the windows, draped the room in black velvet, and adorned every vertical surface with Grandfather's precious icon collection. The tiny, austere faces of several hundred saints pondered the imponderable from their golden rectangles. According to Grandfather, the newest icons were several hundred years old, and some well over a thousand.

"Alexandros, glad you could join me." Grandfather sat in a small wheelchair. He looked the fleshiest Alex had seen him since they left Europe.

"Basil the Confessor." Grandfather cleared his throat and pointed to one of the icons. "Martyred for preaching the gospel during the reign of Julian the Apostate, in 363. Each day, his executioners made seven belts from strips of his skin. When there was no more to flay, they pierced him with wooden stakes. His relics rest in a monastery on the slopes of Mount Athos, not far from where we lived when you were young."

Basil glowered — and no wonder. His image held aloft a belt made from his own hide. Alex tried to remember Mount Athos. He was rewarded with images of old trees, crumbling mosaics, and headaches.

Grandfather scanned the walls for another saint, the criteria known only to him. One cruel fate was merely an appetizer, but several made a proper meal.

"Here," the old man said, pointing a long white finger at an icon depicting a saint conversing with a hideous devil. "This is Theophilus of Adana. He's said to have summoned a powerful demon and made a pact to secure his election as Archdeacon of Adana. Satan demanded he renounce the Virgin and her Son in a contract signed in his own blood."

"He won the post?"

"The vote was unanimous." Grandfather chuckled. "But Theophilus, fearing for his soul — obviously with good reason — repented and prayed to the Virgin. He confessed to another bishop, who burned the unholy contract, and the ill-fated Theophilus instantly expired."

"Did he go to heaven or hell?"

Grandfather shrugged. "You could go to his tomb and ask him."

Alex noticed an icon of a tall, thin, regal saint labeled as Constantine XI Palaiologos. One hand held a scroll, the other a cross.

"His name's almost the same as yours. And he has your narrow face."

"Of course," Grandfather said. "We're descended from the son of his third wife, unknown to history."

"So if he hadn't died in May of 1453," Alex said, "you might be Emperor of the Romans even now?"

"That was a long time ago. Some say a beautiful angel turned him to marble and he rests still in a cave near the Golden Gate, waiting to be reawakened. Others say his body was identified in the streets by his purple boots."

Alex looked down at the old man's purple velvet slippers and smiled.

"Is that why you're so obsessed with our bloodline?"

"It *is* a sacred trust!" The old man's voice rang with conviction. "The empty throne of God's Vicegerent on Earth has made our enemies bold."

"Speaking of enemies, Grandfather. You know my new friends, Sam and Anne?"

"I've not met them." The old man continued to stare at St. Constantine.

"They have a younger sister, Emily. She's become the victim of a warlock's curse, and we could use your help."

"You shouldn't get involved. Warlocks cannot be trusted. Remember Theophilus of Adana?" Grandfather tapped the icon.

"I'm not interested in treating with warlocks! I'm interested in saving a girl's life."

Grandfather's eyes blazed. "What's she to me? Now, if it were your friend Sarah.... Her, I like. She has— "

"How can you be so damned cold? Emily is *doomed* if we don't break the spell."

The older man stroked his white beard. "If but one hair on my beard knew what I was thinking, I would pluck it out."

The muscles of Alex's forearms cramped from his clenched fists.

"I didn't cross the ocean to interfere with some petty warlock's seduction of a young girl," Grandfather said. "I came to discover al-Nasir's purpose and put a stop to it."

"All you do is wait!" Alex yelled.

He ran to his room, retrieved the lion-shaped rhyton, and climbed back up the spiral stairs.

"Here!" He thrust the gold cup in the old man's face. "This is action."

Grandfather examined it. "Interesting. Achaemenid Persian. Royal, judging by its weight in gold."

"I took it from al-Nasir's crypt."

"What?" The old man struggled to rise from his chair. He got about a foot off the seat, then thought better and sat down hard. "I'm surprised you're still alive!" He shook the cup at Alex. "You know where the Caliph sleeps?"

"I know where he slept. I don't know what you've been doing with your time, but I found him and slew two of his thralls. If you help us with the curse, I'll tell you what I know."

Grandfather laughed. "You have the Palaogos fire. You're courting death or worse, but ancient as I am, I can still admire a young man's zeal."

"Al-Nasir is working with this warlock," Alex said, "the one who cursed Emily."

Grandfather shuddered and rubbed his arms.

"That changes everything."

"It does?" Alex said.

"Any friend of the Caliph's is a foe of mine. Do you know anything about their activities?"

"You were right about Sarah's father being a practitioner," Alex said. "The warlock broke into their house. Apparently, Mr. Engelmann banished him with prayer!"

"I see." Grandfather stroked his beard. Alex crossed his arms over his chest.

"Why is al-Nasir here?"

"If I were a betting man, I'd say your warlock treats with demons." The old man tapped the icon of Theophilus of Adana a third time. "Al-Nasir has business with one."

"Christ on the cross!" Could this web get any more tangled?

Grandfather smiled. "No need to be profane. Have Dmitri bring me to my library. If I have a suggestion, I'll let you know."

Grandfather woke him in the middle of the night.

"What do you want?" For a moment, Alex wasn't even sure where he was.

"I think I have a spell to break your curse," the old man said.

"That was quick."

"It's always risky to interfere with the magic of another. We'll need the energy of several for even a chance of success."

"But you think you can do it, Grandfather?"

In the light of the candle he held, Alex saw him shake his head.

"I'm far too old for such an endeavor. One of you will have to lead a circle, drawing on the energy of the others. You, your friend Sarah, and the girl's two siblings. Four should be sufficient."

"I've no idea what to do," Alex said.

"I'll show you the appropriate passages," Grandfather said. "But I'm not sure you're the ideal choice. Sorcery requires a certain attunement, one I'm not convinced you possess."

Alex ground his teeth.

"Don't worry. Our line has other talents. Have Sarah lead the ritual — she might be a mere girl, but I suspect she has the proper faculties."

"What makes you think that?" Alex asked.

"An old man's intuition."

Thirty-Five:
Sickbed

Salem, Massachusetts, Wednesday, November 12, 1913

WHEN EMILY STILL HADN'T returned to school by Wednesday, Sarah dropped by the Williams house. The light in the bedroom was dim, and in the three days since she was last here, the air had acquired a new smell, so unpleasant that she found herself breathing through her mouth.

Emily didn't respond when Sarah and Anne slipped inside. She lay in bed looking pale and sweaty, propped up on a pile of pillows, her hair damp and matted.

"One of her calm phases," Anne said. Sarah could hear tears in her friend's voice. "She's feverish all the time now."

Anne crossed the room and took a damp towel from a bowl to wipe her sister's forehead. The scene was so reminiscent of Judah's room near the end that Sarah wanted to curl in a ball and cry.

Emily's eyes opened, the whites bloodshot.

"Mom-my?" She moved her tongue as if it was too big for her mouth.

"It's me, Emily," Anne said. "Sarah's come to visit."

Emily's gaze drifted to Sarah. "Hi." She made a halfhearted attempt at a smile.

"How are you feeling?" Sarah asked.

"Thirsty. Tired."

Anne poured her a glass of water and told her about what had happened with the bracelet last night.

"Sam couldn't get through it with a pair of gardening shears — the darn thing's hard as steel. But that wasn't the worst of it. She started coughing up blood, and her eyes filled with it."

"I've been reading a lot," Sarah said. "It's not like there's a manual, but Emily said the pastor was trying to draw on her energy. I think the bracelet is rooted in her life force." She put an arm around Anne. "I also think there's a second physical anchor for the spell. That thing Emily saw the pastor dry by the fire."

"How does that help us?"

"I'm not sure yet. But—"

"I hate being sick," Emily said.

"Everyone does, you'll be better soon," Anne said.

The three girls were quiet for just a few minutes when Emily grew restless. She squirmed and twisted, grasping feebly at the blankets. Her movements were wild and uncoordinated but not fast or forceful. And she moaned.

"Emily!" Sarah took hold of her arm. The only response was louder moaning.

"What are you doing?" Anne asked.

"Just trying to see if she knows we're here," Sarah said.

Anne bent over her little sister and smoothed her hair.

"I wish we'd never gone riding that day," she said. "Although Emily was spending time with Pastor Parris before then." She straightened up and turned to Sarah. "The vampire-pastor connection doesn't make any sense."

Sarah considered whether to burden her with the story of the Horn. Her friend deserved to know, but it might push her over the edge.

"There's a pattern here, but we keep missing it," she said.

"Why'd this happen to her?" Anne said. "She's the only Williams kid who actually reads the Bible."

On her way out, Sarah found herself blocked by Emma, the Williamses' big colored cook.

"You going to help her?"

"I'm trying," Sarah said. "I don't know what's wrong. Hopefully the fever will break soon."

"'Tis no fever," Emma said. "I throw *Ifá*, and you gots to fix what you broke."

She couldn't save Charles, but with Emily she had a chance. She slumped against a kitchen counter.

"I don't know how, Emma."

She didn't know what *Ifá* was either, but Emma knew things. If Papa's prayers worked, maybe the cook's did, too.

"Lady Tituba have big *ashé*." Emma cupped one of Sarah cheeks. "You ask her."

Emma always talked about *ashé*, which apparently meant life force, a kind of magical energy. This Lady Tituba must be some kind of mystic woman.

"Where do I find her?"

It was stupid to go alone, but Sarah did it anyway. She had to walk the better part of an hour to reach the address Emma gave her.

The Point was a poor section of town, mostly four-story wooden tenement buildings crowded so close a man could spit on his neighbors. As she climbed the narrow wooden stairs to the fourth floor, she smelled an array of foreign spices. Loud laughter and conversation echoed through the thin walls, little of it in English. This was an immigrant neighborhood, where you rented if the steamer passage that brought you here was all the money you had.

A small colored boy answered her knock. "What you want?"

"I'm looking for Lady Tituba," Sarah said.

"That be my grandmama," the boy said. "Come."

The apartment was tiny, dark, and smelled of a thousand things. Bundles of dried herbs hung from the ceiling, shelves of jars lined the walls. A preserved cat floated in pink liquid in a tank and dead frogs filled a container to bursting.

The boy left, but a lady returned in his place. If she was his grand-mother, she'd been a young mother. Rail thin and barefoot, she wore a long white dress that set off her dark skin and striking features.

"So what's a nice white girl doing in my fine upstanding neighborhood?"

Her southern accent made Sarah think of wind chimes hanging from a willow tree.

"I want to know about a bracelet made of hair. Oily, smelling of licorice and calamus." No point in being coy here.

Lady Tituba cocked her head. She must iron her hair straight, something Sarah had almost done last year after some girls at school teased her about her 'Jew curls.'

"Oil of bend over?" the lady said.

"Huh?"

Lady Tituba drifted to a shelf. The brightness in the room seemed to follow her. She broke the paraffin seal on a jar and held it out.

"Put this on your lover, and he'll bend over and take it anytime you want."

Sarah felt herself grow hot. She couldn't shake the image of Alex bending over. But she gave the jar a sniff.

"This smells like what I'm talking about," Sarah said.

It was hard not to stare into the wells of Lady Tituba's eyes. What gazed back seemed older than the woman before her — much older.

"What would the oil do on a bracelet?" Sarah said.

"Make a bracelet of bend over. Some call it a commanding bracelet." She held up the jar again. "I put grains of paradise in mine, for extra potency." The woman's smile revealed perfect white teeth. "Is it power you seek? In the back room I have the mummified hand of a king."

Sarah shook her head. "The oil, would it make someone sick?"

"Nothing comes without a price." The lady stepped closer, close enough for Sarah to smell her — spices fried in a skillet. And then, far in the distance, she heard the slow and mournful tone of the horn.

"No, you haven't come for power."

"Wh-what if a man put the bracelet on a girl," Sarah said, "formed from both their hair braided together?"

"Then she be bound to him. Body and soul." The lady blinked. Green tadpoles swam in the muddy ponds of her irises.

Not good, but she might as well buy some oil. "How much?"

"Five dollars a pint."

"That's outrageous."

"You can't put a price on quality." Lady Tituba leaned closer still. "But it's not just the three of us in this room, is it?"

Sarah's eyes darted about. Was the boy still here?

The lady lifted her free hand to caress Sarah's cheek. The horn droned louder and louder.

The lady froze, her pupils consumed her eyes, and she jumped back.

"Mighty *Eshu*, forgive me. I didn't recognize you." Now she looked away.

"I just want to help my friend," Sarah said. "I need to know how to remove the bracelet— "

"The passage is unlocked. What is lost will be found."

Lady Tituba tossed the jar to Sarah and shrank back the way she'd came.

"No charge. The oil is a gift."

She slammed the door behind her.

Sarah's found herself alone with the medicinal jars and their occupants. A dead possum gave her the evil eye. The horn continued to blare.

In her mind's eye, she saw Charles mouthing: *The passage is unblocked. What is lost will be found.*

Thirty-Six:
The Painted Man

Salem, Massachusetts, Wednesday night, November 12, 1913

AL-NASIR LEFT HIS NEW LAIR by the fourth-story window. Truth be told, this one was much better than the last, at least after Tarik had cleansed the sarcophagus and decorated the crypt.

He circled Salem, tasting the cool night air. This was his third night hunting. The thieves' scents — two men and two women — were burned into his memory. But the process of finding them was tedious, sniffing them out street by street, house by house.

Then again, what did he have if not time?

He flew over his former home and turned south, searching new areas as the mood struck him. At one point he was obliged to cross the estuary that separated Salem proper from the Marblehead Peninsula. Flying over deep water was uncomfortable at best, so he bled height in exchange for extra speed.

Once on the peninsula, he inspected each dwelling, circling one then flying to the next. It might take weeks, but he would find them.

Then he felt the call.

Fouad. The Moor requested his return. The nature of their bond didn't allow for a specific message, but he knew the old servant wouldn't summon him idly.

Thirty minutes later, the vampire was close to home, flying over the surrounding neighborhood. Fouad waited in the townhouse crypt, but al-Nasir hadn't eaten in two days, and hours of searching had rendered his appetite sharper than a Saracen's blade.

The ancient blood gods looked after their own. A boy of perhaps twelve, a chimney sweep, struggled with his long brushes on a nearby roof. The vampire dropped from the sky, one hundred and forty pounds of dead weight. There was no time for finesse, nor did al-Nasir bother to return to human form. He yanked the boy's neck to the side and tore it open with his razor-sharp incisors. He savored the sweetness of the kill, the warm flesh, the hot salty rush of blood. Haste made him sloppy, allowing some of the liquid to splash the wooden roof tiles. No matter. He fed perched like an enormous gargoyle, wings wrapped around his spasming prey.

Al-Nasir liked to toy with his food. Ideally, each meal was to be savored over several evenings. Even if it was to be a one-night affair, he liked to dance with death. Every human had his threshold, the exact amount of blood loss beyond which no recovery was possible. To bring prey to that limit, pull back, then return to it again and again was to court the sublime. When finally the point of no return was reached, the blood took on a thick syrupy quality, like oasis water siphoned from a palm. Tonight, however, he plunged right through to the brutal end. It was not the most enjoyable meal but it did provide a kind of quick and dirty satisfaction. He likened it to the difference between a lover savored all night in the harem and a virgin sodomized during the bloody sack of a city.

Each had its appeal.

He raised his crimson-stained mouth from the body and surveyed the rooftops. His townhouse was only four buildings away, so it wouldn't do to leave behind the broken empty husk. 'Never eat where you sleep' was an ancient tenant of vampire survival. He'd have to drag the corpse back to the crypt and let Fouad dispose of it.

He clutched the cooling body in his talons as he flapped from rooftop to rooftop until he alighted on his own, an exhausting but brief ordeal. He shifted back to human form, grabbed the cadaver by one ankle, and dragged it across the roof until he was above a window.

Fouad waited inside.

"Master, he's been asking for you most urgently." Al-Nasir had no need to ask who *he* was.

"I'll speak to him in a moment. First, I'm going to lower a body down for you to pull inside."

Al-Nasir crawled back up, gripped the dead boy's hand, and pulled. Clinging to the brick, he adjusted himself so the body dangled in front of the window. Fouad grabbed the corpse by the belt, tugged it inside, and was wrapping it in a large sheet when the vampire entered.

"Master, may I dismember and feed him to my carrion bugs? I know the sawing is messy, but I've not so feasted since we left Morocco."

"I suppose you could use the bathtub in the fourth bedroom," the vampire said. "Just make sure the warlock doesn't walk in on you. He might die of fright."

Fouad's chest shook with mirth. "Thank you, Master." He threw the sheet-wrapped form over his shoulder and lumbered away. No blood dripped, one of the advantages of al-Nasir's diet.

A faint bell tinkled from elsewhere in the apartment.

The vampire sighed and hurried to the study where he kept the encaustic painting. Fouad had hung it on the wall and covered it with black silk curtains. The vampire pulled these aside to reveal the heavy wax portrait.

It glared back at him.

"You made me wait long enough," the portrait said.

The man in the painting had a negroid complexion, almost dark green, a bird-like nose, and soft, boyish brown eyes. His hair was dark and curly in the Hellenistic style. The beeswax and pigment mixture was slathered on three dried and ancient boards whose integrity had been much compromised by the years. Although nearly two millennia old, the artist's thick strokes still retained their intense and lifelike color.

"I was hungry," the vampire told the Painted Man. They spoke French mixed with bits of North African dialect. Although an Egyptian, the man disdained Arabic.

The painted mouth opened to speak. "The witch will—"

"Mr. Parris is a warlock," the vampire said. "I've been waiting three days to tell you something important."

The portrait steepled his greenish fingers. "On October eighteenth, at the close of the wretched one's Sabbath, you made a kill in the manner I instructed?"

Even when fired high into the air, the old sorcerer's arrows struck their target.

"As you requested, I selected a mortal at random and crucified him upside-down upon a tree." The vampire neglected to mention he'd given the boy the dark gift. That had been his own personal nod to chaos.

"I knew it was so."

Then why'd he ask? "Mortals assaulted my lair. At least three or four. One's blood reeked of the archangel."

The man in the painting quivered with excitement. Al-Nasir had the impression of a ram's horn curling about the man's left ear, and a stump where the right horn should have been.

"The feint has been answered," the Painted Man said.

"No coincidence, I assume."

The face grinned. "Coincidence is what mortals call the knots in Klotho's weave they cannot comprehend."

"The warlock located a dwelling that once contained the Horn. He's a coward, but skilled. He believes the object is no longer in the material plane."

"So I thought," the painting said. "That insufferable mass of feathers has returned it to more angelic haunts."

Things might've been easier if al-Nasir had been told that from the beginning. He pointed to the floor — Parris was confined two levels below.

"The warlock says we need a key to open the passage and enter this other place."

"The passage is unlocked, the key has been found," the man said.

"Which means?"

"All part of the Great Plan." The image tapped the stump where his horn had been. "When I recover what that upstart archangel stole, he shall rue the very day of his creation." The painted mouth cackled. "The witch will need to speak to you the night of November fourteenth."

"I told you," al-Nasir said, "he's a warlock."

"Don't forget, November fourteenth. By then, he'll know what to do and will require your services."

"I'll talk to him then."

"But not on the fourteenth, on the sixteenth. Visit him on the sixteenth."

Dealing with the old sorcerer's prophecies required the patience of the dead.

"You must gain access to the Horn before November twenty-first," the Painted Man said. "Otherwise, I'll be forced to send the beetle. He's now strong enough to cross the ocean. My vassal is most dogged."

Al-Nasir harbored a fantasy of giving the beetle's little jackal a swift kick. The last thing he wanted was sharing — or worse, yielding — his glory to Khepri.

"I never fail. Keep the bug away from me."

"I'll keep an eye on the situation." The man in the portrait chuckled at his own joke. The chuckle soon became a giggle, and then a cackle.

"I'll see what the warlock needs when it's time." Al-Nasir closed the curtain on the laughter. He knew the Painted Man's fit would last for hours. Many centuries they had known each other, and he seemed to be getting worse. It was hard to tell.

Almost dawn, and Fouad was undoubtedly taking his glory with the carcass. Tomorrow night, he'd try a different tack. The *magi* Parris had fought must know something. Al-Nasir smiled. It was time to invite himself over.

Thirty-Seven:
Unexpected Visitor

Salem, Massachusetts, Thursday evening, November 13, 1913

PAPA'S STUDY GROUP was near Boston, and he and Mama were staying the night with friends. This left Sarah home alone — which was fine by her — although, technically, Mary was there, but she rarely left her attic room in the evenings.

Sarah had in mind to use this time to practice what her father had taught her, so she changed into her special white prayer shirt and crept into his study. She was freezing, particularly her feet, and it felt quite naughty to walk around the house with no underwear.

She rifled through Papa's books for anything that might help Emily and was about to give up when she found a false backing behind which he'd hidden several volumes. The most interesting was handwritten in medieval Spanish Hebrew, encoded in a cipher that required her to hold a hand mirror up to the pages so she had to read the text inverted.

It was worth the trouble. While the book was anonymous, she thought the author might be Rambam, the famous mystic from Córdoba — odd to think the vampire Nasir was from the same city and might even have known him.

She had no idea how long she'd been reading when she heard an odd thunking at the front door. When she rose, her legs were numb. Thoughts of protective circles constructed from concentric rings of the divine consciousness filled her head. Only when she opened the door to the freezing November night did she remember she was only wearing a thin shirt.

A small man stood on the sidewalk, twenty feet away. His face glowed like alabaster in the light of the streetlamp, but his dark-clad body was lost in the night.

"Good evening," he said, his accent melodic, familiar yet not.

"May I help you?"

"Oh, I'm certain." His nostrils flared. "You can be of great assistance."

It was him.

The horn rang in her ears, slow and mournful. For a moment she lost herself in the dark pits that passed for eyes.

She took a step back. He couldn't enter unless she let him.

"You're Mr. Nasir?"

He smiled, teeth yellow white. "You have me at a disadvantage. It's not every night I meet such a lovely young lady, particularly one clad like a slave girl."

A frigid gust made her nipples stand hard against the thin material. When she didn't give her name, he continued.

"You have something I need. We can come to an accommodation."

"I doubt that."

His nostrils flared again. "I can smell it from where I stand."

The Strength of God sings in our blood. The horn sounds our sacrifice. Did the smell of the Archangel Gabriel's Horn linger in the house like last week's liver and onions?

"I was once a man of honor." He smiled again. "If you give it to me, I'll let you and yours live."

She noticed a number of small rocks scattered on the porch and remembered the odd sound that had drawn her to the door. She forced her face into a smile.

"If you want it so badly, why are you standing so far away?"

He took a step — then snarled and covered his face.

"I'll take an invitation if you don't mind," he said.

Sarah was numbed by more than the chill. She hugged herself and used the sole of one foot to cover the toes of the other.

"When I was a boy," the vampire said, "my father would pull me from the tent to name the constellations. I know the desert wind was cold on our faces but I can't remember how it felt."

"You're from Córdoba?" she said.

"You know me?"

The blackness of his eyes bored into hers. Stupid. She'd over-played her hand.

"I'm good with languages, your accent," she said.

"I think not. No one remembers al-Andalus."

When Alex had told her he was from medieval Moorish Spain, she'd found a book in the library called *Tales of the Alhambra* by Washington Irving. She quoted from memory:

"Behold for once a daydream realized; yet I can scarce credit my senses, or believe that I do indeed inhabit the palace of Boabdil, and look down from its balconies upon chivalric Granada."

"You surprise." He spread his arms wide. "While the kings of Europe accused your people of blood libel, I let your doctors treat my own sons."

She had to remind herself to stay on the offensive. "Bread baked with the blood of children is more to your taste then mine."

"Your eyes betray your curiosity. Ask anything of me."

"All you know is death."

"I've seen kingdoms rise and fall, yet I remain." Part of her wanted to step forward and fall into his eyes. "Tales of forgotten days dance on my tongue."

Her mind was drawn back to the book she'd been reading. "Did you know Moses Maimonides?"

He caressed his pointy little beard, not so differently from the way Papa stroked his.

"The mystic and I met several times in Fustat. He wished to study me, even gave me a urine flask so I could provide him with some of my blood. I didn't oblige him, but I still have the flask."

"You kept it?"

"You stood in the same room… when you slew Nabil. Last year he celebrated a centennial in my service, and you made worms of him." A dark tear came to his eye.

Could this ancient creature feel grief? Could he love?

The horn's long note droned on, reminding her of what was at stake.

"Why do you want…." She couldn't bring herself to say *the Horn*.

"To right old wrongs."

Her surge of anger surprised. "You'll have to step over my dead body to get it."

The gentlemanly expression melted. Now only nothingness stared back at her. *Invite me in*, his voice screamed from everywhere.

Sarah collapsed to her knees, holding her hands over her ears.

Invite me in!

But she didn't. She slammed the door shut, then ran to the window and peered out from behind the edge of the curtain.

The black pits of his eyes found her anyway.

Eventually you'll tire of hiding. And I'll be waiting.

The dark shape took to the air and was gone.

Thirty-Eight:
Exorcism

Salem, Massachusetts, Sunday, November 16, 1913

ALEX DROPPED A STACK OF BOOKS on the breakfast table in front of Sarah.

"We need two ingredients," she said, looking down at an open volume she'd brought herself. "*Oil of bend over* and *red brick dust,* extra strength. Who comes up with these names, anyway?"

"I don't know, but you can bend over if you like." He reached behind her and placed a hand on her bottom. She shook him off with her evil eye.

"We only have a couple of hours until the twins bring Emily."

"I couldn't help myself."

Sarah returned to the book. "I bought some of the oil. It's made from calamus, licorice, and damiana. Similar to the commanding oil used in the original spell but it has a few extra ingredients. Hopefully they'll lend a little more potency, enough to dominate."

"You bought it?" he asked.

"Emma knew a lady."

"A store for witches?"

"Alex, we do live in Salem. Any idea about the brick dust?"

"Ahead of you there." He'd been slogging through Grandfather's generous occult library. "I have everything. We can make it now, but you aren't going to like it." He brought over two bowls filled with powder.

"The white is lye, the red is crushed brick I smashed with a sledge-hammer yesterday. It's a symbolic substitute for the original, more powerful ingredient."

"Which is?" Sarah asked.

"Um. Dried blood, from a woman."

"Why are you looking at me all funny?"

Alex couldn't decide if he was uncomfortable on principle or because the subject was secretly fascinating.

"Special woman's blood, you know."

"I'm well aware," she said. "The brick works though?"

"It's supposed to."

"What do we do with the powders?"

"This is the part you won't like," Alex said. "We mix them with urine to form a paste."

She laughed but turned red. He found it fetching.

"Take them to the outhouse and do your thing," she said.

"Well… it needs to be from whoever's controlling the ritual."

She rolled her eyes. "Point me to a room with no windows and a locked door."

Alex mixed the powders, led Sarah to the canning pantry, and placed the bowl on the floor.

"It doesn't lock from inside," he said, "but I swear I'll stand guard."

Sarah entered the tiny room. "If you fail, you won't have a life to swear on." She slammed the door closed.

By the late afternoon they were almost ready. Yesterday, Sarah had given them all an earful about the importance of ceremonial white clothing, but he'd no complaints as hers was a sheer white dress. The house was fairly cold, so she'd thrown her overcoat on top and pulled on dark stockings. It was a peculiar look. Alex tried not to stare, but he found himself looking forward to the time when she'd remove the jacket. He went to kiss her.

She pushed him away. "Not tonight. You'll upset the purity of the ritual."

Grandfather wheeled his chair into the room.

"Sir," Sarah said after greeting the old man, "none of these occult books agree on how this is done. They either have no details or they're full of incomprehensible instructions. Do I pick one to go with or do I combine elements from each?"

"I've seen a wizened patriarch banish leprosy using only the desiccated finger of a saint," Grandfather said, "and I've seen an African witchdoctor knit a broken bone with mud, a boar femur, and his own blood. Each man was a conduit for a power greater than himself."

Sarah sighed. "I hadn't thought of it that way. Still, I'm confused. What power did Pastor Parris use to curse Emily? My father is convinced that he himself couldn't break the spell because he doesn't believe in it, at least not the way the pastor does."

"The pastor is a Lutheran of sorts, but witchcraft is not a Christian magic," Grandfather said. "Some demon or other power must have brokered his binding. There's always an exchange, and nothing's ever free."

"I've heard that before," Sarah said.

The old man chuckled.

"As for your original question — you should include those elements *you* think will be the most effective." The clock chimed.

"Alex," she said, "the Williamses will be here soon. Go upstairs and dress. All white, and no metal, jewelry, or leather."

He went to his room and changed into some old linen Feast Day clothes. He debated what to do with Grandfather's wolf's head medallion. Sarah had been clear about no metal, but he didn't want to part with it, so he tucked it under his tunic.

Returning, he paused at the door.

"Sir," he heard Sarah say, "I'm going to be blunt. When your wife Isabella died, did she become a vampire?"

Alex didn't dare walk in now. Jesus only knew how the old man would react.

"I was wondering if you might think that," Grandfather said.

"I'm right?"

"My brother arranged my earlier marriages, but with her…. We fell in love the night we met."

"I'm sorry," Sarah said. "Is that why you hunt the undead? Because they killed her?"

"Her death is behind everything I do."

"She isn't still around, is she? Undead, I mean," she asked.

Alex's head was beginning to pound. These blasted headaches. Images flashed through his head. A wolf with bloody jaws. Dmitri wrestling with it.

"No," the old man said. "The monsters destroyed even that a long time ago."

"Who are they? Was it Nasir, or the beetle—"

Alex swooned. The room spun and he crumpled to the floor.

After Sarah helped him up, Alex ate a whole plate of *dolmades* and tossed down a glass of wine. His headache was mostly gone — as long as he didn't think too hard.

He heard the sound of gravel under the Model T's wheels. When he opened the door, Sam carried Emily inside, bundled in blankets. Alex hadn't seen the poor girl in a week, but she looked like she hadn't eaten since then.

"What did you tell your parents?" he asked Sam.

"Anne convinced Aunt Edna to invite them to dinner."

"This better work," Anne said.

Sarah led them to the room Dmitri had cleared. Even the rugs had been removed, so only the wall decorations and a too-large-to-move cabinet remained.

"Put her on the floor," Sarah said. "I know it's not the most comfortable, but we don't need any extraneous elements intruding into our ritual space." She pulled off her jacket and stockings and folded them in the hall outside the room. As Alex suspected, the white dress was thin, and its sleeves ended at the elbows. He wasn't sure he'd ever seen Sarah's elbows before.

She knelt barefoot to light the circle of candles. He could just make out the shape of her knees and thighs, which forced him to fight down an unseemly erection.

"Nothing impure can cross the line of candles," Sarah said when she was done.

He hoped thoughts didn't count.

"Mr. Palaogos," Sarah said, "please remain outside the circle, as your chair might pollute the space."

"Happy to oblige," the old man said.

Sarah pointed back at the door. "I need you men out of the room so Anne and I can prepare Emily."

In the hall, Sam pulled off his jacket, belt, and shoes. The white pants and shirt he wore underneath were several sizes too small, absurdly tight.

"Yeah, I know," he said. "I look like a guy who stole a midget sailor's suit."

"Aye aye, matey!" Alex said.

When Sarah let them back in, the bedroom reeked of *oil of bend over*, sweet and medicinal, like a tonic so bad it could scare the cough right out of you.

"Step carefully over the candles," Sarah said, "and sit on the cardinal points of the compass. Alex here on the north, Sam here on the south." She tapped their spots with the ball of her foot.

Alex sat crossed-legged, facing Emily in the center. She was curled on her side in the fetal position, wearing only a white nightgown. In the flickering candlelight, her skin looked slick and shiny. Alex had never seen so much girl-leg. This was going to be a problem.

He tried to use a nearby painting by Caravaggio to distract himself. According to Grandfather, this 1601 rendering of Saint Peter's crucifixion was intended for Santa Maria del Popolo in Rome. Apparently the church had forced the artist to paint another version, where the saint's face didn't so viscerally reflect being nailed upside-down to a cross.

"In case you're wondering," Sarah said, "Anne and I smeared the *oil of bend over* on Emily's skin. It's supposed to help us compel her to reject the curse." She held the bowl containing the paste of lye, red brick, and urine. "I'm going to make a circle around her with this to contain and reflect the evil essence of the spell. No matter what happens, stay inside the candles and outside the circle of paste."

Sarah grimaced as she worked. The reddish stuff probably smelled like piss, but the cloying odor of calamus had pretty much killed Alex's olfactory sense.

"Everyone hold hands," Sarah said after she finished her circle.

They all had to scoot close to the red line to reach each other. Sarah was on Alex's left, Anne to his right. The hand holding started to excite him again — that *oil of bend over* had some powerful aphrodisiac qualities. He tried a second time to distract himself with Saint Peter's final hours.

Grandfather wheeled into the room and positioned himself outside the line of candles. Sarah began to chant.

Emily stirred. She looked feverish, not fully conscious. Alex found himself focusing on her legs again and had to close his eyes. She was sick, and far too young. He watched Sarah instead. Her hand was soft but slick, hopefully not because of any lingering piss paste.

As Sarah continued chanting, Emily's body began to thrash.

"Look at the bracelet—" Anne said.

"Shhh," her brother said.

Emily was kicking her feet, but Alex thought he saw tiny tendrils of black smoke coming off the anklet, writhing about like snakes on a Gorgon's head.

His hands grew warm. At first there was just an itch on his palms, but it gained intensity, then subsided, then again became fierce. Emily's twitching seemed keyed to these pulses. As each wave crested she extended her limbs, and as it declined she relaxed. She began to moan, then pressed her hands across her chest and belly, caressing. Then moved her hands between her legs and began to rub.

Alex was horrified — and aroused. Everything felt so wrong. Sarah's eyes were closed, but her expression looked concentrated. The twins both stared at their sister in horror.

Anne pulled on Alex's hand, trying to free herself. She leaned forward on her knees.

"We have to stop this. Look what she's doing!"

"Don't break the circle," Grandfather said. "The evil spirit must be exorcised before she can be free."

Anne settled back.

The tendrils of smoke were at least six inches long now. Diffuse, they whipped and coiled back and forth around Emily's foot. Angry welts ran up her leg.

The energy crested again. Emily gripped her groin, spread her legs and pressed her feet outwards. Impossibly, they found purchase at the border formed by the red brick paste. One foot hung in the air in front of Alex's face, the flesh indented as if pushing against some unseen wall.

Sarah increased the volume of her chant with each rising tide. As the latest wave rose, Alex had a distinct impression of rising with it to stand in a tiny bedroom. The vampire sat on the bed, a taller man in a ragged clerical suit before him. This man — he assumed it was Pastor Parris — had patchy white hair and his skin was red and blistered. He gesticulated wildly, holding a doll-like bundle of rags in one hand.

Alex's vision wavered, the energy crashed, and his consciousness returned to the room and the ritual.

For a moment Emily was calmer, although the welts on her leg now pulsed, ugly and unnatural, and the black tendrils of smoke had grown a foot long. She was panting and her eyes were rolled back into her head.

The next time the energy mounted, Emily arched up off the floor. She was grounded at one end by her head and shoulders, her feet braced on the barrier created by their spell. The rest of her was suspended. She pressed her hands into her crotch with frenetic energy. Alex's erection now stood at full mast, bracing his pants like a tent pole. All attempts to banish it proved futile.

The red welts now reached up through the collar of Emily's nightgown. The vessels in her neck throbbed.

Alex felt a burn at his breast where the silver amulet rested against his skin. He had the sensation of floating outside his body. Sarah's hair was plastered to her forehead with sweat. Sam's jaw was locked, as if seeing this finished was his only road to salvation. Anne just looked scared to death.

Grandfather alone seemed caught in the normal flow of time. He waited, watching the scene before him, expectant. Alex had seen that expression before.

With a snap, he returned to himself and attempted to yank his hands free. Anne released, but he couldn't shake himself from Sarah's grasp so he used his right hand to sweep aside the line of red powder, severing the circle.

The door flew open and the air was sucked from the room. The candles snuffed out, and Emily collapsed in a whimpering heap. The black tendrils vanished, and the red welts began to fade.

"What did you do?" Sarah's face was a furious mask of red.

"I had to stop it," Alex said. "It was killing her. If we kept on, she'd have died."

"But it was working!" Sarah said. "You ruined everything."

"The curse would have broken," Alex said, "and maybe turned on the pastor, but Emily wouldn't have survived. Isn't that right, Grandfather?"

The old man looked at Sarah, who started to speak but he held up his hand.

"A hex of this sort is stretched tight between two points. Break the anchor at one, and it will snap back to the other with great force."

"Enough force to kill her," Alex said.

"You were a part of the circle," he said. "If you feel so strongly, perhaps it was so."

"That wasn't natural," Sam said. "There has to be another way."

Sarah gave Alex an anguished, angry look. It hurt like hell.

"You ruined it!" She grabbed his hand and tugged him out of the room, around the corner, and down the hall. Her face was still crimson. "Not only did you destroy the spell, but I saw — no, felt — you looking at her."

He'd never seen her mad like this.

"It was the oil," he said. "I couldn't help it."

"I can't take this anymore." She put her hand on his chest, pushing the wolf's head medallion into his skin. "And what about this?"

"What about it?"

"I told you not to wear jewelry. You ruined it!"

She'd never used this tone of voice with him, but that hardly mattered. Slow to rouse, his own anger grew.

"You should thank me for saving Emily's life."

"It's done." She walked away, stopped only to grab her coat and stockings.

He wanted to go after her.

Anne poked her head out of the room. "Is it safe to help Emily?"

"Go ahead," Alex said. "Hopefully she's no worse off than before."

He heard the door to the house slam. Running to the front hall he opened it and caught a glimpse of Sarah's white form reaching the gate. He started to go after her.

"Wait!" he yelled.

She paused for only a second. "Leave me alone. I can't see you right now."

This froze him on the steps. Black clouds gathered over his head as he watched her go. It was dark out. Jesus, please let the vampire not be out tonight.

"If this ritual thing won't work, what will?" Sam was asking as Alex crept back inside.

"Perhaps you need to secure the other end of the anchor," Grandfather said. "With both ends they can be destroyed simultaneously, and their negative energies will cancel. Do you know what or where it is?"

"It must be that thing the pastor was holding in the room I saw," Anne said. "Mr. Engelmann really did a job on him, he looks terrible!"

So Alex wasn't the only one to see the pastor.

Grandfather chuckled. "Nevertheless, he remains a warlock of unknown skills and intent, and he's in league with a nine hundred-year-old vampire. Caution would seem prudent."

"Damn caution! He's killing my sister!" Sam swept Emily up and carried her from the room.

Anne turned to Alex. "What was that business between you and Sarah?"

"She's just mad I broke her spell."

Anne put her hand on his arm. "It was the right thing to do, but an apology never hurt anyone."

Thirty-Nine:
Grave Robbers

Salem, Massachusetts, Sunday night, November 16, 1913

THE PAINTED MAN MIGHT HAVE his bowmen crossed with his nobles, but he was rarely mistaken, so after waking on November sixteenth, al-Nasir fast-stepped downstairs to the pastor's room.

His knock went unanswered and the door was locked. The vampire sniffed — the warlock was inside. Perhaps he slept.

Al-Nasir tried to relax his mind and concentrate on diffuse qualities. It was like groping around blindfolded in a junk-filled chest for a particular item, one he'd never felt before. For a moment he thought he might have it, then it slipped from his grasp. For several years now, he'd been trying to transform into a vaporous mist. He knew of only two vampires who had mastered the skill, and they were both over a thousand years old. Still, it was never too early to hope. He'd always been precocious.

Sighing, he pushed the door with a finger and snapped the lock. There were so few things to look forward to.

The warlock was in his cot, and his snores grated on the vampire's sensitive ears. The Hebrew *magi* had blasted half the hair from the man's head and turned what remained white as bone. The vampire brushed his long yellow fingernails against Mr. Parris' blistered cheek.

The pastor jerked upright and gathered his legs up to his chest.

"Get away from me!"

Al-Nasir fast-stepped to the far side of the room. No need to antagonize the man. Besides, he loved showing mortals his unnatural speed. Fast-stepping was something one could begin to learn not long after death, but it took centuries to acquire his level of mastery.

"No harm intended. I already ate. My partner said you'd have need of me tonight."

The pastor's brow furrowed. "I suppose he was right. I finally know how to break those magical protections."

He opened a steamer trunk and rummaged until he found an object wrapped in black silk.

"A brass knife?" al-Nasir said.

"After a week of research I've figured it out," the warlock said. "That esoteric ward is based on a model of the Temple of Solomon, built in Jerusalem to house the tablets Moses received on Mt. Sinai. This weapon will help us destroy it."

"Care to shed some light on how?"

Mr. Parris waved his arms like a man swarmed by bees. "That ward isn't just a spell," he said, "it's a mystical building coexistent with the physical building, an occult or celestial temple."

"So?"

"I stole the blade from the ward's creator. It even has the Mr. Engelmann's name on it. This makes it a perfect fulcrum for my art. Well, one of my arts, anyway, as technically I practice two."

Spittle flew from Mr. Parris' mouth and the vampire fast-stepped to avoid it. The man had initially seemed dry, but once you found the oasis, the water pooled deep.

The pastor pulled a brown doll out of his pocket. It smelled like shit.

"Witchcraft makes use of the great principle of sympathy, or 'like equals like.' Say I was to make a likeness of some poor sap in clay and bind it to him with his hair and blood. It's the likeness of *form* and the likeness of *nature*, derived from the hair and blood, that bind the doll to the man. Once bound, sympathy prevails. Burn the doll, burn the man."

Actually, this made sense to al-Nasir. His dead flesh worked no spells, but over the centuries he'd seen his share of the dark arts.

"So we make a little model of this building and destroy it?"

"Precisely! The home will then cease to exist, in an esoteric sense. Not only will the ward be broken, you won't even need an invitation to enter what's left."

Fouad and Tarik had their orders for tomorrow, but it was good to have options. Al-Nasir only had five nights left. That dark-haired girl at the house had reeked of Gabriel, clearly the same trollop whose blood he'd tasted near the old lair. Even if she herself didn't know how to open the way to the Horn, she would provide irresistible leverage against the infidel *magi*.

"If the form is the building," al-Nasir said, "what's the nature? Spiritual temples hardly have hair and blood."

The pastor beamed. "But they do! Mr. Engelmann made this guardian temple, and he has a body!"

"But how do we get it? You're too much of a coward to face him again."

The warlock grimaced. "Not like you'd let me out of the house in any case. Yesterday, I stooped to rolling bones with Fouad!"

"He take all your money?" Fouad was quite the shark.

"Anyway," the warlock said, "I had the ugly hulk fetch me some papers from City Hall. Mr. Engelmann had a son who died years ago. I found a record of his grave."

"So?"

"Blood and flesh. A son is as good as the father. Get me that corpse, a clean ritual space, and I'll build the model."

Al-Nasir's eyes narrowed.

"No hidden costs or consequences?" Practitioners were notorious for whitewashing over the details.

"Of course it won't be free," Mr. Parris said, "but I have standing credit." He glanced at the hearth where only a few embers smoldered.

Al-Nasir slid over to the fireplace and inhaled. He smelled charred ash, woman-stink, and brimstone. A fitting blend.

"You combine witchcraft and demonology?"

"There are many ways to skin a cat."

The pastor was smirking. Inside his mouth, al-Nasir felt his fangs begin to extend at the prospect of success. "You must be ready in three turns of the sun."

The pastor grimaced, then doubled over. Surely the deadline wasn't that problematical!

But he rolled around on the floor, sweat beaded his blistered skin, and he clutched the stinky little doll to his stomach.

"Are you all right?" al-Nasir asked.

The pastor moaned.

The vampire waited until his patience emptied — perhaps two minutes — then turned to get one of the Moors.

"Wait," the groveling mess on the floor whispered.

"Yes?"

"I'm under attack…" The pastor tried to shake the doll in his hand. "Someone's using it against me."

Al-Nasir nudged him with a boot toe. "Is that dangerous to us?"

The warlock didn't answer, only contracted in pain. But soon his color returned and he sat up.

"What happened?" al-Nasir asked.

"It just went away. I think they botched the spell on their end. My bond to the girl-vessel is secure."

"Then my slaves will get the body tonight," the vampire said.

Forty:
Scruples

Salem, Massachusetts, Sunday night, November 16, 1913

As planned, the Williamses stayed the night for fear of the vampire. Alex situated them in a pair of rooms on the second floor.

"Thank you," Sam said when he and Alex were alone.

"For what? Things didn't exactly go well."

"But you stood up to Sarah to protect Emily. That had to be hard."

"The field is certainly level now."

"Friends." Sam punched Alex in the arm. "Truth is, I've had bossy girls in my face since nine months before I was born. As much as I love Sarah and Anne, someday I want to be the man of the house."

Alex climbed the stairs to confront Grandfather. He found Dmitri wheeling the old man into his sitting room.

"You knew that spell was going to kill her, didn't you?"

Constantine turned to face him. "One can never predict the future, but certainly such procedures are dangerous."

The old man could be so infuriatingly... ambiguous. The last hour kept replaying itself in Alex's mind. He was angry at Sarah, angry with himself, and really angry with Grandfather.

"Don't shovel me that load of fetid goat-shit, you *poutanas yie!*"

"Bigger things are at stake." The old man shrugged. "If it makes you feel any better, I'm sorry."

"Sorry?" Alex said. "Sarah hates me and Emily could have died!" On top of it all, the throbbing in his head was back.

"I intended none of that. The warlock's spell stands in powerful defiance of nature. If the anchor here had been broken, he'd likely have been killed or crippled by the backlash."

There it was. The naked truth of the man's cold practicality.

"And this would make Emily's death acceptable how?" Alex asked.

Grandfather shrugged. "Al-Nasir needs this oath breaker. He would never include another in his schemes unless it was critical, the talent substantial. The monster didn't come west for his health."

"But—"

"Tonight's ritual might have worked!" The old voice was full of energy now. "Your Sarah, she's a surprisingly competent practitioner with a razor sharp intellect. I sensed she had talent but I didn't anticipate this preparedness, this degree of control or strength from an untrained girl-child—"

"What do you know about her?"

Grandfather pointed a finger at him. "Where's my full account on al-Nasir and the warlock?"

Alex's temper reared again. "Give me an answer first!"

The old man looked at him for a long moment, then sighed.

"Remember our conversation returning from the Engelmanns? Well, the day of that fire in 1895, Mr. Engelmann and I weren't the only ones in Vienna. An associate of al-Nasir's, an Egyptian — someone you and I both have great reason to despise — had been there. He was searching for something but he left disappointed."

"Sarah told me her father fled Vienna because he found something," Alex said.

Grandfather was all grins. "I thought so."

"What is it? Do you think he still has it?"

The man shook his head. "If it were nearby, I'd know it."

"But what is it?"

"I can't say, but it doesn't belong to any mortal man."

"Can't or won't?" Alex said.

"They are the same. Not to worry, I promise to do my best to keep the Caliph and his ilk away from your Sarah."

The old man glanced at Dmitri, who nodded. Alex couldn't decide if this was a good thing or not.

"This other man in Vienna," he said, "was he perhaps like a beetle or a ram?"

Grandfather rewarded him with a rare expression of surprise.

"Twice in one day he rears his ugly black-shelled head. I shall drive the beetle back into the filth from which he came."

He tapped his chest to drive the point home, and Alex felt each touch pummel his own skull. He saw fleeting images of the wolf, bloody sheets, and an arrow slicked with red.

"I don't understand, Grandfather. What'd he do?"

"He left me with nothing."

Which was exactly how that statement made Alex feel. His head continued to pound. He remembered a creature of nightmare, black bladed claws gripping a ball of fire. Had he met one of these monsters before?

"What do these Egyptians have to do with the vampire?"

Grandfather settled back into his chair. "For at least several centuries the Caliph has lent his aid to their cabal, served their same dark ends."

"Can you vague that up for me?" Alex said. "Come on, Grandfather, you always say evil is selfish. What do they *want*?"

"They serve the old gods. Fallen and forgotten. They wish to tear down the very heavens and rebuild them as they were."

"That sounds rather apocalyptic," Alex said.

"Exactly."

Forty-One:
Tipping Point

Salem, Massachusetts, Monday afternoon, November 17, 1913

THE PHONE RANG and Sarah picked it up.

"This is Mr. Weiss from the Levine Chapel in Brookline," the voice on the other end said. "Is Mr. Engelmann home?"

As it happened, Papa had just returned from work. She traded the phone for his coat and hat. When she returned from the closet Papa still held the receiver, but his face had turned the color of ash.

Sarah waited, chewing on her tongue. The Levine Chapel was the cemetery near Boston where Judah was buried. They went there a couple of times a year to put stones on his grave.

"Thank you," Papa said, and returned the earpiece to the base.

"What's wrong?"

"Last night, someone apparently exhumed Judah's body." Sarah backed into the green armchair and sat. "The warlock," Papa said. "It has to be. I think he's trying to find a new way into the house."

"Why would they need Judah?" Her voice shook.

"They didn't take your brother," he said. "Only the clay God loaned him for a time. Still, the warlock may have unholy uses even for that."

"How do we stop him?" Her emotions felt near the breaking point. Preying on the living was one thing, but—

"Perhaps a trap can be set." Papa drummed his fingers on the wood and brass telephone casing. "I need to think on it."

He pulled her from the chair into his arms. She leaned into his tobacco-scented bulk.

Eventually, he hugged her, extracted himself, and drifted from the room.

At school today, Sarah had barely spoken to any of her friends, and not at all to Alex. She was still coming to terms with the fallout from last night's failed ritual. Endlessly she tore apart the evening in her head, performing an aggressive series of autopsies on the corpse of her budding romance.

She was still mad at Alex. Not the furious kind of mad that had overcome her last night — God only knew where that had come from — but more a vexed anger, like a throbbing gum that made you want to press on the tooth. His improper thoughts about Emily were disquieting, but they weren't really the source of her anger. Mostly it revolved around the spell. Was she mad at him because he'd stopped her? Or because he'd been right, while she blindly charged ahead, putting Emily in peril?

Perhaps. But there was more to it than that.

She'd never felt so alive or so powerful as during the ritual. The strength of four people had flowed through her, everything enlarged and magnified. Having the circle broken had tossed her back into her own little one-person self.

Was that the reason she was still angry?

Meanwhile, the vampire and the pastor were still out there, and Emily — not that Sarah had dared ask — was probably even worse.

Sarah lifted the phone and asked the operator to connect her.

"Alex, I'm sorry I was so mad at you last night."

"You are?" The phone made his voice seem distant. "I'm sorry, too. Does this mean—"

"Don't be rash, cowboy."

"I was worried about you. I admitted as much to Grandfather — I think he might've asked Dmitri to follow you."

She sighed. "I think there's enough lurking in the shadows."

"I'm sorry," he said.

This wasn't helping her hold onto her anger.

"Let's meet tomorrow evening at the Williamses," she said. "I'll call them. Make sure to arrive before sundown. Don't take any chances."

"I'll be there. Let me know for sure tomorrow in school."

"Okay," she said.

"And Sarah?"

"What?"

"I don't know if what I did was right," he said, "but I care about you and I tried my best."

"I know," she said. Still, things were different than they had been. Not just between them, but with her.

Forty-Two:
Memorials

Salem, Massachusetts, Monday night, November 17, 1913

AL-NASIR DREAMED OF TILED COURTYARDS ringed with bubbling fountains whose agitated waters ran red with blood. A few minutes before sunset he woke and gnashed his teeth in anticipation of the night. But until then, there was little to do but rub his naked body into the sandy soil that lined his grave.

Life — or unlife — was a game won by the longest survivor. Centuries ago, al-Nasir had concluded that sunlight, simple as it would seem to avoid, was the leading cause of vampire destruction. Fire was a close second, large conflagrations being fairly common in cities. An unexpected blaze, particularly during daytime, could easily be fatal. In fact, it was his long-held opinion that accident, ennui, and carelessness were significantly more dangerous to the vampire than assault by hostile mortals, the reversal of the predator/prey relationship being rare. Having no intention of meeting such an end, he hid his resting places carefully, and could count on his long pale fingers and toes the days he'd slept in some makeshift grave.

He felt the last sliver of sun slip below the horizon. Fouad and Tarik were waiting when he pushed open his sarcophagus.

"*Salam alechem*, most powerful, glorious, and illustrious Master." Of all his recent servants, Tarik was the most obsequious, especially when seeking forgiveness.

Al-Nasir's anger mounted. Formalities, however, could not be forgone.

"*Salam alechem*." He paused for a few seconds, then allowed himself to extend his teeth and claws. "Where is the girl?"

Both slaves threw themselves on the floor.

"Master, most grievous apologies." Fouad's voice was muffled, his face pressed to the hardwood.

"Your orders were to bring her, regardless." Al-Nasir spat once on each of their heads. His thralls had clung to their pathetic half-lives so long they'd forgotten that some things were worth a little risk.

"We would have taken her, great Master," Fouad said, "but another prevented us."

"Who?" The vampire let his growl expand his ribs.

"A big man. I followed him myself once the girl returned home."

Fouad dared to lift his face. A speck of bloody spittle gleamed in his hair.

"Sleek and deadly Master," his oldest servant said, "we located another dwelling. Inside live the big man, a boy, and an old cripple. The boy passed near my hiding place — he was one of those whose scent you shared with us, one of the defilers who slew Nabil and Ahmed."

"At least you have not failed utterly," al-Nasir said.

The big slaves preened and smiled. Fouad rose from the floor and dusted himself off.

"Tonight I'm hungry," al-Nasir said, "Tomorrow, I'll attend to the young man myself."

He would prosecute this new angle, but he had only a few days left before the Painted Man sent the beetle. The warlock's plan remained crucial.

"Our beloved brothers must be avenged." Tarik revealed his teeth, cut in imitation of his master's. "We've made memorials for them. Do you have time to see?"

"Of course." Al-Nasir couldn't have cared less what little votives the superstitious Negros had devised for their dead brethren. Small gestures, however, served as the foundation for loyalty's fortress.

"Thank you, Master!" Tarik more or less ran from the room — quite a feat for a man who weighed over four hundred pounds. He returned carrying two glass jars, each about a foot tall. "This, princely Master," the slave said, indicating the jar in one hand, "is for Nabil, and the other is for Ahmed. I put what's left of them inside."

Indeed, the jars contained various insects and spiders, a few of which still moved. Scratched crudely in Arabic characters were the names "Nabil" and "Ahmed," though the first of these was misspelled. Behind the amateur calligraphy, the vampire could see "Samson Farm Peach Preserves" embossed on the glass. He attempted his best approximation of a soulful look.

"I'm deeply touched."

The huge slave beamed.

"Once the Great Plan comes to fruition," the vampire said, "I shall rescue your brothers from whatever hell in which they reside and crown all of you as princes to serve at my feet."

"Thank you, most glorious and merciful Master," Fouad whispered.

Tarik, being younger, was more willing to impose on the vampire's patience.

"When you slay the defilers, might you bring me some of their flesh so I may feed it to Nabil and Ahmed?"

Al-Nasir sighed. They meant well.

"That would pleasure us both."

He took to the night to feed. Two or even three lives would be good. He'd been neglecting himself and he needed to be at his best.

Forty-Three:
Breaker of Horses

Salem, Massachusetts, Tuesday evening, November 18, 1913

ALEX WAS SADDLING BUCEPHALUS as the sun slipped down near the horizon. Fitting the horse with tackle was fine work — he had to remove his gloves — and his fingers quickly grew numb from the cold, wasting precious time. Thick white clouds of breath formed in front of both their faces.

It was a twenty-minute ride to the Williams house, so once he set out he alternated between walking and trotting. Bucephalus liked to canter, but earlier today, daggers of frozen rain had left icy patches on the road. Now the sun was gone, leaving only a lingering glow. Grandfather said that most vampires wouldn't even dare that. Halfway to the edge of town the brightest stars revealed themselves. Orion and Sirius loomed overhead — the hunter ever a faithful companion, even if he stunk of dog. Far above, Alex heard an avian cry. Below him, Bucephalus tossed his head and whinnied.

A dozen yards ahead, a black shadow darted across the road. Alex urged Bucephalus into a trot. The shadow crossed again, going the other way. Then he felt it pass behind him.

Not good.

Bucephalus must have felt it too, for he reared. Alex struggled to retain the saddle. As soon as the horse brought his forelegs back to earth, he leapt forward. Alex clung to his neck and whispered a prayer to Saint George.

Stop, come to the trees, a voice whispered in his head — silky, seductive, slippery as ice. Alex felt the wolf's head medallion warm against his chest. *Ai sto diaolo.* He rode on.

A figure stood before him on the road — a man, he thought, but his shape bled into the darkness. *Stop*, the voice whispered.

With his horse now at a gallop, he couldn't have stopped if he'd wanted to. The charging animal should have collided with the shadowy man, but he'd vanished. Alex glanced behind him. Nothing.

He startled to find the man beside him, keeping pace with the galloping horse. The stranger cocked his hooded head, and now Alex glimpsed the face — skin yellowy white, like ivory left too long in the sun. The vampire smiled at him, an endless procession of long yellow teeth.

You are just a boy, the voice said. *Who sent you to my home?* The creature swiped his clawed hand across Bucephalus' hind quarters.

The stallion let out a whinny of pain and stumbled but maintained his footing. Alex twisted himself to free his leg from the stirrup and kicked at the vampire, who veered off and vanished.

He was under no illusion that he'd seen the last of the creature. His best chance was to reach town as quickly as possible — hopefully the vampire wouldn't attack in front of witnesses, and if he made it inside the Williams house it wouldn't be able to follow.

But getting there alive was going to be the problem. That awful shriek wasn't reassuring. Nor the leathery flap of wings above him.

Highland Avenue was close now, lit by electric lights. Only one long loop of unpaved road to go. He pulled Bucephalus hard toward the field on his right, the vampire screaming from above as they streaked across tall grasses toward the lights. Bucephalus breathed in ragged pants, and sweat flecked his neck. Alex brought him alongside the fence that separated them from the paved street and at a low section squeezed his knees. The stallion jumped and landed heavily on the frozen shoulder of the road.

A man driving a horse-drawn buggy cursed when Alex spooked his team, then glanced skyward in bewilderment as the vampire shrieked again, higher this time.

Alex slowed Bucephalus to a trot, weaving between carriages and cars until he crossed right into the heart of town. The Williamses lived only a few blocks away.

He paused at the corner before turning from the busy road. The side street was well lit with only a single pedestrian in sight. He patted his horse. Three blocks to go. He pushed Bucephalus back into a trot. The exhausted animal obliged without complaint.

Alex smelled spices and the smell of decay. As he turned to look over his shoulder, Bucephalus reared again. A black shape swept past him, swirled about the road, and coalesced into the black-clad vampire.

Alex slid backwards. The saddle stayed with him, but the straps that bound it to the horse snapped loose — the vampire must have slashed the leather as he passed. Alex crashed into the icy cobblestones shoulder first. He thrashed his legs to untangle the stirrups. The vampire strolled toward him, his long white fingers twitching.

"Tell me everything," he said. This time, his lips moved as he spoke. His accent sounded a little Turkish but not exactly. He looked more human than before. "Start at the beginning. If you tell me everything, I might not kill you."

Alex shook his head as if to clear it. His legs free at last, he leapt to his feet and sprinted toward Bucephalus, waiting down the street.

"There's no point in running, boy," the vampire called from behind him. "Your hands are stained with blood, I could track you to the ends of the earth."

Alex ran anyway. But before he reached his horse, he collided with the small man, now in front of him and hard as an iron post. One cold hand grasped his neck, the other his waist.

"I know you didn't slay Nabil and Ahmed alone," the creature said. His breath smelled of damp rotten earth. *Who was with you, and why did you come?*

Alex hung in the vampire's grip, paralyzed with terror, his chest burning. The coal-black eyes bore into his. They looked surprised, as if their owner had really expected Alex to answer.

The vampire was using his glamour, and it wasn't working. And then he smiled. His yellow pointy teeth multiplied and lengthened and sharpened, row upon row of fangs. The hand at Alex's waist reached up and tore his shirt and jacket.

There was a flash of heat, a sharp acrid tang mixed with a whiff of putrefaction. The vampire jumped back, opening and closing his fist. His snarl with all those teeth was hideous.

Again the wolf's head medallion had proved its worth.

Alex ran. He closed on Bucephalus and flung himself onto the horse's bare back. He kicked hard, and they galloped down the street. Behind him, he heard shrieks and the leathery flaps.

Two blocks to go.

They turned the corner onto the Williamses' street. The black shadow whipped past. Alex felt a searing pain across his back but clung to Bucephalus with all four limbs. In front of him, the vampire pivoted to make another pass. His airborne form was dark and indistinct, its motion that of a huge bat.

Alex drove Bucephalus straight up the Williamses' front porch, then yanked on the reins. The horse stumbled and slowed. Alex jumped down and grasped at the door. It was unlocked. He threw himself into the foyer and slammed the door shut behind him.

When he turned back, the vampire's face was at the adjacent window, grinning, teeth glimmering in the light from the porch lamps. Taloned fingers tapped the pane. The face vanished. For a moment, there was silence. Alex knew better than to feel relieved.

The quiet lasted for perhaps fifteen seconds, then he heard horrible snarls — and then, mixed with the snarls, equine screams that broke his heart.

Alex sank to his knees. Tears streamed down his face as blood streamed down the windows. Bucephalus had been his since he was nine, had come with them to each of their homes, even following him across the Atlantic.

A new emotion all but overwhelmed his terror and heartbreak: the hot white burn of pure rage.

The other residents of the house poured into the room. Mr. Barnyard was first, foregoing his usual slobbery greeting to attack the front door. He scratched and pawed at the wood, emitting a constant, low growl. Next came Sam, followed by Anne and Sarah. After them were Mr. and Mrs. Williams and two boarders Alex didn't know.

"What in creation is going on?" Mr. Williams asked.

Everyone stared at Alex.

"Alex!" Sarah said. "There's blood all over your back."

He stood there, frozen, mute. Sarah started to come to him, and he held up a hand, palm out.

"He attacked me." He wiped his eyes with the back of his hand. "He followed me. I think he just killed Bucephalus."

"Who attacked you? Who's Buphacephalus?" Mr. Williams said.

"Bucephalus is his horse." Sarah said. "Was it more than one *man*?" She widened her eyes at him, a kind of reverse wink.

"I'm calling the police," Mr. Williams said. "Sam, get the shotguns." Both left the room.

"It was *that* man," Alex said. "The one with the creepy friends. He followed me here, and he had a knife." His body unwound and the pain began in earnest. His back burned.

"How'd he find you?"

"He just came at me on the street, Sarah. I think he followed me across town."

"Can one of you translate that into plain language?" Mrs. Williams said.

"It's this crazy guy from the mill," Anne said. "He's been bothering the boys, bullying them. We didn't think he would really hurt anyone."

"Why didn't you say something?" her mother said. "First your sister gets terribly ill, now some horse-killing lunatic is chasing you?" She seemed to really see Alex for the first time. "Get that boy off the floor and let's take a look at his back."

All three women helped Alex to his feet as Sam and Mr. Williams came back into the room. Sam carried two shotguns.

"The police will come when they can," Mr. Williams said.

A heavy thump sounded from the window. Anne screamed.

Bucephalus' face was pressed against the glass. His tongue lolled to the side and a huge gash crossed his forehead. The vampire had destroyed one of his eyes and laid the flesh open to the bone.

Alex heard a chorus of screams behind him.

Oh, Jesus. The vampire had torn his head off.

The disembodied horse head traveled back and forth across the windows. Alex thought he could just make out the vampire's black sleeve holding it like some demented puppeteer. Bucephalus disappeared from the left window and reappeared at the right. Mr. Barnyard chased the head from one side to the other, barking and growling, inciting ghastly shrill laughter from outside.

Mr. Williams grabbed a shotgun, broke it open, and inserted two shells.

"Let's teach this lunatic a lesson." He stepped toward the door, but Sarah leapt in front of him.

"Sir," she said, "let the police handle it. We shouldn't make a bad situation worse."

He considered, nodded, then threw the deadbolt. It didn't matter, of course. It wasn't the lock that was keeping out the monster.

"Sam," he said, "check all the doors and windows."

Sam left again. The girls helped Alex out of his jacket and shirt, shredded beyond repair. He couldn't raise the arm with the bruised shoulder.

"That's a pretty nasty cut," Mrs. Williams said. "You'll live, but you need some stitches. I can do them if you don't mind a bit of a scar, or I can call the doctor."

"I'd rather you just get it over with," he said. Any doctor who came out tonight would end up in the grave.

They relocated to the library and Anne brought her mother a pile of supplies and a bottle of whiskey. Alex took a couple of quick swigs, but the cleaning and sewing still hurt like hell. Much more painful were the memories: Bucephalus nipping his shoulder while being groomed; whinnying when he saw Alex approach; circling the paddock, his muscles liquid energy under his sleek ebony coat, running for nothing but the sheer pleasure of it.

The police came and went — two of them, the older with an Irish accent and a bushy silver mustache. Alex told them a slightly more polished version of the half-lie he'd given the Williams. They'd promised to look into it, horse-killing being a felony. Alex hoped they waited until the morning.

With the intruder apparently gone, the Williams parents went to bed, and the rest of them gathered in Sam's room. The pain in Alex's back had subsided to a dull throb. He felt like he'd been pushed through one of the mill's picking machines, his mind packed into a brick of senseless cotton.

Out Sam's window he could see the front porch. Dark stringy shapes hung from the trees. Lord Jesus, they looked like horse guts. He closed the curtains.

"How's your sister?" he asked the twins. "Any better?"

Anne sighed. "She hangs on, but she's buried so deep we're lucky to get five minutes of Emily in a day."

"Sorry to hear that," Alex said.

Sam closed the door to the room.

"Can it get any worse?" he said. "First we fail to kill the vampire, then Emily's cure doesn't work, and now the vampire kills your horse and knows where we live."

"Are you sure it was him?" Anne said. "The bugamoor guy?"

"It was him."

"How'd he find you?" Sarah asked again.

"No idea," Alex said. "I was riding down the road into town and there he was."

"So you led him here?" Sam looked more depressed than angry.

"I'm sorry," Alex said. "I didn't exactly have time to think. I was outside, under attack. If I hadn't run into the house he would have killed me."

Three pairs of eyes seemed to accuse him. He looked down at the floor. And then, with no warning, from nowhere and everywhere, he heard the voice.

It is the Greek's fault, he brought the trouble upon you. Kill him!

Alex's breast burned as if someone had dropped a hot coal down his shirt. Glamour again. He looked up to see Sam lunging through the air. They collided hard, and bowled Alex out of his chair. The back of his head slammed into the floor, and his stitches pulled painfully.

The voice. The vampire could make them think whatever he wanted.

Sam punched him in the nose.

He saw an explosion of stars.

All his fault, kill him, the voice shouted soundlessly. Alex's chest flared once more with heat.

Sam's weight pressed down on him. He strained to breathe. The other boy's face wore the red mask of murder. Blows rained down on Alex while he struggled to get his arms between the heavy fists and his face.

Forty-Four:
Donation to the Cause

Salem, Massachusetts, Tuesday, November 18, 1913

PARRIS WORKED NAKED WHILE he and Betty labored to finish the model. The fewer extraneous influences, the more potent the sympathy. And why sully one of his few suits?

Mr. Nasir had brought the body as promised and allowed Parris to use his dining table as a makeshift workspace. Not that the vampire was much for eating in. Betty volunteered to help him scrub the place and extract the iron nails from the floorboards. Watching her rump bob was great fun, even if he did have to double-check her work. One nail would be more than enough to ruin his model. He arranged a little crate for her in the corner, outside his ritual circle, scrubbing her feet himself every day to reduce *impurities*.

She still wore her ancient corset but today she'd removed her skirts and knickers to facilitate the display of her *filthy temptations*. Such distractions were useful, for they generated concupiscence he channeled into his masterpiece.

And a masterpiece it was — the degree and depth of sympathy profound.

"Observe," he said. "Stay on your crate, don't break the circle — the temple is square in shape, oriented cardinally. Here is north."

"And how is this important?" she asked.

"The devil's in the details, my love. Both this model and the physical home we intend to enter are sympathetic analogs of the ideal celestial temple."

"Solomon's Temple?" she said.

"Depends on your point of view. There was once a historical temple in Jerusalem where the ancient Hebrews stored the Ark of the Covenant. But more important is the pure and abstract *form*."

"*Form* as in Plato?" She smiled, cracking the sores around her mouth. "The perfect version of something, transcending the flawed shadow cast into the real world?"

"You've read Plato?" Betty was clever but hardly educated in the formal sense.

"One of my lovers in the 1820s was a philosopher."

"So when I'm dead and gone you'll regale your twenty-first-century boyfriends with tales of your witchy paramour?"

She tapped her dirty fingernails on one knee, and opened her legs to give him a glimpse of what lay between.

"In the meantime, Toy, I'm all yours."

"Good to know succubi are exclusive."

"We usually aren't, but I'd never cheat on you." She blew him a kiss.

"You probably say that to all your lovers."

"But with you, I mean it."

He wanted to believe her. "Anyway, my model — like the real temple — has both an outer and inner wall. The outer courtyard was accessible to anyone, the inner yard only to priests. And along the west side is the central sanctuary itself, flanked by two great pillars."

He pointed at the other end of the table, where the moldy corpse of the donor lay. The small body had hardly been pristine when Mr. Nasir delivered it, but now it was just a pile of loose parts.

"Tell me what you used to make it." Betty humored him in so many ways.

"The walls I built with a mortar of ground bone. The columns are mostly finger bones, but the big central pillars were cut from a femur."

"And the slabs of roof?"

"Rectangular sections of skull."

"What else is in there?" she asked.

"The pavement is made from donor teeth. And I used what remained of the liver for the Molten Sea, the big tank of holy water that sits in front of the sanctuary."

"Can I have the extra parts? Nothing like a severed penis to put an incubus in his place."

"Don't play with the donor!" he said. "Maybe after the book is in my hands."

Betty spat, fortunately outside his ritual circle.

"That damn book is going to get you killed, or worse. Look at your hair."

He ran a hand through the whitened patches that clung to his scalp.

"When the Moors were out yesterday and the vampire asleep, you looked for the book?"

She kicked her bare heels against the crate. "Too yellow to search yourself?"

"You know he can smell where I've been, and I had to work on the model."

"He keeps it in the room with the painting." She shuddered. "It's just sitting on an end table."

"At least we know where it is."

"You can't trust the bloodsucker, Toy. Look how he's treated you."

She'd never liked him associating with other people — he tried not to think about what she'd done to that girl he favored in '02.

"Mr. Nasir needs me to treat with his demon," he said.

"Treat with me instead!"

She put a bare foot on a corner of the crate so as to spread her legs wider and pressed first two, then three fingers inside herself.

Damn. This column was too tall. Parris carefully worked it loose, then stepped over the circle, his chest splattered with dusty flesh and bits of bone. He locked the remains of the finger bone inside the carpenter's vise the Moors had provided then began to file down the end.

Forty-Five:
Light in the Dark

Salem, Massachusetts, Tuesday night, November 18, 1913

SARAH CHEERED SAM ON as he pummeled the spineless betrayer. To think she'd ever liked him, even kissed him. She spat on the floor.

Ladies, open the drapes, the voice whispered. Now the lips that spoke *those* words, those she could kiss forever, locked in eternal bliss. She lurched toward the window, but Anne was closer and moved to open the curtains. How dare that hussy? *He* wanted Sarah to open them. She shoved Anne aside and finished the job herself.

The back of Sarah's wrist stung. Anne had clawed it, jealous bitch. Sarah pushed her back into the wall.

She returned to the window, hoping to catch a glimpse of him, but she was disappointed. She called to memory his delicate features.

Kill the Greek, kill the Greek now. He required proof of her devotion.

She turned back to the room. The traitor struggled underneath Sam. If she found something sharp she could jab him in the kidney. The desk, Sam must have a pen or a knife there.

But the desk was swathed in unpleasant light. She pushed herself closer but felt like she was swimming against the current. The source of her difficulty hung on the wall: Sam's cross.

Why would a cross bother her?

Behind her, she heard the Greek cry out. "It's the vampire. Don't listen to his voice!"

Now conflicting desires swirled in her head. Jealous little boy, one said. Alex could never be the man that *he* is. But another, rebellious part of her grasped the silver *mezuzah* beneath her blouse.

"The Lord is my light and my help; whom should I fear?" she cried in Hebrew. Cool white light shone through the heavy wool and the flesh of her hand. The sinister voice was quelled.

"The Lord is the stronghold of my life, whom should I dread?" Oh my God, what had she done? What would she have done?

The room reeked of a thousand rats dead behind the walls.

She tugged the *mezuzah* out from her blouse and raised it as high as the chain would allow.

"When evil men assail me — to devour my flesh — it is they, my foes and my enemies, who stumble and fall. Should an army besiege me, my heart would have no fear; should war beset me, still would I be calm."

White light bathed the room, burning off the foul miasma. She stumbled, dropped the *mezuzah,* let it bounce against her chest. The sour taste of bile rose in her throat.

Sam sat astride Alex but had stopped hitting. He looked bewildered as he slid off.

"I'm sorry, Alex. I don't know what happened."

As terrible as the whole business had been, Sarah felt elated. She'd done it, used Papa's techniques to cast out the undead. Her prayer had worked!

"The vampire was pushing his thoughts into our heads," she said, "but I shut him out."

"How?" Anne asked. "He made me open the curtains, didn't he? I wanted to kill you to open them first."

"I protected the room from magical influences," Sarah said, "so I don't think he can do that again."

Alex sat up and wiped the blood from his mouth. Nothing looked broken, but Sam had added to his collection of bruises.

"One of the spells your father taught you?" he said.

Their eyes met. She hid her face in her arms. Two minutes ago she'd been searching for a letter opener to jab between his ribs.

Anne screamed.

From the top of the window, an arm waved, then dropped and fell past the glass. No body attached.

My hand is stretched out to you, the silky voice said. *Open the window and invite me in.*

No one moved.

A face appeared where the arm had been. Upside down, the grinning rows of teeth looked as if they were frowning. He tapped at the glass. *Open the window and invite me in.*

The face disappeared, and now a blue-clad leg dangled in the window like a butcher shop display. Severed at mid-thigh, the stump showed a ragged bit of bone. The foot still wore a black leather shoe.

My hand is in your belt. Invite me in, please.

The vampire dropped the leg. It fell out of sight, but he pressed something against the panes with his other hand: the severed head of the older police officer. The man's pupils had rolled out of sight, and blood stained his silver mustache.

Sarah stared in mute horror. The vampire's own face was a grotesque exaggeration of the one she'd seen last week from her door. Only the coal black eyes were the same.

No invitation, ladies and gentlemen? The vampire's mouth didn't move. He held the head by the hair, thumped it against the thin glass, then sniffed, his delicate white nostrils flaring.

You stay my will with infidel magics, but they will not protect you from the consequences of your sacrilege. The creature turned the head upside down and extended his tongue. He licked the bloody stump like a child might enjoy an ice cream.

Isabella's words came back to her: *My first killer and yours.*

The vampire tossed aside the head and leapt into the night.

In the wake of the vampire's display, Sarah reeled physically and mentally. After the destruction of Charles and even after the debacle with the bugamoors, she'd felt a mounting sense of confidence and power. But now, between Emily's curse, her dark dreams, and the might of the vampire, she felt dizzy, swept along toward a fast and bitter end.

"Shall we count the ways in which the apocalypse is upon us?" Anne said. "First, Emily's going to die a horrible wasting death. Second, the police are going to come looking for their missing officers and may well arrest, convict, and hang us all. Third, neither of the first two will matter, because if we leave our houses at night for any reason that *thing* will tear us apart and use our bones for toothpicks."

"Emily!" Sam was out the door before Sarah could blink, Alex on his heels.

Sarah looked at Anne, grabbed her hand, and together they raced after the boys to the sisters' small bedroom. Sarah pushed past the others — she hadn't seen Emily since the failed attempt to break the curse.

She looked even worse. Her skin was pasty white, her body alarmingly thin, her cheeks hollow. Formerly shiny blond hair lay flat and waxen, and her open eyes stared vacantly at the ceiling. The tip of her tongue poked from her cracked lips.

Alex reached down to feel her pulse. "The vampire must have gotten to her somehow, drained her blood." He shook her gently. "Emily, wake up."

"It won't do you any good," Anne said. "After the night at your place she won't even eat. We have to spoon soup down her throat."

"Oh," Alex said. "Sorry."

Anne was right — Sarah could see that Emily wasn't going to last much longer, a couple of days at most. The pastor was sucking the life right out of her. She looked just like Judah had at the end, her—

There was a ruckus outside in the yard. It sounded like a dog had caught a bird — a big bird. Sarah darted to the window. The others crowded behind her. No sign of the vampire, but the streetlight's yellow glow revealed his handiwork. Coiled intestines draped from trees, gruesome decorations hung in advance of the holidays.

"Everything we do just makes things worse," Anne shook her head back and forth like a horse trying to escape the bridle. "If we hadn't killed Charles, hadn't gone to the vampire's house—"

"Emily would still be cursed, and Charles could have murdered dozens." Sam sat down on the edge of the bed. "We had no choice. This thing can be slain. We killed its men, we killed its baby vampire, and it can't come into the house or go out by day. It has weaknesses, limits."

"The vampire can clearly use that weird voice to control people," Sarah said. "But I prayed to God to protect us, and it worked. Sam's right, he can be beaten." *Only you can stop us.*

She'd always believed in God, but tonight He'd listened to her prayer — really listened. A curious elation still streaked her somber mood.

Anne said, "That voice…. I wasn't just angry with Alex, I hated him. I didn't even stop to question why. When he asked us to open the drapes, I couldn't help myself."

Sam nodded. "I was a little mad before, but the voice made me so furious I think I really could have killed Alex. When you yelled whatever you yelled, Sarah, the anger just went away."

"What he did is called a glamour," Alex said. "My grandfather warned me about it. Not all vampires can do it, and it takes them years to learn how, but it's a way to control people's thoughts. I didn't feel it, though — I heard the words in my mind, but that was it. Same thing when he tried it on me outside."

"Why not?" Anne said. "The rest of us were controlled, why not you?"

"I think it's this." Alex unbuttoned his shirt and fished out a silver amulet on a leather strap. "My grandfather gave it to me, told me it would protect me against *them*." He nodded at the window.

Sarah took a look. The medallion was shaped like the head of a wolf, its eyes made from tiny rubies. A cold shiver ran down her spine. *Trust the wolf.*

"What makes you think it was the necklace?" she asked Alex.

"Whenever the vampire used that insinuating voice," he said, "the amulet grew warm and burned my chest."

The silver wolf face gleamed. Where had old Mr. Palaogos gotten the thing? If he was the wolf, the vampire was the bat, and Khepri was the beetle, who was the ram? *The ram looms behind them all.*

"Can I touch it?" Sarah said.

"You can touch anything you want."

Sarah glared at him but placed a finger on the wolf. The silver was warm to the touch. She thought about it snuggled against his chest.

"What did your grandfather say exactly?"

Alex looked past her for a moment. Since the medallion was around his neck, she'd been forced to step in close. She could smell his sweat. It reminded her of the kissing.

"If I remember correctly, he said it would protect or hide me from vampires or their minions."

"Alex," Sam said, "remember in the basement with the bugamoor? I noticed something strange — the big guy knocked my gun away before I even saw him coming. But you came up behind him carrying the holy water, and he never noticed."

"The medallion must have hidden me," Alex said.

Sam leaned back on the foot of the bed. "But the vampire certainly saw you today. He came after you, cut you—"

"The vampire's much more powerful than the Moors," Sarah said. "Maybe the medallion has less effect on him. Alex, did your grandfather say where he got the necklace? Are there more?"

"I can ask, provided the vampire doesn't come back and finish us off—"

"That's our lot now," Anne said. "Sheep waiting to become lamb chops."

"That's it." Sam stood up. "We have to stop letting him control the situation. The guy's ancient, I'm sure he's killed hundreds of people—"

"Thousands," Sarah said. "A century has thirty-six thousand nights in it. If he kills someone even every couple of nights, just think how many it must be if he's really old."

"And we know he's relentless," Sam said, "so one thing we can count on is that he'll attack again. We need to be ready."

"What about Pastor Parris?" Anne said, "We have to get that doll or make him break his curse."

Time to tell them.

"I know exactly where the vampire and the pastor are going to strike," Sarah said.

All eyes turned to her.

"At my house."

"Because of the thing your father brought back from Vienna?" Alex asked.

"What thing?" Anne said.

"The Archangel Gabriel's Horn." There, she'd said it.

"This isn't the time for joking," Sam said.

Sarah kicked at his foot. "I'm not. God told my father to keep it safe, and he did — it's gone. But the vampire won't take our word for it." Sarah slumped onto Anne's bed, across from Emily. If she hadn't been so exhausted she might have cried.

"She isn't making this up," Alex said.

She could have hugged him.

"It fits with what my grandfather says. That the Caliph was sent here to find something incredibly important."

"Sent by whom, the devil?" Sam said.

Alex shrugged. "Ultimately, perhaps so. I don't know."

"It doesn't matter who sent him," Sarah said. "We can't let them win. My father will know what to do."

Anne put her head back into her hands. "What about *our* parents?" she said. "Who's going to protect them?"

"We can tell them to stay inside at night," Alex said. "But we aren't going to be able to walk that line for long. All the more reason to act fast."

"I hate to say it," Sarah said, looking at Emily, "but she doesn't have much time."

Forty-Six:
Lone Wolf

Salem, Massachusetts, Tuesday night, November 18, 1913

AL-NASIR CLUNG TO THE CLAPBOARD siding not five feet from the infidel crypt-breakers. They'd surprised him, these light-handed whelps: the Greek boy had denied his glamour, and the dark-haired girl had invoked her god against him. He shouldn't have lost his temper with her last week.

Now, how to enter the house? Perhaps the girl's prayer-ward didn't extend to the entire dwelling. He could hear almost a dozen heartbeats inside, and some of these others might be more amenable to persuasion. The vampire was climbing down when he sensed something hurtling toward him. He fast-stepped off the wall, throwing himself clear.

Quick as light, the blur corrected its trajectory and collided with al-Nasir as he landed in the yard. Pain jabbed his leg, and he toppled to the frozen ground. Instantly he found himself in a furious bite-and-claw match with a ball of silver fur. As soon as he could, he wrenched the creature off, fast-stepped around the corner of the house, and leapt up to an overhanging tree branch.

Below him circled an enormous wolf, its ruby-red eyes matched by the blood on its silver muzzle. No ordinary animal, of course. A real wolf would have run, tail between legs, at a mere whiff of the vampire's scent. Al-Nasir checked his wounds. The scratches were nothing — they would heal in minutes — and even the gash on his leg would vanish as soon as he fed. Still, he needed to be careful. The pastor was almost finished with his model. Tomorrow night or the next they would strike, and he couldn't risk being in anything less than perfect condition.

"To what do I owe this unprovoked attack?" al-Nasir called down.

Below him, the wolf shimmered and was replaced by a lanky white-haired man, eyes still scarlet. Another vampire.

"You offer me parley?" the man said in Ottoman Turkish so perfect it could have been Suleiman himself.

Vampires that favored the wolf form were always several centuries old, but al-Nasir didn't recognize this one.

"Name yourself and your line." Al-Nasir's Turkish was rusty but still serviceable.

"You may call me Wolf," the man on the grass said. "As to my line, it is your own, spawned that dark night in Ravenna."

Ah, the Greek. They'd never met — al-Nasir wasn't much for family.

"The Dung God told me he killed you at Mount Athos."

"He tried," the wolf said. "I'll have to return the favor."

Al-Nasir's laugh sounded like a bark even to himself.

"I've no quarrel with you. I always liked Isabella." He had, but he never should have sired the bitch.

He hopped down to the ground. The other pulled a pair of purple suede gloves from his jacket and tugged them on. The wolf was half al-Nasir's age and no match for him, but such confrontations were always dangerous.

"I claim blood-right," the other said. "Two of those inside the house are my property."

Al-Nasir leapt back to the window and sniffed, careful to avoid being seen by the occupants. He couldn't be sure of the other humans, but the dark-haired she-bitch and the Greek boy did have the foul stench of wolf on them.

"I, too, have claim," al-Nasir said. "They killed my thralls. But swear blood-oath to me now and I shall withhold my vengeance."

"The Dung God killed my mistress and tried to kill me." The wolf spat. "I forsake your line."

Al-Nasir had only seen Isabella a handful of times — again not much for family — and although he'd felt her die, he hadn't thought much of it. Khepri claimed the Greek had followed him for decades. Al-Nasir had always assumed it a matter of vengeance, but the stink of archangel on the girl inside told a more complicated story.

Al-Nasir gnashed his teeth. "Did your humans attack me with your knowledge? If so, you inherit their debt, and there can be no peace between us."

"I swear I forbade them," the wolf said.

For this one to admit such weakness meant truth. He could deal with the wolf later, after they had the Horn. For now, he'd have to rely on the warlock's plan.

Al-Nasir thought back to Isabella in Ravenna. Her girlish form lying naked in the pool of her child's bloody afterbirth. Her white skin, her red hair, and the red red blood. The stink of it had excited him so. To give her the dark gift had seemed so delicious, so perverse.

"Tonight, because of flame-haired Isabella, I offer you truce."

The other vampire grimaced but nodded. "Because of blood shared, I agree. Both of us are to leave and neither return until the sun has risen and fallen."

"But if you want this mess cleaned up," al-Nasir said, indicating the dismembered policemen, "do it yourself."

"Fouad?" Al-Nasir pulled himself into his townhouse window. "Has the portrait been asking for me?"

"Not that I am aware of, Great Master. Shall I look?"

The Moor looked to be praying the vampire would spare him the task.

"No matter. I'll check myself."

Al-Nasir hurried to the portrait chamber and pulled back the curtains. The painting snored gently, eyes closed and lips slack. Asleep, the Painted Man looked vaguely translucent.

The vampire patted an ancient cheek with the back of his long fingers. It would be satisfying to slap the man, but he dared not damage the delicate image. As it was, a few chips of colored wax flaked free and tumbled onto the rugs below.

The Painted Man yawned and rubbed his eyes. When he spoke, his voice was rough with phlegm.

"That you, al-Nasir?"

"Who else?"

The painted eyes narrowed. "Soon the passage shall open. The lost Horn shall be found."

"The warlock's convinced the Horn lies within this celestial temple," al-Nasir said.

"It is true that such a place exists."

"Are the defenses and the hiding place one and the same?"

"It may be so," the Painted Man said. "I think the witch keeps or is kept by some kind of demon. A hell-bitch. The aura was familiar."

The ancient sorcerer was so old everything must feel familiar.

"Isn't that why you selected him?" the vampire said. "We knew he swims in those waters, likely he was bitten."

"Undoubtedly correct," the painting said.

"I called for a reason," al-Nasir said. "The wolf that haunted Khepri is in Salem, sniffing around like he smells a bitch in heat."

"Indeed." The portrait rubbed his hands together. "Your sounding call has drawn an unexpected player back into the game."

It was hard to imagine how bleeding a boy on a tree could have such an effect, but he wasn't the magician.

A female voice from inside the painting called out, "Grigori."

The Painted Man turned and mumbled something to an unseen listener. Al-Nasir didn't understand the language, but it sounded like Russian.

The vampire rapped on the wall. "Sorcerer, in which king's ear do you whisper now?"

"Not a king — a *czarina*." The Painted Man made an odd palsied gesture with his large hands.

"One of the wolf's humans — a girl — is the one who reeks of archangel. Three times has she escaped my grasp." Al-Nasir felt his lips quiver at the words.

The portrait's skin glistened green and his single curling horn grew more apparent.

"The beetle crosses under the Western Sea as we speak—"

"Goat-fucker!" Al-Nasir cried.

"He will emerge in your basement the dawn after next."

"Accursed bug!" Only two days and the vampire could lose control of everything.

"You must prepare. He needs a human form to assume so that he may walk among his forgotten flock. You remember the details of the ritual?"

The vampire nodded, teeth extended but clenched.

"This should do poor Khepri a world of good," he said. "He still isn't feeling his old self after his little romp in Vienna. No fun, baking his dung."

The portrait snickered. "Fun! Dung!"

Bother, the old man was coming apart again, and it wasn't even a proper rhyme. Al-Nasir reached over to the painting and pinched the waxen lips closed.

"Sir," he said, "keep yourself together. We've not finished our discussion."

But the battle was already lost. The painted image laughed hysterically, tears rolling from his eyes. He grew fainter, almost like a water color, then so translucent al-Nasir could barely make out his features.

Forty-Seven:
Confessions

Salem, Massachusetts, Wednesday, November 19, 1913

ALEX INSISTED SARAH CLOSE HER EYES while he led her to the street, hoping to spare her the grisly sight of Bucephalus' remains. But she cheated, peeping through her lashes at the yard in the dim light of dawn.

All she saw were dark stains on the patchy snow.

Had the vampire cleaned up his mess for some perverse purpose? Or had ghastly police-part-theatre merely been forced into their minds by some undead power?

On the way home she considered what to tell her father. He'd let her stay over because returning after dark hadn't been an option. But she owed him a full accounting.

She slunk in by the back door.

"Sarah, that you?"

"Yes, Mama?" She finished pulling off her boots as her mother entered the mudroom.

"We don't mind your staying over at the Williamses', but you left us sleepless with worry. What kind of daughter does that?"

One who doesn't want to be ripped apart by a malevolent demon.

"I know, I'm sorry," Sarah said. "It got late."

Her mother clucked her tongue. "If you expect me to believe that's the whole story, then I've got a bridge in Prague to sell you."

Sarah and her mother hadn't exchanged a word about this whole business, but Sarah was sure Papa kept her informed, at least to some extent.

"Your father's already canceled a class waiting for you," Mama continued. "Go, and feel free to share everything with him. I'm not hurt. Who am I? Just your mother."

Sarah cringed. "That's not fair, Mama, it's not like I tell him everything either."

Papa stood in his office, his briefcase on the desk.

"Last night, Sarah?"

She told him about her chat with the Caliph, then last night's horrors. As she spoke, the image of the vampire licking the man's severed neck sprang to mind. She squeezed her eyelids closed. Tears welled in the corners of her eyes.

"What you just told me — having unwisely withheld it — confirms my suspicions. These monsters are convinced the Horn is here, or that we can lead them to it."

"But they're wrong?" she said.

"The passage to the archangel's realm is very narrow and requires specific celestial alignment. Gabriel celebrates his feasts in September and March, not November."

"Still they come, Papa."

"You must ask your friends to sleep here until they do. We can't afford to be picked off one by one. We must provide a single tempting fruit — but a poisoned one."

"Won't that be dangerous?"

"And chatting with a vampire at the door isn't?"

Sarah tried to look contrite.

"I'll send your mother to the Hoffmanns in Boston. They have their own defenses." Papa jabbed his pipe at her. "You've been reckless, young lady."

"I know." It was true.

"And I've been blind."

He opened his arms and she fell into them. He was solid and warm, smelling of pipe smoke. She was going to have to watch herself with Alex. One little slip-up and Papa would see right through her.

They pulled away. "We know from your dreams," Papa said, "that this undead Caliph is allied with the Egyptians I faced in Vienna. Mr. Parris is mortal, a newcomer. So we ask ourselves: why did they involve him?"

Sarah called to memory the only image she had of the pastor, from her vision the night of the failed ritual.

"He's ugly?"

Papa nearly choked on pipe smoke laughing.

"That may be true, but no. I made inquiries among my esoteric colleagues. It seems our Mr. Parris' romantic life is more sordid than one might have supposed — word is he has a demon lover."

Sarah scrunched up her nose.

"Vile indeed." Papa smiled. "But demons who consort with mortals are able to walk between worlds. I think that is why the vampire needs him. They must know the Horn isn't in this universe."

"And how does that help us?"

"The household defenses are modeled on the Temple of Solomon. Which should make it possible to open a gateway to the real celestial temple. If we encourage the villains to think the Horn is there, they'll enter, and we can trap them." He pointed out the window. "God's aspect is a tree growing from the layered soil of reality. The mortal realm is the lowest node of the *Sephirot*, and God's incomprehensible secret self the highest."

"The Temple is closer to God?" Sarah said.

"Most certainly. The Temple is the House of the Lord, and the very presence of these fiends — particularly the vampire — will draw God's wrath."

Sarah stifled a yawn.

"I think you should get some sleep," Papa said. "One cannot fight the undead in such a state."

"What about school? I'm already an hour late."

"Sleep, Sarah. The Lord's work will have to take precedence."

Sarah smiled. "Then I'm all for God's wrath."

The bath water burned. She scrubbed herself so hard her skin turned pink. Nothing had actually touched her last night, but all the same....

After washing, she relaxed in the warmth. The air in the room was chilly, in fact cold, so she scrunched low into the water. This exposed her legs and feet, so she braced her toes against the foot of the tub and pushed back to compensate. Now her breasts were above the surface, which made her feel not only uncomfortable but embarrassed, despite the locked door in a room with no windows.

She gazed down at her small pink nipples and beyond to the submerged dark wedge. What would it be like to be with a man? For all she knew, the vampire or the pastor would kill her first. Grim, but all too possible.

She sighed and cupped her breasts. Were they too small? What would Alex think of them if he saw them? Not that she wanted him to — yet. They'd have to be married, and that was impossible. Still.... Had he been with a woman before? She didn't dare ask. The only girl he'd ever mentioned was the little vampire on Santorini.

Sarah felt herself smile. She didn't have to feel bad that one was no more.

The bath felt cathartic. The horror of the last twelve hours seemed to be washing away with the grime. Maybe they could win. God was, after all, on their side, and He'd listened — not just once, but several times.

Alex came over before dusk, and they installed him in Judah's old room. Sarah was glad Mama had taken the noon train to Boston. She might not be able to handle a boy sleeping just down the hall from her daughter. While they got him settled, Anne phoned. Her father had been called to his sister Edna's on some emergency, so she and Sam had to stay with Emily until tomorrow.

Lying in her bed that night, Sarah prayed for the Williamses' safety. She felt the warm presence of the protection she'd thrown over their house in her belly, almost like an extension of herself. It might not be even a tenth as strong as her father's, but it had kept the vampire out and it was still there.

Sarah dreamt that she and the wolf ate lunch on a blanket spread across a hilltop. A gnarled sycamore sheltered them, its branches bare but for a few wilted leaves. Below, the hillside swept down to a junction of two rivers. An ancient city of domed buildings occupied the peninsula between. Red banners festooned the fortified walls, and thin streams of smoke from countless kitchen fires wound their way into the clear blue sky.

"Your home is beautiful," she said, feeling radiant in Isabella's gold and burgundy velvet dress, the red and white doe embroidered on her breast.

The wolf wore purple silk studded with diamonds, sapphires, and emeralds. His ruby eyes looked warm and weary.

"So the poets and saints always tell me, but a great foe approaches from the east."

Sarah looked across the larger of the two rivers. Far in the distance, angry green clouds roiled in the shape of a ram's head.

"Still, there's cause to celebrate," the wolf said. "Do you see the city decorated with red? Today is the Orthodox Feast of Saint Gabriel." He poured her a glass of red wine from a jewel-encrusted decanter. "The vintage is exotic and ancient, quite lovely."

Sarah took the goblet from his hands and sipped, knowing how it would taste: meaty, salty, perfumed.

They enjoyed the soft quality of the air as it wafted up the hill. Small galleys rowed themselves every which way across the confluence of waters.

Then she saw the beetle, large as a house. He entered the river on the far shore and began to swim across, an island of approaching blackness.

The wolf's red eyes glowed. "Our ancient foe wishes to join the feast." *The beetle is the ram's pawn. They seek to rob God of his Strength, but that can be their undoing.*

The wolf nodded as if he'd heard Isabella's voice in *his* head.

"This time, I'll be ready for him."

Trust the wolf. His revenge shall unite us and unlock everything. The passage is almost open, beyond lies Paradise, and the dark gift redeemed.

The wolf stood, pulled Sarah into his arms, and kissed her bare neck.

Sarah woke, her room lit only by the feeble yellow glow from the streetlights. She was cold. Her neck hurt. The window stood open and the wind rattled its frame.

Someone else was in the room.

Forty-Eight:
Bump in the Night

Salem, Massachusetts, Wednesday night, November 19, 1913

DINNER WITH SARAH AND MR. ENGELMANN had been strange, to say the least. How different he was from Grandfather, though nearly as cryptic. This afternoon, after Sarah had invited him over, Alex went so far as to climb most of the way to the icon room. But he paused on the stairs, still angry over Grandfather's role in the failed ritual. Did he really want to live in a world where a young girl's life was less important than secrets he wasn't even allowed to know? In the end, he left without saying a word.

The bed the Engelmanns had put him in was so short he had to sleep half upright, propped on pillows. Perhaps it was the early morning hour and his full bladder, or perhaps it was the thought of Sarah just a wall away, but he was as hard as a rifle barrel. He rose and tiptoed to the hall where he heard Mr. Engelmann's snores drifting down from the floor above.

Sarah's door creaked as Alex slipped in and closed it behind him. His flannels were riffled by a blast of cold air. Thinking he saw something — someone? — leap from the open window into the street below, he rushed over and peered out. Nothing.

"Who's there?" It was Sarah.

"Just me," he said.

She looked pale as a ghost.

"Thank God. I thought for a moment the vampire somehow got in. I was having a nightmare."

Alex crept over. "I couldn't sleep. I'm sorry I'm here."

"I'm not."

He sat on the edge of her bed. She took his hand.

"What we had was nice," she said. "Scary, too. In some ways, more frightening than *him*."

Her hand, held in his, sat in his lap. His erection, having subsided on the way to the room, returned. Alex tried to move her hand away before she noticed.

"Did he really make you hate me?" he said.

She glanced down. "While I was glamoured, it was awful. But it didn't feel right."

He raised his other hand, caressed her cheek with his thumb. She reached for him and he kissed her. It was different this time — slower, yet somehow more urgent. Better than before.

She pulled the covers over herself and he slid under with her. He kissed her chin, then her neck. She tasted of salt and copper. She made little noises and they made him want to hold her tighter, to just inhale her. Her feet were cold, but he rubbed his against them anyway.

He kissed her on the lips again, sliding a hand down from her neck to her breast. So soft and yet firm through the single sheet of fabric. Gently she pushed the hand away.

"Are you mad at me?" he whispered.

He felt her shake her head. "We'd better stop. I don't want to do anything we'll regret."

"I won't regret it."

They kissed some more, her body pressed against his. She stopped him again.

"You might — regret it, I mean. I don't know what we're doing, but with so much evil surrounding us, this is one of the things that feels right."

He nibbled at her neck. "So I'm just a comforter?"

"I've always loved goose feathers."

Forty-Nine:
Waxen Images

Salem, Massachusetts, Wednesday before dawn, November 19, 1913

AL-NASIR WAITED WITH EMPTY PATIENCE in his townhouse basement.

"Khepri always emerges just before dawn," Fouad reiterated needlessly.

Not very convenient. As if hunting those murdering thieves and tomorrow's expedition weren't enough to contend with.

The prisoner's whimper only sharpened the edge of his mood.

"Fouad. Shut that thing up."

The human was wrapped in strips of linen cloth, as requested. The Moor delivered a swift kick, and the whimpers turned to loud moans.

"Fool," the vampire said, "the beetle needs it unharmed. Just stuff its mouth with extra linen."

"My humblest apologies, Great Master." Fouad did as instructed.

Al-Nasir was letting his irritation get the better of him. Really, Fouad and Tarik had seen to most of the preparations, but it was sharing the glory with Khepri that truly chafed.

The topsoil began to shudder, and the vampire felt the ground vibrate under his feet. The Painted Man claimed the beetle could tunnel across the world in a night.

"Stoke the fire," the vampire said. "He nears."

Fouad threw more wood into the flames. Al-Nasir took a step away. An enormous copper pot had been brought to the cellar, filled with wax, and set over fire to melt.

The center of the basement gave way, opening a pit large enough to ride horses through. He heard Khepri's hideous chitters and covered his sensitive ears.

Allah, cursed be His name, how he hated the creature.

Jutting from the sides of the shaft were bits of bone and decayed flesh. Fouad had buried a dozen corpses down here. Al-Nasir hoped the beetle enjoyed them.

For an insect the size of a cow, Khepri moved swiftly. His pincher-like mandibles emerged first, followed by bladed obsidian legs and the hideous dark carapace. The stench of dung filled the room.

Khepri settled beside the hole and shook off the dirt. He began to preen, all the while making that ghastly high-pitched sound. His mouth opened — dark, but something in there glinted.

"Where is the Horn?"

"*Salam alechem* to you as well," the vampire said. Several of Khepri's limbs were still swaddled in ichor-soaked bandages.

"The burns from the Hebrew God still pain you?" al-Nasir said. The beetle removed a femur snagged on his black-bladed body.

"You live in decaying squalor, Caliph."

This from the Lord of Dung? At least the beetle no longer dragged a sun when he burrowed. Al-Nasir hadn't seen it — he wouldn't be here if he had — but he'd heard the beetle could still conjure a diminished solar body when so inclined.

"We have the things you require," the vampire continued, taking the opportunity to kick the captive himself — hard enough to bruise. The Painted Man had said Khepri would inherit any blemishes when he copied the man's form. Oh well.

"I must begin immediately," the beetle shrieked, his voice so high it brought al-Nasir's hands back to his ears.

The vampire glanced at Fouad, who dragged the squirming human to the vat of boiling wax. The slave got the man's shoulders over the lip but was having a hard time with the legs. Khepri's hideous Egyptian chanting filled the room.

He fast-stepped over to help Fouad. How low must he stoop in the name of the Great Plan? They tossed the victim into the simmering whiteness.

The screaming further grated on the vampire's nerves.

Quick as a cat, Khepri sprang across the room and squeezed into the vat. Thick pale wax bubbled over the sides and sizzled in the fire. At least the beetle didn't scream — in fact his chanting stopped as he submerged, dragging the victim with him.

The vampire and his thrall continued to wait. After a few minutes, a man-shaped figured clambered out of the cauldron, his limbs spasmodic and uncoordinated.

Khepri in disguise was tall, almost seven feet, and thin. He looked unformed, his skin a waxen caul drawn over obsidian edges. And he had no mouth, eyes, nose.

"Where's your mutt?" the vampire asked.

The faceless thing beckoned toward the hole. Al-Nasir heard a shrill bark, and little Anubis climbed out of the dirt, panting heavily, tongue lolling, his silver fur and pointed ears caked in filth. The tiny jackal wandered to the corner and lifted his leg.

A black claw surfaced from the lower half of the waxen face to slice open a gash of a mouth.

"Now tell me where I might find the Horn!"

Al-Nasir sighed. "The Greek boy lives in the house outside of town, but I saw the horn bearer and her friends at another dwelling. This body you grow used to live there, so you should be able to find her." He didn't mention the wolf or the house the girl lived in. Let the bug iron out some wrinkles on his own.

Underneath the thing's face, dark knives sculpted liquid wax. A crude nose erupted first, then the eye sockets began to pool. A likeness of sorts, but a long way from resembling the victim.

"I require a day for the wax to set," the high voice said, "then I go to this Salem. The timing is perfect. Tomorrow is the archangel's Feast in the East, and sunset is his hour."

The vampire felt that feverish itching of the skin that signaled daybreak.

"I must retire to my coffin. At first dark tonight the warlock and I unleash our own gambit for the Horn."

The white skin betrayed no emotion, but the seething pits of the eyes began to take on a hint of color.

"Either way, I will row my boat across the sky to hail our victories."

"Poor company that you are," al-Nasir said, "I would that it be so."

Fifty:
Model Citizens

Salem, Massachusetts, Thursday, November 20, 1913

"DON'T CROSS THE RITUAL CIRCLE," Parris warned the minute his guest entered the workroom.

"What do you take me for, a neophyte?" Mr. Nasir said.

Unlike Betty, he didn't seem interested in testing any boundaries. Tiptoeing up to the chalk line, he inspected the remains of the donor and the magnificence of the model.

"Interesting." He sniffed. "You've quite an eye for the details. The decorative trim on those central building walls is etched with shellacked strands of hair?"

"Indeed," Parris said. "You can actually smell that?"

"Even when I was alive, I had refined senses." Mr. Nasir inhaled again. "They've only improved with age. Are those altars dabbed in bile?"

Color him impressed. "I reconstituted it from powdered residue."

"Delightful." The vampire's nostrils flared wide. "Did you have a woman in here?"

The creature's nose was uncomfortably keen.

"One glimpse of your decor," Parris said, "and any girl would run screaming."

Mr. Nasir grinned back.

"I don't begrudge a man his pleasures. Allah, cursed be His name, knows I have mine. But nothing is allowed to leave my lair alive."

"What about me?"

Those dark eyes were examining him. Intently. "If we acquire the Horn, I'll make an exception. How do we transport this construct?"

Parris had modified a case intended for a tuba, painstakingly forming blocks of compressed straw into various shapes and covering them in velvet from Lyon — only the best for his masterpiece. The real trouble had been replacing all the metal fittings with leather ones, but it was done now.

Mr. Nasir held the case steady while Parris situated the model inside. They carried it out together. One person could manage the weight, a mere twenty-five pounds, but keeping it level by oneself was another matter. Mr. Nasir seemed to have no trouble. Evidently dead muscles didn't suffer the same fatigue as living ones.

Mr. Nasir flew Parris then the case to the roof of Mr. Engelmann's house. He seemed unwilling to come close and so hovered a few feet above. The flapping of those terrible wings stirred up the already frigid air.

"Hurry," the vampire called down.

Parris wedged the case above a chimney. Everything he needed was inside. He sketched a powerful amplifying circle on the roof. The one in the workshop had been designed to keep out impure influences, but this one should intensify the synergy between the model and its arcane form.

The thought was so exciting he had to place his tools on the shingles to allow his hands to dance by themselves.

"What's the plan once we get inside?" he called up to the vampire.

"No offense, but ritual magic is an art requiring preparation. Once I get up close and personal, it's no antidote for the speed and chaos of physical violence."

Parris had to agree. His little trinkets hadn't done him much good against even Fouad alone.

Parris uncovered the model and crouched inside the circle. The ugly doll that bound him to the Emily-vessel was still in his pocket. He took a healthy gulp of its energies and picked up the stolen blade, being careful not to touch it except through his silk handkerchief. He lifted the knife and slammed it into the center of the model.

A gasp escaped his lips as he watched his masterpiece shatter and collapse.

The whole house rumbled and shook, a deep and pervasive quaking. He released the letter-opener and wobbled to keep his balance on the canted roof. Blackness expanded outward from the model and it melted into the roof like a hot coal dropped onto a sheet of butter.

Fifty-One:
Into the Maelstrom

Salem, Massachusetts, Thursday evening, November 20, 1913

JOSEPH THOUGHT IT PRUDENT to keep Sarah home from school.

"Given," he said, "the potential life-and-soul-shattering consequences."

Pompous and pedantic, Rebecca called him, although she meant it in a loving way. Probably the Electra principle at work. Rabbi Epstein — her father and his mentor — had certainly deserved the same epithets.

Today, he and Sarah had worked together not just as teacher and student but as collaborators. She didn't have his depth of knowledge or experience but she did possess a certain creative unorthodoxy. Not that he was entirely comfortable with her attempts to introduce ideas from other disciplines. And when she tried a synergistic technique borrowed from a book on witchcraft, he'd drawn the line.

Still, it was Sarah's idea to use *Binah*, the aspect of God representing the 'womb of wisdom,' to allow the ward's energies to literally give birth to the realm of the celestial temple. He in turn had used his more analytical male conceptualizations to bind this power into the silver *mezuzot* they each wore about their necks. That way, when the need arose, either of them should be able to open or close the gateway. If they succeeded in luring the vampire and his demon-loving disciple into the esoteric realm, it would be essential to make sure they stayed there.

The Williams twins arrived just before sunset.

"Our father finally came home an hour ago," Anne said as Joseph took their coats.

"How's Emily?" Sarah asked.

"Worse."

Sam said, "Dad brought her a new puppy from Aunt Edna's but she didn't even seem to notice."

Alex helped him drag in a steamer trunk filled with a frightening array of crosses, sharpened sticks, and firearms.

Joseph was not comforted.

About an hour after sunset, the house shuddered as if hit by a round of heavy artillery. Joseph felt the strike to his wards like a bullet to the gut. Around him, the temple-like structure rippled and wavered. A huge hole had been punched through the esoteric roof and entire construct threatened to unravel.

Joseph lurched toward the sitting room, where the children were gathered.

He'd failed to consider what havoc a warlock's spell might wreak on his personal defenses. By the time he stumbled in, his ward was in shambles and the pain even more intense.

There were only three teenagers in the room. Alex carried a long stake in one hand and a pistol in the other.

"Where's Sam?" Joseph said.

Anne pointed. "And he's always saying my bladder's a pea—"

The plaster ceiling shattered and a creature of nightmare fell into the room. A shadowy raptor plunging from the sky, black wings buffeted away all hope.

Joseph's hands moved in prayer, but the thing was far too fast. Alex's stake and gun were thrown out the window in a gout of shattered glass. The shadow blurred and solidified behind Sarah.

Joseph had never seen a vampire before and he looked not unlike a Goya caricature — a man's shape with a demon's face. But this cartoon held Sarah's arms behind her with one long taloned hand. The other gripped her hair, pulling back her head to expose her throat.

"One twitch, one word, *magi*, and your daughter's blood will flow like a river!"

No one moved.

"You will open the passage to the Horn. Now."

Joseph's insides twisted. Not again! Why was *Hashem* always testing him and his children?

"The gateway is in the cellar," a new voice said from above.

Joseph glanced up to see a pair of suited legs dangling from the hole in the ceiling. Pastor Parris awkwardly lowered himself down. His hair had thinned and whitened since Joseph saw him last.

Parris backed out of the room. The vampire dragged Sarah after.

Joseph and the others had no choice but to follow. His debilitated wards hammered his head like a migraine headache. The vampire was so fast, there was little Joseph could do before he'd kill her. He'd have to hope that if he opened the passage, the creature would take the bait and enter. But what incentive did the monster have to leave Sarah unharmed?

The pastor led them to the back of the cellar, where the roots of the great sycamore protruded from the earthen wall. He lit a candle and its green flame filled the chamber with putrid light.

"Here," the ungodly man announced.

"Open the passage," the vampire said, "or I stop playing nice."

"Let her go and I'll do it," Joseph said.

Open the passage to the Horn!

If he'd thought his headache bad before, now it felt as though a dagger plunged into his eye. He fell to his knees. The fading strength of his wards allowed him to resist compulsion, but any other action was impossible. He—

Someone stepped into the swamp-colored light. Sam placed the barrel of his cowboy pistol to Pastor Parris' skull and thumbed back the hammer.

"Let Sarah go or the warlock loses his head," the boy said.

That's when things began to move fast.

Joseph felt the gateway to the celestial temple open and give way. Sarah — she'd triggered the portal.

The very fabric of reality cracked and shattered like glass. The cellar wall burst outward. Earth, brick, and wood fell away into a gaping hole — an empty place of only orange sky and chalky clouds.

A howling wind siphoned through the room. The teenagers and their two captors were drawn into a vortex of dirt, stone, and roots. Sarah and Sam tumbled away into nothingness, taking Joseph's heart with them.

The pastor managed to catch hold of a root, but his weight and the sucking wind snapped the branch and he was lost, buffeted about like a newspaper caught in a storm.

The vampire let out a shriek and transformed, his huge wings struggling against the gale. For a moment it looked as if he might prevail, then a chunk of masonry tore free and knocked him too into the void.

Joseph knelt. Emotional and psychic punishment rendered him only marginally capable of thought. Earth pelted him from behind, drawn into the vortex. For a moment he could still distinguish the tiny dots of his daughter and her friend, then even these were lost in the distance.

Alex and Anne crouched nearby, struggling against the howling gale.

"Anne?" Alex screamed. "She'd go in after you."

Sarah's best friend looked terrified. "You would have to say that." She reached her hand out to Alex.

"The Holy of Holies!" Joseph screamed. "Try to get the monster into the Holy of Holies."

Alex pulled Anne into the maelstrom and they pinwheeled away, Anne's scream lost in the roar of the wind.

Joseph wanted to plunge after but felt the shape of the power coursing through him. He was the lever holding the dike open. If he went in, the passage would close forever, Sarah would be lost forever.

He settled himself on the dirt and began to pray.

Fifty-Two:
Grand Entrance

Unknown Locale, Thursday, November 20, 1913

SARAH LAY ON HER BACK, half propped up. Someone must have rolled up a towel and shoved it under her shoulders. Her eyes were closed, but the glow of the sun penetrated her eyelids.

"Sarah, wake up." A hand shook her.

The last thing she remembered was the cellar. Reluctantly, she opened her eyes—

And shut them against the blinding glare. She opened her eyes again, but only a crack. Sam knelt beside her, dressed in an odd brown robe with a metallic breastplate.

"Where'd you get that crazy costume?" she said.

"I don't know," he said. "It came with a helmet, sword, and spear — hey, *your* clothes have changed too. This whole place is really weird."

Sarah sat up. Sam's outfit looked handmade — and heavy. She glanced around. No sign of the vampire. Or anyone else.

They were on a sandy hilltop. Scruffy vegetation and a few scattered olive trees sprouted from the dusty earth. In front of them the slope dropped off, revealing a strange sky, intensely bright and sunset orange, but everywhere, not just in the west. Even stranger, the sun itself was nowhere to be seen. Queer clouds churned like milk poured into a draining sink, and huge white birds circled overhead. The orange glow rendered everything in this world more intense.

She hoped Alex, Anne, and her father were safe back in Salem. Opening the gateway had been the right choice. The vampire wouldn't have let her — or anyone else — live. She knew that now, should have known it the first time she saw the merciless pits of his eyes.

She placed a hand against her breast and felt the *mezuzah* beneath the thin fabric. Her father felt far away, but Sarah could sense the bond between the pair of silver boxes.

When she'd fallen out of the cellar, she'd been dressed in a heavy wool skirt and jacket. Now she wore only a thin linen gown of some sort. Much too short, only to mid-thigh, and her pale legs and feet lay bare on the sandy soil. The creamy fabric was sheer, and she wore nothing at all underneath. She crossed her legs and tugged at the gown. Sand rasped against her naked buttocks.

"Sorry, I didn't see anything." Sam turned red. "Well, not much of anything."

"Who dressed me?" Sarah asked.

"I've no idea. I woke up only a few minutes before you. I think we might be dreaming."

"This isn't a dream," she said. "I should know. We fell through a hole between worlds."

She stood up, trying to keep her hands over crucial spots in the translucent fabric. Her legs wobbled, but Sam caught her forearm.

A hot dry breeze hit her face. The sand burned under her bare soles. She recognized her garment as a tunic, the kind of thing you saw sometimes in ancient Greek art. The wind blew right through it, flattening the material against her naked form. If there had been a viable way to die peacefully of embarrassment, she'd have taken it.

"You're wearing something on your back," Sam said.

Could it get worse? She twisted around and saw a feathery pink mass, some kind of... plumage? She tried to touch it, but the awkward location and her reluctance to contort in the tiny gown made it impossible.

"What is it?" she asked.

"Um, I think they're wings. They make you look like an angel — not that you don't always."

Sarah twisted again. She felt the subtle drag on her shoulders.

"What holds them on?"

Sam stepped closer, touched them gently, then moved around behind her.

"I don't know how to tell you this, but I don't think anything does. Your dress has little slits, and the wings grow right out of your shoulder blades. Let me tug on them, see if they come off."

Her heart beat fast. She felt him tugging at her arm — her other arm, the mysterious winged one growing out of her back.

"So now I'm an angel?"

He shrugged. "What am I, then? Julius Caesar?"

"No, your outfit isn't Roman."

He picked up his helmet and weapons. The helm looked bronze, with engraved writing.

"Let me see that," Sarah said.

He handed it over. The writing was Hebrew, or maybe Aramaic, archaic regardless. Some kind of dedication to God, and to King David and King Solomon. She gave it back.

She inched forward to the edge of the cliff, and Sam followed. Their hill descended steeply into a large valley. Below the churning clouds and swirling birds, on another hill, stood an enormous temple. She squinted, wishing her eyes were better, or her glasses weren't lost in some inter-dimensional limbo.

The temple was rectangular, ringed by outer walls that grew from the hill like extensions of the cliffside. Inside the outmost perimeter was another set of walls, far thicker, with four huge gates. Within that, separated by a great courtyard, was a square-shaped arrangement of stone buildings. These structures ringed a central courtyard from which thick black smoke wound its way skyward. A single building near the middle glinted bright, like a single gold tooth lording over its enamel neighbors.

"Sam?" Sarah said. "Back in the cellar, you appeared out of nowhere and grabbed the pastor."

"I was leaving the bathroom when I felt the explosion, and before I got to you I heard the pastor say, 'in the cellar,' so I ran ahead and hid down there."

"Quick thinking. Thanks." His face could have outshone the golden building.

A series of horn blasts shattered the quiet. Short notes first, then a long mournful tone. The note faded and hung in the air long after the sound itself was gone.

Sarah shivered. "Papa's magic worked. That's the *Beit HaMikdash*, King Solomon's Temple."

Sam chuckled. "An angel ought to fit right in."

"You'll be fine, too," she said. "You're some kind of royal guard."

"We should go down there. If nothing else, we'll need water."

Looking down at the long winding trail into the rock-strewn valley, Sarah decided what she really wanted most right now was a pair of shoes.

Fifty-Three:
Scapegoat

Temple of Solomon, Thursday, November 20, 1913

WHEN PARRIS WOKE it was daylight, a weird orange daylight, and he was sprawled on the floor of a massive limestone courtyard surrounded by stone buildings. The aroma of roasting meat and incense filled the air.

He got to his knees — covered in dense brown fur like the rest of his legs, which terminated in a pair of cloven hooves. Thick patches of the fur covered his chest, too. He grasped about for the shitty doll and found it at his waist, securely knotted onto a long curl of hair.

Celestial realms all had their own peculiar rules, but this was certainly—

Men in purple and white vestments and high turbans poured from the surrounding buildings. Their babbling and milling revolved around a gentleman with an enormous white beard. He wore baggy linen pants and long overlapping tunics, purple and yellow, bordered with brass bells that jingled as he strode toward Parris.

A breastplate with a grid of twelve gemstones, each a different color, adorned the man's chest. His head was crowned with a larger turban, not unlike a chef's hat, fronted by a brass plaque engraved with Hebrew letters. Although far from infirm, he carried a long staff topped with an ivory finial in the shape of a pomegranate.

The vestments and insignia of a High Priest of Israel.

He knew it! Mr. Engelmann must have hidden the Horn inside the Celestial Temple of Solomon. Somehow the gateway had opened and they'd crossed over.

"What manner of demon are you?" The High Priest raised his pomegranate-tipped staff and pointed it at Parris. "Only the faithful shall pass unburned!"

A blinding white light radiated from the gilded fruit. When it faded, Parris felt like he'd spent an entire day roasting in the sun. Tendrils of smoke drifted up from his reddened torso.

He turned and fled.

Behind him, he heard the High Priest say, "Just as the Temple circumscribes the true nature of the works of the Lord, so too does it reveal the workings of the antagonist Baal."

"So it is written. So let it be done!" a chorus of men exclaimed in unison.

Parris found running on a pair of hooves surprisingly natural, and he made better speed than he ever had on his clumsy human legs. Behind him, he heard the slap of bare feet on stone.

He sprinted down the wall of the enormous courtyard, past one ornate stone building after another. Dense black smoke rose from a huge rectangular altar in the center. Beyond that, he saw a gold portico flanked by a pair of columns.

A corner loomed before him, and a line of curious structures. Each was approximately six foot cubed and consisted of a bulbous bronze vessel on an elaborate wheeled stand of sculpted lions, oxen, and cherubim.

The cacophony of jingling bells was gaining on him.

Some instinct particular to his transformed nature bid him veer left. He obliged, and a hot white bolt of energy shot by to his right. The very air sizzled at its passing, and the hair on his nearer arm singed. The bolt struck the tiles and exploded, showering him with shards of stone.

Parris neared the row of strange bronze canisters and sensed the biting cold of the metal and the water within. He narrowly dodged another bolt of energy that instead struck a bronze tub. The metal glowed a dull red, and steam poured off in thick white clouds.

Parris leapt. The strength of his new body carried him fifteen feet or more into the air, right over the wall of bronze basins. Looking down, he observed himself reflected in the surface of the water tanks. Two large goat horns grew from his forehead.

That explained the cold reception.

He landed hard on the far side, his hooves jarring against the stone. Two additional bolts slammed into the bronze tubs between him and the priests. The impact tilted them on their stands and threatened to slosh him with boiling water.

Trapped in a narrow corridor between the tanks and the wall, he raced toward the only opening. Without supplies or materials he didn't have a lot of occult options.

He was only halfway down the stretch when the High Priest and a number of others moved to block the entrance.

Parris skidded to a stop.

The High Priest stepped forward, holding his staff high. The air around it crackled with energy.

"Spawn of Azazel, surrender yourself, or face the Wrath of the Lord."

Fifty-Four:
Burnt Offerings

Temple of Solomon, Thursday, November 20, 1913

ALEX WOKE WITH HIS CHEEK PRESSED against something soft. He opened his eyes and saw the something soft was Anne's arm.

He sat up. She wore a garment of saffron wool, a yellow head scarf, and gold bracelets. Between the peculiar golden robe and her gleaming blond hair, she seemed to be glowing.

His movement woke her. She looked at him and her eyes narrowed.

"That's some costume — though you're a bit underdressed."

Glancing down, he saw only a leather diaper and sandals. The leather thongs weren't even sewn to the soles, but merely wrapped around and underneath. Tucked into his belt were a wooden sling and a small leather bag.

He looked back at Anne.

"You're a bit overdressed," he said.

She got to her knees and leaned toward him. He smelled jasmine. Did she normally wear perfume?

She giggled. "You're wearing makeup, blue and black around the eyes."

He studied their surroundings. They sat on a sandy stone surface at the edge of an acropolis. To the left was a gate in a massive limestone wall. Crowds of dusty people, many leading farm animals, drifted through the portal. But no sign of Sarah, Sam, the vampire, or the pastor.

"I think this is the temple," he said. "The trap Mr. Engelmann set for the vampire."

Anne stood up. "We need to find Sam and Sarah."

They walked toward the gate. The air was hot and dry, like Rhodes in the summer, and his throat was already parched.

"I've never seen painted toes before," she said.

He looked down at her bare feet, the toenails a dull reddish brown.

"And stop staring at my ankles." She cuffed him on the arm. "What would Sarah say?"

He focused on himself. Along with his clothes, his keys and wallet were missing. His wolf's head medallion was the only object to make the transition into this place.

Anne reached over and pinched him hard.

"Ouch!"

"Just to check we aren't dreaming."

Alex eavesdropped shamelessly as they merged with the crowd drifting through the stone gate. No one spoke English, Greek, or any of the other languages he knew, but he had no trouble understanding them. It seemed he knew an extra language here, although its name eluded him and he couldn't call to mind any of its words. While they stood in line, a deafening series of horn blasts ripped the air. As best he could tell, the sound came from the walls above. After the final note faded, he asked a peasant about it. The man looked at him like he was a complete idiot.

"That's the call to worship. Have you never offered sacrifice?"

Before he could respond, he heard a familiar voice behind him.

"Alex! What are you two doing here?"

It was Sarah — and Sam, dressed like one of the soldiers at the gate.

He stared. Sarah crossed her arms over her chest. Her exposed skin — and there was a lot of it — was turning pink.

Anne didn't help matters. "That's one tiny dress."

"It came free with the wings," Sarah said.

"Look, they flap!" Sam said.

"Can you fly?" Alex asked.

"I haven't tried yet." She raised one, then the other. So strange.

The milling crowds parted around them. People were backing away, heads lowered.

"They're all staring at you," Anne said. "I bet they think you're an angel."

"Then maybe we can cut the line," Sam said.

At least a dozen guards stood on each side of the towering gates, dressed in bronze scale armor and carrying spears and short swords. As Alex and the others entered, several people dropped to one knee.

The gate was decorated with carvings of cherubim, palms, calyxes, oxen, pomegranates, and lions. Alex knew many ancient carvings had originally been painted but he hadn't expected them to look so... garish. Still, they were impressive.

They passed under the gate's vaulted arch and emerged into the courtyard beyond. Here there was a line of basins, a small trickle of water descending into each. Long lines had formed, and he could see people at the head of the queue rinsing their hands and feet.

Sarah grabbed his arm. "Alex, what's that thing in your belt?"

"It's a sling. I have rocks, too."

"Let me see them," she said.

He reached into a pouch on the belt and handed her five small stones. Now that he studied them, he saw each one had some incomprehensible word written on it.

"This is Hebrew," she said. "One says Jesse ben Obed, this one says David, and this one is a name for God."

"Does that make me ready to kill Goliath or something?"

"The young king uncrowned." She performed a little curtsy, her wings furled behind her like a swan's.

They skipped the basins. It seemed odd to wash your feet and then walk barefoot in this dusty square. But religious customs weren't exactly the bastion of logical thinking.

"How are we going to get back to Salem?" Sam asked.

Sarah clutched the silver thing around her neck.

"We may be able to use this to contact my father, but I think God sent us here for a reason."

The courtyard seemed to be filled with a mix of worshippers, guards, and priests. Alex watched with horror as pilgrims offered goats and rams to priests who slit the necks, splashed the blood on all four sides of an altar, then cut out chunks of flesh to grill above hot coals. Below, thick rivulets of red drained away into stone gutters.

"Dinner, anyone?" Sam said.

"Shut up!" Anne said.

Yet another goat was squealing and thrashing its life away when they heard the explosion. Distant and muted, it seemed to come from the center of the temple. Beyond the inner wall, Alex saw a shining gold building. A bright white light flashed and two more rapid explosions struck counterpoint.

People fled toward the outer gates.

Sam pointed. "Stands to reason that's our villains."

They crossed the courtyard against the flow of traffic until they reached the inner wall.

"Look," Anne said, "see that little passageway between the buildings?"

They ducked into the small tunnel. In the shade the temperature plummeted. The walls were adorned with relief registers depicting mythological scenes, including a fruit-laden tree with a serpent looking down on a naked human couple, presumably Adam and Eve.

Alex felt convinced the snake was watching him.

Fifty-Five:
Death from Above

Temple of Solomon, Thursday, November 20, 1913

FOR THE FIRST TIME IN NEARLY nine-hundred years, al-Nasir flew through the air and took in the daylight world.

He remembered *Ramadan* 1017, his third and final *Hajj*. He'd knelt on his filthy prayer rug facing west into the powerful Arabian sun. Before him, sacred Mecca. Thousands of others worshipped around him, barefoot in dusty white robes. The air was choked with the sour smell of humanity and the joyous intensity of shared faith.

He shook away the memory and banked, wheeling high above rolling green and yellow hills dotted with olives and cedars. The only man-made structure in sight was a massive temple complex. In his youth — before the infidels had forced him from al-Andalus — his world had been dotted with the shells of such structures. But this was no dilapidated ruin, nor was the central building fitted with cross or crescent. In fact, it was similar in shape to Parris' delightful little model. They'd entered the *magi's* hidden world, and the Horn would soon be his—

As if in answer, a tremendous trumpet sounded below. It sent a shiver down his dead spine as he recalled cavalry charges, battle smoke, and burning flesh. He tucked his wings and dove lower. Now he could see hundreds of mortals milling about and smell the tang of sacrificial blood.

The Horn would be there.

He flew nearer. A series of small explosions caught his attention. He felt larger and more powerful than usual, flying faster than ever before. Come to think of it, his vision was better as well. He could see all around himself, having only a small blind spot behind his head. Most convenient.

Below, a group of priests had trapped a goat-man in one corner of the central courtyard. Al-Nasir was startled when his vision sharpened enough to see their faces. Most convenient indeed. Was this a new power recently awakened or just a feature of this bizarre place?

In either case, the trapped man looked to be Parris. He'd transformed into some kind of satyr, but whatever his form, the vampire's erstwhile employee was in need of some attention. Nasir fell faster than expected, landing forcefully on a pair of priests. Instead of grabbing them from behind and snapping their necks he'd crushed them instantly. No matter, dead was dead.

Their surviving fellows regarded him with horrified expressions as he dragged another victim close enough to savage the man's throat. So great was his excitement that the head flew free of the neck. Blood sprayed in all directions, and he gulped down what he could. The man's occult talents lent the blood a spicy flavor, and even this small taste infused him with energy.

Al-Nasir focused on shifting to a form more suited to melee. His bat-like shape was too delicate and clumsy for ground combat against multiple opponents. Oddly, his arms remained winged, although he was able to lengthen his limbs and more important, extend his fingers into claws.

Making the best of the situation, he fast-stepped to nearby prey. He was more careful this time, hardly spilling a drop. He let the lifeless body fall, raised his winged arms, and roared at the orange sky.

Burning the energy boiling in his blood, al-Nasir fast-stepped over to another plaything. This one tried to dive away, but al-Nasir caught him by the leg. He ripped open the femoral artery—

A white light flashed and pain seared across his skin. An invisible force tossed him back across the pavement to slam into a wall. Agony burned along one wing, small flames smoldered on charred flesh. Despite the pain, al-Nasir enjoyed himself immensely. Usually he avoided confrontations with a crowd, but once engaged, they could be delightfully intense. He sized up his opponents.

Most of them had fled in terror — always a pleasure — but one with a staff stood his ground. He, al-Nasir suspected, had been the cause of his burn. The priest raised his staff again, his breastplate momentarily distracting the vampire. And what a distraction! Twelve great gemstones were embedded in a grid, each a different color, each huge — perhaps two-hundred carats. They were uncut, polished cabochons in the old manner. He must claim this prize.

His greed nearly cost him his unlife. The priest's staff glowed white, and the vampire fast-stepped sideways, narrowly avoiding the powerful bolt. The blast was distressingly *holy*.

Al-Nasir screamed, flexed his claws, gnashed his teeth. The priest retained control of his bodily functions but turned and ran in a most pathetic show of cowardice. All of his compatriots were either dead or fading into the distance.

Approximately two minutes had passed since he'd landed.

Al-Nasir fast-stepped over to the pastor-turned-satyr, startling him. He attempted to relax himself into a less threatening aspect, but although his claws and teeth receded, he remained a hulking bat.

"The Horn is close, I can taste it!"

"Is that you, Mr. Nasir?" the satyr said.

Al-Nasir towered at least three feet over the transformed pastor.

"Of course, fool!" he roared. Violence and blood always left him tense and agitated, in a good way.

"You look different, and you have hideous insect eyes," Parris said. "Of course, given what happened to me… I'm not that surprised."

"Indeed. Why has this realm transformed us?" al-Nasir asked, glowering.

The satyr cowered pleasingly. "This sort of place is like purgatory, or the outer planes of hell. Each has its own rules."

The thought made his dead flesh crawl.

"Will we be able to return home once we've found the Horn?"

"Of course," Parris said. "I've always used fire or flame as a gateway."

The vampire grimaced. Fire wasn't exactly his favorite element. He used his sharpened sight to scan the area.

"The Horn will be over there." He pointed at the center of the temple.

"The big gold structure?" the pastor said.

"Treasures always are. The Romans called it a *cella*, the Greeks a *naos*," the vampire said.

"You seem sure of this."

"Priests have no imagination. We'll travel together to the portico. Meet me in front if we're separated."

He flexed his wings. The burned one was partially healed. He lifted into the air and clamped his foot talons roughly into the thick pelt covering the man's buttocks.

Parris flailed and made feeble sounds of protest. Al-Nasir ignored him and lurched aloft. He flapped furiously, and they soared across the courtyard. They passed a huge altar mounted upon a high stepped platform. The vampire smelled burning goat. A few priests scattered in terror below. Enjoying himself tremendously, al-Nasir shattered the air with hideous screeches. Parris added his own scream, perhaps not entirely by choice.

Soon they approached the great stairs to the holy building. A vast metal water tank mounted on twelve bronze oxen occupied the courtyard.

Al-Nasir dropped Parris into the tank — if he tried to land so laden, the warlock would be crushed — and flew straight for the heart of the temple.

The portico was flanked by two bronze columns adorned with pomegranate-shaped capitals and festooned with chains. The olive wood doors were painted gold and carved with cherubim, palms, and calyxes. Al-Nasir gained speed, tucked his wings, and smashed shoulder-first into the portal. The colossal doors cracked and burst open.

Al-Nasir's eyes took a moment to adjust to the gloom. The sanctuary was impressive — walls paneled in carved cedar, covered in gold. Two massive cherubim overlooked the chamber, facing each other, wings reaching out to form an angelic arch. He saluted them with a wing of his own and began his search.

Satisfied the room was free of humans, he closed the outer doors to afford himself some privacy. Several altar tables were covered in beautiful gold cups, bowls, lamps, and candelabra. He took his time examining each item.

No sign of the Horn. It had to be here! The doors to the inner sanctuary were unlocked, so he nudged them open.

The interior space was thick with scented smoke. He discerned a flickering flame and the glint of gold within. A holy of holies, sacred to the god it honored. Could his prize be inside? He backed away, leaving the doors open. It would be unwise to enter and offend the deity any further. Such beings were remote but if awakened could obliterate him as easily as a mortal might crush a fly.

He gnashed his teeth. Time to rejoin the warlock. If the Horn was in the sacred chamber, perhaps some spell could retrieve it. He took one last glance around the outer space. It required all his willpower to abandon the gold relics, but he strode to the outer doors and pulled them open.

Fifty-Six:
Water and Flame

Temple of Solomon, Thursday, November 20, 1913

"Damn, would you look at that thing?" Anne said as they entered the inner courtyard.

Sarah's eyes followed her friend's hand. A titanic bat, carrying a man, flew west across the space.

She shivered. The bat from Isabella's dark delivery — only larger.

They watched the beast swoop over to the golden building, drop the man out of sight, then fly straight into the portico. A distant crashing sound echoed back to them.

"What the hell was that?" Sam said.

"Al-Nasir," Sarah said.

"And his cargo was probably Pastor Parris," Anne said.

"How come he's flying in daylight?" Sam asked.

"Maybe sunlight doesn't kill vampires here," Alex said. "We're not in Massachusetts anymore." He smiled, his eyes covering Sarah like chalk on a blackboard.

He was wearing the least clothing she'd ever seen on a man, even at the beach.

"And Papa thought this place would even the odds," she said.

Alex grabbed her arm. "The holy holy," he said. "Your father yelled something about it, just before we left the basement."

Sarah tried to concentrate, not easy to do since he was still touching her.

"The Holy of Holies?" she said.

"Yes, that's it! He said to get the vampire there."

Sarah pointed at the golden building where the monster had gone.

"He's way ahead of you. *Beit HaMikdash,* the House of the Lord. Inside is the room with the tablets Moses brought down from Mount Sinai. Only the High Priest is allowed there. God's supposed to strike down anyone else."

"If anyone needs smiting, it's those two," Anne said. "Let's make sure they get what's coming to them."

They jogged toward the temple, Alex and Sam in the lead. Sarah might be an angel, but her feet still hurt.

After a while a stitch in the side forced her to stop.

Anne, also barefoot, was limping badly as she caught up and leaned against her arm.

"I... no... farther," Sarah said.

Anne's fingers tickled softly against Sarah's skin. Out of the corner of her eye she saw a flickering light.

Her pain gave way to a curious euphoria.

"Let's catch up," Anne said.

They ran arm in arm to the western end of the courtyard. A bronze basin with legs like giant bulls dominated the front of the sanctuary stairs.

"I think that's the pastor running behind that metal thing," Anne said.

"It's called the Molten Sea," Sarah said. "Are you sure that was him? He looked... really different."

"So does everybody here," Sam said. "Alex, why don't we each take a girl and go around different sides — cut him off."

Anne grabbed her brother's hand and went left, Sarah and Alex went right.

Coming around the corner of the Molten Sea, they found the man in front of the steps. He stared at the twins, his back to Sarah and Alex. The plan, such as it was, had worked.

The man shuffled his feet. Not feet, Sarah realized, but cloven hooves, and what they'd taken for pants was actually fur. He looked like Pan, but his face belonged to Pastor Parris.

"Flee while you have the chance!" he yelled. "He'll be back soon."

Anne yelled back at him, "Release your spell on my sister, Pastor Parris, by everything that's holy."

Sam — never much the talker — hurled his spear at the pastor. The man dove to the side, but the wooden shaft caught him in the thigh. He screamed and went down.

Anne was on him in a second, kicking his gut with her bare feet.

"Release her, you bastard!"

The pastor scrabbled upright, then sprang into the air, leaping unnaturally high. He caught himself on the edge of the tank and pulled himself onto the lip, then yanked the spear out of his furry thigh and tossed it down, screaming.

"*Ex meus vita cruor, serpens.*" Sarah recognized the Latin. *From my life blood, snakes.*

The bloody spear writhed and twisted on the stones, then broke apart into tiny red snakes.

"Back up!" Alex grabbed her arm. "I'm betting he conjured the poisonous variety."

Sarah heard the pastor splashing about in the tank. Off to the side, Sam was wrestling with the top of a burning brazier. He managed to pull the heavy thing free and run it to the tank, then lob it up and over, into the water.

It splashed without much of an effect, but Sam ran to another brazier, grabbed it, then threw that one in as well.

Sarah heard a whoosh, and half the Molten Sea erupted into flame. She saw the pastor twisting in the inferno, screaming.

He dove under the water and emerged a few seconds later free of flames. Anne streaked around to the far side of the tank and climbed a ladder to intercept him.

"Anne, get away!" Sam yelled as he chucked another brazier into the water.

But Anne was already grappling with the pastor at the rim and screaming.

"Give me the doll!"

Sarah slid to the left to get back to the tank without nearing the nasty little serpents.

The pastor looked terrible, the skin on his upper body reddened and blistered — again. Anne jammed a thumb into one of his eyes and now it was he who screamed. The scuffle didn't last long.

"Got it!" Anne called out. "Sarah?"

She threw a small object high into the air—

Sarah spread her wings, leapt, flapped wildly, and found herself aloft. In no time she swept across the space to intercept the doll then beat her wings and fluttered back to earth. She ran up the stairs to peer into the pool. The pastor was gone. The twins perched on the lip of the tank, staring into the water, Sam holding sword in hand.

"Where'd he go?" Sarah called down. "Never mind, we can free Emily." She held the doll high. It was an ugly little thing made of rag and wax, and it smelled awful.

"He vanished," Alex called back. "Just splashed himself with water, said something in Latin, and vanished."

Behind her, Sarah heard a creaking. The air swirled. She smelled cinnamon and almonds.

My first killer, and yours.

She tried to leap into the sky but found herself yanked back through the sanctuary doors. Cruel talons wrenched her wing. She screamed. Pain consumed her consciousness as hideous gray arms lifted her high.

Fifty-Seven:
Enemy at the Gates

Temple of Solomon, Thursday, November 20, 1913

FROM THE BOTTOM OF THE STAIRS, Alex saw the vampire emerge from the sanctuary before Sarah did. He had no time to warn her — the monster snatched her up before she even knew he was there and her scream cut Alex to the core.

The awful scene unfolded before him. Anne and Sam were caught on the far side of the tank. At the top of the stairs, the vampire lifted Sarah over his head and shook her. Her scream poisoned the air and one of her wings fluttered loose and broken.

Alex pulled his sling from his belt, grabbed a stone, and started up the stairs.

The vampire reached under Sarah's thin garment and raked her belly. Her screams redoubled and blood soaked the white linen.

"No!"

The vampire's laugh sounded like a bark. "How the verse is turned around! Three great insults you have offered, and three times you will repay in blood."

Alex stopped on the second step to aim and fire. The shot streaked forward, trailing orange through the air. But inexperience sent it wide to explode against one of the big pillars. He had to get closer. He loaded another shot and resumed climbing. Above him, the vampire brought the winged talon to his face and extended a crimson tongue to lick Sarah's blood.

The creature threw back his head and laugh-barked.

"Perhaps Allah, cursed be His name, still favors me, for He has placed into my hand the Horn the Dung God sought for centuries." He shook Sarah for emphasis, and Alex winced at her soft whimper.

Halfway up the stairs, he launched his second stone. The vampire dodged, but not fast enough, for the rock caught his wing. There was a tiny burst of orange flame, and the stone ripped clear through the thin membrane.

The creature roared. Sarah flopped about in his talons like a toy in a toddler's hands.

"So you wish further debt?"

At the three-quarter mark Alex paused for another shot, but the vampire was dancing around so much he might hit Sarah. He ran up the last few stairs to the top, where the vampire cavorted about the entrance to the sanctuary.

"Consider this the first of your payments." He hurled Sarah into the air.

Alex watched in horror as she arced through the sky to crash like a limp doll on the stairs below. She lay still, a heap of feathers and bloody linen.

He willed himself through a forest of black and red thoughts. He couldn't look at her, not now, but instead turned from Sarah's lifeless form to the vampire. The fanged mouth opened and the beast crouched to leap.

Alex loosed his third shot. It struck the vampire square in the chest, bursting into flame. He bellowed and screamed, beat his wings against his burning torso, and shuffled back into the dark chamber.

Alex strode across the porch and from between the two gold columns released a fourth shot, which caught the vampire in the shoulder and spun him about in a swirl of fire. The creature retreated to the wooden doorposts at the far end. There, a dancer of shadow and flame.

Alex raised his sling and loaded his final pellet.

Tears furrowed his dusty face. "This stone," he whispered, "has written on it the true name of God." He released his grip.

The sling twanged like a divine note plucked on some cosmic harp. The stone burned forward to strike the vampire's head as he cowered at the entrance to the room within a room. He was lifted off his feet and hurled into the smoky rear chamber.

The vampire vanished into the mist, taking with him all sound, all sensation. The next thing Alex knew he was transfixed by a beam of the purest light. Nothing moved, nothing sounded, nothing felt. There was only the light.

Fifty-Eight:
Seventy-two Virgins

Unknown Locale, Thursday, November 20, 1913

THE SWIRL OF INCENSE AND THE STING of al-Nasir's wounds gave way to the bubbling eddies of fountains and the smell of honeyed dates. Palms shaded tiled courtyards. Rich robes caressed his body and naked virgins pressed jeweled dishes into his hands.

In those last moments, denied his revenge, had he stumbled into *Jannah* and its byways of delight?

He sucked the jasmine air, bit into the sweetness of a fruit, and reached down to fondle the soft buttock of a youth.

But the silky skin burned hot against his hand, and the winsome flesh crumbled into dust. All around, trees and slaves dissolved into dervishes of sand. The sun hammered down to ignite liquid air. And it was not the tongues of young lovers but the fiery fingers of *ifrit* that grasped his limbs. His body seared and cooked. His skin blackened and crisped. Thumbs of flame ripped muscles and tendons from bone.

The surface of the earth cracked and breached. No breath carried his tumbling screams.

Down to *Jahannam.* The inferno.

Fifty-Nine:
Climbing into the Light

Temple of Solomon, Thursday, November 20, 1913

A STORM OF BRITTLE OBJECTS PELTED Alex about the head and shoulders. Silently, the inner doors to the Holy of Holies closed, snuffing out the glow. Sensation faded back into the world.

Minutes before, the sanctuary had been in disarray, but now it was meticulously arranged. He glanced down to discover what had struck him and found the area littered with bleached bones. A femur here, ribs there, even a misshapen skull studded with razor-long teeth. Not a single shard remained on the inner side of the threshold.

God, it seemed, had settled accounts with Ali ibn Hammud al-Nasir.

But Sarah?

Alex ran down the stairs to find Anne crouched over her crumpled form. The swirling clouds had turned dark and ominous. From the courtyard, priests streamed toward them.

"She's not breathing!" Sam squatted beside Anne, his face as white as the vampire's bones.

Alex knelt. Something was wrong with the angle of her back, and one of her wings lay smashed beneath her. Brittle bones jutted from the feathery mass. Dark red drooled from her lips. He felt nothing but desolation.

Anne held one of Sarah's hands as she rocked back and forth. Then a beatific expression lit her face, and her body began to emit a soft white light. A nimbus spread from her hands to Sarah's body.

Sarah shifted, and her mangled wing twitched and straightened. Her eyes shot open. She coughed and sprayed her friends with bloody spittle.

Alex didn't care.

The wounds on her stomach healed and faded in front of their eyes, leaving only dried blood on clean white flesh. She released Anne's hand and tried to pull down the tunic to cover her legs. The glow around both girls faded.

"Remind me never to get mauled to death by a vampire again."

Alex watched Sarah's wings waving behind her as she talked with the High Priest. In the background, the giant tank of water still burned with white flames. Dried blood still edged Sarah's lips, but she seemed in great spirits, full of energy even. She put a hand to her mouth.

The gesture was so unconsciously cute that Alex spun her around and kissed her full on the lips before he'd quite decided to do it. Her eyes went wide, just inches from his, but she was kissing him back when they heard the High Priest.

"Please remember we stand on God's holy ground."

Sarah pulled away. "Emily's doll! Where is it? I had it when the vampire attacked me."

She blew him a kiss, then raced up the stairs, stopped midway, flapped her wings and more or less flew to the top. She paced the portico, searching the ground.

"Disgusting!" she yelled down. "I'm getting vampire bones stuck between my toes."

Alex joined her. He found the doll perched on the base of a pillar.

"Its name is *Boaz*," Sarah said.

"The doll?" Alex said.

"No, ninny, the pillar." Somehow, he even enjoyed her little insults.

"The pillar has a name?"

She nodded. "The other one is *Jachin.*"

Alex supposed God could name His pillars if He was so inclined. Sarah and Alex walked down the stairs together. He took her hand. If the cat was out of the bag, he might as well enjoy the advantages.

Sarah showed the doll to the High Priest.

"This evil thing was constructed to steal the life from their little sister." She indicated the twins.

The High Priest held out his hand toward the little bundle of rags, hair, and wax.

"May I?" He brought the doll close to his face. "Although expertly built, it's a straightforward sympathetic binding. The form analogizes the nature...."

Alex watched Sarah while the man blathered on about how to unravel the warlock's curse.

"I'm going to do it here," she said when he was finished. "Magic works better in this place, I don't think I'll even need any paraphernalia."

"Is it safe?" Anne said.

Sarah sat cross-legged on the stone, clutched the little doll in her lap, and chanted some prayer or another.

There was a brief white flash, and the doll unraveled into a handful of rags and hair. She let the pieces drift from her hands to the pavement.

"Is that it?" Sarah asked the priest.

"Your sister should be free."

Anne rushed in and hugged Sarah, then the man — who turned bright red and tried to back away.

"No, no, my oaths!"

"What's the matter?" Anne released him.

"The priests took oaths not to touch women," Sarah said. "Speaking of touching..." She jabbed a finger at each of the twins. "Not a word about me and Alex to my father."

Sam slapped Alex on the back. It wasn't the most gentle of taps.

"We'd best look to finding our way home," Alex said. "I don't think it's a good idea to dawdle here."

"What about the warlock?" Anne said. "He just disappeared—"

"As far as I'm concerned, he can go to hell," Sam said.

"That's a certainty," Alex said, "but hopefully sooner rather than later."

Sarah fished her little silver necklace out from under her tunic and showed it to the priest.

"My father used this *mezuzah* to build a magical bridge to this place. Would you know how to get us back?"

The High Priest squinted at the tiny amulet. He touched it with the tip of his staff and both emitted the same soft white light.

"An elegant construction. I think he left the door cracked for you. That must be exhausting."

The priest started chanting.

The white glow from the amulet and staff intensified.

The world began to white out—

Alex tumbled onto the dirt floor of the cellar. His friends, dressed now in their normal winter clothes, were sprawled nearby. Mr. Engelmann sat on the ground cross-legged. He looked old and tired.

Sixty:
Awakenings

Salem, Massachusetts, Thursday night, November 20

EMILY WOKE EXHAUSTED. Her room smelled stuffy and the curtains were drawn — odd, since she liked sunrise to wake her. She felt feverish and dizzy. How had she gotten into bed, anyway? The last thing she remembered was Sunday services at church.

She threw back the covers, intending to turn on a light. Hopefully Anne wouldn't wake. When she tried to stand, her legs gave way and she toppled to the floor. She bit her tongue and pulled herself up to the nightstand for a candle.

She fumbled with the matches, gripped the table for support, fumbled with the matches again. Finally she got one lit.

Where'd Anne gone in the middle of the night? Her bed was empty and made. The room was completely rearranged. The dresser was covered in folded piles of nightgowns and towels.

She was wearing a nightgown her mother must have picked — pink with lacy white trim. Her arms and legs looked thin.

Images jumped into her head: a hideous purple-faced woman touched her in ways both soft and painful, and a dusty skeleton lay on a table. She shuddered. Too tired to stay upright any longer, she slid to the floor with her back against the wall.

A funny bit of something was around her ankle. She tugged and snapped it free, tossed it aside into the darkness. She had no energy to move, so she sat, spreading her toes and relaxing them, trying to bring feeling back to her stiff muscles.

The clock in the hall chimed twice — hours till dawn. She felt too tired to even try to stand.

"Mommy!" Her voice sounded hoarse, her throat dry.

In seconds she heard footsteps hurrying down the hall. Hopefully they wouldn't mind being woken. The door to her room opened. The light came on, and instead of being upset, Mommy hugged and hugged her, Daddy hovering behind in his checked flannel robe.

"Emily! You're up, darling! Has the fever broken? Let's get you back to bed."

Emily's half-closed eyes turned the twinkling flame of the candle into little stars. She looked up through it at her parents. Mommy's round face showed only relief, but the flickering light made Daddy's skin look like a bowl of clam chowder filled with squirming black crawfish.

"I'm fine, Mommy, just tired and a little dizzy. Have I been sick?"

Sixty-One:
Retreat into Fire

Temple of Solomon and Unknown Locale, Thursday, November 20, 1913

WATER, PARTICULARLY HOLY WATER, was an effective magical shield, and Parris had wrapped it around himself, becoming practically invisible. Back in the material plane, the spell would have taken time and reagents, like the bay leaves and opal. Here he only needed the water itself and a simple incantation. Small blessings.

He tasted blood and pus, his burned face and arm throbbed, and he couldn't see out of the eye the Williams girl had poked. Wading in the center of the tank didn't give him a great vantage point, but as the children and the priests gathered below, he knew the outcome couldn't be good. No sign of the vampire. Soon enough, the priest raised his staff and the meddling teens vanished.

Parris remained, drifting alone in a sea of misery, until the priests wandered off. If he didn't act soon, he would succumb to the pain and drown in this wretched realm. Fixating on some of his own blood he chanted:

Power of the warlocks rise, course unseen through the skies.
Come to us who call you near, come to us who call you here.
Down roads of fire and flame, come forth to bring pain.
Blood to blood I summon thee, blood to blood return to me.

Betty must have been waiting for him. She parted the flames to perch on the lip of the tank.

"Toy, I find you a bit worse for the wear."

"I'm not even sure I can walk."

She hopped down and waded over to him. Her dirty corset was soon soaked, and his eyes tracked the saggy curves of her breasts. She reached out and caressed his burnt peeling face.

"My poor, poor Toy. I liked both your eyes." She extended her purple tongue to lick the burned half of his face. It was agonizing, but when she was finished, the pain receded.

He clung to her wet skin, the texture of a fish washed up on shore days before. She helped him to the edge of the tank, carried him down the ladder and up to the portico, where it was obvious that Mr. Nasir's long unlife had finally come to a tragic end. She fetched a golden coffer from the outer sanctuary, and they collected every fragment they could find, including the hideous skull. Mr. Nasir would wish to be buried in his homeland or, failing that, one never knew when the bones of such a creature might come in handy.

Then down the stairs and into the flame.

Crossing through, Betty brought him to the muddy shore of a misty lake. Far in the distance, he heard the sounds of clashing arms and the screams of the dying. On the shoreline squatted a tiny hovel with a roof of dried dung.

Inside, Dr. Faustus' lost grimoire lay on a filthy pallet pushed up against one wall.

"You got it for me?" he asked.

"You left the fire burning in the vampire's hearth," she said. "I thought it the least I could do."

He tried to kiss her, but the pain made him swoon.

"You can recover here," Betty said. "Then I'll take you back to your world. Unless you decide to stay, of course."

Desiccated fish heads hung from the rafters of the tiny dwelling, and flies buzzed thickly about discarded piles of offal.

She'd never before invited him home.

Sixty-Two:
Bedwarmer

Salem, Massachusetts, Friday before dawn, November 21, 1913

Sarah finished in the upstairs bathroom. It was after three in the morning, and she should try to get some sleep.

Anne was outside waiting when she opened the door to the hall. She held a candle — the electricity had shorted. Sarah's room had been spared the worst of the destruction, but her parents' bedroom was open to the sky, and snow fluttered down through the gaping hole in the roof above the stairwell. Anyway, for tonight, Papa slept on the living room couch. Snoring.

"What did your mother say about Emily?" Sarah asked.

"We didn't talk long," Anne said, "but apparently she's up and chattering away like nothing happened. She's thin and weak but 'has a healthy appetite.' Which for my mother is the definition of wellness."

"That's wonderful." Sarah had been tense with worry for so long, she hadn't quite let it go.

"Come to our house tomorrow. See for yourself."

"I'll ask Papa."

"Lovely," Anne said. "But now I want to know about you and Alex — you haven't mentioned him in days and you've *never* really given me the story. When did it start and how far has it gone?"

Sarah was surprised Anne had waited this long before cornering her.

"Since the night on the boat. Not *that* far. And it hasn't all been smooth sailing."

"Tart!" Anne smacked her arm. "Is the kissing good?"

Despite the freezing air, Sarah's face felt hot. "With everything that's been going on, I've hardly had time to think about it."

"Are you going to tell your parents?" Anne asked.

"I just can't," Sarah said. "I care about him, more and more. But if we got married, Papa might disown me."

The wind whistled through the hole in the roof, so raw it cut through Sarah's robe.

"I don't think he'd go that far," Anne said. "But would you?"

Alex slipped into her room before she fell asleep.

Sarah let him under the covers. Sam had turned off the boiler because broken pipes were spraying water, so the whole house was freezing.

She curled against his chest, and as she hoped, he kissed her. The feeling didn't compare to anything else, except maybe magic. The sensation of their lips pressed together wasn't that special, but she just wanted to keep on doing it, long past the point where any other activity engaged in for so long would have bored her.

"Aren't you afraid your father will catch us?" Alex asked.

"Holding the gateway open exhausted him. I think he's out for the night."

He ran his fingers through her hair, tangling them in the curls.

"Why does something so wrong have to feel so right?" she said, nuzzling his neck.

"I'm all for moral rectitude, but in this case I have to cast my vote for impropriety."

"Tomorrow, I'm going to visit Emily." She gave his neck a little nip. "You should come."

"It's a date, then." He kissed her again. And again.

Sarah put her legs around one of his and pressed them together. She'd never felt like this before. Reckless. Excited. Maybe almost dying did this to you.

They kept kissing. When he unlaced the tie around her neck and slid a hand underneath her nightgown, she held her breath but didn't stop him.

Just a few minutes more. Then she'd make him go back to his room.

Sixty-Three:
A Surprising Gift

Salem, Massachusetts, Friday, November 21, 1913

DADDY HAD SEEMED A BIT STIFF this morning when he brought Emily the new puppy, but two dogs were going to be so much fun. This one came with a weird name Emily shortened to Nuby, which suited his delicate silver limbs, and she'd tied a blue ribbon to his collar. Daddy didn't know his breed, but she'd fetched the kennel club book from downstairs and Nuby looked like a funny Mexican dog called the Chihuahua except his ears were pointier and his snout longer.

The door to her room opened and Mr. Barnyard zoomed in, followed by her mother.

"Emily, the gang of four has come to visit you."

Mr. Barnyard stood beside the bed, a low growl in his throat. Jealous already!

"I'm feeling great, Mom," Emily said. "Send them up."

Nuby was on his feet now, his little tail held rigid. He growled at Mr. Barnyard, tiny teeth bared, but the pitch was so high he sounded silly.

Mr. Barnyard started barking. Not silly.

"You two," Mommy said, grabbing both dogs by their collars, "are going out back to settle your differences."

Sixty-Four:
In the Land of Moriah

Salem, Massachusetts, Friday, November 21, 1913

AFTER VISITING EMILY, Sarah and Alex held hands as they descended the stairs into the Williams foyer.

"We can leave in a minute." He looked embarrassed. "But I need a quick visit to the outhouse first."

He left and she noticed Mr. Williams standing near the coat rack.

"I didn't see you there, sir," Sarah said. "Congratulations on Emily's recovery." She stepped forward to give him a hug.

He skittered back. "You'd best keep your distance. I've brought home a bit of a bug from my sister's."

He did look pale, and stress over Emily's illness had made him thinner, emphasizing his height.

Alex stomped back into the room.

"Ready to go?" He noticed Mr. Williams. "Sir, your new dog killed a squirrel in the back yard. He's making a mess of the innards."

Mr. Williams sighed. "He thinks himself something of a ratter."

Alex whispered to Sarah, "We could go over to my house, if you like."

"I promised Papa I'd be right home." He had that puppy dog look. "I'll come over this evening," she said. "It's *shabbos*, so I'll be there right around sunset."

"I'll see you both soon," Mr. Williams said, backing out of the room.

Sarah followed Alex out to the car.

"I can't wait to get you alone," he said as he pulled out into the street.

"We're only talking about a few hours."

"We'll have privacy," he said. "Grandfather's hardly going to get out of his chair and harass us."

The ride was only about two minutes long.

"Don't you have services tonight?" he said when he pulled up to the curb.

"I'm feeling reckless," she said.

He raised an eyebrow.

She didn't dare kiss him in front of the house.

"Maybe you'll get lucky."

Sarah found Papa in his study. Mama had once compared him to a spider, waiting in the middle of a web for prey to come to him.

"You still look tired, Papa."

He set his pipe on the desk to come around and hug her.

"Even God's aid is not without cost," he said. "You're sure the vampire's dead? And Pastor Parris?"

"The pastor vanished, so we don't know what happened to him. But even if he's alive, I doubt he'll dare return here. As to the vampire — given that the creature was literally obliterated by the wrath of God, I'd say we've seen the last of him." She sighed. "I just don't understand why *Hashem* even allows the existence of such a beast."

"I form light and create darkness, I make weal and create woe— I the Lord do all these things," Papa quoted in Hebrew.

"Isaiah 45:7?"

He looked pleased. Sarah didn't.

"So that's it. God has a plan? That's just—" He held up a hand, and she stopped.

"Admittedly," he said, "the divine scheme can be perplexing to the rest of us."

"One of the things I don't understand — and there's plenty — is the aspects we assumed in the Temple. I like to think I'm a good person but I wouldn't exactly call myself angelic."

He didn't say anything for a couple of minutes. Sarah waited him out.

"I think I finally owe you the truth about what I did," he said.

She felt her heart pound faster. "With the Horn?"

"You remember in September of 1909, when your mother had influenza?"

"Of course." Mama's fever had taken over a week to break.

"September 29 is celebrated throughout the Christian West as the Feast of Saint Gabriel," he said.

Today is the Feast of Saint Gabriel, the wolf had said to her.

"The Horn was in my desk," Papa continued, "and from it spoke a voice of cold red flame."

"Like Moses at the burning bush?"

"More like the *Akedah.*"

An angel of the Lord had asked Abraham to sacrifice his son Isaac in the land of Moriah. The very spot where Jerusalem was founded, where Solomon built his Temple.

"Why don't I remember?" She felt so cold. Like she had lying broken on the temple stones, until Anne touched her with so warm hands.

"God's small mercy, I suppose."

"He's mean — *Hashem.*"

Papa tried to smile. "God tested Abraham. Why should it be any different for us?"

Sarah heard the horn, slow and mournful. *The horn sounds our sacrifice. My death, your blood, your death, my blood. I save you and you save me.*

She remembered now. Papa had taken her down to the cellar. She was cold then, too, wearing only her nightgown. He'd seated her on the roots in the back, her bare feet resting on the dry wood.

Then a voice spoke. It was a whisper, yet the loudest sound in the world.

"Joseph, Joseph."

"*Hineni*," he said, "here I am," and kicked off his shoes.

"As surely as your blood and your voice know my name," the angel said, "my voice shall know the blood of your blood."

Pain twisted Sarah's innards then. Her first blood ran warm down her calves, slicked the roots and her toes.

She followed Papa's hand to between her feet.

He placed a horn there. A most glorious Horn, about a foot long, engraved with Hebrew letters and encircled in gold. Her blood — black in the dim light — dripped onto it.

The long trumpeting note droned on and on.

Beneath Sarah, the roots began to glow and shimmer. They grew brighter, more vibrant, transforming from dirty tubes of wood into the verdant branches of a living tree. Leaves emerged from buds unseen, opening themselves. Soon she felt like a queen seated on a glorious living throne. The tree continued to swell around her, buds giving way to glorious orange and red fruits. She breathed in the intoxicating smell, akin to orange blossoms yet indescribably grander.

"Papa, can I have a fruit?" she heard herself say.

"Don't touch them, little *malka*."

Her skin tingled. She looked to the side and saw the expanse of Paradise, the Garden of Eden. This was no ordinary tree, watered and fed with her blood. There, in that dark basement, the tree of wood and tree of knowledge became one and the same. The layers of God's creation compressed together.

Twelve year-old Sarah had tapped her foot. "I'm going to get down if that's okay."

Papa took her hand as she stepped down to the dirt floor, had hugged her close, not caring about her blood-soaked garment.

Before their eyes, the tree withdrew. At first the fruit shrank to nothingness, then the leaves folded, and finally the glow faded. When it was no more, the blood on the roots and the Horn itself were gone, too. Nothing remained but the limbs of an old sycamore.

Sarah shook her head to clear her thoughts, trying to focus on the four walls of Papa's study. The trumpeting of the horn faded from her ears.

"God had you do that?"

"Obedience to the Lord is not bondage but righteousness." His eyes looked so sad. "It's less than he asked of Abraham."

"God's still mean," she said. "What happened to the Horn?"

"The Lord used us to return it to Paradise, to the Garden of Eden, where it belongs. Now it waits there with Gabriel, so he may bring it to Elijah."

"That's why I had the wings in the Temple?"

Papa toked on his pipe, but it had gone out. "The object we perceive as the Horn," he said, "is but a protrusion of God's Strength into the world. Such a powerful force has likely tugged on us, just as the moon pulls on the ocean to create the tides."

The Strength of God sings in our blood, Isabella had said. *The passage is almost open, beyond lies Paradise, and the dark gift redeemed.*

"And the monsters? What do they want with the Horn?"

Joseph clicked his teeth on the tip of his pipe. "They keep their own council."

"But God won't let anything really bad happen, right?" Sarah asked.

"He saw to the vampire's end, did He not?"

"So we've postponed the End of Days?"

"Given that all men must be righteous first," Joseph said, "I think we still have a bit of time."

They both laughed.

"I have a train to catch," he said. "Are you sure you don't want to come?"

She shook her head.

He was going to stay with the Hoffmanns until the house was repaired — there went his money for a car — but Anne had offered to put Sarah up. Boston was too far from school… and Alex.

"What about the Sabbath?" he asked.

After what God had put her through, she really didn't feel like praying just now.

Sixty-Five:
The Toast

Salem, Massachusetts, Friday evening, November 21, 1913

SARAH RODE THE TROLLEY OUT toward Alex's house, not even trying to stop thinking about him. She'd never felt this way about a boy — a man, really — and wrong religion or not, Alex was a good man. She hated to disappoint her father, but really, after everything that happened, didn't she deserve something for herself? The worst that could happen was his being upset with her for a couple of weeks. If he expected her to forgive him, she could hope for the same.

And she *had* just survived near death at the hands of a nine hundred-year-old vampire. What was the point of following all the rules if God was just going to test your faith regardless?

With voices and blood in the basement....

She shuddered then hopped off the trolley at the junction. Her boots crunched in the snow, already packed hard. Walking west, she watched the sun crawl downward. Did Khepri really drag it across the sky? Was the sun a ball of dung pulled by a cosmic beetle?

In any case, the temperature would soon drop. She picked up her pace.

She still had questions. Was Alex the wolf in her dream, or Mr. Palaogos? Was everyone part of some giant cosmic plan? None of it made any sense, but if Mr. Palaogos *was* the wolf, he should have some answers.

Sarah let herself in through the gate as the last sliver of sun dropped below the horizon. She knocked on the front door. Unlocked, it drifted open at her touch.

"Alex, are you home?" Sarah called out. The foyer was dark. When she heard nothing, she edged closer to the stairs. "Hello?"

She heard a soft voice from the library and followed it.

"Good evening, Sarah."

It wasn't a large room, and the sheer mass of bookshelves further cramped the area. Old Mr. Palaogos sat alone in his chair by the window. He had a book on his lap but stared at the drawn curtains.

"Good evening. Is Alex home?"

The old man looked frail, his skin almost translucent.

"Call me Constantine. I'm sure he'll be downstairs momentarily."

Had Alex said anything to him? The old man seemed so ancient it was hard to imagine him even thinking about such matters.

"I hear congratulations are in order," Constantine said. "You've saved your friend and vanquished Ali ibn Hammud al-Nasir. This is no small matter. For nearly a millennium, he stalked the earth. No small matter indeed." He reached for a dusty decanter and crystal glasses, poured red wine into two.

"A toast, to the first of old debts settled."

"I think you owe me the truth about Isabella," Sarah said.

He pointed behind her, at a small painting on the wall. Sarah had once seen an Italian Renaissance exhibition in Boston, and this portrait would have fit right in. Isabella's red braids were bound tightly about her head and fresh garlands of red roses hung from the gold frame.

"I agree," the old man said.

When she turned back, his smile as he offered the glass looked every bit the wolf.

"This vintage is exotic and ancient, quite lovely." *Try some* echoed oddly in her head.

Part of Sarah wanted to scream. She felt hot and flushed and didn't know why. The other part of her wanted to accept the glass. She reached for it. The wine was exotic: meaty, salty, perfumed. *Finish your glass, dear.*

"It would offend the gods to waste it." He threw back his own goblet and emptied it.

She couldn't think clearly. She backed up and reached a hand out to steady herself against a bookshelf but still lifted the glass to her lips and finished it.

She looked over at Mr. Palaogos, but his chair was empty. Instead, a wolf stood on all fours in the small space between them. His eyes glowed like rubies. She held out her hand, and he sniffed at it delicately. Everything seemed to rotate as he curled about her knees, pressing into her skirts like Mr. Barnyard.

Then the wolf vanished, and Constantine stood behind her. Looking down, she saw his purple slippers — always a touch of purple, color of kings. His hand took hers. Part of her wanted to flinch, part of her wanted to grasp him back. His hand wasn't that of an old man, his touch smooth and cool.

He spun her to face him, pulled off her overcoat, and unbuttoned her jacket and scarf. They fell to the floor.

"The passage draws near. Remember the city decked in red? Today is November 21, the Orthodox Feast of Saint Gabriel."

"March..." she muttered. So dizzy. Papa had said it was March.

"In the west, my dear. We Greeks are slow to change our calendars."

He looked forty years younger, just as in her dreams, except her sleeping mind must have added the fur. He and Alex bore a strong resemblance, one that hadn't been so evident in the old man's visage.

Sarah staggered back against the hard shelves. Her mouth felt filled with cotton.

"You were in my dreams?"

"You invited me into your home. I'm afraid I couldn't resist returning for the occasional drink." He was smiling, his teeth very long and white. "You and Isabella have so much in common, I'm glad you chose each other."

"For what?" The room continued to spin.

"I'm sorry it comes to this." He cupped her chin in one hand and rested the other on her bare neck. "The passage grows near, and I only know one way to bring her back, to make old wrongs right. The beetle has forced my hand."

Constantine caressed her neck. The pulse of her blood rang in her ears, her body refused to run, and even the will to do so froze in her veins.

"What was in the wine?"

"The dark gift," he said, "the blood of my long dead lover, my wife, my mother, my Isis — Isabella's life, her soul."

If another were to share my blood, I might find my way back.

He smiled and his canines, already sharp, lengthened.

His wife hadn't just been killed and risen a vampire, she'd made him one herself.

Gently, he pulled Sarah's head to the side, leaned in, and nipped her neck. The pain was brief.

Sixty-Six:
Dogs

Salem, Massachusetts, Friday evening, November 21, 1913

LYING IN BED IN HIS SCRATCHY underclothes, Alex relived each fleeting moment in Sarah's bed. It had taken every bit of his strength to leave her at her house, but he understood she needed to talk to her father.

He didn't know if he could contain himself until she arrived. As he lay there, hard and excited, he rolled on his side and imagined that she was facing him without—

"Alex, are you home?" Her voice drifted up from below.

He sprang up and began to dress.

"I'll be there in a minute," he yelled down, doubting she'd hear. For some reason, the stairwell conveyed sound upward better than down.

After donning the minimum acceptable clothing, he pounded down the two flights of stairs. She must be talking to Grandfather, because the library light was on and he heard murmurs from inside.

He entered — and froze.

She hung limp in Grandfather's arms. Blood streaked her neck. His eyes glowed ruby red.

No. *No!*

He collapsed to his knees. Pain hit Alex's temples like a tamping iron hammering his skull. His brain seemed to explode as forgotten fragments surfaced.

He remembered the high-pitched yipping of dogs. He was a little boy watching his black-haired grandfather storm out of their cottage, sword in hand. Beyond, he saw a creature of nightmare: a man with the head of a beetle clutching a ball of fire. He saw Dimitri drag Grandfather back inside, his teeth now long bright fangs.

The stark horror of it stared him in the face.

Grandfather was a vampire. He knew so much about the undead because no life beat in his own chest.

Alex tried to rise but enormous arms clasped him from behind, dragged him from the room, away from her.

Alex struggled in Dmitri's iron grip, but it was useless. The hairy giant might have thought the blows rained on his head the buzzing of flies. He carried Alex downstairs and hurled him into the wine cellar.

The heavy oak door slammed shut before he could get to his feet. He heard the bolt slide home. His head hurt so bad he could barely think.

Dmitri was Grandfather's thrall. How could he have been so blind?

Because his grandfather, his grandfather the vampire, had glamoured the memories out of him, that's why. But they came now, and they hurt like hell.

The cottage on Mount Athos. His parents had lived there too. When Dmitri dragged Grandfather back inside, flaming arrows protruding from his chest, Father helped him to the bed and Mama wiped his brow. But the wounds were too great, the beast within too strong. The wolf surfaced, bringing with him blood and death. Dmitri tried to stop the animal, but it was too strong, feasting on the blood of its kin to save its wretched unlife.

His parents.

Perhaps the old monster hadn't meant to, but Grandfather had killed his parents, then killed Alex's every memory of them. His whole life had been a lie.

Except Sarah. Jesus, no.

As it had on the stairs in the Temple, rage swelled at the back of his head, driving out the pain, clearing his mind. Rage at the betrayal, rage for his parents, rage at what was being done to Sarah.

Maybe it wasn't too late. Sarah had been bitten but she was still alive. It took death to create the undead.

Alex slammed his shoulder against the unyielding door until it ached. He pulled a bottle of wine from a stone niche and smashed it against the planks. Red juice splashed across the oak and drooled down like blood.

He sat on the cold stone floor with his head in his hands and cried. Broken glass cut his palms and the room stank of sour grapes. He had no notion of how much time had passed when he noticed the ladder lurking in the shadows.

Its sides were wood, but the rungs were not. He hurled it to the floor and stomped and twisted the brittle parts until he pried free an iron bar.

Then he went to work on the door.

Sixty-Seven:
Sacrifices

Salem, Massachusetts, Friday night, November 21, 1913

SARAH WOKE SHIVERING. The sky was still orange, and she lay in the snow. At her feet, Constantine tugged off her stockings. He'd already removed her boots, skirts, and petticoats. They lay heaped on the dirty white ground. A huge tree stood near, bare of any leaves.

She struggled to move, but her limbs remained frozen.

"Don't make this harder than it needs to be," he said. He finished removing her undergarments, and she felt the searing chill of snow on her bare bottom.

How had she spoken with him, shared *Shabbos* dinner with him, and never known he was a vampire? She felt ill. He'd used his glamour to make her drink blood. Had her dreams been no more than the icy touch of his dead fingers on her mind?

He moved forward and set to work on her corset.

"I'm not going to rape you," he said. "You needn't worry about that. I really am sorry, but *they* can never be allowed to have it."

She found she could talk. "Please, let me go. What would Alex think?" A horrifying thought crossed her mind. "Or does he know what you are?"

He shook his head as he tugged off her corset and began unwinding the band of cloth wrapped around her breasts.

"The poor boy witnessed our departure — Dmitri had to restrain him. He may never forgive me. This night will be costly for us both, but only you can stop them."

"Who are they? Say what you mean." She tried to scream, but what emerged was a tiny moan. *Trust the wolf. At the moment of the passage, his cruelty and kindness shall unlock everything.*

Constantine clicked his tongue at her. "You nearly died at the hands of the Caliph. Now the beetle god has crossed the Western Sea." He spat blood on the white snow. "He'll be here soon. He ripped my love limb from limb, bathed her in fire, and left me only dust."

"Why don't you just fight him?"

"He commands the sun. He would burn me as he burned my love then take the Horn from you anyway. He paused. "Perhaps if I stop them, the Son will see fit to redeem me." He shrugged. "But not even the lamb is so merciful."

But Papa had hidden the Horn. "They want to end the world?"

"Close enough." He lifted some rope from the ground. "They would rip your prize from you and use it to open the gates of heaven."

She stared at him. "And you want different?"

"I would see them stopped and Khepri obliterated!"

How did he know all this? "Who are you?"

He paused in tying cords around the tree and bowed. "Kōnstantinos XI Dragasēs Palaiologos, last King of the Romans. At your service, my lady. The rumors of my death were unfortunately completely true." He spoke Greek now, lending yet one more touch of unreality to the moment.

Thanatos. Nekros. Of course he was dead. She'd misjudged the timing. The dreams had been her clues. He and Isabella had lived and died not decades ago but centuries.

"Are you even related to Alex?"

The vampire shrugged again. "He's my living heir. Blood of my blood. The uncrowned king."

It always came down to blood.

He finished with the rope, took her arms, and pulled her onto her feet. Her naked back burned from the coldness of the snow, but now she felt the freezing wind on her whole body. She'd never been naked out of doors before, or in front of a man. She began to cry.

He brushed at her tears. "I am a man no longer, and the blood gods' magic is never gentle, but I'll try and make it brief."

We must both die twice before we save each other. Oh, God, please. She wasn't ready to die.

He took her in both arms, flipped her upside down, and slammed her back into the trunk of the tree. He secured the ropes around her ankles and stepped back.

She flopped down painfully against the trunk, the rough uneven surface pressed against her bare back and limbs. She felt dull pain in her ankles. The smell of burning wood clogged her nostrils. Below her, the brilliant sky was lit with an intense red and yellow light. Her head craned up, and she saw the gnarled roots of the tree overhead, ascending into the snow.

"*Aima*," he said. "From the moment I tasted your blood, it sang with the hidden Strength of your God."

The passage is unblocked. What is lost will be found.

Constantine's fingernails grew into long talons. He stepped forward to swipe one hand across her belly, and the pain tore through her abdomen. He was doing something to her, something she felt only as a series of deep wrenching motions.

"You drank the dark gift first," he said. "It will save you both."

Together we can stop them, but the price will be steep.

Sarah swooned. Warm tickles crawled across her face, and dark liquid dripped slowly off her and fell upwards onto the twisted canopy of roots. The moment stretched, and she felt the welling presence of something approaching, something massive and primal. Then she heard the horn, the long mournful tone, loud and gigantic but at great distance.

The horn sounds our sacrifice. My death, your blood, your death, my blood.

Oh, God, no!

"The realms merge," Constantine said.

Sarah felt intensely thirsty. She wondered if she should pull her chin up to see what he'd done. How bad was it? Blood poured down her face. No, it would be best not to look.

The horn continued, louder and louder. She'd heard it in the basement, too, when Papa bent his knee to God's inscrutable will.

Those roots too had been bloodied. Above her, the wood began to shimmer as the tree came alive. From its dead wood, luminous leaves sprang.

She remembered the actual Horn. Remembered it between her legs in the basement. Oh Lord. *You're the key. The passage is almost open, beyond lies Paradise.*

She saw it again now, nestled in the roots. A ram's horn sheathed in gold. Papa's Horn, the Strength of God.

"Why? Why?"

The vampire's laugh seemed to echo in the garden.

"When heaven is besieged, even gods must use what weapons they can." He gestured at the great living tree on which she now hung. "After all the centuries, the world still contains wonders. *Etz haDaat tov V'ra* you would call it: the Tree of the Knowledge of Good and Evil."

The tree from which the serpent had tempted Eve.

He stepped forward, so close she could have grabbed him if she had the strength. He reached below her head and plucked the Horn from the roots.

"A small thing, is it not?" he said. "But lovely in its own way."

She gasped. "There was no need! It was hidden."

"They'd have found it," he said. "The beetle approaches as we speak."

She was fading.

"I might as well borrow a few of these." He reached up again and brought forth two orange and red fruits, which he slipped into the pocket of his robe. "You never know when the fruit Eve offered Adam might come in handy."

Snow whirled about her, and mixed with the blare of the horn she heard high-pitched yelps. She found her vision crowned by an inverted ugly little canine.

"The trap has been set," the vampire said, "now the vermin will be crushed."

The little barking dog was held by a man. Sarah struggled to see his upside down face.

Mr. Williams? No, for his hideous voice sliced sharper than a knife.

"Wolf-cub, you've done half my work, but still, I thought your heart filled with shafts of ash."

"The dead do not die so easily, Dung God," Constantine said. "For over a century I've waited for my revenge. Isabella's gift will be redeemed tonight."

The thing that looked like Mr. Williams laughed in a way no human could.

"I need not even touch you. I shall name the sun and collect the Horn from your ashes."

Hail to me! Hail to the Nine Gods with hidden faces who dwell in the Mansion of Khepri, said a voice to make stones bleed.

Constantine raised the archangel's Horn to his lips.

Time ceased. The vampire stood there, smile frozen. Not a hair on the mean little dog ruffled in the breeze. The beetle-man didn't move. Even the snowflakes halted in midair.

But the trumpeting continued, louder and louder, and from behind Sarah a flickering light began to wriggle bright filaments across the vampire's shadowy form.

The light shifted, and a dazzling figure stepped from nothingness to join the others before her.

Sarah's mind couldn't fully comprehend the new arrival. All soft feathery fire, neither masculine nor feminine. Yet so beautiful, the perception of it was ecstasy and agony combined. Their eyes met and she knew.

The Archangel Gabriel.

The awesome face turned to Sarah, a whirlpool of cold red flame surrounding a gaze as old as eternity.

Though you walk through a valley of deepest darkness, would you still serve the Lord, the God of your fathers, the God of Abraham, the God of Isaac, and the God of Jacob?

The angel's voice faded into the dirge-like crescendo of sound. Sarah felt the passage close back in on itself. Tree and garden all collapsed through her, and her consciousness thinned to imperceptibility.

Sixty-Eight:
A Man of Means

Salem, Massachusetts, Friday night, November 21, 1913

ALEX RACED UP THE BASEMENT STAIRS and into the library. Grandfather was gone, and so was Sarah. The clock read past seven. He turned to go then spied the coffer on the floor.

Grandfather kept his most personal things there, and it was usually sealed in the baroque cabinet. Alex had never seen inside. He nudged the top. It was unlocked.

And filled with papers and jewels — rubies, diamonds, emeralds. A golden cross with a sapphire bigger than a robin's egg held down a single folded sheet of paper, scrawled with his name.

Hands shaking, he opened the note to reveal tight lines of handwritten Greek. Blood from his cut fingers stained the cream-colored paper.

> *Dear Alexandros,*
>
> *I know at this moment you will find it impossible to understand what I am and what I have done, but I hope one day you shall find it in your heart to forgive*

me. Beneath all the layers of half-lies, it remains true that you are all that is left of my blood and our noble line. Out of blood was I born King of the Romans, God's Vicegerent on Earth, and in defense of my faith was I sacrificed, cut apart in the streets of Constantinople. The dark gift of blood restored my will to motion, but sacrificed my faith to darkness. Long have I stood in shadow, hidden from the grace of God. Perhaps now, in the autumn of His need, blood and sacrifice may redeem us all.

Your loving ancestor,

Kōnstantinos XI Dragasēs Palaiologos,
Basileus kai autokratōr Rhomaiōn

Alex dropped the letter. He felt hollow. He fumbled through the other papers — vellum sheets covered in archaic Greek, property deeds, bank statements. They had never wanted for money, but the numbers were staggering. Bloody plunder of the long centuries.

From behind the house he heard dogs barking and a horrible chittering shriek. He followed it out to the back porch. Though the night was bitter, he took no jacket. The hunter's moon was low in the sky, and by its reddish light he saw two figures at the yard's lone tree. One in purple.

Grandfather.

He leapt down and ran. The vampire raised his arm to his face, a glimmer of gold in his hand.

And there came a sound. Slow and mournful, a titanic horn blast resounding from everywhere and nowhere.

A flaming figure materialized from nowhere. Alex's feet slowed and came to a stop. Despite his desperation, his legs refused to close the distance to this awesome form.

Grandfather vanished and a silver blur arced down the hill toward the house. A wolf. It stopped when it reached Alex. Ruby eyes met his. The wolf held in his powerful jaws a crescent of bone and gold.

"What have you done with her?" Alex screamed.

The pendant around his neck burned hot. *Flee while you can,* Grandfather's voice cried in his head.

A smaller creature caught up to the wolf and pounced. A tiny gray dog, all furious teeth that bit and tore at the wolf's belly, its muzzle dripping blood.

Recently dredged memories churned in Alex's brain, acquiring details. The wolf howled and thrashed about his parents' bed, arrows embedded in his breast, his muzzle red with Mother's warm blood. The pointy-eared dog nipped at Dmitri, the giant stomping and kicking yet getting bit again and again.

And here and now the wolf twisted, trying to evade the dog's needling nips but hampered by the object in his mouth. Finally he broke free and kicked the dog aside.

Alex watched the thing he'd called Grandfather flee toward the woods to join a hulking figure waiting there. The little dog followed, barks fading into the night.

A renewed bout of shrieking brought Alex's attention back to the tree. Before the winged brightness stood a man whose head exploded in a gout of red and white.

Alex forced himself up the hill. While the winged form was silent, the headless man remained on his feet, emitting the terrible tweets. From his severed neck, black insect legs poked forth. The base of a giant beetle's body stayed rooted in the man's shoulders, the dark and shiny legs waving like snakes on a Gorgon's head.

At their Mount Athos cottage, with his ball of flame, this same creature had set arrows afire. With a bow of yew, he had launched them into Grandfather's chest and set the roof of their home ablaze.

Now, using his spindly limbs, the insect-headed man gathered strands of heavy air to bundle into a growing ball of hot yellow fire. The beetle chanted:

> *Re sits in his Abode of Millions of Years.*
> *The doors of the sky are opened for me,*
> *the doors of the earth are opened for me,*
> *the door-bolts of Geb are opened for me,*
> *the shutters of the sky-windows are thrown open for me.*

The bright warmth of daylight spilled across the yard. The beetle-man held a tiny sun in his black claws. Alex's eyes struggled to adjust as he searched for Sarah. His gaze closed on something white hanging limp against the dark outline of the tree.

The beetle-man shrieked again and hurled his sphere at the seraphim. The angel caught the little sun in its wingtips, where it shrank, diminished, and was gone.

The beetle howled and pulled himself free of the human body, an empty husk, which collapsed to the ground. Expanding to the size of a motor car, he twittered and rushed forward, slammed his carapace into the angel. The pair rolled sideways across the yard.

Crimson flamed wings struggled with obsidian bladed limbs. Hideous chitters played a painful counterpoint to the horn's distant blare. Throwing the beetle free, the angel spread its wings and launched into the air, exquisite features clenched in fury.

Gossamer extensions levered from the back of the insect, who took chase. The two great forms wrestled as they rose in the sky, throwing peculiar shadows across the yard and its solitary tree. Soon they were high above, as if riding through the heavens on some celestial chariot, the shrieks and trumpets slowly fading.

Alex climbed through the crunchy whiteness toward the tree, barely aware of his feet inside his boots. The ground sloped upward, the moon above him, the leafless tree black against this blood-stained coin.

In the moonlight he recognized the white form bound to the trunk.

Sarah.

A thin layer of windblown snow clung to her body like peach fuzz. Her hair hung down from her lifeless face. Her torso gaped open to the cold.

He sank to his knees. Eyes turned up to the cruel heavens. Like the future he'd imagined they might have, the stars seemed to glimmer, then fade.

Sixty-Nine:
Shroud

Salem, Massachusetts, Sunday, November 23, 1913

SARAH STOOD NAKED in the cool mist, her bare feet half-submerged in the muddy banks of the river. The water was warm, almost hot. Everything was devoid of color. Far across the water, the gate to the celestial kingdom beckoned, its golden doors standing open. On each side stood an angel formed of flame, one blue, one red. They beckoned to her with wings of colored fire.

The river itself ran silent, but she became aware of soft splashes. Out of the mist, a thin figure coalesced. He wore a dark cloak and poled a skiff.

"The ferryman," a feminine voice said.

Isabella. She wore only a thin white dress, a white and orange doe embroidered on her breast.

"Charon?" Sarah nodded toward the man on the boat. Fear tightened her voice. "I don't even believe in him."

Isabella chuckled. "You're dead, and by the hand of a Greek."

Was she? Or was this another dream? It seemed different from the others. Sarah looked across at the glowing gate. Perhaps it would be easiest to cross.

"That's not the way you're going," Isabella said.

The ferryman drew closer. His cloak was torn and patchy, his boat just a large slice of raw tree.

Sarah looked at Isabella. She was pretty, her alabaster skin flecked with small freckles, her red hair glorious. She was the only source of color in this place.

"You've no coin," she said, "but Charon might take you anyway." She gestured at the luminous gateway. "You've earned the right, I haven't."

"What do you mean?" Sarah said.

"The dark gift will take us back to the world of the living." She reached out a small hand to Sarah. "Blood is life. Eternal life."

"As a vampire?"

I save you and you save me. The dark logic was finally clear. Sarah took Isabella's hand in her own. It was cool to the touch but soft. So soft.

"We stand between worlds. Dead and undead. The ancient song of the blood gods is strong, but only the dead buried beneath the earth will rise to greet the night."

Sarah glanced back at the heavenly gates. "It's my choice?"

Isabella shrugged. "Not usually, but you carry within you God's Strength." She looked away into the darkness. "Maybe enough to open a way for us both."

"If I go with you, will Alex be there?"

"He's living, is he not?"

Alex was alive, Papa and Mama were alive. Sarah didn't want to die. After Judah, losing her might destroy them. It seemed so unfair. But to become a vampire? Were they all soulless evil monsters?

Sacrifice is strength, and strength will save our souls.

Had God set her on this dark road?

She could see the ferryman better now. Inside his dark hood, his face was that of a lifeless skull. Nothing felt right. She prayed for an answer.

"Come with me, sister, leave the kingdom of Hades to others." Isabella tugged again. "We may live again."

"I'd like to see Alex and my parents," Sarah said. "I didn't have a chance to say goodbye."

"There'll be time for that. With the dark gift, there's always time."

Was it a trick? The Last Temptation of Sarah Engelmann?

Isabella tugged again, and this time Sarah followed. If God intended her life to end this way then she was done with Him.

They turned from the boatman and walked up the bank into the mist. Dry leaves crackled under their feet. There was blood on the other girl's mouth and chin. Sarah hadn't noticed before. There was nothing wrong with wanting to live, was there?

Sarah woke. It was dark and very cold. There was no pain, but there was hunger and thirst.

One and the same now, hunger and thirst.

She could see nothing. Her entire body was wrapped in cloth. She strained against it, but an unyielding pressure kept her immobilized. She smelled wet earth. She tried to scream, but only a snarl came out, and all that got her was a mouth filled with grit. They had buried her alive, without a coffin, as was proper, naked in a linen shroud. How deep was she? Six feet?

She struggled, not in the least tired. Even straining, she couldn't feel her heartbeat. The darkness blinded her, and the only noise was the sound of her struggle. The touch of the linen was vibrant, more intense than any caress she had ever known. Where was Isabella? She'd said everything would be fine.

Time passed. The hunger and thirst mounted, but her energy didn't slack. In the end, soft cloth yielded to hard teeth. Once she worked a hole open, the dirt poured in. She contracted and relaxed her whole body in great spasms until she was able to shove her sharp-nailed hands past the soft material and into the soft soil beyond.

She must feed.

Find

THE DARKENING DREAM

online at:

the-darkening-dream.com

IF YOU ENJOYED *The Darkening Dream,* please consider taking a few moments to leave a review at the retailer where you purchased it. It need not be long. A few sentences and a rating are all that's required. These reviews really do matter.

Acknowledgements

First and foremost, I'd like to thank my wife Sharon, my mother, and my "story consultant" Bryan Visintin for reading each chapter hot off the presses as I finished it. Then reading again. And again. Then discussing each and every possible alteration.

I owe a great debt to the thousands of Fantasy, Science Fiction, Paranormal, and Horror novels, movies, games, and television shows I've consumed over the years. The details in this book wouldn't have been possible without several hundred writers of histories, occult books, and whatnot that I gobbled up over the course of my writing. Not to mention the ever handy Google and Wikipedia.

This novel was a big learning curve for me. A breadth of reading and a decent ear for prose do not alone make for a great first draft. Or second. Or sixth. So I'd like to thank my professional editors: the incomparable Renni Browne, Shannon Roberts, R.J. Cavender, and Jen Howard. Renni and Shannon in particular made me take a hard look at everything and not only illuminated the big changes that needed to be made, but also pointed a flickering torch toward the exit.

Proof reading was by Dan Grubb, typesetting and book design by Chris Fisher, e-book layout by Morgana Gallaway, and jacket copy editing by Beth Jusino. Thanks also to The Editorial Department champs Karinya Funsett-Topping, Ross Browne, and last but not least, Jane Ryder.

The awesome cover illustration is by Cliff Nielsen with Dana Melanie serving as the model for Sarah. The cover and logo design are by Pete Garceau. The cool interior engravings are by Original Force with additional art direction by Erick Pangilinan. The print edition is formatted in Arno Pro, an Adobe font family designed by Robert Slimbach. Thanks also to my long time business partner Jason Rubin for help with my working cover and logo. I used Lulu.com to print private draft editions during development. I'm not sure this was their business model, but if they didn't make a lot on the printing, they made up for it in shipping. Further thanks to Stephen Rubin for pro bono intellectual property advice.

This novel was written entirely on Apple products (thanks Steve!) and in Scrivener, a specialized word processor for writers. If you write long form prose and are still using a dinosaur like Word, look into it. The paper version was typeset in Adobe InDesign and the e-book converted with Calibre.

I also very much appreciate my loyal beta readers, especially those who read many drafts or offered up comments: Scott Shumaker, Jane Mullaney, Keren Perlmutter, Ben Stragnell, Lara Shanis (my third grade teacher!), Owen Rescher, Brent Askari, Bill Guschwan, Andrew Reiner, Brian Roe, Danny Pickford, David Cotrell, Jason Kay, Don Gavin, Lauren Lewis, Tilly Reniers, Avram Hirschberg, Abbe Flitter, Greg Cooper, Valerie Flitter, Jerry Meadors, Joe Labbe, Dinorah Mayton, Lindsay Gerber, Michael Perlmutter, Sam G., Mitch Gavin, Lisa Pivo, Michael Flitter, and Grant Thompson. If I missed any of you who finished the book, I apologize, or you forgot to tell me!

Lastly, I'd like to thank you, the reader, who's eyes on this page hopefully mean you made it to the end.

All sorts of additional info can be found at my website: http://andy-gavin-author.com

Andy Gavin,
California, December 2011

About the Author

ANDY GAVIN is an unstoppable storyteller who studied for his Ph.D. at M.I.T. and founded video game developer Naughty Dog, Inc. at the age of fifteen, serving as co-president for two decades. There he created, produced, and directed over a dozen video games, including the award winning and best selling Crash Bandicoot and Jak & Daxter franchises, selling over 40 million units worldwide. He sleeps little, reads novels and histories, watches media obsessively, travels, and of course, writes.

For more information, check him out at http://all-things-andy-gavin/bio.